A LONG R

Library of Congress Co
Softcover 978
ebook 978-1

All rights reserved. No part of this book may be reproduced or transmitted in any form or by any means, electronic or mechanical, including photocopying, recording, or any information storage and retrieval system, without permission in writing from the copyright holder.

This is a work of fiction. Names, characters, places, and incidents either are the product of the author's imagination or are used fictitiously, and any resemblance to any actual persons, living or dead, events, or locales is entirely coincidental.

Rev. Date: 10/11/2025

TERRY DAVIS
A Long Road Home

Foreword

Every journey home begins with a single moment of loss

Every story has its beginning, though some are buried beneath the wreckage of what came before.
This one begins with a storm — a road, a family, and a little girl who should not have survived.

From that single moment of ruin came a lifetime of echoes: the kindness of strangers, the weight of loss, the stubborn light of hope that refused to go out. Years later, on a quiet stretch of Kentish farmland, that same light would find its way back — through love, through labour, through the people who would come to call Ashmore Grange their home.

But before the warmth of the hearth, there was the sound of rain on glass, and the cry of twisted metal on the M2.

Prologue
Farthing Corner, 1963 — The Storm

The rain had been relentless that morning, a silver curtain sweeping across the M2 near Farthing Corner Services as the little Morris Minor fought its way through the spray. Julie sat in the back seat, her rag doll clutched tightly, half singing to herself while her father hummed along to the crackling radio.

"You singing again, poppet?" her father said warmly, glancing at her in the mirror.

Julie looked up, smiling around her thumb. "Rain, Daddy," she said proudly. "Rain song."

Her mother laughed softly. "It is a rain song, isn't it? Clever girl."

Her mother turned to smile at her, reaching back to straighten the blanket that had slipped from her knees.

A sudden glare of headlights flashed in the mirror.

"What the—? He's coming up fast—" her father started.

The roar of a diesel engine filled the air—then everything shattered. The foreign truck slammed into the back of their car, the impact forcing them forward through the sheets of rain. The sounds of twisting metal, breaking glass, and a woman's scream echoed into the storm and disappeared.

The Morris Minor flipped several times before stopping on the grass verge just below the service station. Rain hissed against the crumpled shell as people from the café and passing motorists hurried down the bank to help. But it was hopeless. The car was too badly mangled, the doors crushed, the windshield shattered. Through the broken glass, they could see the motionless figures inside and believed no one could have survived. None of them knew a child was in the back.

By the time the fire brigade arrived, steam rose from the wreck like breath in the cold air. Working under the glare of floodlights, they started cutting through the twisted metal to reach the couple in front.

"Careful with that torch—watch the fuel line!" someone called through the hiss of rain.

Another firefighter leaned in, peering into the back. "Wait—there's a child in here! Under the seat—look!"

It was only then, as one of the crew pulled aside a tangle of torn upholstery, that they saw a small hand beneath the seat.

"Hold it—stop cutting!" the lead man shouted. "She's still breathing. Get the medics here, now!"

Julie was still alive — unconscious, barely breathing, tangled in the wreckage. The firemen could hardly believe it. When they freed her, she was handed carefully to the waiting ambulance crew, who worked frantically to stabilise her before racing her to hospital through the rain-soaked night.

"She's a fighter, this one," one of the crew muttered, checking her pulse. "Come on, sweetheart… stay with us."

In the ambulance, the driver glanced across at his mate. "Not a mark on her face," he said quietly. "You'd never know what she's come through."

"Luckiest child I've ever seen," the other replied, eyes on the road. "Let's hope she stays that way."

But when they wheeled her into A&E, the truth told its own story. Her tiny body was covered in bruises, her ribs cracked, a deep gash along her temple hidden beneath her matted hair. Her breathing was shallow, one lung collapsed, and yet — somehow — her heartbeat held steady. The doctors said it was a miracle she'd survived the night.

But luck, as it turned out, would come and go from Julie's life in waves — leaving its mark not in scars, but in silence.

In the weeks that followed, police pieced together what had happened on that stretch of highway. Witnesses described the lorry drifting between lanes before the collision, with its brake lights never turning on. When they pulled the driver from the cab, dazed but unharmed, the smell of alcohol told its own story.

At the subsequent inquest, the details were laid bare — the empty bottles found in the cab, the hours he'd been driving without rest, the tachograph showing speeds far above the limit. The court fell silent when the photographs of the wreck were shown.

The judge's voice was cold as steel when he passed sentence: twenty-two years for causing death by dangerous driving.

Julie would never know his name, nor the face of the man whose carelessness had rewritten her life before it had even begun. But somewhere in the background of her story, his shadow remained — a quiet, unspoken truth buried in the noise of the past.

Julie remained in the hospital for several months following the accident, wrapped in silence and bandages, a mystery child with no family left to claim her.

When she was strong enough, she was moved into a foster home — a temporary stop in a world that didn't quite know what to do with her. It was there she stayed until three years later, at the age of five, when she was taken to the orphanage that would come to define her early years.

The nurses said she was lucky to be alive. Julie never thought of it as luck — though later, she would remember none of it.

Luck had saved her once, but it would not always be kind. And though the storm had passed, its echo would follow her for years to come.

CHAPTER ONE – *The Orphanage*

The car doors slammed, and the sound echoed through the courtyard like something shutting behind her forever. Julie clutched her rag doll tight, its hair matted now from weeks of travel, and looked up at the tall brick building. The windows stared back — square, watchful eyes — and somewhere inside a bell rang that made her stomach twist.

A woman in a grey uniform stood waiting at the steps. Her shoes shone so much they looked wet.
"Come along," she said without smiling. "We don't dawdle here." Her voice was crisp as frost. Julie didn't know what *dawdle* meant, but she knew she was doing it.

Inside smelled of polish and cabbage. The floorboards creaked in long sighs, and every sound seemed too loud. A clock ticked somewhere high above her head.
The woman — Matron Prentiss, someone had called her — bent down just enough to peel the doll from Julie's grasp.
"Toys aren't permitted outside the dormitory," she said. "Rules are rules."
Julie's fingers reached after it, but the matron had already turned away.

Down the corridor, another door opened. A younger woman in a blue apron stepped out, wiping her hands on a towel. Her hair was soft brown, escaping its pins, and her smile appeared like sunlight through clouds.
"Oh, you must be Julie," she said kindly. "Don't worry, we'll look after you."

Julie wanted to believe her. She wanted to ask if her mummy was coming soon, but her throat ached too much to try.
Ellen crouched to her level, eyes warm. "You've had a long

journey, haven't you? Let's get you some warm milk."
Behind her, the matron's heels clicked sharply on the tiles.
"No fuss, Nurse. She'll settle soon enough."

But Julie could already tell the difference between their voices — one that made her chest tighten, and one that made her breathe again.

That night, lying in the narrow bed under thin blankets, Julie listened to the building sigh and shift around her. The wind tapped at the panes like someone trying to get in. In the cot beside her, a small voice whispered through the dark.
"Don't cry. She can hear you if you cry."

Julie turned her head. Two pale eyes glimmered back at her in the faint spill of light from the corridor doorway.
"Who are you?" she whispered.
"Maggie," came the reply. "I've been here ages. If you keep quiet, she leaves you be."

Julie swallowed hard. "Will she be cross if I ask for my doll?"
"She's always cross," Maggie murmured, rolling onto her side. "But you can share mine if you want. It's only got one arm."

For the first time that night, Julie felt something shift — not warmth exactly, but the small, steady presence of someone who understood.

She reached across the narrow gap between their beds until her fingers brushed Maggie's blanket.
"Thank you," she breathed.

Neither girl spoke again. The silence grew softer around them, and Julie kept her eyes open until the dark became shapes, then dreams, then nothing at all.

From that night on, she and Maggie were never far apart — two small hearts learning to survive together in the shadow of Matron Prentiss.

Days turned into weeks, then months. The seasons outside the orphanage windows shifted, but inside, everything stayed the same — the waxed floors, the echoing corridors, the smell of boiled cabbage and disinfectant that clung to the air.

Matron Prentiss ruled the place like a clock: strict, unbending, and always watching. Her footsteps could be heard long before she appeared, sharp and measured, the sound that made children straighten their backs and lower their voices.

Julie learned quickly. Learned to eat what was put in front of her without flinching. Learned to fold her clothes perfectly square. Learned never to ask twice for anything.

Maggie became her shadow, her laughter soft and quick, her loyalty fierce in the way only childhood can make it. The two of them shared everything — whispered stories under the blankets, bruised shins from playground scuffles, and the secret language of children who have no one else.

But as they grew older, Matron's temper seemed to harden like the ice on the windows in winter. A dropped cup meant a slap. A tear was met with scorn. Julie, quieter than most, became her favourite target.

"You, girl — look at me when I'm speaking."
Julie would lift her eyes, trying to hide the fear. "Yes, Matron."
"Always moping about. Do you think the world owes you something?"
"No, Matron."
"Then stand up straight and stop feeling sorry for yourself."

The punishments were never savage, but they were cruel in their precision — standing in the corridor for hours, missing supper, being made to scrub floors until her fingers bled. Nurse Ellen tried to intervene once, gently suggesting that Julie was only a child. The matron's reply was thin as wire.

"Children learn through discipline, Nurse. You'll see I'm right."

Ellen didn't argue again, but she found small ways to help — a warm drink left waiting, a quiet word of comfort, a bandage when no one was looking.

By the time Julie turned ten, she had become the still point around which the matron's moods revolved. Maggie would squeeze her hand when the woman passed, whispering, "Ignore her. She hates what she doesn't understand."

Julie didn't answer, but sometimes she wondered what there was about her to hate.

As the years turned, the orphanage seemed to grow smaller. What had once felt endless now became a cage of routines.

The older girls worked in the laundry, the kitchen, or out in the gardens under Nurse Ellen's softer supervision. Matron Prentiss still watched from the upper windows, her hands folded behind her back, waiting for an excuse to remind everyone who ruled the place.

Julie had long stopped crying. Her face had learned stillness, her voice control. She could polish floors until the boards shone, stitch torn hems neatly enough to please even the matron, and move through the days without leaving a trace of herself behind.

Maggie was the only one who ever saw the spark that still lived somewhere deep inside her — the quiet defiance that time hadn't managed to grind away.

By fourteen, they were inseparable, sharing a narrow bed on cold nights when the frost crept across the windows.

They whispered about the world beyond the gates: towns with shops still open after dark, people who laughed without lowering their voices, fields that went on forever.

Maggie dreamed of finding work in one of those towns, maybe as a housemaid.

Julie said little, but she listened with her whole heart.

The matron seemed to sense their bond and resented it. Julie could feel the woman's eyes on her at mealtimes, in the chapel, during chores — measuring, waiting.

The punishments became subtler. Letters that other girls received from relatives were withheld "by mistake." Julie's sewing work was unpicked and handed back without comment. Small cruelties, perfectly aimed.

Nurse Ellen did what she could, but her kindness had limits within those walls. She was older now, quieter, careful not to draw Matron's attention.

Sometimes, when Julie passed her in the corridor, she would see the apology in Ellen's eyes — the sorrow of someone who wanted to help and couldn't.

At fifteen, Julie and Maggie were moved to the attic dormitory with the older girls. The air was thin and cold, the rafters full of pigeons. It should have been lonely, but up there they found a strange sort of peace.

They began to make plans — not yet real, not yet possible, but plans nonetheless. Maggie kept a small tin under her bed where she hid coins found in coat pockets and dropped by careless visitors.

Julie wrote the names of places on scraps of paper: *Rochester. Maidstone. Canterbury.* Somewhere — anywhere — that wasn't here.

Matron Prentiss noticed, of course. Nothing escaped her. One evening, she summoned Julie to her office.

The room was neat and bare, the ticking clock loud enough to fill the silence between them.

"You think I don't see you," the matron said, her voice smooth as glass. "But I see everything. You think you're better than this place. You're not."

Julie stood very still. "No, Matron."

"Ungrateful girl. You'd be dead in a ditch if it weren't for this home. You'll remember that."

"I do remember," Julie said softly, and for once, she didn't look away.

The slap came fast — a clean, deliberate strike that left her cheek burning. The matron's breath caught as though she'd surprised herself. Julie didn't cry, didn't flinch. That, somehow, seemed to unsettle the woman more than tears ever could.

After that, something shifted. Matron Prentiss no longer raised her hand, but her dislike turned colder, quieter, more poisonous. Julie and Maggie became ghosts, moving through the halls with care and watchfulness, biding their time.

By the time Julie turned sixteen, her beauty began to shine through her plainness — with long blonde hair and blue eyes that appeared older than they truly were. The matron's bitterness worsened each month. She called Julie a bad influence, too proud, too aware, not suitable for the younger girls to look up to. But the truth was simpler: Julie had outgrown her reach.

That winter, as the snow pressed against the dormer windows and the pipes groaned throughout the nights, Julie and Maggie started talking seriously about leaving. Not someday — soon.

They met quietly after lights-out, wrapped in blankets against the cold. Maggie had saved a few pounds; Ellen had quietly passed on an old coat and a pair of boots that would fit. The plan was rough, desperate, but real: they would wait until the matron's rounds were finished, slip out through the laundry door, cross the yard, and take the path that led down to the main gate and freedom.

"What if we're caught?" Maggie whispered one night.

"Then we try again," Julie said. "I can't stay here another year."

Maggie looked at her, eyes wide with both fear and love. "Then neither can I."

The wind rattled the windows, but the girls lay side by side, silent and certain. For the first time in years, Julie felt the faint beat of something that might someday become freedom.

In the days that followed, the atmosphere inside the orphanage grew heavier. Matron Prentiss's eyes lingered longer when she passed them, as if she could sense something forming just out of sight. Julie and Maggie worked side by side, silent, careful, pretending nothing had changed.

Each night, they whispered plans under the blankets — what to take, which door to use, how far they could walk before dawn. They waited for the perfect moment, when Matron was tired, when Ellen was on duty, and when the heat of the day had drained all sound from the house.

Ellen said nothing, but Julie caught her watching them once with a look that seemed almost like understanding.

By the end of that week, the air felt heavy and close, filled with dust and the faint smell of polish. The days dragged on in thick, unmoving heat, and the nights were too warm to sleep. Even the birds outside had fallen silent.

On the last evening, Matron went to bed early, complaining about the heat. The girls lay in the dark, their thoughts racing faster than their breath.

"Are you sure?" Maggie whispered. "We could wait a little longer. Till it's cooler."

Julie turned on her side to face her. "Cooler won't make her kinder. You know that."

Maggie nodded slowly. "She'll know by morning."

Julie smiled faintly in the dark. "Then we'll be gone by then."

For a long time, neither of them spoke. The window creaked as the warm air pushed against it. Somewhere down the corridor, a door closed and footsteps faded away.

When the house finally stilled, Julie sat up. "Tomorrow night," she whispered.

Maggie's hand found hers in the dark. "Tomorrow," she said.

The next day was endless. The matron's temper frayed; the smallest thing drew her anger. Julie scrubbed, polished, and folded all without a word. By evening, her arms ached and her nerves felt raw.

When lights-out came, the dormitory fell quiet one bed at a time until only she and Maggie were awake. The clock in the hallway struck eleven, then twelve.

Julie sat up. "It's time."

Maggie didn't move. "Already?"

She reached for the old coat Ellen had left folded by the laundry door a week before and slipped it on quietly. Then she picked up the small backpack she'd kept hidden under the bed, holding it close against her chest. Inside were the bare essentials: a crust of bread, a bottle of water, a spare pair of socks, underwear, and the little purse of coins Maggie had collected.

Maggie sat up slowly, her hands twisting the edge of the blanket. "What if it's locked? What if someone hears us?"

Julie shook her head. "We'll be careful. We can do this."

They crept through the dormitory, each step heavy with fear. The air smelled of soap and summer dust, and the boards whispered softly beneath their feet. Down the corridor, the faint line of light under the matron's door had gone dark.

"She'll be making her rounds soon," Julie whispered. "We have to go before she comes by."

They sneaked out of the dormitory, the hallway dimly lit by moonlight streaming through the high windows. The air smelled of polish and candle wax. Every sound — the ticking of the hallway clock, the faint groan of a pipe — seemed loud enough to give them away.

Halfway down the staircase, Julie froze. The beam of Matron Prentiss's torch slid across the lower landing, slow and searching. The matron was doing her rounds, moving from room to room, the sharp click of her shoes echoing like a warning.

Julie pulled Maggie back into the shadow beneath the stairs, pressing a hand over her mouth. The torch's glow passed over the wall just feet away. They could hear the matron's breathing, the rustling of her keys, and the low sigh she gave before turning away.

When the sound of her footsteps finally faded, Julie exhaled. "Now," she mouthed.

They moved once more, carefully stepping until they reached the laundry room on the ground floor. It was cooler there, with damp air filled with the scent of soap and ironed linens. The small window above the sinks had been their plan from the beginning— low enough to reach and half-hidden behind the water tanks.

Julie placed the backpack down and ran her fingers along the frame. The latch was stiff, having been stuck tight for many years because it had not been opened. She tugged once, twice, but it wouldn't budge. Her pulse quickened.

"Is it stuck?" Maggie whispered.

"Just stiff," Julie muttered, fingers slipping on the metal. She tried again, pressing her shoulder against the frame until the latch suddenly gave way with a loud squeal. Warm night air rushed in as the sash lifted, carrying the smell of cut grass and soap from the yard beyond.

Maggie hesitated behind her, whispering, "What if she hears?"

"She's gone to check the dormitories," Julie murmured. "We won't get another chance."

The open window looked out onto the rear courtyard. Beyond it lay the vegetable garden, the fence, and the path leading to the main gate. Freedom was less than fifty feet away.

Julie turned to Maggie. "You first."

But Maggie didn't move. Her face turned pale, and her hands trembled at her sides. "I can't," she said. "I thought I could, but I can't."

Julie stared at her, heart pounding. "If you stay, she'll never let you go. You know what she's like."

Maggie shook her head, tears welling. "At least here I know what to expect. Out there... I don't."

For a moment, the only sound was the ticking of the laundry clock and the faint chorus of crickets outside. Then Julie leaned in close, her voice barely a whisper. "I'll come back for you. I promise."

Maggie gave a trembling nod. "Go."

Julie lifted the backpack, pushed it through the gap, and climbed onto the sill. The night waited, heavy and silent.

Suddenly, they froze when they heard movement outside in the hallway. Maggie quickly looked over her shoulder, as if expecting Matron to suddenly burst in and catch them. The footsteps approached, then receded, and the girls exhaled in relief.

As the girls exchanged glances, the moonlight cast a soft glow over their uncertain faces. "This is it, then," Julie whispered. "You haven't changed your mind, have you?"

Maggie shook her head. "No. You know me—I'm a mess in a crisis." She tried to smile, but her voice trembled. "But get in touch—okay? I'll worry."

Julie nodded sadly. She had no idea how to reach out without being discovered and caught, and that was a risk she couldn't take. The two hugged tightly, tears streaming down their faces. Then Julie eased her backpack through the window, where it landed with a soft thud. She climbed onto the windowsill, slipped out through the gap, and dropped just a few feet onto a flower bed. She loved and appreciated all the hard work the old gardener put into caring for the plants, so she was careful not to damage any of them.

Maggie stuck her nervous, white face out of the window and looked down. Julie asked Maggie one last time if she'd come with her, knowing the answer already.

"Can you shut the window, please, Mags?" Julie whispered, slinging her backpack over her shoulder.

It wasn't far to the locked gates, and she ran toward them. Halfway down the driveway, she glanced back briefly and waved to Maggie's ghostly face pressed against the glass.

The gates were nine feet tall with spikes on top. *How the heck am I ever going to get through them? I should have thought of this earlier.*

She panicked when she saw a light turn on in the orphanage and hid among some rose bushes, almost yelling as the thorns pierced her skin.

She froze at the sound of a car starting, thinking, *God, have they already noticed I'm missing?* No, they couldn't have had enough time to see she was gone and reach a car.

As the car reversed and headed toward the now-opening gates, she wondered, *Should I leave now or wait? No, I should wait until it passes, then run through afterward.*

As the car slowly drove through the gates, she was horrified to see it stop just outside. It only took off after the person driving was sure the gates had closed behind them.

Julie, in agony from the brutal thorns, was sobbing—free yet still a prisoner.

She carefully freed herself from the rose bushes as best she could in the dark. *Stop, think—there must be a way out.*

Her heart was racing, and she was bleeding from the thorns she had just encountered. She started walking around the tall brick wall that enclosed the orphanage, cringing with each step, which echoed like a herd of galloping horses on the gravel.

At the back of the property was the old gardener's shed, where she hoped to find a ladder. She saw two, but they were padlocked to the shed. Panic was now setting in as she began to realise she might never escape.

Not one to give up, Julie kept searching and found some apple bushel boxes. She wonders if she could stack them to get over the wall.

She notices a spot with overhanging trees, thinking the low branches could help her climb over the wall. She moves the boxes toward the wall one by one, trying to stay silent in the quiet moonlit night. The wall is like the gate, nine feet high. Luckily for Julie, it doesn't have barbed wire or glass on top.

She stacks two boxes on top of each other, but there are still six feet to reach the top. So, she flips them over, reducing the gap to just 4 feet and making it easy for her to reach the top. She then stacks another box beside them and uses it as a step, allowing her to get onto the other two, which aren't very stable.

Once again, the lights in the orphanage flicker back on, revealing her position, and she remains frozen in fear, unable even to breathe. She watches the matron walk down the hallway, thinking to herself. *Does that woman ever rest?* She probably checked that everything was secure before heading to bed. The lights go out again, and Julie lets out a deep sigh of relief.

She climbs onto the first box and grabs a branch to steady herself as she slowly moves onto the other two wobbling boxes, feeling she might slip if she lets go of the branch and holds on tight.

She tries to climb over but realises she left her backpack behind. She muttered some choice words, climbs back down, grabs it, and goes up again. Holding onto the branch, she quickly tosses the backpack over the wall and follows closely. She scrapes her knee and twists her ankle on landing, but it's a minor injury she can walk off soon. Afterwards, she disappeared from the orphanage forever.

CHAPTER TWO – *The Long Hill Ahead*

She walked along the beach for miles until she reached Hastings Pier at 6:20 am. Feeling exhausted, she couldn't go any farther. The sun was rising in the east, casting long shadows past the pier's structure. People started appearing; she saw dog walkers and a postman on the road in the distance. This made her even more nervous, and she had been seeking cover for the past half hour. She rested under the pier, tucked into the triangle of space near the promenade, trying to hide from the people walking on the boards above her on the pier. From what she could see, they looked like fishermen hoping to catch dinner.

She realised she couldn't hide forever, not even until it was dark again. That would be a waste of time and accomplish nothing. She needed to move forward and seem less guarded and suspicious. She had to appear confident and as if she belonged.

She looked down at the blood on her arms and the scraped knee that was still bleeding a little. She reached into her backpack and grabbed a handkerchief. She used the water she had with her to clean up as best as she could, but one of the deeper cuts was slow to stop bleeding.

Once her aching legs felt better and the bleeding stopped, she sipped the little water remaining in the old lemonade bottle she had brought. Julie stood up, shook off the sand, and headed toward the road. She noticed a town map on display and realised she wasn't far from Hastings Railway Station.

Even though she was exhausted, her adrenaline still surged, propelling her forward. She started down Schwerte Way, turned right onto White Rock Road, and then suddenly froze, her shoulders instinctively tensing in panic at the sight of a police car passing by. She stayed frozen, mid-step, holding her breath, expecting them to pull over and confront her, but they continued on without a second glance.

Oh, you silly cow, she thought to herself. She stopped dead in her tracks at the sight of the cops! *That's not suspicious at all!* She kept walking until she reached the station.

She'd only ever ridden a train once, which was when they took her to the orphanage years ago, but at the age of four, she had no memory of it.

She wandered around, unsure how to proceed, until she found the ticket office, where she checked the fare prices and realised she had enough money to get to Maidstone in Kent. All she knew about Maidstone was that it was far from Bexhill and the orphanage, and that was enough for now.

The train arrived on time, and she carefully opened one of the doors, not entirely sure what she was doing. She tried to close the door gently, only to be shown by another passenger that the doors were slam doors and had to be slammed shut.

The old steam engine slowly started to move off with a whistle, a chug chug, and smoke rising high into the sky, while the smell of steam and smoke crept into the carriage.

"At least I'm going somewhere," she whispered to herself, clutching the strap of her bag. "Anywhere but back there."

Although she was excited to ride the train for the first time she could remember, its gentle rocking lulled her to sleep in just five minutes. She luckily woke up at 2:15 p.m., right before reaching Maidstone East. When she exited the station, she was unsure of which direction to take, so she started walking without a clear destination.

After wandering aimlessly for almost an hour, she paused in a small park, where a charming pond and a group of ducks attracted her attention. She had only enough food for herself, but decided to share some with the noisy ducks. As they competed for the crumbs and quarrelled, she finally smiled for the first time that day. She then took a few sips from her small water bottle, which she quickly finished.

"At least someone's happy," she muttered, watching the ducks flap and squabble.

After spending half an hour with the ducks and taking a break, she felt ready to continue and kept wandering until she reached a dual carriageway, where she saw a sign pointing right (A249 Stockbury, M2, Sittingbourne and Faversham). With no idea where she was or which way to go, she decided to turn right and climb a steep hill. But halfway up (Detling Hill), her legs aching, she wished she had taken the other path, not realising it would have taken her straight back to Maidstone.

She pressed on toward the top, and the steep climb lasted over an hour. She hadn't even reached the summit when, out of breath, she sat on the grassy shoulder. Tears welled in her eyes for the first time as genuine fear overtook her. It was getting late—past 6:30 p.m.—and she had nowhere to stay that night, which terrified her.

"What have I done?" she said softly, her voice trembling. "What have I got myself into?"

What have I got myself into? Where could I find food and shelter now? It was finally sinking in that she'd made a huge mistake and was in real trouble.

She paused, a chilling thought suddenly hitting her as she imagined Maggie taking the full fury of Matron. "Oh, God, Maggie... I hope she's all right." *Should I turn back?* But that wasn't very reassuring. It was better to keep moving, distract herself, and focus on what lay ahead.

What kind of future is that, you idiot? Here I am, all alone and terrified in the middle of nowhere, with only six pounds to my name and no idea what was around the corner.

She continued climbing the long, steep slope and spotted a transport café at the top of the hill. Exhausted and hungry, she kept going and eventually arrived after what felt like ages. Inside, she felt relieved to find the place almost empty. The sandwich and tea she ordered gave her a much-needed boost. The tea tasted especially good—hot and sweet, with a big spoonful of sugar. Since it was free, she decided she needed the extra energy.

She sat sipping her tea, leisurely enjoying her moment, hesitant to leave the comfort of this place, but aware she couldn't remain indefinitely.

A police car pulled up, causing her terror, and the constable entered the café. Without giving her a second glance, he went to the counter and bought something she thought was a Coke and left.

"Thank God," she breathed out quietly, her hands trembling as she set her cup down.

She took a moment in the restroom to freshen up and change into clean underwear, which made her feel more like herself. Then, she tied her long blonde hair into a ponytail, making her look several years younger than her actual age.

As the light began to fade, she continued walking along the A249, following the signs to Stockbury. She came to a road that led into an abandoned World War II airfield, now a busy industrial park. In front of her was a low, concrete building that turned out to be an old World War II pillbox.

She had no idea what it was, but she hoped it would offer safe shelter for the night.

"Please let it be dry," she whispered to herself. "Just one night without rain… that's all I need."

She cautiously approached what she guessed was the entrance, and her mood lifted. If she could squeeze in there, she might finally get some rest. At least it would be dry, she hoped, as she peeked inside.

She was surprised to find the space dry and warm, which wasn't unexpected since it was summer. It looked like someone had stayed there before, judging by the old mattress on the floor. She touched it with her hand, hoping it wasn't damp. The mattress was dirty, but surprisingly, it wasn't stained and felt dry to the touch.

"Well, that's a first," she muttered under her breath. "Something actually going right today."

Beggars can't be choosers! She murmured, forcing a small smile. Not sure where she heard that saying.

"Maybe matron used to say that," she added softly, her throat tightening. "Or someone at the home… I can't remember."

Nothing was blocking the entrance, but she was too tired to care, and she soon drifted off to sleep, completely drained from walking all day with only a little sleep on the train.

"Just a few hours," she murmured as her eyes closed. "Then I'll keep going… promise."

CHAPTER THREE – *The Stranger in the Pillbox*

Julie woke up suddenly in the morning, disoriented by the grey concrete walls and unsure of her whereabouts. Then it all came back to her, and she glanced at her watch: it was a quarter past seven. She felt stiff but rested after a good night's sleep. Rubbing her eyes, she moved toward the doorway, nearly tripping over an elderly man sitting with his back against the entrance, his feet flat and his knees bent.

She looked in horror with thoughts flashing through her mind. "What the hell?"

He turned around and grinned. "Good morning, sweetheart. Did you sleep well?"

"Who are you? What are you doing here?" she gasped, pressing herself against the wall. "Don't come any closer."

Julie was stunned. Unwelcome thoughts intruded into her mind, especially after everything the matron had done to her at the orphanage. The man sat in the doorway, blocking her way out, and she panicked as her thoughts spiralled out of control.

"Don't worry, love. I usually sleep in here, but I showed up a bit too late last night and found the room had already been rented out." He chuckled at his joke.

"That's not funny!" she snapped, her voice trembling. "You scared the life out of me."

Julie's face was still a picture of fear, so he tried to explain it as gently as possible. "I figured the best thing to do was to block the door. We don't get many intruders, but you never know." Better be safe, etc.

"Block the door?" she echoed, her tone caught between disbelief and relief. "You mean… You were guarding me?"

He had stumbled in late last night, lost in darkness with just a small torch to guide him, and was stunned to see a sleeping beauty whose face appeared almost otherworldly in the torchlight.

She slept so soundly that he stood over her for a few moments, marvelling at her beauty. Then, an overwhelming urge to protect her washed over him, and he blocked the doorway with his own body, dozing lightly and sitting up like a sentinel guarding a fairy-tale princess.

Julie gulped. "Who are you?"

"My name is Giles – and yours?"

"Julie," she replied cautiously, searching for a way to move past him.

"Julie," he repeated softly, as if testing the name. "Pretty name. Suits you."

As Giles stood up, he stretched his long limbs, revealing that he was younger than he looked despite the dirt and grime covering him. His rough exterior didn't match his middle-aged years, which were probably around forty, though it was hard to tell with his long grey beard and scruffy appearance. He wore a worn-out trench coat, rugged boots, and faded jeans. Standing over six feet tall, he had a muscular build, with hands that seemed disproportionately large for his frame. Julie couldn't help but notice his impressive size, and she felt a bit uneasy.

Giles could sense this. "Please don't worry, if I were a threat to you, I would have done something last night when I found you in my hotel!" he smiled again, reassuringly.

"Weren't you freezing outside all night?" was all she could manage to say.

"No, I'm okay with sleeping under the stars. It's not cold right now, anyway."

Julie believed the man wouldn't be a problem, at least she hoped so. The thought of how vulnerable she had made herself was unsettling. She was still tense from his tall stature and those huge hands, but he seemed harmless enough.

"Now, young lady," he said kindly, stepping aside so she could leave the pillbox. "What brings you out here sleeping on the streets? You're too young to be out on your own like this."

"I'm seventeen, soon eighteen."

"Very old," quipped Giles."

"Old enough to look after myself," she said quickly, folding her arms.

Julie was nervous; she didn't know what to say to him. But his eyes shone with kindness, and his smile was sincere and comforting. She was young and inexperienced, and it was hard for her to lie, so she told him how she had escaped from the orphanage and shared everything about the matron.

Giles listened and felt a lump in his throat, imagining what this poor girl had gone through. "I don't blame you. That Matron sounds like a real nightmare to me."

"She was," Julie said bitterly. "If I never see her again, it'll be too soon."

"Forget about your past. What about your future?" he questioned.

"And where are you headed?"

"I'm not sure. I just needed to get out of that situation." He gazed into her sad, serious eyes and felt a pang of empathy.

What a courageous, strong little girl.

But he thought about it for a moment. Despite her youthful appearance, she was clearly a strong-willed young woman, beautiful and seemingly unaware of the influence she had on men. He hoped she could take care of herself. He felt a surge of protective feelings; her story and determination having struck a chord with him. He offered her the one thing he could.

"Do you fancy a cuppa?"

"Yes, I would love one." She frowned, "Have you got some tea here?"

He chuckled at her confusion. "No, but come with me. This hotel has a nice breakfast area." He gave Julie a reassuring smile. She was confused. "There's a mobile café just over there called Fred's."

"Oh, okay."

"He's a great guy who always makes me a cup of tea. I do a few small things for him, so I'm sure he'll be generous to you as well. If not, you might have to do the dishes for the week!" he laughed again at his own great sense of humour.

Poor Julie didn't know what to make of him. Was he serious or what?

The smell of bacon sizzling on his hotplate was irresistible! A few truckers already sat at Fred's café eating breakfast. A couple looked up from their papers and bacon sandwiches, curious about where this young, pretty girl had come from.

Fred was a chubby, cheerful-looking guy. "Hi, Giles. And who's this? I didn't know you had a daughter."

Giles snorted with amusement, shaking his head. "This is Julie, my new friend. I found her squatting in my place last night, and she would dearly love a cup of tea."

"Free, huh?" laughed Fred, good humouredly, "Who needs customers like you, Giles? I'd be rolling in dough by now!" He turned to Julie. "Alright, my love, how do you have it?"

"Milk and two sugars, please," Julie shot him a genuinely grateful smile. "And thank you so much."

"It's a pleasure, sweetheart," Fred said with a warm smile. "Want some breakfast?"

"I'd love some. I'm starving, but I'm short on cash." She was already figuring out what she could afford, but hoping he would extend the same offer as the tea.

"Don't worry about that. I'll find Giles some jobs to do later to pay for it." Fred winked, placing two steaming mugs down in front of them. "OK, Giles?"

"Aye," smiled Giles. "It keeps me busy – and fed, of course!"

Within minutes, Fred arrived with a large plate of eggs, bacon, sausages, and baked beans, placing it in front of Julie along with two slices of bread and butter. Julie let out a delighted gasp. Fred did the same for Giles, who looked up in amazement.

Julie dove right in, ravenous. She was just a little girl, but with a generous amount of ketchup, she finished the whole plate in record time, using the single slice of bread she had to mop up the leftovers.

She leaned back, rubbing her full belly, feeling satisfied. "Wow, that feels great. Thanks again, Fred."

"You're welcome, my little darlin," Fred said as he began gathering the dirty plates. "So, what brings you out here, squatting in poor old Giles's house?"

"Well, I'm on my way to…" she hesitated. *Where the hell am I headed?* She had seen the name of a town, so she lied, "I'm trying to get to Faversham, I have a sister there."

Giles's eyes widened in surprise. This was the first he'd heard of it. He studied her face and quickly realised she was making it up as she went along. But he had no right to say anything. He'd run away from plenty of things himself and knew what it felt like to walk off into the unknown.

"That's quite a trip," said Fred. "How do you plan to get there?"

"Walk," said Julie, "but I don't know how far it is."

"About twenty miles."

"Oh," she shrugged. "I should be able to walk there in a day or two."

"Excuse me," a voice behind her said. "I couldn't help overhearing your conversation."

She couldn't place the accent – it sounded Scottish or Irish. Julie turned and saw a balding middle-aged man, who continued,

"I'm in my truck on the way to Dover and would quite happily drop you off at Faversham, if you would like."

She wasn't liking this one bit. She'd only said 'Faversham' because she had seen the name at Maidstone Station.

"I'm not sure,' she said quickly. "I've never hitch-hiked, and I don't know you. So, I don't think so, but thanks anyway."

Giles imagined her on the road, wandering. If she wanted to get away at all, if she had her sights set on Faversham, this was a better option than most. It wasn't as if he was in a position to keep her where she was. Freedom had driven him on the road, and freedom was what Julie wanted.

"Hey, it's no problem," urged Giles, seriously. "I know George and you'll be safe with him."

"I don't know," she muttered shyly, not wanting to offend the trucker.

"Okay," George said, raising his hands in a gesture of innocence, "but I'm here for another ten minutes if you change your mind."

Giles spoke softly to Julie, his gentle blue eyes comforting her. "It's a simple choice, Julie. If you want to get to Faversham, you can either walk for a day or more or take a half-hour drive."

Julie let out a sigh. Maybe it was for the best—to put more distance between herself and Bexhill. She remembered all the walking she'd done the day before and couldn't bear the thought of more days like it.

So, thanking George, she reluctantly accepted the ride.

She hugged Giles goodbye, tactfully ignoring the smell of his dirty clothes and the dirt embedded in the folds of his skin.

She held onto him tightly, overflowing with genuine gratitude and compassion. Giles was moved in ways he never could have imagined; he saw a teenage girl show such kindness to an old vagrant, and tears welled up in his own eyes.

CHAPTER FOUR – *The Road to Faversham*

George guided her to a huge Foden S39, which had a forty-foot trailer hitched behind it, and helped her climb into the cab. Julie burst out laughing, excited to be riding in such a big truck, towering high above everything.

"There you are then, Julie."

"Is that an Irish accent, George?"

"That's right. I'm from Dublin," he said, revving up the engine. "A great city on the banks of the Liffey, and of course, it has the best Guinness in the world. But I'd guess you've never actually tasted a Guinness."

Julie had trouble understanding everything he said over the noise of the large Cummings diesel engine pounding away, but she inferred the rest.

"No, I've never tasted any beer," she admitted. "Or, in fact, any alcoholic drink."

"Never?" he said, half shocked. "You haven't lived yet, girl! A pint of Guinness'll put hair on your chest."

Julie laughed. "Don't think I need that, thanks very much!"

George grinned. "Fair enough — but maybe someday, when you're not riding around in strangers' lorries, eh?"

"You mean when I'm old and respectable?" she teased.

"Exactly that," he chuckled. "Though respectable's overrated, if you ask me."

He raised his eyebrows and smiled, as they headed down the road past the Three Squirrels Pub, nearly colliding with a car that pulled out without looking. He slammed on the brakes, almost shooting Julie onto the front windshield, but she managed to stop herself by grabbing the dashboard.

"Bloody hell!" she gasped, clutching the dashboard. "That was close!"

"Jaysus, some people shouldn't be allowed behind a wheel," George muttered, shaking his head. "You all right there, love?"

"Yeah... I think so," Julie said, laughing nervously. "I nearly saw my life flash before my eyes!"

"Let's hope it was a good show," George winked, easing the truck forward again. "Would've been a shame to lose you before Faversham."

Apologising, he continued and turned onto the M2 at Stockbury Roundabout.

They talked about nothing in particular, and Julie felt a sense of relief. He did point out, when they came to a clearing, that the land in the distance was the Isle of Sheppey, but Julie had never heard of it and just nodded politely. George seemed just as harmless as Giles had said. She started to unwind, glad to be putting more distance between herself and the orphanage.

"You got family in Faversham, then?" George asked after a while.

Julie hesitated. "No... not really. I'm just hoping to find work — maybe a café or something."

He nodded slowly. "Good place for that. Folks down there are decent. Just keep your wits about ya, all the same."

"I will," she promised. Then, after a pause, she added softly, "It's nice, though... someone caring enough to say that."

George smiled at that, a little sadly. "Ah, well — every girl needs someone to keep an eye out, eh?"

Twenty minutes later, George exited at Junction 7 to take the A2 to Dover. He slowed down the truck and pulled into a layby, saying, "This is as far as we go now, Julie. Faversham is that way, about three miles. The safest route would be down that lane over there – Homestall Lane, through Macknade. Head to the end of the road, turn left into Graveney Road, and keep straight on until you get to Faversham."

She struggled to open the heavy door and finally slid down to the ground, laughing. "Thanks, George, and be safe on your journey."

"You are very welcome, Julie, and take good care of yourself out there, too."

"I will," she said. "And if I ever make it big, I'll buy you a pint of that Guinness."

George laughed loudly. "I'll hold you to that, girl! Now off you go, before I get sentimental and drive you all the way there myself."

"I will," she called back, waving as the lorry thundered away. "And thank you!"

Julie headed down Homestall Lane with no idea where she was going.

For a moment, she stood watching the red taillights disappear into the distance, the sound of the big engine fading into the hum of the countryside. It struck her how rare it was for anyone to be kind without wanting something in return — and that thought stayed with her as she started walking again.

She had only walked about a quarter mile when she came across a group of people outside an old, converted coach, halfway down the lane in a field next to a cherry orchard. They had long hair and wore hippie-style clothing. Most of them climbed into the vehicle, but one person stayed outside, just a few yards from where Julie was standing on the road.

Another girl, wearing a long, flowery skirt and a tie-dyed top, was busy cooking over an open fire. Her long black hair was tied up in a bun. Julie was staring, and when the girl met her gaze, she said hello. "Hi," said the girl, smiling as she approached her. "Where did you come from?"

She was articulate, and Julie, feeling embarrassed to be seen as ordinary, found herself trying to adopt a fancy accent as well.

"Oh, I got a ride to the end of the lane, and I'm on my way to Faversham," she said, waving her hand casually.

"Nice little town, Faversham," the girl said. "Did you know Faversham is the only town to use the Royal Arms of England as its own? They appear on the town council's seal, which was approved by the heraldic authorities."

Julie stood there, her mouth agape, unsure of what to say, but she finally managed to utter, "No, I didn't know that."

Standing before her, the tall, slender girl grinned. "That's the history lesson. That's about all I know about Faversham's history anyway," she said. An old farmhand told me about it while we were cherry-picking last summer."

"I've never actually been," Julie admitted. "Got friends or family there?" the girl asked. "No," replied Julie coyly.

"What then? A job?"

Julie shook her head, her voice small. "I don't really know. I just needed to get away."
The girl studied her for a moment, her expression softening. "Yeah," she said quietly. "We've all had a reason to run at some point."

Julie seemed to be getting a little flustered, so the girl said softly, "Sorry, I didn't mean to pry."

Julie, feeling lost, began to cry, and the girl wrapped her slender arm around her, the bangles clinking. "I'm sorry, are you okay?"

"Not really!" Julie said, then she blurted out her story to the hippie girl as they slowly walked toward the campfire.

"Oh, dear," the girl said. When Julie had finished, "Been there, done that, just like most of us here. I left home when I was fifteen—three years ago."

"By the way, I'm Margaret." The girl introduced herself.

"I'm Julie," she said, looking at Margaret gratefully as a weight lifted off her shoulders. She had found someone who understood.

"Come and sit down – have a nice cup of hot tea." Margaret took the kettle off the fire and poured, while Julie slumped down on the grass. "Here, drink this, and you'll feel a lot better."

"Thanks." Julie wrapped her fingers around the mug, finding comfort in it.

"Got a place to stay in Faversham?"

Julie made a face. "No, I haven't. I have no idea what I'll do. It's getting pretty scary now."

Margaret gave her a warm smile. "Don't worry, love. Faversham's full of good folk. And if it comes to it, there's always room by the fire here. We look after our own."

Julie blinked back fresh tears, managing a shaky smile. "You don't even know me."

"I don't need to," Margaret said simply. "You just look like someone who deserves a bit of luck."

"Just a minute," the girl said. "I have an idea that might help you."

She climbed into the old coach, leaving Julie to stare into the flames, lost in thought about her future. A few minutes later, Margaret came out with four others, all of whom were very friendly. They introduced themselves. Tony and Barrie were in their twenties, while there were two more girls, Sammy and Christine, who seemed to be in their late teens, similar to Margaret.

"I just filled everyone in on your situation, and we're all on the same page," Margaret said with a smile. You're more than welcome to stay with us until you sort things out, if you'd like."

"Really?" said Julie, almost laughing in relief. "That would be fantastic."

"You'll need to help out with the chores around here, though, and we all do a couple of days fruit picking," said Tony, his voice filled with a natural ease. He stood about 5 feet 10 inches tall, with long, dark hair pulled back in a ponytail. He had a scruffy appearance but was clean overall. "If you're okay with that, then it's all good."

"Yes, yes, of course, I'll do whatever!" Julie exclaimed. "I appreciate your help. I have no idea what might have happened."

"C'mon, then," Margaret reached out and helped Julie up from the grass, guiding her toward the coach.

"Let me look at those cuts, Julie." She reached for the first-aid kit in the kitchen. "They don't look too bad, but I'll clean them up for you just in case they get infected," said Margaret.

"Thanks, Margaret. Most of the scratches are from a rose bush; the one on my knee is the worst."

Margaret continued whilst cleaning Julie's wounds.

"Tony bought the coach, which was in a bit of a mess, but he had it customised," Margaret explained. "He's from Canterbury and has wealthy parents: both lawyers."

Julie's eyes widened. She had never mingled with wealthy, sophisticated people before, and she was starstruck.

"But Tony's lack of enthusiasm for the profession has left them disappointed," Margaret said, with a sly smile. "He dropped out of college in 1965 and took to the hippy trail."

Julie was stunned. These people were different from anyone she'd ever met before, and she felt honoured by their kindness.

As she entered, the old coach looked quite worn down, with belongings scattered everywhere, but it was dry and reasonably tidy. What immediately caught her eye was a small kitchen just inside the door. Further back, there was a fold-down table in the dining area. Then, she noticed what seemed to be a large, cluttered bedroom area, with mattresses and bedding strewn across the floor in front of a double bed at the back.

"We all sleep here, Julie. I'm afraid it's all open plan. I hope you're not too shy."

"N...no," Julie lied. She was, but she'd have to get used to it. She was out in the big, wide world now, and surely it couldn't be any more wicked than being with that woman at the orphanage?

Julie was quickly accepted into the group and immediately felt at ease, listening to their stories and discovering they had more in common than she initially thought. Margaret was eighteen, from Sandwich, and had a solid education, but made a wrong turn at a critical point in her life.

Sammy was a beautiful girl, but she was pretty short. She had a scar over her right eye, was slightly overweight, and had short, curly hair. Born in Glasgow, she moved to Strood with her family at age fourteen, which marked the start of her troubles.

She noticed Julie looking at the scar and decided to share her story with Julie and the others, who had never heard it before. "It happened when I was sixteen at a barbecue. A drunk boy kissed me, and I was so shocked. What made it worse was that he stuck his tongue in my mouth and rubbed his hands on my backside. My dad saw what was going on and was furious, grabbing the boy by the throat and nearly choking him. All hell broke loose when the boy's dad got involved, and they all crashed into the barbecue, destroying it. The boy's dad got burned on both arms, and I hit my head on a corner. Although I wasn't burned, I got a nasty cut above my right eye, leaving this scar."

CHAPTER FIVE – *First Awakening*

Life with the hippies brings Julie a strange new freedom — a community built on peace, music, and pleasure. As she grows close to them, curiosity stirs within her, and she begins to learn what it means to truly belong.

As time went on, Julie got to know them better. Barrie, whose name meant "spear" in Gaelic, came over from Ireland, but he didn't talk much about his past, except that his parents were killed in an IRA bombing in 1965. He carried that loss quietly, like a man always half-looking over his shoulder.

Barrie's long, scraggly red beard and wild hair gave him the look of someone who had spent a lifetime outdoors. He was skilled at catching rabbits and the occasional pheasant, which meant they rarely went hungry. Julie admired his quiet competence and easy humour. He was a mystery — but a comforting one.

Christine, or "Chris" as they called her, was twenty and the oldest in the group. Born in 1948, she had grown up in London's East End, in the shadow of Jack the Ripper's old haunts. Her father, a soldier, had been one of the last evacuated from Dunkirk. Her life had not been easy — she had left school at fifteen, fending for herself, learning to survive in a harsh world. She was outspoken, bold, and seemed to live entirely by her own rules.

Chris's free spirit fascinated Julie. She was striking — long blonde hair, confident smile, never afraid to draw attention. She had a way of holding court around the fire, talking about music, London nights, and the thrill of freedom. Julie found herself listening, mesmerised.

She had an abortion at thirteen and was forced to leave school at fifteen. A true rebel, she openly explored her sexuality with both men and women. She was slim, with long blonde hair and large breasts, often walking around the camp naked, which drew attention from the boys.

They spent a few days each week picking fruit, just enough to cover their basic food and essential meds. Julie hung out with them, mostly avoiding the drugs but sometimes trying them. Although the coach was a complete mess, with clothes, bedding, and junk scattered everywhere, and no place to store anything, Julie was happy in her new life, free from the nightmare of the orphanage. Still, there were moments when she grew restless. The endless summer nights carried a rhythm she didn't yet understand — a mix of laughter, whispers, and closeness that seemed to fill the space between everyone but her.

Back then, it was the era of free love. At night, after getting high on weed or other substances, they'd pair off and have sex, often falling asleep together—usually Tony with Margaret and Barrie with Sammy. Christine would go with whoever was in the mood at the time, regardless of gender. Julie was always invited, but she always declined, still too nervous and afraid. She kept to herself, turning her face to the wall and pretending to be asleep. But hearing and seeing the others engage in it most nights, she found herself strangely intrigued and wondering what it would be like to have sex.

One night, as she lay in bed, she overheard the others having a good time. Wondering again what it would be like, she felt a strange sensation spread between her legs. At first, she thought it was just an itch, something she could scratch to make it go away.

She always went to bed with a blanket and underwear on, so she lifted her hand from under the pillow and reached down to scratch the itch. Her hand slipped inside her underwear, and she touched the spot where the sensation was coming from. It felt like she'd gotten an electric shock; the sensation shot up her body to her head, and her heart seemed to stop.

She let out a soft yelp, but no one heard. She quickly released, terrified of what had just happened. She lay there panting and confused, trying to understand what had just occurred.

She finally came to her senses, recalling the group's sex session, and remembered them discussing how intense their orgasms were afterward. *Did I have one?* she wondered. *No way*, she thought. *You have to have sex to get that kind of release, surely.*

She felt both confused and curious at the same time. A sensation lingered between her legs, and she wanted to try again but felt afraid. With her heart racing, she decided to touch herself again.

She hesitantly slid her hand back inside her underwear again and touched the spot where the sensation was coming from. As soon as she did, the electric sensation was overwhelming, and she immediately brought her legs together.

Still, this time she didn't pull back. It was pleasant; she relished the sensation, and she knew she would want sex if she ever got the chance. Even though the others had each made a move, she had never given in.

Two nights later in August, on Julie's eighteenth birthday, they gathered around the campfire after finishing a rabbit stew, drinking plenty of booze, and getting high on cannabis. Barrie leaned back on his elbows, took a long drag on his joint, his eyes half-closed against the smoke, watching her with a grin. "So, birthday girl — what's it feel like to be eighteen and free?"

Julie laughed, shaking her head. "Feels the same — only hungrier."

That brought another roar of laughter. Margaret passed her a tin mug and said, "Then eat, drink, and laugh with us. You're one of us now, Jules. No going back."

They toasted to freedom, to friendship, to love. The night became softer, the air heavy with summer heat. Julie felt it all at once — the closeness, the belonging, the pulse of something new rising in her chest.

Later, as the fire dimmed and the guitar fell quiet, she sat staring into the embers. A hand touched hers. She didn't pull away. For the first time, she let the moment happen — not with fear, but with trust.

Barrie looked straight at her with a twinkle in his eye and said, "How would you like to join me and Sammy tonight?"

Julie was taken aback, shocked at the suggestion, and could not answer.

She remained silent, her eyes fixed on Barrie and Sammy, who were now intensely focused on the one-sided conversation.

She was paralyzed with shock when Sammy joined in and sat down next to her, taking her other hand and gazing into her eyes, saying, "It's just a suggestion, Julie. You can say no, and we won't be offended."

"I'm not offended; I'm just caught off guard and surprised by the sudden offer. I wasn't expecting that as the best present." Taking a deep breath, Julie asked if she could have a few minutes to think it over.

"Of course," Sammy said, "no pressure here."

Having put this off for weeks, and after the experience two nights ago, and now eighteen, she was still a virgin and nervous about the unknown. Her friends had made it seem natural, and she knew she couldn't refuse forever. They had been kind, and her curiosity was growing. She shrugged noncommittally—this was a step forward from her usual rejections. They had a couple more bottles of homemade wine and smoked some more weed. Julie had a few extra drinks too and got a little tipsy, but she relaxed.

"What do you think, Julie?" Barrie asked, smiling encouragingly. Julie nodded shyly, and Sammy stood up, reaching for her hand. The two of them casually walked to the coach, with Sammy leading her inside to the double bed, where they sat down together. Sammy wrapped her arm around Julie and kissed her softly on the lips. Julie was surprised, but with a bit of help from the alcohol, she didn't pull away. This was Julie's first time kissing someone, especially someone of the same sex, but she found herself responding. Sensing Julie's slight tension, Sammy held her more gently and kissed her again, until Julie began to relax. As Sammy's tongue entered Julie's mouth, she was initially alarmed but soon started to enjoy the sensation.

Not long after, Barrie showed up, and by that point Julie was getting pretty worked up and excited, and the drink and drugs had lowered her inhibitions. She knew she was about to lose her virginity, but it didn't matter to her anymore.

Barrie wrapped his arms around them, and the three were locked in a passionate kiss: their tongues entwined, hands caressing, all intertwined in bed. Barrie's kiss with Julie was intense, his hand cupping one breast, while Sammy's tongue circled Julie's ear, sending shivers down the other. With no bra on, Julie's nipples instantly hardened under their touch, and the teasing sent her into a gasp, her eyes nearly rolling back. She let out a low moan: nothing had ever felt this exhilarating before. She was in a different realm, her body quaking with pleasure, and she didn't care what came next.

Everyone else was gathered outside, peering in through the open door to see what was going on, but the three on the bed appeared oblivious.

Sammy was also getting worked up and wet, one hand rubbing Barrie's crotch over his trousers. Hungrily, they lifted Julie's blouse, revealing two pert little breasts. Both girls were now topless, and Sammy put her arms around Julie, rubbing their breasts together, while Barrie looked on, idly playing with himself, trying not to cum. Sammy's hand went down to Julie's pert little bottom over her flowery skirt, rubbing it, her finger following the crack down between her legs. Julie tensed. Barrie dragged Sammy's elasticated skirt down, then did the same to Julie's, so both girls were now just in their panties, and he fondled their cute little butts. Sammy guided Julie's hand to Barrie's trouser belt and eagerly helped her undo his jeans, pulling them down. Noticing the bulge in his underpants, Julie was aware that she had never seen a real penis so closely before, only from a distance when Barrie was drunk or stoned and pissed up the side of the coach, and she was a little afraid.

Julie and the two girls were lying on the bed with Barrie in between. Since this was his first time with Julie, he rolled over and started kissing her, his hand tracing over her breasts, down her stomach, and then fingering her belly button, before stroking inside her underwear. Julie let out a gasp. She was on fire, shaking with anticipation, and very, very wet between her legs when his hand arrived there. He was enjoying this new girl. His finger soon found her lips, and she let out a low, loud moan as his finger stroked and then gently entered her well-lubricated entrance.

Sammy pulled down Julie's knickers, giving Barrie better access, and it didn't take long before he started rubbing. He eventually found her G-spot, and despite her nerves, pleasure surged through Julie's body, sending electric shocks through her brain and making her toes curl up. She almost burst out laughing. She'd never experienced such intense pleasure in her entire life.

Sammy was so wet, Barrie inserted three fingers into her, as she leaned over him, hard nipples brushing his nose, and an eager mouth. He managed to catch hold and suck one of them, while Sammy removed his pants and revealed his large member. She could not resist taking it into her mouth, sucking slowly at first, then harder. Now out of his mind with pleasure, Barrie rolled Julie over, lifted his head, and started to gently lick Julie's outer lips until she was gasping with delight, especially when Barrie inserted his tongue right inside her, tasting her sweet juices.

Tony, Margaret, and Christine, who had been watching from the doorway, couldn't take it anymore and stepped into the coach.

Christine was the first to strip off completely to join in the orgy, going up to Sammy, who was on the bed with Barrie's manhood in her mouth. Chris put her tongue into Sammy's mouth, and their tongues greedily engaged. Tony and Margaret were kissing each other and stripping each other naked, their tongues spinning around each other's.

Now there were six naked bodies intertwined, squirming, on and off the bed. There were no rules – anybody with anyone, doing anything. Fingers anywhere.

Everything fell silent as Barrie parted Julie's legs, kneeling between them with his huge member in his hand. Julie was horrified: it looked massive, and she was worried she wouldn't be big enough to take it. But she was also intensely excited – she wanted him inside her, right then!

Sammy lightly pushed Julie onto her back, dipping her head between her and Barrie, and she started to use her tongue on Julie's clitoris. Julie wriggled, almost overwhelmed. Opening her eyes, she realised that Tony had put his manhood near her mouth. She knew what he wanted and licked it gently. He pushed forward, and she took it in her mouth, gripping it with her hand to stop him from going further down her throat in case she gagged.

Then Sammy stopped what she was doing to Julie and moved away, as the tip of Barry's manhood began lightly pressing against Julie's throbbing, wet flesh. She tensed up, not knowing what it would feel like. Sammy helped by gently spreading Julie's lips whilst Barrie pushed a little harder. The head entered Julie, and she tensed up; it hurt. Luckily for her, Barrie was a gentle lover. He slowly entered her, withdrawing, then gradually entering a little more each time, until he had at least four inches in her. Julie gasped. So, this is sex!

With one slow, hard thrust, she had all his manhood inside her.

Once he was certain she was okay, Barrie started to thrust in and out, faster. As Julie became more relaxed and uninhibited, she eagerly lifted her hips, trying to get more inside her, but she had it all. She was soon thrusting with him. Barrie eventually withdrew, and Sammy took him in her mouth and finished him off, swallowing his cum.

Julie was still on her back, recovering but still frustrated and excited, when Tony lay astride her and stared pleadingly at her, as if asking permission. There was no resistance from Julie: in fact, she pulled him towards her, and he entered her. Tony was bigger than Barrie, and more enthusiastic, so it hurt Julie a little at first, but she quickly lost herself as Tony brought her to a massive orgasm – and to her shock and surprise, she gushed all over him.

Tony quickly took out his manhood and put it in Julie's mouth, where he came in seconds. Poor Julie had not expected it to taste so salty and spat it all out.

Julie was clueless about what was happening with the others. All she could hear were noises as she lay, exhausted, her eyes closed, feeling warm, buzzing, and a bit sore.

Julie's first experience of sex was her first — but not her last — orgy.

CHAPTER SIX – *The Shadow in the Field*

An afternoon of peace turns into horror when danger comes too close to camp. Julie learns how quickly the world can take from her what little safety she has found — and how strength sometimes comes from simply surviving.

One Sunday afternoon, while the others were in town grabbing supplies, Julie and Barrie were lounging when they heard shouting and laughter from the nearby woods.

"What's that?" Julie asked, a wave of unease washing over her.

Barrie shrugged but got up, his eyes fixed on the source of the noise.

Barrie frowned, shading his eyes. "Could be poachers… or just drunk lads out from the town."

Two men stumbled into the field, looking like they had been poaching. They had a rabbit and a couple of pheasants, so it was apparent they had been, and they were probably drunk, based on their loud voices and aggressive behaviour. They came over and started yelling at Julie and Barrie.

"Yah! Fuckin" beatniks!" shouted one.

"Filthy bastards," said the other, laughing.

Julie stiffened. Barrie stayed seated but tense. "Just ignore them," he muttered.

The two guys moved closer and started to mock them. Barrie and Julie did their best to ignore them, but it wasn't easy.

"Peace, man!" the smaller one mocked, flashing two fingers in the air.

"That's what you call yourselves, eh? Peace and dirt!"

"Fuck off and die, you useless unwashed slobs," the taller, broader one seethed, right in Barrie's face.

Despite being a big guy, Barrie knew he wouldn't stand a chance against the two of them, so he decided to keep his mouth shut. He hoped they'd move on, but he wasn't about to get that lucky.

The two guys circled them again and started making lewd comments to Julie. "No tits, but I'd give 'er one."

Barrie stood up and said, "We're a peaceful people, and we don't want any trouble. Please leave us alone."

The taller man sneered. "Look at this one, preaching love in his fancy boots."

"Peace, man!" The smaller one sarcastically flipped two fingers in the air, his eyes blazing with anger.

He touched Julie's hair. "A bit greasy, this one."

Barrie stepped forward. "Come on, buddy. Just leave us alone."

There was no way those jerks were going to do that. One of them shoved Barrie backward, sending him sprawling into the mud. The pair burst out laughing.

Julie gasped. "Stop it! Leave him alone!"

Barrie quickly got up and chased the guy who pushed him, but he was soon overwhelmed by the two of them. They forced Barrie face down in the mud and started beating him brutally, with one boot striking his head. Julie began screaming, so one of the guys grabbed her and covered her mouth.

Barrie was out for the count.

The lad holding Julie said, "I bet this slut loves a gang bang."

Julie had no idea what a gang bang was, but she was certain it wasn't good. They forced her inside the coach, where she screamed out in protest. One of them tore off her clothes, leaving her completely naked, while the other held her down.

"Let's just fuck her and get out of here before anybody else turns up."

Julie was helpless. She was terrified and crying for them to leave her alone, but that didn't bother these scumbags. Every time she screamed, they slapped her in the face. Although she was only a slight girl, she fought like a tiger, grabbing anything she could lay her hands on, screaming, fighting, punching, and kicking, with both of them, catching her shin on one of the cupboards, but felt nothing in her adrenaline-fueled rage.

The cowards hit her back, knocking her to the coach floor, and one of them kicked her in the head. "Fuck this," the bigger one said, "she ain't worth it, let's piss off." They walked past Julie, curled up naked on the floor in a foetal position, sobbing, spitting on her on the way out.

As Barrie regained consciousness, the two scumbags were leaving the coach. He realised they had taken anything they could find but had no idea what they had done to Julie. He grabbed a piece of wood and charged at them, no longer caring about his safety. He tried to swing the wood overhead at the nearest thug. However, the tight space wouldn't allow it, and the wood instead hit an overhanging branch, jolting his wrists. This gave them the chance to tackle him again, and they knocked him out for a second time.

They had ransacked the place, stealing three shillings and drugs from a kitchen drawer, leaving Julie curled up on the floor and Barrie unconscious, face down outside, still and bleeding.

One of them glanced around the coach quickly, making sure they hadn't missed anything. Then, he spat at Julie again, who was still sobbing on the floor, as he walked away laughing. They also gave Barrie one last kick for good measure as they walked past, calling them "stinking beatniks."

Julie pulled herself together, still sobbing, grabbed some clothes, and rushed over to Barrie, who was still unconscious. She went back into the coach, soaked a towel in water, and pressed it to Barrie's face. She had no idea what else to do.

After a few minutes, Barrie began to stir, his eyes glassy and unfocused for a moment. He sat up straight, taking in his surroundings. "Are they gone?" he asked.

"Yeah, just barely. Are you alright?"

"I think so," he replied as he got up with Julie's help, battered and bruised, bleeding, and feeling faint.

"Sit down, and I'll grab something for those cuts."

She limped back into the coach without thinking and grabbed the first aid kit Margaret had used on her. Then she went back outside to Barrie, who had noticed Julie's torn clothes and the swelling on her face, and that she was limping.

"My God, they've beaten you up too," he said, voice loud and worried.

"Are you alright? Why are you limping?"

"Don't worry about me; let me look at those cuts." She was holding back tears, in pain, especially from the nasty cut on her shin, which was swelling quickly, and blood was running down her leg, but she was more worried about Barrie, who had been knocked out twice.

She tended to his worst cuts and applied some bandages; one was especially severe and needed to be wrapped up. She also gave him some aspirin for the pain, but it would take a while before those injuries stopped aching. She discreetly took a couple of aspirin herself, not wanting to worry Barrie.

She had tried to hide her face from Barrie, but he noticed the bruises again, and they were growing larger.

"Come on, Julie, my turn to be the doctor, let me look at your face."

She turned to face him, and he went into a fit of rage. "The bastards, what have they done to you? Why beat up a girl? Fucking cowards!"

Julie, sobbing again and barely able to speak, told him they had beaten her because she resisted them while they were trying to rape her, and that she had hit her shin on the cupboard.

Barrie tended to Julie's bruises, but all he could give her was a damp towel to put on them. Luckily, she didn't have any broken skin, except for the nasty bruise and cut on her very painful shin. Barrie wrapped it up after putting on some antibiotic cream.

Julie limped back into the coach, trembling from thoughts of what might have happened. She changed into her nightclothes and lay on her bed, reflecting on how fortunate she was not to have been raped or harmed more seriously. She decided that the cuts and bruises were worth it, even though she still felt traumatised.

When Tony and the other three girls returned, Barrie, his face battered, was sitting on an old log inspecting his injuries, and Julie was in shock inside the coach.

"What the hell has happened here?" asked Tony.

Barrie explained the situation, but what were they supposed to do about it? They were outcasts, and the police wouldn't take them seriously. Plus, with their secret stashes of drugs and way of life, they didn't want the police poking around anyway, so they'd just have to hope the thugs didn't show up again.

Meanwhile, the girls went to check on Julie, offering her gentle comfort as they stroked her hair and whispered softly while she cried and shared her story.

"You're safe now, love," Margaret murmured, stroking her hair. "You did nothing wrong. You hear me? Nothing."

The guys were unsure of how to help, so they tried by bringing her tea and offering her the first hit on each joint - it was all they could think to do.

For the next few weeks, the group moved more cautiously, taking turns to watch the camp at night. Barrie carried guilt like a shadow; he believed he should have protected her.

It took Julie a few weeks to physically recover from the trauma, but the cuts and bruises faded. However, the emotional and mental scars remained. The incident would always stay in the back of her mind, haunting her thoughts and feelings about what could have been. She needed some time to get past her fear of intimacy again, as the idea of anyone touching her made her uneasy. Her friends were understanding and waited for her to heal. They offered gentle hugs when she needed them and rocked her to sleep like a child would be rocked. Julie's bruises faded, but the memory did not. Some nights she woke with a start, her heart pounding at a sound in the dark. But she refused to give in to fear. Each morning, she rose, tended the fire, and helped with the fruit-picking as if nothing had changed.

In truth, everything had.

She had survived.

And somewhere inside her, beneath the ache and exhaustion, a quiet determination began to grow — that she would never again let the world decide who she was or what she was worth.

CHAPTER SEVEN – *A Room and a Key*

Winter bites, money thins, and Julie chooses a different life. A chance meeting with LeeRoy opens a door to work, a room of her own, and the first real shot at independence.

Winter arrived, and with the dole money and what they had saved from picking fruit, they managed to get by, just barely.

Julie was too scared to go to the unemployment office, worried that the authorities would discover her and report her to the orphanage. Even though she was eighteen now, she still feared the Matron and what might happen, so she played it safe. She felt guilty taking money from the others and tried to make up for it by cooking and cleaning as much as she could. But the cramped coach and cold weather were taking a toll, and with no money, she was getting restless. In the spring of 1971, she decided it was time to find a job, so she headed to Faversham.

She enquired at a few shops, but no one seemed to be taking on any new staff. Maybe she came across as too relaxed and uncool, with her unkempt hair and bohemian style. Frustrated, she stumbled upon Bushe's Café on Court Street and decided to grab a cup of tea and clear her head. Little did she know, it would be a turning point in her life.

As she sipped her tea, contemplating her options, her eyes met a black man's eyes across the room. He offered her a wide, friendly smile that caught her off guard – she'd never seen a black man in person before, only in books or magazines. At first, she looked away, but she couldn't help glancing back. He was still there, looking at her with a hint of flirtation.

"Don't be shy, love — I don't bite," he called across softly, his voice warm enough to make her smile despite herself.

She flashed him a shy smile, and that was all it took. A surge of nerves hit her as he got up and walked over to her. She couldn't help but notice how handsome, tall, and athletic he was, probably in his twenties, she figured. When he sat down, a waft of expensive cologne enveloped her. She'd never been around a man who smelled so incredible!

He pulled out a chair and sat down, never taking his eyes off her. "What's your name?" he asked, a hint of mischief in his smile. She told him, and he flashed a grin. "Nice to meet you, Julie. I'm LeeRoy, LeeRoy Alonso." "Nice to meet you, too, LeeRoy Alonso," she replied.

"That's a name you won't forget, huh?" he teased, and she laughed.

Julie lowered her eyes to her cup, trying to hide the blush rising in her cheeks. "You talk like you know that already," she said. "Maybe I do," LeeRoy chuckled. "You've got that look about you — like you're pretending not to be curious."
"Maybe I'm not pretending," she said, half-teasing, half-trembling.
He leaned in just enough for her to catch the soft scent of aftershave again. "Then maybe I'll give you a reason to be."

"You're almost done with your coffee; would you like me to grab you another?" His eyes sparkled with genuine happiness.

Julie hesitated, glancing toward the counter. "If I say yes, does that mean I'm in trouble?"
"Only if you don't," he grinned. "I promise, it's just coffee... for now."
She laughed softly, surprising herself. "All right then — but just one."
"Deal," he said, standing to order, and for the first time in a long while, Julie felt the weight of the past lift just a little.

Delight! That's the word, Julie thought. *He looks delightful.* Julie smiled to herself. It was great to feel appreciated, and she had a good vibe about LeeRoy.

He returned with his coffee and Julie's tea and sat down with her. "I haven't seen you around before. So, what brings you to Faversham?" She told him she was in town looking for a job.

"Oh, what kind of work are you looking for?"

"Anything. I need to get out of the place I'm living now."

"And where might that be?"

"Macknade. We're living in an old coach in the orchard, near the motorway."

"Ha, yes. I've seen that." He smiled. "So, where are you from?"

"Well," she said, "it's a long story." She told LeeRoy about the accident and the orphanage in Bexhill, and said to him she hated it there. His smile fell as he looked concerned. "Why? What was wrong with it?"

"What was right with it?" Julie snorted. "It was super strict, and there was this awful matron who was always on my case. I couldn't take it anymore, so I took off and ended up with the people I'm living with now. However, things are becoming increasingly challenging over time. We've got nothing—just drugs and sex. When she mentioned sex, she looked down at the floor, though I don't use drugs. I've tried a few, but I'm not keen."

"Sounds alright to me," LeeRoy said with a teasing tone.

"It's not every day, week in and week out. They're sex-crazed. It was fun at first, but you never know who you might end up with in bed, male or female."

"It just keeps getting better!" LeeRoy said with a grin.

"Anyway," Julie said quickly, "I need to move on. I'm eighteen now and I'm ready for more in my life."

LeeRoy nodded slowly, deep in thought. "Have you ever worked in a pub?" he asked.

"I've never done anything except picking fruit," she said, "but I'm willing to learn. Why?"

"Well, there's a pub on Preston Street, and I know they're looking for a barmaid. They've been looking for a while now. I know the owner pretty well. I'm sure he'd give you a shot."

"Do you think so?" Julie beamed, getting excited. Then she added, hesitantly, "And would he be okay with a hippie behind the bar?"

"Maybe not," LeeRoy said. "But to be fair, it's just your clothes." He looked her over from head to toe. *With a fresh haircut and a new outfit, she'd be breathtaking. Scratch that. She's already breathtaking,* he thought!

Being somewhat of a ladies' man, LeeRoy didn't want to let this one slip away. He realised she was vulnerable and was going to do his best to get to know her better.

"Hey," he said hesitantly, aware that what he was about to say might sound weird, since they had only just met ten minutes ago. "My sister lives with me, and I'm pretty sure she has some regular clothes she's no longer using. She's super frugal and tends to hold onto everything, and she's around your size."

"Hmmm." Julie gave him a sceptical look, taking him in. Her instincts told her he was the real deal. "That's all well and good," she said, "but I still have to go back to that awful brothel. To be honest, they've treated me well in many ways. They took me in without asking any questions. But I can't do it anymore."

"Then don't go back," he said gently. "You've done your share of surviving — now it's time to live."

"Okay, let's take it one step at a time. You might have to stick around for a while, but I'm sure Chas—"

"Chas? Who's Chas?" Julie interrupted. LeeRoy chuckled, explaining that Chas was the landlord of the pub. "I'm sure if he offered you the job, he could also provide you with accommodation if you wanted it."

"Chas has a spare room; well, he did a week ago, and I'm sure it would work for him if you moved in, especially if things get busy."

"I don't know," Julie said, biting her lip. "It's all happening so fast, and I've only just met you. Don't get me wrong. You seem like a nice guy," she hesitated, then looked at him and threw her hands up. "What the heck? Why not? I've got nothing to lose. In fact, I have nothing. Anything is a plus."

"Great," LeeRoy said, his dark brown eyes shining with happiness. "Let's start by visiting my sister." They stood up, and LeeRoy helped her put on her coat. "It's only a five-minute drive."

Julie hesitated, uneasy about getting into a car. But she knew worse things had happened. LeeRoy seemed like a decent guy, and she hoped she could start trusting people again.

"If I scream, you'd better stop," she said half-jokingly as they walked.

"You won't need to," he smiled. "But I'll stop anyway."

They walked past the Guild Hall, down the alleyway beside the bank, to the car park. A nearly new silver Rolls-Royce was parked there, and LeeRoy stopped.

"Here we are," he said, taking out his keys and unlocking the driver's door.

Julie almost died. "This? This is yours?" she stuttered. "Whoa, what do you do for a living?"

"Oh, this and that," LeeRoy said, and left it at that.

Julie was over the moon. She had only ever seen a Rolls-Royce in magazines, never mind riding in one. LeeRoy opened the passenger side door and held it for Julie to get in. "Thanks," Julie said politely to LeeRoy, impressed. When he got behind the wheel, he noticed Julie running her hands over the leather seats and couldn't help but smile. LeeRoy turned the key and started the engine, but you could barely hear it – it was more like a purring kitten. Julie stroked the leather upholstery again and burst out laughing, which just made LeeRoy smile again. He decided he had never met a nicer, more down-to-earth girl.

"You're laughing at my car?" he asked.

"No," she said, "I'm laughing at my life. Yesterday I was sleeping on a coach — today I'm sitting in a Rolls-Royce."

He drove past the cottage hospital and then turned left, followed by a right into Preston Street.

"The pub is just down there," he said, "but that's for later – first, let's get you some interview clothes."

He drove over the M2, telling Julie that he recalled when it was under construction and how much it had improved his frequent trips to London. They then headed to Sheldwich, where they pulled up to a massive house with electric gates. As they slowed down, LeeRoy used the remote to open the gates, which looked like something straight out of a sci-fi movie to Julie. She figured he must live in some gated community.

As LeeRoy drove down the driveway, he pulled up in front of the impressive mansion, which had large stone columns on either side of its massive oak door.

"What? Where?" Julie exclaimed. "Is this yours? You bought this?"

"Sort of," he said.

"What does 'sort of' mean?"

"Just sort of," Julie. That's all." He smiled, speaking firmly enough to let her know not to push it.

With its luxurious gardens and grand entrance, the mansion was the ultimate symbol of a lifestyle she could only imagine visiting, never mind living in.

As LeeRoy stepped ahead and held the door open, Julie felt as though she was receiving special treatment. It was something new for her, and for the first time in her short life, she felt like a real lady.

As they entered, Julie was taken aback by the decor. The imported marble floors and walls, combined with the intricate hand-carved woodwork and gilded staircase, showcased LeeRoy's extravagant style.

The mansion's spacious living areas, including several sitting rooms, a grand formal dining room, and a large chef's kitchen, offered plenty of space for hosting big gatherings and entertaining guests in style.

As LeeRoy called out for his sister, a lovely young woman appeared at the top of the impressive staircase. She seemed to float down the stairs, and LeeRoy introduced her as Rosina. She had the same warm smile as LeeRoy, and at 19, she was about Julie's height, with long, jet-black hair that looked soft and full, almost like a black thundercloud. Her skin was a rich, autumn brown and as smooth as glass. Her eyes, unlike LeeRoy's, were a unique lake green - a colour Julie found interesting but didn't mention. Rosina didn't seem to mind a random hippie girl dropping by her place.

"This is some place you have here!" Julie exclaimed, taking in the spacious entrance hall. "I've never seen anything like it in my life."

"Oh, it's cozy," Rosina said, raising one eyebrow with a hint of amusement on her face. "It's home, and we love it, even though I'm not here all that often."

"If this is cozy," Julie laughed, "I can't wait to see what you call fancy."

When LeeRoy filled Rosina in on the situation, she happily took Julie upstairs. When they entered one of the main bedrooms, Julie was again awestruck.

The pièce de résistance was one of the mansion's luxurious suites, featuring a private balcony overlooking a large lake and vast countryside with the Isle of Sheppey in the distance, a Jacuzzi tub, and a spacious walk-in closet.

"This is amazing," Julie stuttered.

"It's nice," Rosina agreed, "especially on a warm morning, a great spot for breakfast."

"You have breakfast on a balcony?" She gasped. "I usually have mine on a crate outside the coach."

As Julie gazed out at the view, feeling as though she were in a dream, Rosina found her some suitable clothes. After getting dressed, Julie stared at herself in the mirror, which stretched from floor to ceiling, and thought, "Wow, what a difference nice clothes make." She wondered if she'd miss the hippie, colourful swirl of flounces and cheesecloth, feeling a little out of place in regular clothes, but was sure she'd get used to it again.

They made their way back downstairs, and the transformation took LeeRoy by surprise. Rosina had styled Julie's hair, and the olive-green dress hugged her like a second skin. She had never worn a dress with the hem above her knees before. She looked absolutely breathtaking—like a beautiful, delicate blonde princess. LeeRoy was utterly captivated by her beauty, especially now that she was clean and polished. At first, he was speechless, his eyes wide with admiration, and his jaw dropped open in astonishment.

Rosina's lips curled into a smile. She knew her brother well, but she'd never seen him like this before, and he was speechless.

As LeeRoy came back to life, all he could manage was a whisper: "Wow!" "You're stunning! I don't think you'll have any trouble getting the job."

She twirled around, giggling, and he was enchanted, unable to take his eyes off her long, slender legs. When he regained his speech, he said, "Let's take a drive up there now."

"If I don't get the job, can I still keep the dress?" she joked, and LeeRoy laughed.

Saying goodbye to Rosina and thanking her several times, they set off to The Hole in the Wall.

On the way to the pub, Julie mentioned to LeeRoy, "I saw one of your pictures in the lounge and noticed your name is spelled with two capital letters, the 'L' and 'R', and two e's." She asked, "Isn't that a bit unusual?"

He chuckled, "Yeah, it is. They messed up my birth certificate; I should have been called 'Lee' and given the middle name 'Roy'. My mother thought it was easier to leave it as is rather than deal with the hassle of getting it changed, so here I am, a LeeRoy with two capitals and two e's."

I think Leeroy or LeeRoy originated from the Normans in France, but I'm not sure.

"Well, LeeRoy-with-two-capitals," Julie said, "that's a name I won't forget."

They turned onto Preston Street, a narrow road lined with old shopfronts and lamplight glowing on the wet pavement. A few locals were walking in the same direction, collars turned up against the evening chill. LeeRoy slowed the car and pulled over next to a low, whitewashed building with hanging lanterns and a sign that read The Hole in the Wall. The faint sound of laughter and clinking glasses drifted from inside.

"Here we are," he said, switching off the engine. "Looks quiet now, but it'll be packed later."

"This place has a bit of history," LeeRoy said as they walked toward the entrance. "It was built around sixteen hundred — used to be a coaching inn back when horse-drawn carriages stopped here overnight. They've added to it over the years, but it's still in great shape. There are three bars now — one with a snooker table and a dartboard, another they call the posh bar, and then the public bar for the regulars."

"Three bars?" Julie murmured. "Blimey... I'll need a map."

As they walked in, only three old guys were sitting in the corner, chatting away and not even looking up.

One of the barmaids said, "Hi, LeeRoy, what can I get you?"

"Nothing, thanks, we're here to see Chas."

"OK, no problem, he's just down in the cellar changing a barrel. He'll be up in a sec."

Julie asked, "Excuse me, may I use your toilet, please?" Yes, of course. It's just through that door, past the fireplace." Julie replied, "Thanks," and walked away.

"Go ahead," LeeRoy said lightly, "I'll wait here."

Chas came up the stairs from the cellar and immediately spotted LeeRoy. "Hey LeeRoy, how's it going today, buddy?" "Great, thanks, Chas. Everything alright with you, I hope?"

"Yeah, thanks, we had a hectic night last night, and of course, it's Saturday, it's gonna be another crazy night."

"Anyway, what brings you in so early?"

"Are you still hiring a barmaid?"

"Yes, I am. Are you looking for work?"

Laughing. "You couldn't afford me, Chas, but I might have a friend who's interested. She hasn't done any bar work before, but she's willing to learn."

"Okay, sounds good to me, ask her to pop in and see me when it's convenient." "She's here now, just popped out to the loo." "Great, do you want a beer while you're waiting?" "Why not," replied LeeRoy, "pint of Guinness please."

Chas was nearly finished pouring the Guinness when Julie returned. He saw her and almost overfilled the glass, stopping just in time, and he looked at LeeRoy, who had noticed Chas's jaw drop and the Guinness nearly spill over. He just got a sly wink from LeeRoy.

Chas, a Cockney boy with lots of personality, was introduced to Julie. She thought he looked pretty old - he had a beer belly and was starting to go bald, with a strand of hair combed over the top of his head.

"This is my friend, Julie, who's interested in your vacancy."

"Nice to meet you," Chas said, his eyes sparkling at the prospect of getting to know this stunning young woman behind the bar. "What's your background, Julie? Sorry, LeeRoy mentioned you didn't have bar experience, but what kind of work have you done?"

"Only fruit picking," replied Julie, head lowered, feeling a little embarrassed.

"I'm sure she could learn, really quickly," LeeRoy interrupted. Chas thought for a moment, then glanced at the stunning young woman who would undoubtedly win over all the guys in the bar, and said, "What the hell! Yeah, let's give it a shot."

"Thank you," Julie said softly. "I won't let you down."

Just one more thing, you old bastard," added LeeRoy. "She needs a room, too. I told her you run a bed and breakfast. How about a live-in barmaid?"

"Ah," said Chas, "you're pushing your luck now, my old friend, but I believe we can work something out. Just keep in mind, it will affect what she gets paid."

That was okay with Julie. She appreciated what they were doing for her and couldn't believe how kind people were being. Little did she know, they both had their eyes on her, but Julie, still a bit naive, had no idea.

"The full-time pay is fifteen pounds a week, paid in cash, but I'll only give you twelve quid since you have a free room."

"That's fine," Julie said gratefully with a big grin.

Chas grunted. "When can you start?"

"Right away, if that's okay with you. I don't have any other commitments."

"Sounds great," Chas said. "It's Saturday, and we'll be busy tonight. Not the best day to start, but it won't hurt to dive right in. We can get you up to speed early on. Come on."

"Deep end it is," Julie breathed, "just tell me where to swim, even though I hate water."

"Let's go show you the room. Luckily, we haven't rented them all out yet. Do you have any luggage with you?" "No, I'll have to pick it up later. I don't have much, so no worries."

Chas led them to the staircase and signalled for Julie to go up the dimly lit back stairs first, saying, "Ladies first." Julie thought he was being a gentleman, but he couldn't help but sneak a glance at her tiny rear end in that tight dress as he followed her up the stairs. LeeRoy was right behind him. When Chas opened the door to Julie's room, she was over the moon. The room was beautiful, fully furnished, and seemed incredibly spacious, especially after the cramped old coach she'd been sharing with six people. She exclaimed, "This is like staying at a five-star hotel! Not that I've ever been to one, but I imagine it's like this. Thanks so much."

"You're welcome," Chas said, picturing himself lying on the bed with her. "Your bathroom is just through that door."

"Bathroom?" Julie squeaked, and she dashed across the room. "I have my own bathroom – I can't remember the last time I took a real bath!"

Not only was there a bath, but also a shower, sink, and toilet. She almost fainted and couldn't contain her excitement.

Chas grinned. She was easily impressed and looked very grateful. He would soon be in her panties, but how could he manage that without his wife catching him? He guessed LeeRoy had the same idea, if he hadn't already acted on it. "Alright, it's yours. We'll give you some time to get settled in. It's four hours before we open again tonight. I'll send one of the other girls up for you an hour before we open."

"Awesome!" Julie turned her sparkling eyes to her saviour.

"Will you be here tonight, LeeRoy?"

"Nothing can keep me away tonight, my darlin. See ya later."

Good," she said, "because I'll need a friendly face."

Julie was alone. Now she had time to think about the hippies she'd left behind. *What would they think? Or would they not care? People like them come and go all the time.*

So what? I'm happy. At last, I have the chance to make something of myself, even if it is behind a bar.

First, she went to the bathroom and filled the bath with water as hot as she could handle. The bath was stocked with bath salts and other fragrant items she had never seen before. It was a luxury she had never experienced before, either.

She undressed and admired her slim, perfect body in the full-length mirror in the corner of her room, ignoring the scar on her shin. Then she stepped into the bath, flinching as her skin touched the scalding water, and she had to let in a little cold water. As she sank into the warm, scented water, she closed her eyes, still in disbelief about how fortunate she was.

Her mind drifted back to the past. The guys on the coach might not even notice she was gone, depending on how high they were. The only concern was whether she could go without the drugs she'd been taking with the others. She wasn't an addict, and she figured she'd be okay since she wasn't into the heavy stuff – just some smoking and the occasional purple heart.

She soaked in the bath for at least an hour, replenishing the hot water as it cooled, and thought about her brief, pointless life, wondering what the future might hold. If there were even a future. She took her time getting dressed, then wandered around her room, amazed to have a space all to herself. She rummaged through drawers and cupboards, gazed out the window, jumped on the bed, and then lay back, staring at the ceiling, thinking about how far she'd come from that awful matron – not just in physical distance, but also mentally. She was starting to feel more confident and comfortable in her own skin. All the abuse was now behind her.

She started thinking about the new job, feeling a mix of fear about whether she could handle it and excitement, trusting she would succeed. She practiced in her mind, picturing herself as confident and capable.

At 6 p.m., Chas's wife, Valrie, knocked on Julie's door and introduced herself. From her accent, she was also from the East End. She was pretty slim and not a bad-looking woman for her age, which Julie estimated to be about 45.

Valrie quickly gave Julie a once-over, noticing she was very young, sweet, and quite beautiful. Valrie's friendly smile didn't quite reach her eyes, as she was suspicious of this girl Chas had invited to live with them without asking her. But after a few minutes of chatting, Val could see that Julie seemed naïve and had no hidden agenda. She was as genuinely nice a person as this jaded old barmaid had ever seen.

But she still caught herself thinking: *I've got to keep an eye on that horny husband of mine. It wouldn't be the first time he tried to hit on one of the barmaids – and this one is a real cutie.* "Come on, Julie, and I'll show you the ropes before we open at seven."

Julie followed Val to the bar, where she guided her through pulling a pint and using the simple till. Val showed her where the different drinks were and how to find the prices. It was a lot to take in, and Julie's heart raced as Val went to open the doors and let in some customers who had been waiting outside.

"Come over, and I'll show you how to open the doors for future reference," Val said. "There's this lock, then the two bolts..." She demonstrated.

The people outside had started knocking on the door at 7 p.m., and Val rolled her eyes and opened it.

Julie quickly got the hang of working behind the bar and enjoyed the experience.

CHAPTER EIGHT – *The Night She Stood Tall*

After a few weeks of working and sharing drinks after hours with LeeRoy, they got to know each other much better.

"It's easier with you here," Julie admitted softly. "Work doesn't feel so scary anymore."

One night at 7 p.m., when the bar was opening, there was a loud banging on the door. Val told Julie it was probably those two idiots from the estate. She muttered something under her breath that Julie didn't catch. "They're regulars and a real pain, but we haven't seen them in a while. I was hoping they'd found another place to drink." Leaning over, she whispered to Julie as she pulled back the second bolt. "They'll get drunk and be making a nuisance of themselves soon, but don't worry."

The door burst open, and two young men, yelling and complaining, hurried to the bar counter, with Val following to serve them.

Julie's eyes widened in a second glance, and then she stared, her blood running cold. Horrified, she saw that it was the two arseholes who had beaten Barrie and tried to rape her! She felt bile rise in her throat, and she thought she might vomit. She forced it down, feeling light-headed, and made her way to the bar, keeping her head down.

"Breathe, Julie," she told herself silently. "Just breathe and keep moving."

Would they recognise her? Luckily, since Julie was new, Val served the jerks two pints of strong lager, and they sat at the bar chatting and laughing. Gary and Paul were both about twenty years old, and they were total losers. They had never held down a job in their lives, relying on the dole and a bit of petty crime to get by. They spotted Julie within moments but didn't recognise her out of her hippie gear, with her hair up and neat. "And who might you be, sweetheart?" Gary said, grinning. He had a tattoo on his neck that read: "CUT HERE." Julie wanted to oblige.

Val said she was the new barmaid. Julie, who was quiet and panicking on the inside, was worried they'd recognised her.

"Feel free to join us later if things get slow," Paul said with a wink, the taller one who had initially hit on Julie.

"We'll make sure you have a good time, sweetheart."

In that moment, Julie's fear shifted to anger. She was boiling inside and unsure of what to say or do, until the other two barmaids arrived to introduce themselves – Jennie and Jane – and rescued the situation.

Val burst into laughter. "Three J's behind the bar – could be a pop group."

Julie was busy at the other end of the bar, getting familiar with everything and keeping a safe distance from the two scumbags, so she didn't have to deal with them. Still, she was on edge all night. As the bar filled up with around sixty people, the jukebox cranked up as loud as it could go. Julie kept herself busy and started to enjoy the energy of the crowd, having a good time. She liked the mix of people and chatting with the customers – there were some friendly people there.

"You're doing great," Val murmured as she swept past. "Head up."

At 9:15 p.m., LeeRoy walked into the bar and headed straight for Julie's end. He lingered, waiting for her to notice him. She soon spotted LeeRoy and said, in a teasing but joking tone, "Good evening, sir. What can I get you?" He ordered a pint of Guinness, which she poured with ease. As Julie set the pint on the bar, she said, "That'll be two shillings and sixpence, please, sir."

"Daylight robbery," LeeRoy joked.

He was impressed and blended into the crowd, keeping an eye on her from a distance as she worked.

The night was also marked by plenty of dancing, drinking, and obnoxious behaviour, especially from the two jerks, who were now pretty drunk. Gary came over to Julie's end of the bar while she was emptying the overflowing ashtrays and started giving her a hard time. He slammed his pint glass down on the counter and yelled, "Hey! Slut! Want to give us a blow job out back?"

Instantly, Julie slammed him across the nose with the glass ashtray she held. It felt satisfying, and the impact released a lot of the anger that had been building up since the attempted rape. She wasn't strong, but with the heavy ashtray's help, the blow broke his nose open, and he fell to the floor, blood pouring all over him.

The pub fell silent, and LeeRoy quickly got to his feet when he heard the guy talking trash. He pushed through the crowd to help, but he didn't need to worry—Julie could take care of herself.

"Blow job, huh? You won't be blowing anything with that nose anytime soon," LeeRoy said, laughing at the poor bastard crying on the floor. Chas, coming from the East End, had seen it all before and found the humour in it. "Mr. Hard Bastard Gary, brought down by a little, feeble woman!"

Gary slowly rose to his feet, his eyes cloudy with tears and confusion as he struggled to understand why this woman was overreacting so intensely.

"Go fuck yourself. You're a sick bastard," hissed Julie in a low voice, right into his face.

Through the lens of his streaming eyes, Gary fixed his gaze on Julie, and then he recognised her. He let out a roar. "You fucking whore! You want it proper this time, huh? Well, you are fucking well going to get it–right now!" Incensed, he tried to lunge over the bar to attack Julie.

What a mistake! Chas had stashed a baseball bat under the bar, and in a split second, he slammed it down with all his might, crushing two of Gary's fingers and sending him into a fit of screams.

His friend believed he could handle it, but that turned out to be a big mistake. As he approached the bar, LeeRoy threw a perfectly timed left and right, knocking him to the ground.

One guy was out cold on the floor, and another was crumpled in the corner, screaming about getting revenge.

Julie was suddenly grabbed by Val and pulled into the kitchen. "What the hell are you doing?" Val exclaimed.

Julie burst into tears, and Val grabbed her by the shoulders, shaking her violently. She yelled again, "What the hell just happened out there?!" Julie couldn't speak and was hyperventilating when Chas rushed in. "Are you okay, Julie?" he asked.

"Yes, yes," she managed to get out, "give me a moment and I'll explain."

Val looked on in confusion, waiting for a logical reason why one of her staff, a new hire at that, would smash a customer in the face with an ashtray, even though she knew deep down that the idiot must have done something bad to provoke it.

The Hole in the Wall had a back door that led directly into a dark alleyway. By the time Paul came round, LeeRoy and Chas, with help from a couple of other tough regulars, had thrown the scumbags out into it.

"He needs a fucking hospital!" spat Paul.

"Then take him. It's not like I broke his legs!" Chas snarled.

"The Cottage Hospital is only about 600 yards away – carry him if you have to." He then went into the kitchen to find Julie.

Chas pulled up a chair and sat Julie down. She took a few deep breaths and looked at Val. "I'm sorry, Val," she said. "I shouldn't have done that, but if you knew what those two bastards did to Barrie and me, you would've done the same."

"What did they do?" Chas chimed in as LeeRoy knocked on the door and came in.

She explained, through a few small sobs, what had happened at the camp.

"Bastards," Chas said, gritting his teeth. "But well done, sweetheart — those bastards had it coming to them!" Val hugged Julie and apologised for getting mad at her. "If I'd known that before, I would have joined in. Serves those jerks right."

Val found a tea towel, dipped it in some water, and cleaned Julie's eyes. "There, that looks better," she said with a slight smile, then dried them.

She turned to Julie and asked, "How are you feeling? Do you want to go back out or would you rather wrap up your shift now?"

"If it's okay with you, can I get a cup of coffee? I'll calm down, and I'm sure I'll be fine to carry on." "Good girl," Val said, heading back out to the bar. All the customers glanced over at her, and one asked, "Is the new girl alright?"

"Yes," Val replied, "a little shaken up, but she'll be okay and back out shortly."

The regulars at The Hole in the Wall weren't the type to call the cops. Julie, Chas, and LeeRoy had taken care of this one, anyway.

Everyone went back to their drinks, and the conversation and music resumed.

Twenty minutes later, Julie said to Chas and LeeRoy, who had stayed with her, "I think I'm ok to carry on now."

"Are you sure, Julie?" Chas asked. "Yes, thank you. It's best to get back and face it head-on," she replied.

LeeRoy stood up and opened the door to the bar. Julie hesitantly walked in, saying thank you to LeeRoy as she passed by.

She stopped in her tracks when all the customers clapped and cheered upon spotting her.

Chas and LeeRoy were right behind her, gently encouraging her to go into the bar. She did, feeling very embarrassed.

"You'll fit right in here, girl!" one of them winked.

"Thanks for the entertainment!" another grinned.

"Alright, show's over," Val called, trying not to smile. "Pints don't pull themselves."

Closing time was anytime between 10:30 and 11:00 p.m.—whenever the customers finished and left. That night, all the customers left without any trouble; some even congratulated their new barmaid on her punch-up that night.

LeeRoy stayed behind, as he usually did, with a few other privileged regulars for a 'lock-in' and late drinks.

The girls all cleaned up, and the two part-timers went home. Julie went over and joined Leeroy. She was exhausted after her first real job, and her feet were aching.

"Where did you learn to punch like that?" LeeRoy asked.

"I have no idea," said Julie. "It just happened so fast, I didn't think." "Impressive!" LeeRoy said, one eyebrow raised.

"I thought I was going to get fired on my first night, but all Chas did was laugh about it and say, well done, darling. Those bastards had it coming to 'em!"

LeeRoy laughed. "Gary will have a hard time living that one down. Serves the wanker right. It's about time he got fucked over."

Julie's smile dropped, and she stared off into the distance.

"OK, fun over," LeeRoy said, standing up. "Can I buy you a drink, my heroine?"

"Shut up," said Julie, quickly smiling again. "Yes, please. I'll have a vodka and tonic, please."

"We'll bring 'em over!" called Chas, as he carried some empty glasses back.

"Vodka and tonic for Muhammad Ali here," called LeeRoy, "I'll have a pint of Guinness, and take one for yourself and Val."

Chas brought the drinks over and sat down with them, taking a swig from a pint of lager. "So, how did you find it tonight, Julie? Disregarding your boxing match, that is?"

"Oh, shut up. I don't know if Gary will ever live it down, but I'm guessing I won't be allowed to forget it either."

"Probably not," Chas said, grinning. "But other than that, what did you think?"

Julie smiled shyly. "To be honest, Chas, I loved it, despite those two wankers. Excuse my language, but they really are."

Chas and LeeRoy laughed, and both held up their glasses, saying, "We'll drink to that one, darling."

"There was a lot of friendly banter. I loved it, and it will get a lot better once I know my way around the bar and the different drinks."

LeeRoy put down his pint and decided it was time to make his move. "Want to hit a nightclub?" he asked Julie.

"Nightclub," she said, frowning, thinking the night was over. "Where?"

"There's one here – at the top of Preston Street, 600 yards away."

Julie looked at Chas, and he shrugged. "No problem – I'll get you a key and you can let yourself in."

He was a little jealous that she was going out with LeeRoy, but what could he do, with his wife right behind him? He got her the key.

"I need to go to my new room and touch up my makeup before I go anywhere," she insisted, and then she headed off, with Chas and LeeRoy unable to take their eyes off her as she walked away.

"You're a lucky bastard," Chas said to LeeRoy. "Why's he lucky?" Val asked, who was standing right behind Chas, unbeknown to him.

"Bloody hell, woman! You scared the life out of me," he stuttered, not wanting to let Val know what he was talking about. He replied, "LeeRoy's win at the bookies last week," but she knew.

Julie returned wearing another stunning little black dress from Rosina, and the men exchanged glances before looking back at her. "Wow," LeeRoy exclaimed, "you look incredible." "Thanks, kind sir," Julie replied.

They finished their drinks and said their goodbyes. Julie linked her arm through LeeRoy's, and they walked up to the nightclub, just a few minutes away, right next to the train line and the station.

It was £1 each to get in, which included the first drink. LeeRoy paid for both of them and slipped the lady in the booth an extra £5.

Julie picked up on it and was confused, but she didn't speak up. She assumed LeeRoy was just being nice or trying to impress her.

She'd never been to a nightclub before and was amazed. It was dark, with loud music and flashing lights, but the vibe was electric! She felt a rush from it, even though she was tired earlier. The excitement had energised her.

"What would you like to drink?" he asked Julie. "Oh, I'll be happy with a Coke," she replied. "A Coke? This is a nightclub, not a coffee shop! I doubt they'll even sell it alone," he said with a

laugh. "Yeah, okay, can I have a vodka and orange instead?"
"That's more like it," and he headed to the bar to get their drinks.

As he walked back, he was aware of people staring, and he played along. *Look, everyone! See who I've got with me!* he thought proudly. She was the hottest girl in the room, and everyone knew it—except Julie.

People were constantly approaching LeeRoy, shaking his hand, and chatting with him. Julie thought he must know everyone, but then she realised that, even though he kept a low profile, money was changing hands for small packages.

She thought he was dealing, but she brushed it off. *Big deal, right? Someone had to make a living. She couldn't complain, considering she'd taken her share of drugs too. He was paying for a night out and covering all her drinks,* but she finally understood how he could afford the Rolls and the fancy mansion.

Before long, the club was packed with people dancing, drinking, and sneaking cuddles in the dark corners. Julie was relaxing with her drink, starting to wonder if LeeRoy would make a move on her that night, when her thoughts were interrupted and she was shocked to see the two scumbags walk through the main entrance, over LeeRoy's right shoulder. LeeRoy, sitting with his back to the entrance, noticed the change in her expression and quickly turned around to see them walking in with confidence. He couldn't help but notice that Gary's right hand was bandaged and Paul had a strip of plaster across his nose, and he let out a chuckle to himself.

"They must've pumped them full of something good in that hospital," LeeRoy said.

They didn't see Julie and LeeRoy sitting in the dark corner, so they headed straight to the bar to order their drinks.

Julie was shaking. "Do you think they'll start trouble when they see us, LeeRoy?"

"Who knows with jerks like that? We'll have to wait and see."

After getting their drinks, they turned around to scan the nightclub, and sure enough, they spotted LeeRoy and Julie. At first, they just stood there, unsure of what to do. Gary decided he'd had enough for one day and backed off.

Paul walked up to them and snarled at LeeRoy, pointing in his face, "I'm not gonna forget what you did in the pub. You're gonna pay."

That was a stupid thing to say. LeeRoy stood right in front of him, pushed his face into Paul's, and sneered, "Give it your best shot."

Paul was pulling back his right arm to punch LeeRoy, but that was all he knew until he woke up fifteen minutes later in a back storage room.

As soon as his arm moved, LeeRoy knocked him out, and he went down for the second time that night.

Just like the piece of shit he is.

Gary backed off. Two bouncers dragged Paul to the back storeroom. The club didn't want the police involved, so they left him there until he came to, and then he was tossed out again, nursing his wounds.

Gary was left sitting at the bar, his eyes locked on Julie and LeeRoy. LeeRoy was getting frustrated. He had two choices: go over and take him out, or talk to the bouncers, who were all his friends. He opted for the second, and Gary was soon out the door, back with his friend.

Now feeling much more at ease, LeeRoy sold a few more packages and then asked Julie if she'd like to dance.

"Yes, yes," she said with a smile. "I'm really in the mood to dance."

LeeRoy hoped she'd be in the mood for more than just dancing later.

They drank and danced all night, and by 2 a.m., the last slow dance of the evening started. "Would you like the last dance, Mademoiselle?" LeeRoy asked, holding Julie close. "That would be a pleasure, sir," she replied with a quip.

He felt so warm and close that she could feel his large penis pressing against her belly, and she was getting turned on. It was the first time since her terrible ordeal that she'd felt like sex again.

Maybe it was LeeRoy's vigorous defence of her against her attackers that broke the spell and made her feel safe with him.

As he leaned down and breathed hotly into her ear, Julie could feel herself getting turned on, and LeeRoy knew they were going to have fun that night, since she was pressing hard, rubbing herself against him, too.

The music stopped, and the lights came on. LeeRoy groaned and smiled, "Back in a second, babe."

He went over to the bouncers and slipped them a few quid for turning a blind eye to his drug deals and dumping the scumbags out of the door.

They walked back down Preston Street, hand in hand, to The Hole in the Wall. LeeRoy's hands were nearly three times the size of little Julie's. He let out a slight snicker, imagining that his manhood would look even bigger with her small hands around it.

"What are you sniggering at?" she asked.

"Nothing," he told her, too embarrassed to tell her what he was thinking. "I was just remembering you smashing Gary in the face with that ashtray, that's all." "Ha-ha! Will I never live that down?"

"Not for a long time, my darling," he said.

Julie gave LeeRoy the key, and he opened the door for her.

"Would you like me to see you up to your room?" said LeeRoy.

She hesitated, bashful, although she wanted him to. "That would be nice."

It was a large pub, and Chas and Val's main living area was located right at the front of the building, far enough from Julie's room that they wouldn't disturb anyone. Julie climbed the narrow stairs, with LeeRoy close behind, still gazing at her incredible little behind and imagining all sorts of things.

After LeeRoy took the key from Julie and opened the door, he flipped on the light. Julie followed and collapsed onto the couch, exhausted. It had been a hectic day, evening, and now early morning – a lot had happened in a short period.

Julie looked up at the tall, handsome Black man as he reached out his hand. She hesitated for a moment, then took it, and he gently helped her to her feet.

He carefully slid his large right hand behind her head and kissed her gently on the side of her neck. She writhed with pleasure, her body electrified. He pulled back, panting slightly, trying to catch his breath. She was so delicate, like a fragile porcelain doll, and he worried he might hurt her. His eyes locked onto hers, unsure if it was okay to continue. He'd never felt the need to ask a woman's permission before – it was apparent when they were interested, and sex usually came easily. But even though Julie was attracted to him, he sensed something different about her. He felt a respect for her. She was already starting to mean something to him, and he wasn't sure why, since they'd only known each other for a few weeks, but he wanted more than just a physical connection. This was an extraordinary young woman.

She wrapped her arms as far as they would go around this giant, who grasped her head in both hands, gazed deeply into her eyes, and began kissing her on the lips, their tongues intertwined. She was electrified, full of desire for him. He held her tightly and pushed his very erect manhood up against her. She wanted it: she had already decided that she was going to let it inside her that night, while they were dancing in the nightclub.

He ran his fingers through her hair, down her neck, and onto her blouse, over her now-erect nipples. She sucked in a breath and wriggled even more, while he put his hand up her blouse and caressed her right breast in his large hand, moving on to inside her bra.

She had both her hands inside the back of his shirt, digging her nails into his skin. He expertly undid the clip on the front of her bra with one hand, releasing her firm breasts that stayed just where they should, and went back to massaging the right one. Then he removed her blouse and bra, so she was completely topless. He marvelled at her slim, firm body. He wanted sex, yes, but more than that, he wanted to enfold her; protect her. He was already feeling something like love for her, and he was overwhelmed.

She gazed into his deep, dark eyes as she unfastened the buttons of his shirt and slid it off his shoulders, down his back. She had trouble with the cufflinks, and he had to lend a hand, his struggles making it seem like he was in a straitjacket. They saw the funny side of it and were both laughing when LeeRoy pulled her close and started rubbing her bottom with both hands whilst leaning down and sucking her hard right nipple. She groaned, and the guttural sound excited him even more. He unzipped her jeans and put his hand down to clasp her tight butt over her underwear, running his other hand over the front and between her legs.

She was now unable to stand still, faintly swaying and trembling with desire. He held her tightly, pressing his fingers into her, through her underwear. She was extremely wet and turned on. She started to undo his zip, but he had to lend a hand, remarking at her inexperience.

He was left standing there supporting her, his hands between her legs and his trousers ridiculously around his ankles. She grabbed his massive, hard manhood over his pants, squeezing so hard that he let her go. They both laughed and fell onto the bed.

He kicked off his trousers, rolled over, and started kissing her passionately, tongues lashing out, while his hands caressed her breasts. He slid his hand between her legs, inserting just about an inch of finger inside, just enough to tease. She wanted it all, right then, but he was going to make her wait. She had no choice. Her tiny hand was now inside his underpants, and she gasped as she grabbed hold of his hard, hot, throbbing manhood for the first time.

She pulled his underpants off, removing her panties at the same time. They were both now completely naked. He then put as much of his finger as he could inside her. She didn't care. She was so worked up, she couldn't think straight.

He rolled her onto her side and held both cheeks of her butt in his huge left hand. He continued to slide his right finger in and out while sucking on her. She was in erotic heaven. She twisted around and managed to get into a position where she could take his massive manhood into her tiny mouth. Now he was having fun too, her tongue rolling around his head, while he was finger fucking her. She could not hold back and had a massive orgasm, releasing his manhood from her mouth and screaming so loudly that he had to stop and put his hand over her mouth in case she woke Chas and Val.

He held her tightly as she shuddered, and then she opened her shining eyes, breathing huskily, "I want you in me!"

He rolled her onto her back and started to insert his massive manhood into her. This took her breath away – she had never had anything so large in her. He was very gentle and took his time, gradually getting it all in, until she thought she would split in two, but as he moved it gently in and out, she relaxed and started to enjoy feeling so full. She began to move with him, arching her back to take the whole nine inches he had to offer. He started to speed up – in, out; faster and faster, pounding and pounding, until they both came together and collapsed on the bed with him still inside her.

To his surprise, it was all he could do to stop himself from telling her he loved her, there and then.

They were both fighting for breath, especially Julie, with LeeRoy's huge body on top of her. She had to get him off. He was so heavy! She pushed, but if he hadn't helped, she couldn't have moved him anywhere. He rolled off; his member slipped out of her and lay on his belly like a felled oak tree. They were both exhausted.

They lay there for what felt like an eternity, panting. Then LeeRoy rolled onto his side and gazed at her in awe. "What's up?" Julie asked, laughing. noticing the care and appreciation in LeeRoy's soft eyes. She barely dared to express her true feelings; she felt shy and almost embarrassed by the depth of her emotions for this fantastic man.

As LeeRoy brushed a strand of her hair back from her face, he kissed her softly once more. Then, he sprawled out on his back, grinning like a teenager.

Julie returned his grin, then gazed up at the ceiling with a silly smile, feeling an incredible warmth.

Eventually, Julie asked LeeRoy if he wanted some coffee. "That would be nice," he said.

"Well, you'd better get up and make it — it's your job," she said with a smirk. "It says so in the Bible."

LeeRoy frowned, confused. "What are you talking about? It doesn't say that in the Bible." "I bet you a pound it does," she said, sitting up on her elbow.

LeeRoy laughed. "Okay, you're on. Shake on it."

Julie slipped into a nightgown, tiptoed across to the dressing table, and found a Gideon Bible she'd moved from the bedside drawer.

"This is going to be the easiest pound I've ever made," LeeRoy said confidently, lying back with his hands linked behind his head.

Julie opened the Bible, flipped through it, and said, "Got your pound ready?" She showed him the word "Hebrews" and laughed. "There it is! He brews!"

LeeRoy couldn't help but laugh along with her. Then, he padded downstairs to make some drinks reluctantly. He shook his head, grinning to himself. He couldn't get over her.

Julie woke up at 9:30, still on a high from LeeRoy's touch. LeeRoy had left early that morning, so Chas wouldn't suspect he'd spent the night.

She took a shower and headed down to the bar, where she couldn't help but smile and share with everyone how head-over-heels in love she felt — and how incredible the sex had been. Though she decided to keep that to herself for now.

Val was there, sorting out the orders from the brewery.

"Hey, Julie. How was the club last night?"

"It was amazing. My first time in a nightclub!" Julie was thrilled to have an excuse to get excited. But then she got serious, remembering other things. "The only problem was – those two jerks showed up and caused trouble again, but it didn't last. LeeRoy took care of them, and they left with their tails between their legs. Typical losers."

"You can say that again!" Val snorted, still ticking off her list. "I'm surprised Chas hasn't kicked them out, but I guess they spend money and can always be shown the door, you know?"

"They know the drill by now," she said, laughing.

CHAPTER NINE – *Ashes of the Orchard*

Julie needed to grab her belongings from the coach, so she let Val know where she was headed. She didn't have much, but it was all she owned. She had put back on the same clothes she had on while working last night, which weren't even hers. She also felt like she owed it to her old friends to update them on what she was doing. After all, she'd vanished without a word, and it was weighing on her conscience. They'd been good to her, so she should at least let them know she wasn't coming back.

Before her shift, Julie headed to Macknade Orchard, a thirty-minute walk from Preston Street. As she walked down the lane leading to the old coach, she noticed a lot of smoke in the distance and figured Barrie had been a bit too generous with the logs on the fire again. As she rounded the corner, she saw a crowd of people gathered, and when she spotted the blue flashing lights on a van, she realised it was the police. She froze in her tracks.

"What on earth—?" she whispered aloud, her throat tightening. *Oh my God!* she thought. *They're being evicted or arrested.*

For a moment, she hesitated, unsure if she should step back, afraid she'd end up in cuffs too. But she chose to keep going. Police were everywhere. As she approached the scene, her anxiety grew until she saw something that made her stomach turn with horror. The coach was a smoking charred ruin, and now she understood why she'd seen so much smoke earlier when she rounded the corner.

"No… oh, no," she gasped, her legs giving way for a moment. "Please, not them…"

Oh, God!

She then saw that three fire trucks were spraying down the fire, generating a lot of smoke and steam.

She ran toward the burned-out coach, but a cop grabbed her arm and said, "Hey, hold back, it's not safe to go any closer."

"What's happening?" she exclaimed, her breath coming in short gasps as she frantically scanned the crowd and debris. "And who might you be, Miss?"

"Julie Barnes," she said, trying to break free from the officer's tight grip, her eyes scanning the area for any sign of her friends. "I used to live here, but I left a couple of days ago."

"Ah," the officer replied, then called out to his boss, "Inspector!" to fill her in on what was going on. The officers looked serious, which only increased Julie's fear.

"Please!" she cried. "Tell me they're okay!"

"Please! please!" She was in a panic, her mind racing with worry. "What's happened? Where are my friends?"

"Come with me, please, Miss." The inspector gently led Julie to his car and assisted her into the passenger seat. Her eyes were wide with terror. She knew it couldn't be good.

"I'm sorry, but I'm afraid it's bad news," the inspector began. Julie gulped, frozen, as the officer continued to speak. "There was a fire here last night, as you can see. We don't know yet how it started, but people have died."

Julie let out an instinctive gasp, and the inspector gently patted her hand.

"We think there are still…bod'…he corrected himself: people inside, but we won't know for sure until the fire is out and our forensic team has arrived and completed their inspection."

Julie broke down, sobbing uncontrollably and shaking violently. The inspector handed her a handkerchief. She tried to dry her eyes but was too overwhelmed to stop crying.

"They were good people," she sobbed. "They didn't deserve this... none of them."

"I know this is tough on you, Julie," the inspector said, "but I'd appreciate it if you could answer a few questions for me. It would help us enormously."

"I'll try," she sobbed.

"Can you tell me how many people lived in the coach?"

She sobbed that there were five, excluding me. She could only give their first names: Tony, Barrie, Margaret, Sammy, and Christine.

Do you..." Her voice broke. "Are they all dead?" A sob overtook her words; she had forgotten what the inspector told her about the fire and forensic evidence.

"Thanks for helping with the names – it'll be a big help. You mentioned you'd been living here a few days ago. Could you please let me know how to reach you again?"

"Yes," she still sobbed and found it hard to talk. "I'm working and living in a pub on Preston Street called The Hole in the Wall."

"Ah, yes, I know it well. Would you like a lift back there?"

"Yes, please," she sobbed, "thank you."

"Julie, wait!" Val called, but she was gone before anyone could stop her.

The inspector drove Julie back to the pub, accompanying her as she went inside. Still sobbing, Julie ran straight up to her room.

"What's wrong with her?" Chas stared. "Why are you here, Fred?"

The inspector explained everything.

"Bloody hell," Chas said, his voice rising in a high-pitched tone. He called LeeRoy.

LeeRoy was there in minutes, heading straight to Julie's room, where she was still crying her eyes out. He wrapped his arms around her to comfort her, but nothing could soothe her. He held her tightly.

"Oh, LeeRoy, how did it happen?" she gasped between sobs. "They were such lovely people! They took me in when I was at my lowest. They didn't deserve to die like that."

LeeRoy stroked her hair. "I'm so sorry, Julie. I wish there were something I could do."

"Just be here for me, please."

"Not a problem," said LeeRoy, hugging her.

"You don't have to say anything," he murmured. "Just let it out."

Julie didn't work that night, and LeeRoy stayed with her, just holding her close until she fell asleep.

At around 11 p.m., he gently lifted Julie and placed her in bed. She stirred momentarily but didn't fully wake.

He stepped into the bar and spotted Chas and Val, who both asked at the same time, "How is she?"

"She's fast asleep, but my god, I wonder what went on up there. I guess that the campfire spread while they were sleeping, but we'll probably never know for sure."

"Val spoke first, saying, "Poor thing, she was only going up there to get her things. I can't imagine what a shock it must have been to come across that carnage."

"When you see her in the morning, LeeRoy, tell her to take the rest of the week off. She's not going to want to face people for a while."

"Alright, thanks, Val. I think I'll head home and ask Rosina to get some more clothes sorted out for her. Then, when she's feeling better, I'll take her shopping for some new stuff. What are the clothes like at Flair, you know, the place next door?" He couldn't think of the name, but Val corrected him. "Fashions."

"Ah, yes, that place."

"They're okay, LeeRoy. Cheap, but very popular with all the young girls in Faversham and the surrounding towns."

"Good," LeeRoy said quietly. "She deserves something new — something that doesn't smell of smoke."

CHAPTER TEN – *Truths by the Sea*

LeeRoy returned early the next morning with some of his sister's clothes to get her through until Julie was in a position to buy more. He said good morning to Chas when he passed, not wanting to get into a conversation, and quickly moved on, climbing the stairs to Julie's room and knocking gently on the door.

"Who is it?" Julie whispered, her voice filled with sadness.

"It's just me," LeeRoy said, and she hesitantly opened the door for him, turning her back to LeeRoy as she walked into the room.

"I know it's a stupid question," LeeRoy said to Julie, "but how are you?"

She turned slowly, and LeeRoy was stunned by her expression. Physically, she was present, but her vacant stare told LeeRoy she was still trapped in the horror of yesterday. He felt like crying himself, but he held back, instead wrapping his arms around her and silently holding her close.

She softly cried and tried to say something to LeeRoy, but couldn't find the words as he stroked her hair. He wished he could take her pain away, but knew it wasn't possible; all he could do was hold her close and be there for her.

She made a gesture to LeeRoy, signalling she wanted him to let her go. She sat on the settee, looking directly into his eyes with tears in hers, and he could see deep into her soul, feeling her pain.

LeeRoy wasn't sure what to say to make her feel better, so he asked if she'd like a cup of tea, expecting her to say no, but she replied, "Yes, please, that would be nice."

He made her tea and coffee for himself, handed the tea to Julie, and sat down beside her. They both finished their drinks without saying a word.

"You don't have to talk if you can't," he said softly. "I'll just sit here until you feel like breathing again."

"I have no idea how to handle all of this," LeeRoy said, "so I'll just say what I think. How about you get ready, if you're up to it, and I'll take you out for a drive – maybe to Whitstable, what do you think?"

Julie looked at him with sad, bloodshot eyes, pausing for a moment before saying, "Yeah, okay, that would be better than sitting here all day staring at the walls."

He hugged her and gave her a light kiss on the cheek, saying, "I'll wait for you in the bar. Don't rush, just come down when you're ready."

He found Chas in the bar. "How is she?" he asked. "Not good," replied LeeRoy. "She looks awful, and I feel so helpless. I have no idea how to talk to her or what to say. You know what I mean."

"All I can suggest, LeeRoy, based on my own experience, is to try to comfort her, lend a listening ear, express your genuine sorrow, provide as much support as you can, and just be there for her. Don't try to distract her, don't give advice, listen, and avoid sharing your own stories of loss."

After hearing all that, LeeRoy was taken aback and impressed with Chas. He hadn't realised he could show such empathy.

"That's a lot to take in, Chas, but I'll do my best for her, of course. She's trying to sort herself out, and I'm going to take a drive to Whitstable, try to take her mind off it if that's at all possible."

"Good idea, mate. A little sea air can only help." They continued to talk, and after about 30 minutes, Julie walked into the bar still looking sad but ready to face the world.

Chas glanced at her and said, "I'm not going to ask how you're doing, Julie. I can see you're not feeling it, but enjoy the ride and the sea air." "Thanks, Chas," Julie replied. "Can we go now, please, LeeRoy?"

"Yes, of course, the car's right outside."

They drove up Whitstable Road and turned onto Graveney Road, passing Homestall Lane along the way. Julie stayed silent, her eyes fixed straight ahead, unable to look at the road where she once lived and her friends had died so tragically.

They then made their way down Head Hill Road, joined Seasalter Road, and ultimately ended up in Whitstable, still in silence. LeeRoy felt awkward, unsure of what to do or say.

"You don't have to talk, sweetheart," he said quietly. "Just breathe the air. Let the sea do the talking for a bit."

LeeRoy pulled up near The Pearsons Arms, glanced over at Julie, and asked, "Are you okay?" even though he knew she wasn't.

"Yeah, I'm OK, and thanks for being with me."

He glanced over at her, but she didn't notice as she was gazing out to sea, lost in thought. He suggested they take a walk along the seawall.

"Yeah, okay," without even realising what she was agreeing to.

He got out, walked around, and opened the passenger door, holding out his hand to help her out.

Neither LeeRoy nor Julie knew what to say, and she was still lost in thoughts of her friends as they strolled hand in hand, barely noticing the warm onshore breeze. They walked for what felt like ages, almost making their way back to Seasalter.

Another couple with a black Labrador came walking by. The dog rushed over to them, and Julie smiled and cooed over him, "…helping **to** distract her from the tragedy for a bit."

"That's the first smile I've seen all day," LeeRoy said gently. "Keep it — it suits you."

"I'd like a dog one day," she told LeeRoy.

"That's something I've never really thought about," he said, gazing out to sea, lost in thought. He turned back toward her, searching her face. "How're you feeling now?"

"Numb," she replied. "I can't take it in. I need to know how it happened."

"The police will find out soon, Julie. Try not to worry. Easy for me to say, but try."

They strolled along the gravel beach, chatting about the weather and the sea. LeeRoy said, "I'll bring you back here someday, and we can go for a swim." "I don't think so," Julie replied. "I'm scared of water. I can't swim."

"You could give it a try. There's a nice pool in Faversham. How about I take you there and teach you how to swim?"

"No way," Julie said, shuddering. "I'd hate it." She said, not knowing then that she would later regret not accepting his offer.

"We should think about heading back to the car," LeeRoy said, looking up at the sky. "Looks like rain over Will's Mother's." "What?" enquired Julie, looking confused. "Just an old saying meaning it's looking like rain." "Never heard that one before," Julie said. "Stick with me, baby, and you'll learn a lot more," he smiled as they headed back.

"You're a strange mix, LeeRoy," Julie said softly, half-smiling. "Half trouble, half teacher."

On the way back to Whitstable, they walked past a pub right on the beach for the second time. LeeRoy suggested they stop for a bite to eat and a drink.

"It would be great to have a sit-down, but I'm not sure I could handle any food or drink. A coffee would be nice, though."

Since the Old Neptune had tables set up on the beach with a view across the estuary to the Isle of Sheppey and Essex, LeeRoy told Julie, "You sit there, and I'll go get a drink and order some food. You don't have to eat, but you should try it."

LeeRoy ordered a coffee for Julie and a pint of Guinness for himself, along with a couple of sandwiches, thinking she might be more willing to eat if they were right there. When he returned to the table with the coffee and his Guinness, Julie was crying again, but she managed to pull herself together.

"Come on, girl," he said, trying to encourage her. "Drink your coffee before it gets cold. It'll make you feel better."

"Thanks." She absentmindedly traced her finger along the side of the cup, following the path of a coffee stain. "I don't know how I would have gotten through this without you."

"Not at all, sweetheart, I feel for you. I'll do whatever I can." He realised he was struggling to think of anything that could help her, so he added, "But I'm here for you, whenever you need me."

She smiled briefly. "Thanks again."

The sandwiches arrived, and Julie managed to eat half of them, but it made her feel queasy, so she left the rest. LeeRoy finished the rest.

As she gazed out to sea toward Sheppey, she turned to LeeRoy and said, "You've been very kind to me, and I don't want to sound ungrateful, but I know almost nothing about you."

"What would you like to know, Julie?"

She gazed directly into his eyes and replied, "It's clear to me, and I hope to you, that despite knowing each other for such a short time, we've grown remarkably close. You're aware of every detail about me. I know it's not much, but you know it all. Meanwhile, I don't know anything about you."

For a moment, LeeRoy thought to himself. *She's right. We've gotten close, and I hope we can make something lasting work. Should I be honest with her, or tell her what she wants to hear? If I do open up and she finds out I've been holding back, it could ruin everything.*

He figured it might help take her mind off her sadness and grief, so he decided to open up and share his life story.

"Alright," LeeRoy said, "you at least deserve to know who you're getting involved with, so here goes."

He told her that his parents were from the Caribbean and had immigrated together, but his father had left before LeeRoy was born, so he never knew him.

"I was raised in Plaistow, East London, and was always getting into trouble stealing things from school. I was eventually kicked out at the age of thirteen. I joined a local gang comprised of older kids, so I quickly picked up the ropes. By sixteen, I had already done two years in a young offenders' institution."

"You're being very open," Julie said.

"Guess it's easier to talk when someone actually listens," he said quietly.

Yeah, I know, but I feel like, as you said, we're forming some connection, even after such a short time, and I want to be honest with you.

"Thanks, LeeRoy, go ahead. It'll help take my mind off things I hope. But one question: why did you get mixed up with a gang?"

"It's hard to pinpoint exactly, but I think it was the thrill of taking risks, the anticipation of meeting up with the other members to plan some crazy stuff, the excitement of pulling it off, the rush of getting away with it, and the camaraderie that came with it all."

"In the end, we all got caught." "How did that happen?" She asked."

"You really wanna know?" "Yes, of course I do."

He wasn't exactly eager to share, but he was feeling open and could tell she was intrigued, which was pulling her attention away from yesterday's events.

Okay, a couple of our crew went to Minster on the Isle of Sheppey, just over there, pointing to the Island, for a weekend and rented one of those beach huts. It had the basics, but they wouldn't have cared too much since they'd be out partying and hitting on girls most of the time.

They heard about a nightclub in Leysdown called The Starlight, supposedly full of girls looking for a good time.

They took a bus there, arriving around 9:30 after a few drinks at a local pub.

They were there for less than an hour, chatting with a couple of girls, when a group of local guys walked in, accusing our guys of hitting on their girls. You can imagine what happened next."

Julie, a bit naïve, said, "No, what happened?"

"Our two boys had a tough time because there were seven of them, but our lads didn't let that stop them. All hell broke loose. Martin, one of the guys, grabbed a pint glass from the bar and smashed it into the face of the closest one, who let out a scream and fell to the floor, bleeding heavily like a stuck pig."

"How do you know so much detail, LeeRoy?"

He paused, took a deep breath, and confessed he was the other one.

"Honestly, that's awful, but go on."

"As you can imagine, we got the snot beaten out of us, and Martin ended up with a broken leg before the bouncers intervened.

The police arrived just before the ambulance, and the local men had already left.

Martin was taken to the hospital, and the police arrested me and took me to Sheerness police station. However, after six hours, they had to let me go because nobody was talking, and they had no proof of who had started it. It wasn't us, but I wasn't saying anything to them."

Julie was now wondering. *Who is this man I'm with? Am I safe? Yeah, of course I am. He's been nothing but a gentleman."*

"It was 2:00 a.m. when the police let me go, so I had to walk back to Minster, but I had no idea how to get there. The police didn't care and wouldn't help. I guess they were frustrated because they couldn't make a charge stick.

It was only 3 miles to Minster, but it felt like I had walked ten. I got back to the hut around 4 am and that's when I realised Martin had the key."

Julie chuckled. "What did you do?"

"I had no choice; the hut was on stilts, so I crawled under and tried to catch some sleep, but it was impossible. It was freezing cold, and a wind was blowing in off the sea. I was seventeen years old and not at all happy with the situation, especially with all sorts of bugs crawling all over me."

"I think I dozed off and came to around 8:30 am, but for a few seconds, I was disoriented and had no idea where I was. I was starving and thirsty, but since I couldn't get into the hut, I decided to find a phone booth and call Sam.

He had a car and I figured, or rather, I knew that once I explained what happened and that Martin was in the hospital, he'd come straight down." "And did he?" she asked.

LeeRoy was just about to say, "Patience, I'll get to it," but he remembered her situation and carried on.

"Yes, he did, but he took a wrong turn near Sittingbourne and ended up heading to Maidstone before realising it. He eventually arrived around 2 p.m., having stopped at a service station along the way to pick up a sandwich and a bottle of lemonade for me, which I was grateful for."

Sam was furious as I recounted to him what had happened. He then asked if I knew how Martin was doing. "No idea," I said. "We should probably head to the hospital and check," I suggested. "Good idea," Sam agreed, and off we went.

We found out which ward he was in, but they wouldn't let us see him because visiting hours weren't until 3 p.m., so we were pretty annoyed.

"Bloody hell," snapped Sam, "that's two and a half hours away. Let's see if this shithole of a town has a decent café and get something to eat. I'm starving."

"It was only half a mile to the main street, where we found Marettles' Café and parked outside. It was pretty busy, but we were soon served and enjoyed a classic breakfast. Just as we were finishing up, a group of guys walked in.

"I wasn't entirely sure, but I thought some of them might have been involved in the fight last night, so I mentioned it to Sam, who glanced over at them. There were eight of them, and we looked at each other and decided it would be foolish to start anything here in broad daylight, especially since I was battered and bruised from the night before.

Sam whispered to me to get out before they spotted us, and that we could sort it out later. We managed to escape unnoticed. I'm not sure if they would have started anything, but being black and far from London, we stood out like a sore thumb.

We went to the beach and relaxed until it was time to visit Martin. At first, they sent us to the wrong ward, but we finally found him. He seemed pretty down on himself, but his eyes lit up when he saw us—well, one eye did; the other was black and swollen shut."

Julie was still in pain and upset, but she was eager to learn more about the man who had suddenly appeared in her life. "Go on," she said.

"We found it a little funny to see him lying on the bed with his leg propped up by a winch-like device, but he didn't think it was funny and wanted to get out. However, he ended up being there for nearly two weeks.

We stayed with him for about an hour, winding him up like you do, until we got bored and left him to his own devices. He had lost the keys to the cabin, so we just left whatever little was inside and headed back to London.

For a couple of weeks, nothing much happened, but we had been planning our return and seeking revenge on the local boys who had wronged us, especially Martin, who was now back home on crutches and unable to join in our plans.

"And what were you planning?" Julie asked.

"Revenge, of course. Our gang consisted of around nineteen members, or eighteen if you didn't count Martin. Although we were rivals with a South London gang, we weren't sworn enemies. When necessary, we'd work together, so I reached out to them, explained the situation, and shared our plans. They were on board—no issue.

One Saturday afternoon, a bunch of us piled into cars and headed down to Sheerness, parking outside Marettles' and crashing in. We had crowbars and hammers, but no guns or knives.

The local boys who were inside saw us coming and took off through the back, jumping over walls and through a gate.

Honestly, I'm ashamed to say it, but at seventeen, you don't think twice and never consider the consequences.

They were fortunate because they all managed to escape just in time, so we took it out on the café, knocking over tables and chairs on the way out. I'm sure a lot of crockery was also smashed.

Things were getting out of hand. I think the owner or manager was on the phone with the police before we left, but I'm not sure.

Anyway, I got back into the car I had arrived in and we took off, crossing the Sheppey Bridge and heading to a place called Iwade. However, ahead of us there was a roadblock, and the police stopped the car we were in and arrested all five of us. It turned out they had stopped two other cars, too, so they caught fifteen of us out of about fifty.

Everyone was handcuffed and taken back to Sheerness police station, which was my second time there."

Julie interrupted, "That's a fascinating story, LeeRoy, but I'm starting to get a little chilly. Can we go, please?" "Yes, yes, of course. I got so wrapped up in remembering details, sorry. Let's head back to the car, and if you're Ok with it, we can stop at the Pearsons Arms. I wouldn't mind another Guinness, but of course, it's whatever you want to do that matters."

"No, no, that's fine as long as it's warm in there. I could use another coffee."

"Come on then," he said gently, helping her to her feet. "You've heard enough ghosts for one day — *save a little room for the ones still waiting their turn.*"

It was just a short distance, and the trip didn't take long. LeeRoy held the door open for Julie to enter. As she moved toward an empty table, she noticed a picture and a sign that caught her eye. She loved history, so she paused to read it. The sign said:

Kentish Gazette, 17 February 1857.
Fire.
Between eleven and twelve o'clock on Wednesday night, a fire broke out on the premises of Mr. G. Whitnall, the "Pearson Arms," situated near the beach. The inmates were aroused by the smoke entering the apartment in which they were sleeping, and it almost suffocated them. The coastguardsmen were quickly on the scene and soon got the fire under control. It appeared to have originated in a cupboard filled with children's clothes, the contents of which were consumed, but no further damage was sustained.

As LeeRoy read over her shoulder, he said, "They say an East End gangster now owns it. You never know, we might even run into him." "I don't think I'd like that," Julie replied.

They sat down, and LeeRoy asked, "Would you like coffee or something a bit stronger?" She hesitated for a moment, then said, "I think I'd like a vodka and orange if that's okay?" "Sure, absolutely," LeeRoy replied. "I'll go grab the drinks."

He came back with the drinks, took his seat again, and asked her how she was feeling.

She flashed him a half smile and said, "I'm not sure, to be honest, it's hard to process. It did take my mind off things a bit, listening to your spooky past life, though."

"There's more, and I can keep going if you'd like," he said.

"Yeah, okay, it's best to clear the air about your past, just don't tell me anything that could get you in trouble. I don't want to hear anything I have to keep confidential."

He chuckled and said, "Don't worry, I'll keep all that to myself."

"Great, let's hear it then."

"OK, where did we leave off?"

"Was it not when you got taken to Sheerness police station?"

"Yeah, I think so. We were all packed into a cell, hearing the local guys yelling and screaming for our blood outside, which was pretty intense. However, there was no way they were getting in, and they weren't letting us out anytime soon.

They left us to stew in the cell with no food or water; I think they were enjoying watching us suffer. After all, we were black and from London and had messed up their town, so they were not happy.

Julie stopped him and asked, "What's the problem with being black?" "Prejudice, my darlin', prejudice. They don't take kindly to us black guys in some places, especially out in the sticks." Julie looked confused and asked, "You don't seem to have any problems in Faversham, or do you?"

"In the beginning, I did, especially with knob heads like those two idiots that you clobbered. Still a few clumps here and there, and taking care of the right people, if you catch my drift, I eventually gained some respect. Now, I'm fairly well accepted around town and rarely have any issues."

Julie replied, looking sadly at LeeRoy, "I think it's terrible and nasty to behave that way, and it shouldn't be allowed."

"Well, that's just how it is. It's not too bad in London. Anyway, where was I?"

"Oh, right — we were locked up. Early the next morning, around seven, they took us one by one to an interview room, questioned us, and then sent us back to our cell with a solicitor present who was as useless as a wet rag in a pool."

"Later that afternoon, we were taken back to the interview room and charged with affray."

"What's Affray?" she asked.

"Affray is a legal term for a fight or violent behaviour in a public place that disturbs the peace or causes fear to others."

"And you were charged for that?"

"Yes, just like all the others, and they eventually let us go. The cop who tried to pin the fight on me at the nightclub was at the door, smirking, and said something like, 'Not so clever this time.' I could have punched him in the face, but that wouldn't be a smart move in a police station.

"They had given us the car keys back after searching it and found a couple of baseball bats, which didn't help our case. No one claimed ownership, so we all got the same charge.

"It took six months, but we eventually had to go to court. They tracked down and charged seventeen of us. As I mentioned earlier, our solicitor was a disappointment and advised us all to plead guilty, which we did. The case wrapped up quickly, and we were sent to the cells under the court while the judge decided our fate.

We were called up one at a time to be sentenced, and the screw in charge of the cells, with a smarmy smile, repeated to us what each one received: a £50 fine, six months in prison, another six months, two more £50 fines, and a six-month suspended sentence. Then it was my turn. I stood before the "Hanging Judge," and he gave a lot of empty talk about why he was giving me a six-month youth custody sentence."

"You went to prison?"

"Yes, like I said, I got six months but only completed four before they let me out for good behaviour."

"What was it like inside? Was it terrible?"

"Nah, it was a breeze, no problem at all."

Julie frowned slightly. "You make it sound easy, but I bet it wasn't."

He didn't tell Julie that after getting out, he rejoined the gang and learned everything about the drug trade.

By the time he turned nineteen, he was the gang's leader. He effectively controlled the East End of London through intimidation and violence, but he never actually committed murder.

He came close a few times, though. By the time he was twenty-five, he'd made several million.

He told Julie he had decided to leave London, but still kept in touch with his friends, omitting the fact that he maintained control by delegating daily tasks to his best friend, Sam.

He minimised his involvement here in Faversham, saying, "Just to keep my hand in." Julie listened attentively but didn't say much. She was aware of his activities and had concluded that he couldn't have earned that kind of wealth without being involved in something substantial. It didn't add up that he could make that much money by just dealing small quantities at the local club.

She wasn't concerned about his financial status or his alleged crimes. What mattered to her was that he was the kindest person she'd ever met. She gave his hand a grateful squeeze.

He concluded by saying, "That's all that's interesting in my life," then changed the subject, asking her, "Ever been to Herne Bay?"

"Never heard of it, so no, I haven't. Where is it?"

"Not far," he said. "Nice little place — pebbly beach, a pier, some cafés."

Julie gave a faint smile. "After everything you've told me, that sounds like heaven."

She glanced out of the window. "Funny," she added softly, "last time I saw a pier, I was hiding underneath it."

CHAPTER ELEVEN – *Smoke and Shadows*

LeeRoy took the back roads along "Tankerton. The little rain that had arrived from 'Will's Mother'" had stopped and the skies had cleared, so LeeRoy pulled the car over for a moment at the top of the hill to show Julie the stunning view across the Swale Estuary to the Isle of Sheppey, and beyond that, the Thames Estuary toward Essex, with ships chuffing out black smoke as they sailed to destinations unknown.

They sat there admiring it for ten minutes, with Julie breathing in the fresh air, trying to forget, and then headed toward Herne Bay.

They went past the small Hampton Pier and a large hotel on the right, which LeeRoy said was owned by Peter Noone's parents, the lead singer of Herman's Hermits. She didn't look impressed, as she had never heard of the band.

They arrived and parked. "Fancy a walk along the pier?"

"Sounds nice," said Julie, vaguely noticing the beautiful old clock tower along the road.

The pier was 3,787 feet long, and passenger steamboats often arrived, but none were there that day. They walked past the roller-skating rink and onto the central part of the pier, passing a few fishermen who weren't catching much, probably because it was a warm, clear, calm day.

They sat at the end of the pier for what felt like hours, but it was only thirty minutes. The conversation was sparse, but Julie snuggled up to LeeRoy, taking in the view and reminiscing about happy times with her friends. She tried to focus on the good memories instead of their deaths, but couldn't help wondering what had gone so wrong to cause such a fire.

Julie was fascinated watching two children hanging what she thought was string over the end of the pier and pulling up small crabs.

"Why are they doing that?" she asked LeeRoy.

He chuckled and said to her, "It's called crabbing, just kids having fun; they will throw them back later."

"It feels like a waste of time if they aren't able to eat them," she responded.

"Well, occasionally, if they're lucky, they will catch an edible one, but not very often."

"Still seems like a waste of time," she said, then looked up at LeeRoy and added, "Can we head back home, please?" She felt strange calling the pub home after such a short time.

They drove back to Faversham, arriving at the Hole in the Wall around 5 p.m. Julie let herself in, and they walked through the bar.

"What are you going to do tonight?" asked LeeRoy, but before she could respond, the police inspector walked into the bar, which wasn't open to the public yet.

"Hello. How have you been?" he asked.

"OK," said Julie, her tone dull. "Any news yet?"

"Yes, there is," the inspector said, "and I think you should sit down." Julie's heart pounded. The inspector stayed standing, and Julie could tell by his expression that this was bad news. LeeRoy squeezed her shoulder.

"Okay." He cleared his throat. "Forensics found signs of arson."

"Arson?" Julie cried in disbelief. "Somebody set fire to the coach?"

"That can't be right," LeeRoy said under his breath. "Who'd torch a place like that?"

LeeRoy sat down next to her concerned, one hand stroking her back, trying to soothe her.

"Yes," the inspector confirmed. "We're ninety-five percent sure that's what happened. They've taken some material back to the lab for analysis, but that's the conclusion otherwise."

"My God!" Julie exclaimed. "But that's murder! Who would do such a thing?"

"That's what I want to ask you. Do you know anyone who might have a reason to harm any of your friends?"

"No!" Julie said. "They kept to themselves and had no enemies that I know of. Are you saying everyone is dead?" Tears welled up in her eyes.

"Yes, I'm afraid so. At least they've identified five bodies, but they were so badly burned that they haven't been individually identified yet."

"My God!" Julie cried out, reaching for LeeRoy. "He wrapped her in his arms and held her tight as she crumpled."

"It's alright, sweetheart, I've got you," he murmured. "Let it out."

"I know it's hard, Julie," the inspector continued, "but I need to keep asking questions. Are you okay to answer?"

"Yes," she sobbed.

"What about drugs? Did they owe money to anyone? Especially for drugs?" he asked, looking meaningfully at LeeRoy.

"No, no," Julie said. "They weren't into anything heavy and they never bought anything they couldn't afford." She wiped her nose on the back of her hand, and LeeRoy pulled out his cotton handkerchief, handing it to her as she continued to sob, "I have no idea. I wish I did. I can't believe someone would do such a thing. Are you sure?"

"I'm afraid it certainly looks that way at the moment," said the inspector. "OK, that will be all for now, but LeeRoy has my number. Would you please call me if you think of anything?"

"Of course, but I just can't think of any reason or who would do such a thing."

When the inspector left, LeeRoy stayed seated, eyes fixed on the floor. "Arson," he muttered. "That takes planning. Someone wanted them gone."

Julie looked up, frightened. "Why them? Why not when I was still there?"

He hesitated just long enough for her to notice, then shook his head. "No, darlin'. Don't start blaming yourself. You couldn't have stopped it — none of this is on you."

The following weekend, Julie returned to work. She and Chas believed it was better than sitting alone with her racing thoughts; working at least kept her occupied. The pub was attracting a large crowd, with a band playing on Saturday night and filling up fast. The night looked to be lively. Julie appreciated the distraction, which helped her forget her worries.

At around 10 p.m., just as Julie came out of the saloon bar with empty bottles, the two troublemakers who had caused problems the week before walked in. They stopped abruptly, surprised to see Julie. She hesitated too, but kept walking confidently, drawing strength from the crowds, the fact that LeeRoy and Chas were nearby, and her victory over them last time. They huddled together, whispering and nervously glancing around, especially at Julie.

They shifted to the far end of the bar, avoiding her, ordered their regular two pints of strong lager, and entered the snooker room. However, since there was no snooker that night, as the band was playing and the snooker table was covered, they huddled together, whispering, finished their beers, and then left.

"That's unusual," Chas said to LeeRoy. "They normally stick around till the end – or until they're thrown out."

"Yeah, sure is," LeeRoy muttered, staring hard at the door they'd just left through. "Really strange."

Chas shrugged uneasily. "They give me the creeps, those two. Never know what they're plotting."

LeeRoy nodded slowly. "Yeah. Let's keep an eye out, just in case."

CHAPTER TWELVE – *Ash and Reckoning*

The identities of the deceased from the coach fire were verified, families were notified, and funerals were scheduled. It was a challenging time for Julie, knowing her friends' funerals were taking place across the country. She had lost a significant amount of weight, which she could ill afford to lose, and she appeared hollow-eyed and gaunt.

Barrie's funeral was held on a Friday at St. Mary's Church of Charity in Faversham. Since no family members could be found, the local council covered the expenses. The attendance was small, but Julie and LeeRoy were there. Barrie had always been Julie's favourite. She remembered how kind he was to her and how he tried to protect her from those jerks.

Julie stood in the cemetery, looking down at Barrie's coffin six feet below in the open grave, tears streaming down her face. She tossed a handful of dirt, listening to it hit the wood, then placed a bunch of flowers in the grave.

LeeRoy stood quietly beside her, hat in hand. "You deserved better, mate," he said under his breath. "We'll make sure someone pays for this."

Another three weeks had passed before the two jerks returned to the pub. They seemed quieter than usual, ordering two pints, sitting by the door, and drinking quietly. They continued to order more rounds, and this pattern persisted throughout the evening, gradually growing louder and rowdier. Julie stayed back, keeping her distance.

LeeRoy walked in just after 10 p.m. and spotted them near the door. He growled, "So you decided to grace us with your presence again, huh?"

"Piss off!" Gary snarled, drunk on courage. LeeRoy just laughed at him.

Drunk and fired up, they began harassing the staff and customers. "Chill out," Chas warned, "or you know where you'll end up." Gary slurred, "Piss off — or you'll get what she was meant to get!" He pointed his finger at Julie.

The room went still for a second. LeeRoy froze, then said quietly, "What did you just say?"

"Shut the hell up," Paul hissed. "You jerk!" He pushed Gary, who fell backward onto the floor. Gary roared, pulling himself up, then launched himself at Paul. They grappled with each other, too drunk to do much damage.

Chas and LeeRoy pulled them apart, slapped them, and threw them out of the door they knew so well.

"What was all that about?" asked Chas.

"No idea," said LeeRoy, murmuring under his breath,

"What did he mean?"

"What Julie was meant to get?"

The two scumbags stumbled down Preston Street into Court Street, shoving each other and arguing.

"You fucking jerk!" slurred Paul.

A couple of girls who were regulars in The Hole in the Wall were on their way home from a night out, heading towards the two men. They quickly grabbed each other's arms and hurried by, trying to steer clear of them.

"Blondie should've burned alive!" Gary yelled back towards the pub.

"Shut up!" his friend said, trying to rush him past the women, who gave them a wide berth, looking scared.

"The fire shoulda fuckin' killed her!" Gary yelled.

The two girls had rushed across the street to avoid the men, holding onto each other tightly, their eyes wide with fear. One of them glanced back, seeing the now small, dark figures in the distance, wavering just out of reach.

"Did you hear that?" one of the girls gasped, her fingers still digging deep into her friend's arm. "Yes, I think I did. Did he say she should have been burned alive?"

"Yes, he did, do you think it was them that set light to those hippies?"

"The way I heard it, yes."

"We have to go to the police," the other whispered urgently. They knew the only fire recently was the one that had killed people in the old bus at Macknade.

They also knew, from hearing about it at The Hole in the Wall, that the people who had died were Julie's friends.

"Sod the police," her friend replied. "I think we should go to the Hole and let Julie know."

They reaffirmed what they had heard and decided to tell Julie, then ran to the pub just as Chas arrived to lock the door.

"Hey, girls, you're too late," Chas said as they burst in, white-faced. "Just called last orders!" Seeing their breathlessness and shocked expressions, Chas frowned. "What's wrong?"

"We have to talk to Julie!" the first girl panted. "In private." Chas was so surprised, he waved them on. "Julie!" He yelled, "You have visitors."

Julie and the girls settled into a quiet corner of the pub, and LeeRoy joined them, looking concerned. Chas dropped off some brandy, winking, "Looks like you could use these." Then he slipped into the background.

The girls chattered and talked over each other, filling Julie in on what had just happened and what they'd overheard the scumbags yelling.

"You what?" roared LeeRoy, standing up. Julie tugged him down, her hand gripping his leg.

She was stunned. "Say that again, exactly."

"Both of us heard it," the second girl agreed. "They said you should've been burned alive. They said the fire should've killed you."

"Assholes!" Julie sat frozen in shock, her mind racing as she replayed what she'd just heard. LeeRoy, his knuckles white and fists clenched, looked like he was about to explode. He was thinking, trying to process what he'd just been told. Neither of them could speak.

Chas came over, curious and asked, "Are you okay? You look like you've seen a ghost." He chuckled, "Not you, LeeRoy, but Julie certainly does?" LeeRoy's voice was barely above a whisper, his anger barely contained.

"Not funny, Chas. We just found out something that needs some thought."

Chas backed off, hands raised in surrender. "LeeRoy, what did they tell you?" LeeRoy's face was grim. "Sorry, Chas." Julie asked quietly, "LeeRoy, do you think they burned the coach?" LeeRoy's eyes were stern and distant. "It's a possibility. They're troublemakers, but they usually throw punches, not burn coaches."

"Arson? Murder?" LeeRoy went on. "I don't know. Who knows what they're capable of?"

"I do," Julie said, so quietly that LeeRoy barely heard.

"What, darling?" LeeRoy asked, taking her trembling hand.

"Rape," she murmured.

LeeRoy bent down, trying to see through her curtain of blonde hair, peering into her flushed face, which was still bent over. "Julie?"

"They tried to rape me." She spoke up clearly, sitting up straight. Despite her glassy eyes from tears, she gazed directly at him, a challenge in her stare.

His fingers tightened around her hand, and he looked furious and disgusted, making her think he might reject her.

She felt like soiled goods.

"Julie," he said softly, searching her eyes. They held each other's gaze for several seconds, and he saw only honesty and pain in her face. Then his voice grew firmer at the thought of what he wanted to do to the scumbags. "Why didn't you tell me?"

Julie sniffed back tears. "I handled it. I moved on."

"You shouldn't have had to," he said quietly. "No one walks away from something like that without scars."

LeeRoy scrutinised her, unable to believe she could be so strong yet so vulnerable. His teeth clenched at the thought of those guys hurting her.

She wiped away her tears and shrugged, feeling embarrassed to be seen in such a vulnerable state. She'd been trying to toughen herself up. She didn't want LeeRoy to see her as fragile, and the thought of him feeling sorry for her made her sick. She longed for him to laugh again at her swinging the ashtray, nearly knocking one of them out. She also craved revenge for her friends.

"What they said about the fire," she said, her voice strong with resolve. "Should we call the inspector and tell him?"

"No, not yet," LeeRoy said quickly, his eyes narrowing in thought. "Let me think it over for a bit."

"Okay," she said uneasily. "Whatever you think is best, LeeRoy."

"I have to make some calls," he said, standing up and looking preoccupied. "You'll be alright, right?"

"Yes," Julie said unconvincingly, and went to wash the glasses.

The rest of the night dragged on with no sign of LeeRoy. It was 1 a.m., and the lock-in had ended, so she figured he wasn't coming back at all. It must have been an important call.

She knew what he was involved in, so she assumed it was work-related, but she had hoped he would return to comfort her. She was still shaken by the girls' comments and felt exposed and vulnerable after sharing her feelings. Although she hadn't done anything wrong, she wondered why LeeRoy hadn't come back. She shared her experience of nearly being raped, and then he had left. Did she push him away?

Come on, don't be silly! she scolded herself. She went over all the signs that proved he genuinely cared about her. She convinced herself he wouldn't stay away for long, but still had a hard time falling asleep, hoping to hear him knock on the door.

CHAPTER THIRTEEN – *An Eye for an Eye*

LeeRoy had made his phone calls, and the following evening, he was sitting in a new transit van in the car park next to the swimming pool.

He knew the scumbags would eventually come through the car park, and sure enough, at 9:45 p.m., they went through the alleyway by the National Westminster Bank.

As they approached the transit, the back door swung open, and three large black men leapt out, grabbed them, and, before they could protest, shoved them into the back of the van, screaming. The two scumbags started to fight back, but when they were shown the business end of two sawn-off shotguns, they shut up and lay still, their necks held down by the guy's boots.

"What do you want?" Gary asked, his voice barely audible; his mouth was pressed against the cold metal floor of the van.

"Shut the fuck up," said one of the men, pressing his foot down harder. "You'll find out soon enough."

"Where the hell are you taking us?" Paul cried, his voice muffled against the floor.

"Somewhere quiet," one of the men replied flatly. "You'll like the view."

They were freaking out, but they stayed quiet and waited. They couldn't see that the van was heading toward Oare, turning right at the Three Mariners and down to a remote part of Harty Ferry. The van passed the Coast Guard Cottages and continued to the end of the road, up a small hill, and stopped just before the water's edge as the tide was high. From there, the men could see any traffic for at least three-quarters of a mile.

The lights were turned on in front of the van, but the scumbags, both lying face down with boots on the backs of their necks, still couldn't see anything.

The rear van doors opened, and a bright flashlight shone in their faces, illuminating each of them in turn with a blinding pool of light. They couldn't see who was holding the flashlight until he spoke.

"Hey, guys. We meet again!"

"LeeRoy? What the fuck's going on?" said Gary, but he was squeaking instead of doing his usual, reckless blabbering.

"You thought you were finished with me?" LeeRoy said low, letting the words hang. "Not a chance."

"Now shut the fuck up!" shouted LeeRoy. "Get them out," he demanded, and the three monsters practically lifted them off their feet. They were much larger than LeeRoy, but he was the one in control. Two held their victims' faces down on the grass, while the third stood with a gun, steadily scanning from one petrified guy to the other. LeeRoy pulled out a long, very long knife that glinted in the moonlight.

Paul, catching sight of the weapon out of the corner of his eye, whimpered and pissed himself as half his face was pressed into the dirt. The urine hissed and steamed in the cold air. Two of the massive men grumbled and kicked him in disgust.

LeeRoy took the knife and, bending down to each of his captives, one by one, he grasped the hems of their clothing and sliced them up the back. He carelessly caught Gary's skin, causing him to yelp. Paul was bawling like a baby the entire time.

"You'll remember what you did for the rest of your life," LeeRoy told them quietly as he worked, each syllable deliberate.

"Strip them and duct tape them," LeeRoy commanded, and the big guys did as they were told, ripping the lads' clothes off without hesitation. They didn't worry about undoing anything, harshly yanking the sliced things off their limbs, leaving red welts as the lads cried out in pain. Both of them were now completely naked, their skin bone-white in the moonlight.

LeeRoy's men duct-taped their hands behind their backs and bound their feet. They weren't going anywhere.

The sky was clear, and a full moon made it seem almost like day, but it was pretty chilly. Both scumbags' teeth were chattering, partly from the cold on their gooseflesh skin, but primarily out of fear.

"Gag this one," LeeRoy said. They left Gary's mouth free and yanked him to his feet, where he stood wobbling.

"OK," snarled LeeRoy, right in Gary's face. "We know you wankers torched that bus and murdered those friends of Julie's."

"You're mad!" Gary blurted. "We never killed anybody!"
"You set fire to her home," LeeRoy said, his voice low and deadly. "Don't pretend you didn't know who'd be inside."

Fuck! thought Gary. *We're in the shit now. How the hell did he find out?*

"No idea what the fuck you're on about, LeeRoy," he protested, his eyes wild, but his voice loud and steady. "We wouldn't do anything like that. We've never been near the place."

"You lying fuck. I know the two of you tried to rape Julie!" LeeRoy spat, his face twisted in fury. "You are lucky you're still alive, believe me." He pointed the knife at Gary.

Gary's face crumpled, and he started crying.

"Shut the fuck up!" LeeRoy said. "That won't help you. It'll only piss me off more. I'll stamp on your face myself if you don't shut the fuck up."

LeeRoy, furious, booted Gary in the ribs, sending him tumbling over and down onto a small gravel beach. Gary screamed in pain as the sharp stones dug into his thin, bony skin. LeeRoy followed him down and gave him another kick for good measure, making him yelp in agony.

"Bring the other wanker down here," LeeRoy said, "One of you stay up there and keep a lookout up the road."

Paul was shoved down the slope to join Gary, but since he was gagged, the only sounds he made were the muffled thuds of his body bouncing down the hill, along with the hiss and shifting of pebbles as they dislodged under his weight.

"One last chance, you fucking shit," LeeRoy shouted at Gary.

"Tell me what happened, or I'll unleash big Sam on you."

"Fuck off," Gary said. He got another kick in the ribs right away.

"Alright," LeeRoy said. "Let's do this the hard way. Over to you, Sam."

Sam cracked his knuckles and grinned. "Been a while since I had a workout."

"Don't enjoy it too much," LeeRoy warned. "This isn't for fun—it's for answers."

Sam handed his shotgun to LeeRoy and pulled out a mean-looking switchblade. Gary didn't see it at first, but Sam stood over him, crouched and straddled him, one knee on either side, and showed him the nasty blade. Gary started to struggle, but this guy was eighteen stone, and Gary was only half that; he wasn't going anywhere.

"You crazy fuckers!" Gary squealed, his eyes wild with fear.

"You'll get locked up for this."

"Aha," LeeRoy said, "and just who's gonna rat us in?" It won't be you—unless you start talking, because you'll be floating face down out there in the Swale very soon. The crabs and fish will love your scabby meat. Got it?"

"You wouldn't dare," said Gary, tears, drool, and snot contradicting his bravado.

"Just try us," said Sam. He grabbed hold of Gary's earlobe in his left hand and sliced it off without hesitation. Gary screamed, blood running down his face and onto the pebble beach.

"Gag him," said LeeRoy, and Sam quickly stuffed a rag in Gary's mouth, causing him to gag on the rotten piece of material and blood.

"Un-gag this wanker," directed LeeRoy, nodding towards Paul. "Then sit him up so he can see just what's coming his way if he doesn't talk."

One of the other men got out his knife and came straight for Paul's face. He thought he was going to get the same treatment and squeezed his eyes shut, whimpering, but all the man did was cut the duct tape from around his mouth.

"Now just watch that scumbag," LeeRoy pointed to Gary with the knife, "and whatever is done to him is going to be done to you – until you talk. Get it?"

Paul looked crazed: his eyes were blank and staring, his mouth twisted.

"Maybe not," LeeRoy added. "Let me explain. First, you'll lose your earlobe, no matter what." Paul let out a high-pitched cry. "If you want to talk, that's all you'll lose. Next, he'll cut off Gary's other earlobe. Then you'll get another chance to talk. But if you don't, you'll lose both earlobes." Tears streamed down Paul's face. "We'll keep going, cutting off bits here and there. If you're the real hero and still don't talk, Sam here will cut off Gary's testicles and then yours." LeeRoy paused to let the reality sink in. "But I'm sure you'll be more than happy to talk before that. We might castrate both of you anyway, just for fun. I don't think any Faversham girls will be too disappointed, do you?"

"You're sick!" Paul spat weakly. "You're all bloody sick!" "No, mate," Sam said. "We're tidy. You're the mess."

Gary struggled to break free, but it was no use—he was still pinned down by Sam. He was bleeding heavily and terrified, just like Paul. He was in a panic, barely making sense, his cries more like the howls of a wild animal than words. "Go for it," LeeRoy said. Gary kicked wildly, but it was no match for Sam's brute strength. Sam tore off Gary's other earlobe, and he let out a muffled groan through the gag.

"Come on, Paul. That's two ear lobes you're going to lose. So tell me, you wankers, what happened?"

They were both paralysed with terror. Paul couldn't speak, and Gary was still choking on the rag.

"Give 'em both a kick in the ribs." LeeRoy's friends obliged instantly, and both lads gave terrifying, unnatural screams – Gary's muffled through his gag – trying to get away, but they had no chance.

"Alright," said LeeRoy, "slice his nose." "No, no!" Paul, the most cowardly of the two, cried out. "Please! Please! Promise not to cut us, and I'll tell you what happened."

"Can promise you nothing," LeeRoy said. "Just spit it out, or I'll cut the tip of your tongue off if you don't start talking."

"Alright, alright," Paul said, hyperventilating. He sat there, silent.

"Well?" LeeRoy said impatiently, kicking Paul in his already bruised ribs. He screamed out again. "Shut up with that crying and talk!"

"OK, OK," Paul sobbed. "It all started in the pub, when that slag......."

LeeRoy smashed him straight in the mouth with the butt of Sam's shotgun, knocking out three of his front teeth. Blood sprayed everywhere, and Paul was out cold.

"Nobody calls my girl a slag," said LeeRoy. "Fling him in the sea to bring him round."

"Christ, LeeRoy," one of the London lads muttered, half admiring, half wary. "You've got a dark side."
LeeRoy's eyes flicked to him. "You've no idea."

Gary started gagging, the wad of cloth in his throat cutting off his airway. Sam yanked it out. "Don't want you to choke, do we?" he sneered, as Gary coughed and spluttered. "That would be too easy."

The London boys were loving every minute of this – a day out in the country, by the sea, plus all the entertainment they could ask for. They grabbed Paul and tossed him six feet through the air, where he landed on a broken wooden sea break. "Break" was an understatement because it broke two of his already bruised ribs. He rolled off the wall and into the shallow water and stinking mud. Face down, he started to drown.

"Better pull him out," said LeeRoy. "Give him another kick in the ribs when he comes round."

They dragged him up. Paul came to after a few ducking's, three minutes later, and was welcomed back into reality with a kick in the ribs from Sam.

"Right, you fucking arseholes, talk," Shouted LeeRoy inches from his bloody face.

Paul tried, but his mouth was a mash of raw flesh. LeeRoy's slam of the shotgun butt had not only knocked out his teeth but also split both lips and cut his tongue, which was now badly swollen. Even if he had wanted to talk, he couldn't. He was in a bad way, but LeeRoy didn't give a fuck; just like they didn't when they burnt the coach, or tried to rape Julie.

"Get that other wanker over here," said LeeRoy.

Two of them dragged Gary over to the others, cutting his feet on the gravel. All his bravado was gone, and his eyes were out on stalks at closer sight of his friend, his face like raw meat. "Right now, Gazzer, start where toothless finished."

Gary spluttered apologetically to Paul, "I got no choice. They'll kill us if I don't."

Paul lisped, thick-tongued and dazed, "Gonna kill uth anyway."

LeeRoy sneered, "Even if we do kill you, shitheads, it'll be quicker and painless if you talk. Try staying silent, and you'll tell us in the end, but it'll be a very long, painful death," he promised. "In fact, Gazzer boy, if we go down that road, you can watch while we slowly gut your friend for fish bait. But only after we've slowly removed his bollocks, so you will know exactly what's coming to you. Best start talking right now. I'm getting cold and impatient."

The fear in both of them was now so intense that the air was electric. Paul was almost unconscious with tension and pain, the anxiety and terror visible on his ruined face.

"Last chance, Gaz. Talk, and watch your words unless you want the dental treatment too."

Gary swallowed down the bile rising in his throat. "OK," he gasped. "In the pub, that... girl recognised us, and you know what happened."

"Yes," smiled LeeRoy, recalling Julie flooring him with the ashtray. "Girl after my own heart. Carry on."

"We got pissed and went up to Macknade to do some damage." Gary winced, tears welling up in his eyes. "It was Paul's idea," he said.

Paul snarled through his split lips, "Fucker!" and got kicked by Sam.

"I just went along with it!" Gary muttered. We got there just after midnight. Looked through the windows, but it was too dark. We were trying to scare the living daylights out of them by setting fire to some old sacks under the bus. We thought they'd smoulder and smoke them out. But they caught fire fast. We panicked and took off like crazy, running away from there. We heard this massive explosion – it must have been the gas bottles going off." Gary broke off, sobbing more out of fear of what LeeRoy would do now than out of remorse.

"We just ran, scared the cops might come, but we were lucky and got home OK."

"Oh, thank fuck you were lucky and okay," LeeRoy said, sarcastically.

"We didn't mean to do it," Gary's voice cracked. "We just wanted to scare them, thinking the girl was in there. We heard everyone died, so we almost pissed our pants when we saw your bird in the pub..." Gary gulped, his eyes wild.

LeeRoy held up his hand to stop him from talking. He thought for a few minutes, pacing the shoreline, the crunch of gravel loud in their ears.

He spun around and spoke in a chilling, calm voice: "What really got to me was that you thought Julie was in there. If she had been, they'd be finding you in a hundred pieces by tomorrow. As I see it, I have three options." LeeRoy raised one finger, ticking off each one:

"Option one: turn you over to the cops, but that's a problem for us, considering your current state and what you'll be like after more time." He smiled and lifted another finger.

"Or, two: cut your throats, dump you in the Swale, and let the crabs and fish sort you out.

Three: punish you and let you run home with your tail between your legs. That might be the only thing we leave between them, though. But will you go to the police?"

Both shook their heads, murmuring a chorus of repeated "no's."

LeeRoy considered for a moment. "Even if you did, how could you prove we'd done anything?"

"We can't," muttered Gary, defeated.

LeeRoy paced around both of them, lying on the pebbles, still bound. He stopped. "So, I am going for Option three."

Cries and gasps came from both of them. Paul was weeping loudly, this time in relief.

"You see these three boys?" LeeRoy swept his arm through the air, indicating Sam and his henchmen. "You know what they are capable of? Well, if you go to the police, my name is the only one you know." LeeRoy smiled widely, just his white teeth picked up by the moonlight, like the disembodied grin of the Cheshire Cat. "That leaves these gents free to fuck you up. I mean, fuck you up dead. Get it?"

"Yes. Yes!" Paul mumbled and nodded, but Gary only glared insolently now that he thought he was safe, saying nothing.

LeeRoy kicked Gary in the ribs again and repeated, "Get it?"

"Yes, I get it," he moaned, doubled over, gagging. His ribs felt splintered, as if with one more touch, they would explode inwardly.

LeeRoy turned to his men and said, "Cut his ear lobes off."

They turned their attention to Paul's bloodied face. He was trembling in shock, and having suffered already, he barely registered the additional pain as the knife hacked at his ears.

Satisfied, LeeRoy continued calmly, "And poke one of Gary's eyes out."

"No-o-o!" roared Gary, struggling against his restraints but It was to no avail.

The huge guys held him down, screaming. One placed his heavy hand, bearing half of his weight on Gary's forehead and pulled his eyelid open, while the other leaned down on his chest and poked the tip of his knife into Gary's eye. He went berserk, screeching, but was helpless to do anything: the duct tape and two eighteen-stone black men were keeping him just where he was. With fascination, the knifeman twisted the blade in his eyeball, releasing blood and jelly. Gary went rigid, then limp as the men released him where he lay, moaning pitifully.

"An eye for an eye," LeeRoy smiled, but his teeth were set in a tight grimace. "But you're getting off lightly. Maybe you'll think twice before trying to rape or kill anyone else." He let his words sink in before saying, brightly, "Right, wankers. We're going now, and you're staying right here. Hopefully, you'll die of hypothermia, but if not, I'm sure somebody will find you in the morning. Just remember, keep your gobs shut, or you're dead, but only after worse torture."

LeeRoy and his guys got in the van and left their victims lying tied up, naked and bloody, on the small beach.

Fortunately, there wasn't a spring tide, or they would have drowned when the tide fully came in. Although they were freezing cold, they wouldn't die from hypothermia. For a while, the only sounds were soft sobs and moans of pain. They were in a terrible state. Struggling to free themselves from the duct tape only made their injuries worse, and with the strong tape wrapped around them multiple times, they were helpless. All they could do was lie there, drifting in and out of consciousness, hoping someone would rescue them.

On the ground nearby, Paul spotted movement out of the corner of his eye, and his head snapped around. It was a large brown rat, scuffling through the gravelly beach, just a few feet away. The rat hesitated, then made a sudden dash forward, grabbed one of the severed ear lobes, and scurried off.

"Did you see that?" Paul asked, his voice rising in hysteria, barely able to speak through his injuries.

"How the fuck can I see anything?" Gary said in a muffled voice. "They dug my eye out!" His voice wavered with emotion. "There's so much blood in the other one, I can't see a fucking thing."

Paul was staring blindly into nothingness, detached from reality. He was lost in another world, with no fundamental awareness of what was going on. Eventually, both drifted off into exhausted sleep despite their pain as it started to get light.

Just after 5 a.m., an old fisherman and local character, Bill, arrived to take his boat out for the day.

"What the……..?" He started.

He peered through milky, hooded eyes, trying to make out what he was seeing. He couldn't believe that there were tied-up, naked bodies on the beach. He started walking towards them uncertainly, horrified but curious.

"Oh, my God!"

He thought they were dead, until Paul opened his eyes, saw him, and yelled, "Help! Please!"

The old fisherman slowly went down to them but was reluctant to step closer, seeing that they were bound up and encrusted with thick brown blood.

Gary was also shouting by now, "Help! Help!"

Bill nervously glanced all around him, scouring the landscape, afraid that whoever had done this was watching him and would kill him without a second's thought.

"What the hell happened to you? Who did this to you?"

"Don't worry about that for fuck's sake," said Gary, "cut this tape off me."

The old fisherman warily got out a small penknife and cut the tape with shaky hands, the blood flow slowly returning to the two men's body parts. Gary took the knife, cut his own feet free, and then freed Paul. They tried to stand up, but after being bound for so long and with their broken ribs and other injuries, it was tough. Bill saw they weren't in any shape to walk, but he didn't have room for them in his truck, which was packed with lobster pots, fishing nets, and stinking buckets.

"I'll call for help," Bill said. There was an emergency phone nearby, located right on the path edge, thanks to a persistent woman from one of the coastguard's cottages who had pushed the authorities to act after two people had drowned in the Swale over the past few years. The survivors of any accidents always knocked on the woman's door for help in the middle of the night. The most recent drowning had been the last straw, and the most serious incident in a string of similar accidents, so the Faversham council had installed the phone.

The old fisherman walked the twenty yards to the phone as fast as his arthritic knees would allow.

"Fucking sure!" he said out loud when he saw the cable ripped out and the phone receiver lying on the ground. Cursing, he hurried back to the groaning men.

"It's not working – vandalised again. "You stay here," the fisherman told them. "I'll drive up to the cottages and get someone to call an ambulance."

The scumbags were in no position to argue. They were barely conscious and couldn't stand for more than a few seconds.

He climbed into his rusty old truck and headed up the road to the nearest houses: the coastguards' cottages, the lobster pots swaying and rattling as his rough ride shook them on the bumpy road.

At 5:28 am, after Bill knocked on several cottage doors without a response, a man in a bathrobe finally answered in a furious state. The old fisherman was a familiar face to him, but he wasn't happy to be woken up so early. "What the hell's going on?" he demanded. After Bill explained what he'd found, the man hesitantly dialled 999 and requested an ambulance. "And by the sound of it, you might need to send the police, too."

Soon, the ambulance showed up, and the crew glanced at the two boys, who were now cocooned in some old fish sacks from Bill's truck. They didn't exactly smell great, but at least they had some protection from the cold.

The crew tended to the boys and stabilised them as much as possible, then loaded them into the warm ambulance just as the police arrived; they didn't seem to be in a rush. The officers took a peek inside the ambulance, and although they were a bit taken aback by their condition, they couldn't help but snicker when they recognised the two battered individuals.

They weren't in the mood to talk to the police, so Bill confirmed that he had been the one who found them and reported it.

"Yes," said Bill, "I was just about to launch my dinghy when I saw them on that little beach. It scared me half to death; I thought they were dead and I'm surprised they're still alive given the state they were in."

"Yeah, they do look pretty rough. Did they say anything to you about what happened?" "No, they just kept yelling to get them untied, or more specifically, to cut the tape off."

"Alright, thanks. Could you please provide your name and address? I'm sure the investigation team will want to get in touch with you."

"Of course, but I won't be able to tell them anything more than I just told you."

Bill gave his information and launched his dinghy into the Swale, heading toward his trawler anchored offshore as police cordoned off the area. The forensic team was about to arrive, and the ambulance, with its flashing blue lights, headed to Canterbury Hospital.

When they arrived at the hospital, Gary was rushed into surgery after doctors evaluated the damage to his eye. They were able to save it, but they determined that he'd lose about 50 percent of his vision.

Paul was in rough shape. On top of broken ribs and severe bruising, he'd lost five teeth, had fifteen stitches in his lips, five in his tongue, and six in each earlobe. He'd be drinking through a straw for a while to come.

CHAPTER FOURTEEN — *The Long Night*

Julie woke up feeling exhausted and uneasy. LeeRoy hadn't shown up at all, despite her hopes that he would come by early and join her in bed. She hoped work was keeping him away, rather than what she'd said the night before. She'd been falling hard for LeeRoy, and she thought he felt the same way until now.

"Maybe I pushed too hard," she whispered to the empty room. "Maybe he's had enough of me."

She stretched out her arm and grabbed the alarm clock, groaning at the time. She had barely slept at all. Since she didn't have to work until 6 p.m., she took a sleeping pill, then a large vodka and orange, and rolled over, hoping to get a few more hours of sleep.

"Please let him walk through that door when I wake up," she murmured before drifting off again.

It didn't take long for word to spread about the guys getting a good beating. One of the nurses knew Jennie, another barmaid, and had stopped by when her shift ended at noon. "Oh my God, Jen! You should've seen the state they were in! They were practically half dead! They got a real beating for something!"

Even though she was whispering with Jennie, the news was spreading quickly. Someone visiting the hospital that morning had seen two guys being wheeled in on a stretcher when they arrived.

"Who did it?" Jennie hissed. "Did they say?"
"No idea," the nurse replied, wide-eyed. "But whoever it was, they didn't mess around."

One of the customers, Sammy Reed, walked in looking full of it. Stories were getting twisted as the rumour mill churned out tales.

The guys were dead. They'd had so many parts cut off, they'd ended up like two of the three wise monkeys: see no evil, hear no evil, speak no evil. They'd both been castrated, was the latest version. "Shag no evil!" one of the men drinking at the bar laughed.

"Bloody hell, that's sick," Jennie said, half laughing, half grimacing. "But honestly, no loss there, was it?"

"If anyone had it coming, it was those two," muttered a voice from the corner. "Heard one of 'em squealed like a pig."

"Serves 'em right," another voice added darkly. "World's better off without that sort."

By the time Julie started her shift at 6 p.m., the whole place was buzzing with rumours. There was a lot of speculation about who might hate these guys so much. They had managed to upset many people in Faversham, so there were plenty of suspects, although most people were willing to buy the attackers a round of drinks, whoever they were.

When Julie heard the news, her stomach turned over.

"No, no, no," she muttered under her breath. "Please tell me he didn't... LeeRoy, what have you done?"

What had happened to LeeRoy last night? Her silly, girlish fears that he'd gone off her had turned into even greater ones.

At 8 p.m., with Julie behind the bar, LeeRoy strolled into the pub. "LeeRoy!" she exclaimed, both relieved and thrilled. "I thought you'd taken off."

He smiled faintly. "Not a chance, babe. You don't get rid of me that easily."

Julie tried to laugh, though her voice shook. "You've no idea what's been going round today."

LeeRoy leaned closer, eyes steady. "Then maybe don't believe everything you hear."

He leaned casually against the bar, his hands resting on the surface, holding his cash. Julie couldn't help but scrutinise them, searching for any signs of bruising, scratches, or a fight. There was nothing.

"Been busy, sweetie," LeeRoy smiled. "Had to take a sudden trip to London and didn't get back until tonight," he lied.

"London? What were you doing there?"

"Nothing you'd be interested in, my little cherub."

"Okay," she shrugged. "But it's great to see you. I guess you haven't heard what happened to those two losers?"

"What losers?" he said, acting like he had no clue what was going on.

"Those two idiots that I hit with the ashtray."

"No," LeeRoy said innocently again. "What happened?"

"We're not sure," she said, sharing what she'd heard from the regulars. "Jen's friend told her about it earlier today, and then Sammy Reed came in and said he'd heard the same thing tonight."

LeeRoy glanced around. "Is he still here?"

"Yeah, he's playing snooker."

"I'll go check if I can find out a bit more. See you in a minute."

Leaving the bar, LeeRoy found Sammy Reed in the snooker room, casually chalking his cue while his buddy circled the table, searching for the perfect shot.

"Hey, Sammy," LeeRoy said casually. "Julie tells me those two jerks took a pretty good beating."

"Just a little," Sammy said with a grin.

"Hmmm. What happened?"

"Honestly, I only know what old Bill the fisherman said to Harry Jenkins, who passed it along to me, so the story's probably gotten a bit distorted.

"Tell me what you know."

"All I know is that old Bill discovered them this morning at Harty Ferry. "The old Bill?" LeeRoy asked nervously. "No, not the police, but old Bill the fisherman who has a boat moored off Harty Ferry. He found them tied up on the beach. He said there was so much blood they were unrecognisable."

"Wow!" LeeRoy exclaimed, and he was relieved it wasn't the police who had found them, even though he knew they would have been called. "Do they have any idea who did it?"

"Not that I know of," Sammy replied. "But given those guys, there's probably a long list of suspects."

"Reckon they'll live?" LeeRoy asked, forcing a casual tone. "Yeah, just about," Sammy said. "Though I doubt they'll be chatting anyone up again."

"Hmm," LeeRoy said, changing the subject to football. He chatted as he stood and watched the snooker game for a few more minutes before heading back through.

When he returned to the bar, Julie looked at him with a questioning expression. "Yeah. He didn't know much," LeeRoy said, sipping his beer.

"I shouldn't say it, but I'm pretty sure they had it coming - whatever they did. Other than what we know about" Julie mused, scrutinizing him as she spoke, trying to gauge his reaction.

"I'm sure they did," LeeRoy replied. "They got what was coming to them."

"You don't seem very shocked," Julie said softly.
LeeRoy met her gaze. "Takes a lot to shock me these days, sweetheart."

Julie frowned, puzzled, but LeeRoy stayed calm and revealed nothing, so she dismissed her concerns.

Gary and Paul had been at the hospital for three days when the inspector from the Faversham police showed up.

"Hello, Gary, been to war, have we?" The inspector pulled the curtains around his cubicle and marched in. He had already talked to the doctor and confirmed that they refused to say what had happened.

"Piss off," he spat through swollen lips. His head was bandaged, his face half obscured, but his one good eye shot venom.

"Now, now, Gary, not a nice way to speak to someone who's come to help you."

"Help me!" Gary muttered. "You're probably laughing your bollocks off."

"Maybe," the inspector said, "but I still have to figure out who did this and bring them to justice." He despised those scumbags and was glad someone had taken them down. However, he couldn't show it, although Gary already knew.

"Problem is," Gary said, "we have no fucking idea."

"I still have some questions for you, if you can hear through all that bandage," he said. "Can't it wait?" Gary asked. "I'm in agony. I don't even know how I'll get home." "Won't your parents come pick you up?" "They don't know I'm here, and anyway, they don't drive, so I'm stuck."

"How about this, Gary? If you come to the station in the morning and tell me what happened, I'll take you home." Gary thought it over, considering his options.

"Alright, but drop me off somewhere. I don't want to be seen in a "gaver" car." "Deal." Gary had no intention of keeping his promise.

Gary hadn't shown up at the police station the next morning, though the inspector hadn't expected him to. He drove to Gary's house and knocked on the door, noticing the shabby, peeling paint around the council house as he waited.

Gary's mother opened the door, mumbling through lips holding a smouldering cigarette and barking out, "Yes? Oh, it's you, what's he done now?"

The inspector explained to his mother that there had been an incident at Harty Ferry and that Gary and Paul had been taken to Canterbury Hospital three days ago.

"Three days ago! At the hospital? What are you talking about? I hadn't seen him in three days, but that's not unusual. When he came in late last night, I heard him go to the bathroom, and when I checked in a bit later, I noticed some blood on one of the towels. I banged on his door and asked what the hell he had been up to, and he just yelled for me to shut up, saying he was tired and had just had a minor scuffle at the bar. That's nothing out of the ordinary, so I went back to bed. My guess is that wasn't exactly the truth, considering you're at my door and he's still in his room at midday!"

"I only know they were badly beaten and tortured."

"God!" she gasped, snatching the cigarette out of her mouth. "He didn't tell me that! He just said he was in a scuffle."

"Some fight," said the inspector. "They cut off his ear lobes, and the same to Paul."

"My God!" she shrieked. "He didn't tell me that! I'll go and get the little bastard up."

He heard her thunder up the stairs and scream at Gary. "You little fuck! Why didn't you tell me the truth? What the fuck happened?"

Gary winced as she yanked the bedclothes off him and tried to pull him out of bed. He let out a scream from the pain of his bruised ribs, and his mother let go, shocked by the state of his face.

"Who the fucking hell did that to you?"

Fuck's sake, Mother, I'm in pain here. Just leave me alone!

"You'll be in a lot more pain if you don't tell me the truth. There's a copper downstairs that wants to talk to you." "Well, I don't want to talk to him," said Gary.

"Do as you please," his mother replied.

She went back downstairs and pointed to the ceiling above her, saying to the inspector, "All yours. Top of the stairs."

From the pile of bedding came a muffled, "Fuck off!"

"Nice welcome, Gary," said the inspector. "Right, off the record, I couldn't give a fuck about you two. You probably deserved it."

"Bollocks," said Gary.

"However, I have a job to do, and I need to ask a few questions, as I'm sure you realise, as thick as you are."

"Fuck off," Gary said, with his head still buried in his bloodstained pillow.

"Now, now, be a good boy, Gary, and I'll be away in no time. So, tell me what happened to you both?"

"Nothing. We were run over by a train."

"Well, I could almost believe that, seeing the state of you both. I'll ask again, what the hell happened to you?"

"I don't have anything to say," said Gary. "I can't remember. Must be a concussion."

"Okay, Gary, I couldn't care less, but I need to make it look like I'm doing my job."

"No point," the inspector told Gary's mother at the bottom of the stairs, where she stood with her arms folded. "He's not going to tell me anything."

"I'll beat it out of the little bastard, and he is a bastard, should have aborted him, the worthless piece of shit," she said before running back upstairs, yelling, "Right you wanker! What you got there is nothing compared to what I'll do to you!"

The inspector gave a wry smile as he left.

CHAPTER FIFTEEN — *Ashes, Answers, and an Invitation*

Julie and LeeRoy had spent the night together, catching up on lost time. After making love, she lay in his arms and brought up the subject that had been on her mind all day — the news about the two guys ending up in the hospital.

"So LeeRoy, I want you to be honest with me," she began, biting her lip. "Were you involved in what happened to those little shits last night?"

"Me?" LeeRoy raised an eyebrow in surprise.

Julie stared into his dark brown eyes, searching for the truth.

"I never laid a finger on them, sweetheart." In that respect, he was being truthful.

Later that day, when interviewing Paul, the inspector received the same reception as he did from Gary. They weren't foolish enough to discuss it with anyone. There was a lot of speculation and rumour around Faversham, but only those involved knew the truth.

Paul had his jaw wired up and was discharged from the hospital after five nights. Nobody felt sorry for them. Since they didn't want to be seen in such a state, even though they hated not being out on the town, they stayed in, and it was pretty quiet around Faversham for a while.

It was several weeks before they dared to venture into The Hole in the Wall again, doing so very cautiously because they didn't know if LeeRoy would be there or not. They felt relieved to see he wasn't, but Julie was there working behind the bar. They looked away from her, trying to stay out of sight.

She was shocked to see the state they were in. She couldn't help but laugh. Gary was wearing an eye patch and looked like Long John Silver. Then she noticed they both had no earlobes. She burst out laughing and had to rush into the other bar, barely holding herself together.

Chas was in the bar and asked what was so funny.

"Go take a look in the public bar," she choked.

Chas walked over and saw the two scumbags standing at the bar, looking embarrassed.

"Aye, aye, lads," he said in a west country accent, mimicking that of a pirate with a smirk on his lips. "I haven't seen you around for a while. Have you been on holiday?"

"Haha, very funny," said Gary. "You know what the fuck happened."

"Not exactly. What did they do?"

Gary shot Chas a glare; their eyes locked for a couple of seconds. "Mind your own business," Gary said, then added, "and grab us two pints of lager."

"Please."

"Please," he added sarcastically.

Chas pulled the pints. "Have you heard the joke about Van Gogh?"

"No," Paul said, "but I bet you're gonna tell us."

"Van Gogh walked into a bar," said Chas, "and the barman said, 'Hi, want a beer?'" Van Gogh said, "No thanks, I've got one ear!"

Chas roared with laughter at his own punchline.

"Ha, ha, ha," said Gary. "Very funny, tosser."

Others in the bar were sniggering to themselves but didn't have the balls to laugh out loud.

Four rounds later and just after 10 p.m., LeeRoy walked into the bar.

"Hello, lads," he said, smiling as he walked up to them. "Haven't seen you around in a while. Been anywhere good?"

"Fuck you," one of them said.

LeeRoy called out to Julie, "Can I get a Guinness, please?" and sat down with the two troublemakers. They shifted uncomfortably away from him.

Julie found it strange that LeeRoy was sitting with them, but she got distracted when someone ordered a beer.

LeeRoy leaned in close to the table and said quietly but firmly, "I hope, for your own sake you've kept your mouths shut." "Mine was wired shut," said Paul.

"You know what I mean. What did you tell the old Bill?"

"Nuffin," said Gary. "We ain't that stupid."

"That's a matter of opinion," said LeeRoy fixing them with a glare as he stood up and made his way back to the bar to pay for his Guinness.

"Take one for yourself, Julie, and one for Chas," he called over to Julie.

"Thank you, darling," said Julie, calling out to let Chas know he had one in the wood from LeeRoy.

"While you're at it," LeeRoy peeled another fiver from his wad and handed it to Julie. "Get two pints of lager for those two."

Julie stiffened and stared at him. "You're joking?"

"Just take them over to them."

Julie seethed. "No way, if I do, I'll tip it over their fucking heads."

LeeRoy laughed.

Julie couldn't believe her ears. She lowered her voice and hissed at him, "Those bastards tried to rape me! Remember?"

He looked at her with a deeper understanding. He might have gotten his revenge, but he realised that Julie wasn't ready to forgive and forget, which was only natural. "Yeah, sorry. Maybe that wasn't such a great idea after all, so let's cancel it."

"Good," Julie said firmly. She dropped the money into the till, slamming it shut, and threw LeeRoy's change on the bar. "Have you lost your mind or something?"

At 11 p.m., they called time, and to everyone's surprise, the scumbags slipped out quietly. Chas raised an eyebrow. "That beating shut them up." "We should do it more often," LeeRoy said, taking a swig of his Guinness.

Chas fixed LeeRoy with a steely gaze. The last customers had just left, and the girls were busy cleaning up. He circled the bar and took a seat on the stool next to LeeRoy, meeting his eyes head-on and said, "You did it, didn't you?" "Did what?" LeeRoy asked.

Listen, man, I don't have a problem with it. I wish I had been there.

LeeRoy said nothing; he simply took another sip of his beer and offered a small smile, staring into the distance.

"Alright, alright," Chas muttered. "I don't expect you to admit anything, but" he leaned in and said quietly, "good for you, I'm sure they had it coming."

"They did," LeeRoy said. He took another swig, thinking, his eyes scanning the room for anyone who might overhear him. Then he turned to Chas. "I trust you completely, so here you go." He filled Chas in on what he'd uncovered about the coach murders.

"Fucking hell!" said Chas. "Does Julie know?" LeeRoy shook his head, and Chas gabbled on. "So, they thought they'd murdered her too? What about the old Bill? Won't the lads gob off to them?"

"No way. They know what to expect if they do."

"Bloody hell," Chas said in admiration. "And I thought I knew you."

"Well, there ya go," LeeRoy said, finishing his drink.

Julie had finished her clearing up, said goodnight to the other barmaids, and walked over to join Chas and LeeRoy. "What are you two plotting?" She asked.

"Nothing, just discussing the state of the world, that's all," LeeRoy said. "You want to head up to the club, Julie?"

"Sorry, I don't feel up to it tonight," Julie's mouth twisted apologetically. "Maybe Saturday?"

"No problem," LeeRoy said. "Give us a decent bottle of wine Chas and we'll go sit and watch TV."

"Got a nice Chablis," Chas replied. "Three quid a bottle."

"Three quid? You thief!"

"Hey! Cheeky bastard! That's cost price – no markup. I'm doing you a favour, mate."

"Okay, take it out of that," LeeRoy said, handing him a twenty-pound note pulled from a roll he pulled out of his pocket.

Chas's eyes widened. "Been down and robbed the bank tonight, have we?"

"I wish." Chas grabbed the bottle from the fridge and handed it to LeeRoy. "Night. Don't do anything I wouldn't do," he joked.

"Can't promise," LeeRoy said with a wink. "Don't mind me," Julie retorted. "Just pretend I'm not here."

"I'll go run the bath, and you can open the wine," Julie said as they headed upstairs. "It'll be nice to share a glass in the bath together."

"Sounds good to me," LeeRoy replied.

Julie entered the bathroom, filled the tub, and lit four candles she found, placing them around the edge of the tub. It was a romantic gesture, she thought. With LeeRoy, it was more than just a physical connection. She felt a deeper bond, and she hoped he felt the same.

With the bath full, she called out to LeeRoy, laughing, "Oy, you, in!"

LeeRoy walked in fully clothed, swung his foot over the side of the tub and began to clamber straight in.

She let out a scream, "What are you doing?"

"I'm just following orders," he laughed, sitting down in the warm, soapy water, his trousers fully submerged and his shirt soaking up the water like a sponge. "You told me to get in."

"You prick," she said, laughing. "What are you going to wear home?"

"I just need to stay the night while they dry."

"Sure of yourself, aren't you?"

"Yep, pretty sure I'm not going anywhere tonight." LeeRoy stepped out of the bath again, his clothes still dripping. A bit ridiculous, he thought, but he was trying to show off in front of his girl.

My girl, he thought. It felt right somehow, comforting—my girl, all to himself. Nobody else's. He stripped off, wringing out his clothes over the sink and hanging them on the radiator. Then he climbed back into the tub where Julie waited for him and leaned against the cold tap.

"Why do the men always get the tap end?" He twisted away from it, only to end up on the hot one.

"Oh, quit complaining. You can always leave and go home," Julie said, hoping he wouldn't.

"No way," LeeRoy said. "Can't leave you to finish a whole bottle of wine by yourself, can I?"

They were both laughing now, and LeeRoy flicked some water at Julie, who retaliated by throwing a bar of soap at him.

"Ah, fight time is it?" he said, grabbing both her feet and lifting them so quickly that Julie's head went underwater. She spluttered back to the surface but refused to give up. She grabbed his nuts, and he yelped like a stuck pig, immediately releasing her. "You play dirty!"

LeeRoy chuckled as he leaned over the tub, grabbed the wine bottle, and poured each of them a glass of cold Chablis. His face relaxed into a smile as he met her steady gaze, and he handed her a glass, saying, "To us!" as they clinked their glasses together. They sat in silence for a few minutes, sipping and exchanging glances. Then Julie asked, "Can I ask you something?" "Of course," LeeRoy replied, "but it sounds like it might be serious."

"We just toasted to us," she said, looking confused. "What does 'us' mean to you?"

LeeRoy gazed down into his white wine, taking a moment to think. He cleared his throat. "In you, Julie, I've found a kindred spirit. I look forward to seeing you. I love being with you... I think I'm in love with you," he added, a hint of shyness in his voice.

She was speechless. "Oh, LeeRoy, you mean that?" she cried out, feeling flattered and touched.

"Yes, Julie," he said, his voice growing stronger as he responded. "I do. I love you."

Julie was speechless. Tears welled up in her eyes as she smiled at LeeRoy. "LeeRoy, I love you too. When did you realise you loved me?"

"When you whacked Gary on the nose with that ashtray," he said, looking completely serious.

"Be serious, LeeRoy."

"OK, probably just now when you grabbed my bollocks."

"Piss off," she joked. "Get serious."

He grinned. "I love it when you get all riled up!" He gestured with the hand holding his wine glass. "Your little nose twitches and your eyes start blinking like crazy."

Oh, I give up.

"Oooh, that little nose is twitching again!" he teased.

She hurled the soap at him again, but it missed and knocked the bottle of Chablis off the edge of the tub. Luckily, LeeRoy had super-fast responses and caught it by the neck before too much spilled.

"Temper, temper! Come here and kiss me," LeeRoy said, locking eyes with her.

She melted, then began to kneel up and leaned in toward him, sending the bathwater swirling. He wrapped his arms around her and drew her close, taking the back of her head in his large hand and gently kissed her. At first, it was a gentle kiss, but then the blood began to rush. Julie opened her mouth and let LeeRoy's large, pink tongue explore deep into her mouth, searching for her own. Soon they were entangled, Julie's right knee between LeeRoy's legs, and she started to rub against him. He didn't protest at her interfering with his bollocks this time; he was loving it.

"Turn around, Julie, and I'll wash you."

"That sounds nice," she said and did so, now sitting with her back to LeeRoy. He retrieved the soap.

"Get scrubbing," she said.

"Scrubbing? How dirty are you?"

"As dirty as you want me to be."

"Later, later," he snickered. "Now it's your turn to shut up." He lathered the soap and washed around the back of her neck, then slowly down her back. She knew what was coming, but he was going to make her wait. His hands slid around the front, avoiding her breasts, gliding over her smooth, wet skin, one finger exploring her belly button. For some reason, that turned Julie on. His hands were inches from her now-throbbing vagina, but it was going to stay that way for a bit longer; he liked to tease.

He carried on washing her all over, avoiding any erogenous areas, although she was wriggling around in excitement, eager for him to touch her there; most of her was on fire.

"Turn around, baby."

She lay back, closed her eyes, and let him do whatever he wanted. Taking her foot in both of his large hands, it looked like a doll's. He massaged her toes with his thumbs, then in between her toes, and down to the sole of her foot. This was heaven, but all she could think about was him entering her. She couldn't wait; something had to happen. He carried on with her other foot and she was burning with desire. She had to do something. She put her right hand under the water, between her legs, and started to massage herself, her back arching. LeeRoy could see what she was doing, and it turned him on big-time.

His manhood was swollen harder. He slid his hand slowly up her right leg, over her calf, and onto the top of her thigh. His hands met hers, and she guided one of his large fingers into her.

She was now ready to cum and tried to hold back, but all in vain. LeeRoy now had three fingers in her. She squealed, hands grabbing the top sides of the bath as LeeRoy's fingers finished her off. She climaxed like an explosion, limbs thrashing, water splashing everywhere. Her legs crossed and twisted. LeeRoy thought she would break his arm, until she pushed LeeRoy's hand away. She couldn't take any more and sank back in the bath, exhausted.

"You seemed to enjoy that," LeeRoy said. "Just a bit," she panted. "Wow, that was intense—it almost hurt." She gazed at him in awe. "What do you do to me?"

"No idea, my love, but it seems to work."

"Pass me the wine, please." She took the glass but could barely hold it steady, the wine shaking. LeeRoy was staring at her.

"What?" she asked.

"That's all right for you. You've had yours. I'm sitting here with a huge hard-on watching you drink wine."

She laughed. "Who cares? I'm sorted."

"Give me that glass," he snatched it and placed it on the floor.

He stood up, and she gazed at the rigid manhood between his legs. He reached out to help her up, and she took his hands. He pulled her to her feet, turned her around, and bent her over, where she stood. She gripped the end of the tub tightly; she knew what was about to happen. He slipped his hands around her and gently parted the entrance to her body, pushing in gently, just enough for her to feel what was coming.

She gripped the edge of the bath tightly as he entered her. She had been so turned on that he slipped into her easily. Once all the way in, he held her breasts, taking the now-erect nipple in two fingers. She was getting very turned on, yet again.

"Fuck me, LeeRoy. Please, now!"

He obliged. He went at her hard, really hard, nearly knocking her out of the bath. LeeRoy could hold it and did. She couldn't, and climaxed again, screaming his name. He wasn't finished; he had a tight hold on her and fucked her hard.

Eventually, he let it go. She felt it burst out inside her, like a hosepipe on full blast. She collapsed in the bath, and he fell on top of her, the water level slapping almost over the top of the bath. He had to get off, or he would drown the poor girl. He rolled off her and clambered out of the bath, where he lay on the floor, exhausted, trying to breathe. She lay back in the bath, just as exhausted as he was.

Eventually, when she could breathe again, she panted, "Bloody hell, LeeRoy, you're a sodding animal! Not complaining, but bloody hell, man! I'm knackered."

"I'm ready for another go," he said with a grin. "Piss off, you're not getting near me again tonight!"

Thank fuck for that, he thought. *Don't think I could anyway.*

"Oh, you're an old party pooper," he said. The bath was cooling off, so she got out, and they dried off and crashed on the couch.

"You left the wine in the bathroom," he said. "That's your job. You're the man. Go get it. There's a good boy."

LeeRoy laughed and did as he was told. They soon finished the bottle, which still had some spilled on the bathroom floor.

"I'll head down to the bar and grab another one," he said. "I'll leave a note for Chas and pay him tomorrow." He was back in two minutes, opening the second bottle of Chablis.

Julie turned on the radio, keeping it low, and they snuggled up on the couch.

In the quiet, with LeeRoy's arm around her, Julie sat staring at the glowing bars of the electric fire, wondering if he meant what he said.

Did he want to please me? Tell me what he thought I wanted to hear? Make it easier to have sex with me?

"Do you love me, LeeRoy?" she asked softly.

He gazed down at her, taken aback. "Yes, darling. I wouldn't say that to anyone unless I meant it." He swallowed hard. "I've never said that to anyone else, not even my mother when I was a kid."

Julie's eyes widened, but she felt warm and comforted.

"Are your parents still alive?"

"My mother is, she lives in Barbados. She used to live here for twenty years, but she moved back three years ago. She couldn't handle the racism."

"That's awful," Julie said. "Do you ever have any issues with that?"

"Used to at school, but I was a big kid and a few good beatings took care of that."

"What about your dad?"

"Never knew him. He pissed off when I was two, and nobody has any idea where he is."

They sat in silence for a bit, sipping their wine, each lost in their thoughts. Until Julie said, "LeeRoy, I need to ask you another question."

"Sounds serious again. Go ahead."

"Well, tonight with those two bastards in the bar," she started. "It's been on my mind and it's bothering me."

"What is?"

"You know what – offering to buy them a drink. I was," she stopped, exasperated." Look, LeeRoy, don't try to pull the wool over my eyes, you know everything that's going on around here. What happened to them – that kind of thing wouldn't happen without you knowing who was involved. Can you look me in the eye and tell me it wasn't you?" Her eyes flickered from one of his dark eyes to the other, searching for a sign, seeing only herself reflected in the darkness. "You said you were in London that night, but I'm not convinced. Please don't lie to me, LeeRoy. Was it you? Did you do that to them? I'm scared, LeeRoy. If you're capable of that kind of violence, it scares me."

"Listen," he said, turning around to see her face, and gently brushing a strand of her hair behind her ear with his gentle fingers. She flicked his hand away, waiting for the answer. "Yes, I'm into all sorts of things and I can handle myself, but I've never – and never will – hit a woman. Especially not you. I love you."

"I believe that LeeRoy, but if we're going to have a relationship, I need to be able to trust you. You can never lie to me." He let out a heavy sigh. "Okay, Julie, you can trust me with your life. You might not like what I'm about to tell you, but I need you to look me in the eye and promise on your life—and on the lives of any kids you might have, too." "Wow, LeeRoy, that's a pretty tall order," she responded, seeing he was serious. "I promise on my life that I'll never let you down or repeat anything you tell me. But I'm not going to swear on any kid's life." LeeRoy's face twisted as he considered his words. "Okay, but this is going to hurt." He hesitated. "Tell me, whatever it is, please." He looked at her face, waiting for a reaction. "Okay, it was them who set the coach on fire."

"No, no, no!" she screamed, her hand flying to her mouth. "How do you know?" "Believe me, Julie. They admitted it." "Oh my god," Julie was confused. "Are you sure it was them? Why would they do that?"

"Because they thought you were in there."

"Me?" She couldn't believe it. "Why would they want to harm me?"

"Remember the ashtray and busted nose?"

Julie frowned in disbelief. "You mean they tried to kill me – and my friends – because of a broken nose?"

"I'm afraid so, Julie."

"We have to tell the police!" She stood up, started pacing, and wrung her hands together.

"Julie, listen, we can't. I've handled it, and that's the end of it."

"How?" She stopped dead and glared at him. "It was you who did that to them, wasn't it?"

"Not exactly," said LeeRoy, "but yes, I was there."

"My God," she gasped. "I need time to process all this." She grasped a handful of her hair above her forehead, distraught.

"Can you please just go home and give me some space? I don't think I can be with someone capable of such violence."

"Home?" LeeRoy exclaimed. "But my clothes are still wet."

"Fucking hard luck!" Julie snapped, her mind elsewhere. "You should've thought about that when you were pissing around."

"Please go and leave me alone. I need some space, just gooooo!!" she screamed at him.

LeeRoy knew he wasn't going to win any arguments, so he put on his still-wet clothes and tried to kiss her on the cheek. But she wasn't having any of it. She was more upset and confused than angry, struggling to make sense of what was happening. Two bottles of wine didn't improve her mood either. She needed some space.

"Bye, Julie. See you tomorrow," LeeRoy said, hesitant to leave. "But instead of getting mad at me, remember, you're the one who made me tell you."

"You won't see me tomorrow. Just go, LeeRoy," she said, her voice filled with defeat. "You'll probably never see me again – at least, I don't think so. I don't fuckinggggg knowww please just goooo!!" She gazed off into space, her eyes glassy, as if talking to herself, as if he'd already left. "I just need to clear my head and think about all this. My God, it's all just a dream. I'll wake up soon, I hope."

LeeRoy took off in a hurry. Julie made herself a cup of coffee, sat down on the couch, and tried to process everything, but it was still all a jumble. *I can't believe those scumbags, as clueless as they are, would burn five people to death! Six if I'd been there! I refuse to believe it.* She took a sip of coffee, still lost in thought, her mind racing. *But if it's not true, why would LeeRoy say it was? And for fuck's sake! Look what he did to them!*

Why can't we go to the police?

Of course, if they are charged, they'll drop LeeRoy right in the shit. Fuck. Fuck. Fuck! Fucking hell. This is madness.

I could kill those bastards myself.

She couldn't believe LeeRoy was capable of such things, but the more she thought about it, the more she wished she'd been there. *They would've lost more than just their bloody ears.*

Her mind was a jumbled mess, but she went to bed and, with the help of the wine, fell asleep.

In the morning, she woke up in bed and had to think hard.

Did I dream all that? No, I bloody well didn't.

God, what a mess! She got up, took a shower, made coffee and went over everything from the previous night with a clearer head. But it didn't help. She was still completely lost. *How can I possibly be with someone who can hurt others and not give a damn?*

She had to run some errands, so after eleven, she strolled down Preston Street to Woolworth's, grabbed her necessities, and made her way to the café where she'd first met LeeRoy.

At the corner of Court Street, she saw the two men loitering under the Guild Hall, just like they did most of the day. She froze, her eyes locked on them, burning with fury. She took a step off the curb, ready to cross the street to confront them, but she had no idea what she would do or say. She was overwhelmed with rage, her stomach twisting with emotion, and fear was the last thing on her mind; she knew she had to do something.

She was suddenly brought to a stop: a firm hand held her back. She spun around, furious, coming face to face with LeeRoy. After going to the pub and being told she had gone to Woolworth's, he had walked down the street to find her.

"What are you doing?" she cried, struggling to break free of his grip.

"Stopping you from putting me in prison," he warned.

"You in prison?" Her voice rose. "It's those fuckers that need to be locked up."

"Yeah, Julie, I agree, but if they go away, so do I."

Those scumbags saw them and realised this wasn't a safe spot. As the cowards they were, they quickly took off. Who could blame them, considering what had happened just a few weeks earlier?

LeeRoy spoke in a low, urgent tone. "What were you thinking, Julie?"

"I don't know. I just lost it and wanted to kill them with my bare hands." She looked up the road, where the two were now just tiny figures in the distance, vanishing around a corner.

"What are you doing here anyway?" she asked.

"I came by to see if you were okay, and Chas told me where you had gone, so I came to find you. Bloody good job I did; otherwise I dread to think what might have happened."

"They'd be dead," she yelled at LeeRoy. "I would've killed them with my bare hands. Anyway, I thought I told you I didn't want to see you today."

"Yeah, I recall that clearly and spent the whole night tossing and turning, wondering if you were serious."

"I was, I am serious. I don't know, I'm bloody livid and confused," and she started crying.

"Look, Len's café is just down there, let's grab a coffee, give you time to calm down a bit, then we can try to talk this through, okay?"

"Yeah, okay," she replied, trying to hold back the tears." I was on my way there when I spotted those two bastards."

After ordering two large coffees, they sat in silence for what seemed like an eternity but was only a minute. Then LeeRoy said, "Listen, I'm sorry I didn't want you to know what happened."

"Well, now I do. And it serves them fucking right. It's a shame you didn't kill the bastards."

"It was tempting," LeeRoy said, "but that would have sparked a full-blown investigation. As it is, lucky for me, Fred hates the bastards himself."

"Who's Fred?" she butted in.

"The inspector hates them, too, so he's not going to put a lot of effort into finding out who beat them up. Honestly, he probably has a good idea who did it."

"If he did, he would have arrested you by now."

"He needs proof, darling.

"Don't call me darling," she rebuked him.

"Sorry, anyway,' he continued, 'as I said, I don't think he gives a shit."

They sat sipping their coffees, their minds elsewhere. LeeRoy looked at Julie, his face serious. "But do you remember what I told you last night?"

"Of course, I fucking remember," she choked. "How could I ever forget that?"

"No, not about the scumbags."

"Then what is it about?" she exclaimed, exasperated. "I'm sorry, LeeRoy, but I'm still trying to process what you said about those cunts — 'Sorry for using that word, I hate it, but that's what they are — murdering my friends, what you did to them, and then seeing them on the market just now, acting like they owned the place!" Her sharp breath revealed her frustration.

"Okay, darling, I'll leave what I was going to say. But I don't like you using that C-word either."

"Tough!" she seethed. "And no, you bloody well won't leave it. Whatever you have to say can't be any worse than last night."

"What is it?"

"I want to ask you something," he said, playing with the sugar pourer. "It's hard now. I had it all planned, but now I don't know how to ask."

"Just spit it out," she said.

He turned his eyes to her. "Okay, even though it hasn't been that long, will you come live with me?" He raised his hands in the air for a moment.

She tilted her head to one side and gazed up at him with a blank expression. "You want me to live with you? Honestly, I'm not even sure I want to see you again."

"Really," he said, "I thought you said that in the heat of the moment."

"I did, but I meant it at the time."

"At the time," he said swiftly, cutting off her explanation, "but what about now?"

"Now I need to take a step back and try to make sense of all this. Can we go for a walk by the creek, please?"

"Yeah, it's a nice day, and I think the tide's up, so it shouldn't be too smelly."

LeeRoy picked up her bags and carried them for her, and she shot him a sly glance, saying, "So are we creeping now?" "Just being a gentleman," he replied, happy to see her start to relax. The thought of her never wanting to see him again made him uneasy, though maybe he shouldn't have asked her to move in with him just yet.

They walked across the bridge and strolled along the creek wall, passing by the Front Brents and the Albion pub. "That's a nice little pub," LeeRoy said. "If you ever love me again, I'll take you there for a meal someday."

"If I ever do that," she said, her voice laced with sarcasm. LeeRoy knew she was starting to calm down, and he hoped things would get back to normal soon – or at least, as normal as they'd been before the past couple of days.

They stopped and sat on the grassy bank, able to see for miles across the marshes toward Graveney and Whitstable in the distance.

They talked about nothing and LeeRoy gathered his courage to reach out and hold Julie's hand, expecting her to pull away. She didn't, and his heart pounded in his chest. He turned and looked at her; she felt his gaze and turned back to him. They didn't say a word, but both knew they would be together forever. They locked eyes for a few seconds, then wrapped each other in a tight hug, afraid to let go in case the other vanished.

Julie spoke up first, saying, "I'm sorry, LeeRoy, for how I reacted last night." He started to speak, but she raised her hand to stop him. "Please just listen to me. I was hurt, confused, and angry—not just with them, but with you too, for how you responded. I'm still not happy about what you did, but after seeing them outside the Guild Hall and how I felt, I'm not sure what I would have done if you hadn't stopped me. I guess I can understand your anger now."

"So, am I off the hook now?" he asked, with a hint of sarcasm.

"I guess so," she replied.

They had been out for a couple of hours and were almost back at the café, "I could murder another cuppa, how about you?" asked LeeRoy.

"Yes, that would be nice, thank you."

They took their seats in the same two spots as before, when LeeRoy had asked if she'd thought about what he'd asked earlier.

"And what would that be?" she asked, fully aware of what it was.

"Oh, come on, you can't say you have forgotten"

"Forgotten what?" she sarcastically replied.

LeeRoy was starting to feel a little embarrassed, unsure if she was messing with him or just joking around, but he asked again.

"I asked if you'd like to move in with me?" "No rush, take your time and let me know how you're feeling when you're ready."

She paused, letting his heart beat twice before speaking again. "Let me get this straight — you want me to leave that cozy little room in a lovely little pub in the heart of Faversham, along with all my new friends, and move to a house out in the middle of nowhere with nothing but a bicycle to get around, cold, windy winters alone with just you?"

He wasn't sure if she was serious or messing with him, so he just replied, "Yes."

"I've thought about it!" She burst out laughing. "Wow, how could I say no?" He grinned. "But what about your sister? Won't she mind?"

"No, she's only here for two more weeks. After that, she's going back to Barbados. She mostly lives there with our mother."

"Looks like you've got a roommate then!" she laughed.

"Awesome!" LeeRoy said, delighted. He reached across the table for her hand. "I do love you, Julie."

"And I love you too, LeeRoy," she smiled, but then added, "I think I'd like to stick around at the pub until your sister's gone back, though."

"Why?" He looked puzzled. "She won't be a problem."

I know, I know. It's not that. When I move in, I want it to just be you and me.

He shrugged. "Yeah, I can understand that. But I don't think I can wait three weeks. I'll go home and kick her out today!" he said with a smile.

"No, you won't. You wouldn't dare. Anyway, if you did, she'd kill you."

"Think you might be right," he said. "Come on, I'll walk back to the pub with you."

They left the café holding hands. Julie was beaming with excitement, the trauma of yesterday already fading. And although he wouldn't show it too obviously in public, LeeRoy was just as thrilled. As they walked past the Guild Hall, they couldn't help but glance across the street, checking if the scumbags had returned, but they weren't there.

When they got back to the pub, they walked in through the bar where Chas was counting out some change. He looked up, sensing their mood, and said, "Whoa, you two are beaming!"

Julie's eyes sparkled. She turned to LeeRoy, "Can I share the news, please?"

"Of course, you can—I want everyone to know."

"Know what?" asked Chas with a puzzled look.

"LeeRoy asked me to move in with him," she said, beaming.

"Awesome," Chas said. "When's this all going to happen?"

"Three weeks from now."

"Does that mean you're quitting your job?" Chas asked.

"No way," Julie said. "I couldn't do that to you after all you've done for me." Then she gasped. "But how will I get to work from out there? I hadn't thought about that."

"Don't worry," LeeRoy said. "I'll always be around to drop you off – it'll be a good excuse to come back a bit later to pick you up. If not, you can always grab a taxi."

"I'm so excited!" Julie squealed.

Although it had been a whirlwind of a relationship, she loved LeeRoy dearly, and she would also love living in a house like that! What a dream—a true one for someone from an orphanage. *I still can't believe it.*

CHAPTER SIXTEEN — *Keys, Kindness, and Tinky Winky*

For Julie, those three weeks felt like forever, but eventually LeeRoy and Julie drove Rosina to Heathrow and said their goodbyes. Julie was practically bouncing with excitement as they pulled into the airport car park.

"Call us when you get home," Julie called after Rosina.

On the drive home, LeeRoy grinned,

"Alright, girl, now we've got the place to ourselves. You've checked with Chas about taking the rest of the week off?"

"No backing out now," he teased.

"Yes, yes. He was okay with it. I think he loves me too, like a daughter of course," she added.

"He's a softie really," Julie said, smirking.

"Don't kid yourself!" LeeRoy burst out laughing. "Give him half a chance, and he'd be in your knickers in a heartbeat."

"Behave!" Julie shot back. "You're terrible."

"That's ridiculous, LeeRoy. Of course, he wouldn't. He's married, for starters."

LeeRoy couldn't help but smile at her naivety. "That's never stopped him before. In fact, I'm pretty sure he's sleeping with Brenda."

"Brenda?" Julie was caught off guard. "Brenda from the bar?"

"Yeah," LeeRoy said. "Not entirely sure, but the clues are there."

Julie frowned. "Well, I've never noticed them."

"That's no surprise, you've only been there for five minutes, but now that I've mentioned it, you'll be on the lookout," he said. "I'm sure of that."

They returned to the pub to gather Julie's belongings – not that she had many, which easily fitted into the trunk of LeeRoy's car. Chas walked in and asked if they needed any help. Julie looked at him suspiciously, trying to re-evaluate him after LeeRoy's revelation. "What's wrong?" Chas asked, surprised by her expression. "Nothing," Julie said. "Just looking." She'd be watching Brenda more closely the next time she saw her.

They took off and drove to Julie's new home. The electric gates swung open, and they pulled up next to a sleek new red Mini Cooper with a black roof. "I thought nobody else lived here," Julie said, looking confused.

"They don't."

"Whose car's that then?"

"Yours," said LeeRoy, handing her a set of keys.

"Mine?" she squealed. "Mine? What do you mean by mine?"

"Exactly like it sounds, Julie," LeeRoy grinned, clearly amused by her reaction. "It's your moving-in gift."

She burst out of the Rolls-Royce, slamming the door.

Sod the Roller, she thought. I love that car!

She sprinted to the front of the Rolls and came to a sudden stop beside the Mini. LeeRoy was right behind her.

She hesitantly looked up at him. "Are you sure this isn't just a joke?"

"Julie, I wouldn't joke about something like this!" LeeRoy said, slightly surprised that she would think he was capable of such a thing.

"Can I get in it?"

"Julie, it's all yours. You can do with it whatever you want. Just don't drive on the road until you pass your test."

Julie struggled with the keys at first, but she worked it out pretty quickly. Opening a car door on her own was a new experience for her as she settled into the driver's seat—another first—and a huge smile spread across her face. She looked like she was going to burst if it got any bigger.

"I can't believe you did this LeeRoy! I love it!" Her voice was a high-pitched squeal of happiness. "Thanks a million times, thanks!"

LeeRoy jumped into the passenger seat and showed her how to insert the key into the ignition and start the engine which roared to life with a sound reminiscent of a lion roaring.

He let her play with the throttle, headlights, and any other buttons or switches within her reach, all while revving the engine.

"That's enough," he said as he got out of the passenger seat laughing.

"Move over," he said, "and I'll take you for a spin in it."

She didn't need a second invitation and quickly slipped into the passenger seat. With its sporty exhaust, the engine roared to life as he pressed the pedal.

"Just a minute," he said. "I need the key fob for the gates. It's in the Roller."

He jumped out of the new car, leaving the door open, grabbed the key fob, and pointed it, opening the gates.

As he jumped back in the Mini, with the door being much lighter than the Roller, he slammed it a bit harder than he meant to.

"Be careful with Tinky Winky!" Julie laughed.

"Fucking Tinky Winky!" he shook his head, sniggering.

"You've named it already?"

"Yep. Tinky Winky, it is."

LeeRoy reversed it around, drove forward out of the gates, turned left, and drove down onto the M2.

"OK. Let's see what this baby – 'Tinky Winky' – can do," he said, turning onto the motorway. They headed west towards London, the speedometer rising from 60 to 70, then 80, 90, 100, and finally to 108 mph.

"Slow down, LeeRoy!" Julie exclaimed, her face twisting in a grimace and her knuckles whitening with tension. "That's way too fast, and I'm getting scared."

"Don't worry," he assured her, "I've driven a lot faster than this; in fact, I've taken the Roller up to 130 miles an hour."

"I don't care, I'm scared, my parents were killed in a car crash, I don't like it."

LeeRoy immediately let his foot off the pedal, saying, "Sorry, yes, I forgot. I'll slow down — sorry again."

Julie glared at him and shook her head. "Thank you. Where are we going anyway?" "

Not really anywhere special; just up the motorway, then take the Stockbury exit, go around the roundabout, and head back.

"Stockbury? That name rings a bell," she said, curious, but she couldn't quite remember why. They took the exit, and when she saw the turn, it clicked into place. "Is there an old airport up that way?"

"Yes," he said, "Detling, why?"

"I think that's where I ended up after running away from the orphanage. Can we drive up and see if it is?"

"Sure," said LeeRoy with a smile. "It's not far."

Julie recognised the place. "Yes, that's it," she said excitedly. "Let's stop and grab a cup of coffee at the mobile café over there. The owner was really lovely to me that morning; he gave me a free breakfast and tea."

"Really?" LeeRoy said. "So, I'm not the only nice guy around here then?"

"No, you're not," Julie replied. "There's another guy – and an older homeless guy – who was also really nice."

"A homeless guy?"

"Yes," she said, then told LeeRoy the story.

"There," she shouted. "What?" LeeRoy asked, a bit spooked by her sudden loud outburst.

"The thingy where I slept, a pillbox I think."

"Yeah, that's certainly an old pillbox, and you're saying you slept in it?"

"Yes, I just told you all about it."

"Yes, I know, but I had no idea it was something like that. It must be full of rats and shit."

They pulled up and walked over to the old pillbox, its stark concrete structure uninviting.

"This is it, where I slept that night," Julie said, stepping inside and half expecting the old tramp to be inside. But the place was empty, except for the old mattress and some trash – a few crumpled paper bags and empty bottles.

"Lovely hotel," LeeRoy said, peeking over her shoulder. "I can't believe you slept in here – were you not scared?"

"Five-star," she replied, gazing around and considering how far she'd come.

"I guess I was a little nervous, especially when I woke up in the morning and saw a man sitting at the entrance, but as you know, everything worked out okay."

They walked across to the café and sat down at one of the tables. LeeRoy got up and ordered two cups of tea, which came in giant mugs.

Fred, the café owner, glanced at Julie and thought he recognised her, but since hundreds of people passed through, he dismissed it. Julie noticed this, so after taking a sip of her tea, she walked over and said, "Hi, Fred."

He still couldn't quite put his finger on where he'd seen her before. "Your face looks familiar," Fred said, "but I just can't remember where from."

"Right here," Julie replied. "If you recall, I slept in that old concrete thing over there. The pillbox?"

"Yes," Fred said, "and yes, now I remember. Old Giles found you when you squatted in his house."

She let out a laugh. "Yeah, it probably gave him a bit of a shock. How's he doing?"

"He's alright," Fred said. "He's been working at the airfield but just got laid off. You've just missed him. I think he's heading into Sittingbourne to look for work."

"Oh," Julie said, sounding disappointed. "That's too bad."

"What's too bad?" LeeRoy said, having just come up behind her.

"You made me jump!" Julie laughed. "It's too bad we just missed Giles."

"Who's Giles?"

"He's the guy who found me in his bed."

"His bed!" LeeRoy exclaimed. "What are you talking about?"

With a grin, Julie explained. "He slept outside all night. Like I said, I ended up sleeping in that old concrete pillbox over there – didn't know it was already taken." She chuckled at her little joke.

Julie introduced LeeRoy to Fred.

"Nice meeting you, Fred, and thanks for what you did for Julie," said LeeRoy, shaking his hand.

"Not a problem."

LeeRoy nodded. "Come on, Julie, we need to make a move."

"You be sure to look after that little lady," Fred told LeeRoy.

"And feel free to stop by anytime you're in the area."

"We will," Julie said, giving Fred a friendly smile and adding, "Thanks again, Fred."

They climbed back into Tinky Winky and headed down the A249 toward the M2. As they passed a person walking along the side of the road, Julie spun around and yelled at LeeRoy: "Stop!"

LeeRoy jammed on the brakes in panic. "What the fuck's up with you?"

"That guy we just passed! I'm positive it was Giles." "So what?" LeeRoy said, looking confused.

"So, reverse up! I want to say hello to him."

"He's an old tramp, Julie."

"Maybe so, but he's a nice old tramp."

"OK, you win." He reversed back to the old tramp, the engine whining.

Giles was a bit on edge since a car had come to a screeching halt a couple of hundred yards ahead of him and was now backing up.

As Tinky Winky came alongside him, Julie rolled down the window. "It is you, Giles, isn't it?"

"Yeah, it's me—Giles," he said gruffly, keeping a wary distance. "Julie!" She stuck her face out the window, grinning. Giles did a double-take, then burst out laughing. "Ha! Julie the squatter!" "That's right. How's it going, Giles?"

"As good as can be expected," he said, moving closer, and set his duffel bag down as he spoke. "Just lost a decent job at the airport, but that's the way it goes."

"Sorry, Giles, this is LeeRoy," she said, leaning back in the car as LeeRoy leaned forward and raised his hand in greeting, but not wanting to shake the old tramp's hand.

"Hello, Giles, and thanks for taking care of Julie."

"Was a pleasure, man! And it's great to see her again. I often wondered what happened to her."

"Can we drop you off somewhere?" asked LeeRoy. "You're a long way from anywhere here."

"I'm not sure where I'm headed, really," Giles said.

"The guy in the café said you were heading into Sittingbourne."

"Yeah, wherever. That'd be great, if you don't mind."

"Not a problem! Jump out and let the guy in, Julie."

Since Tinky Winky only had two doors, Julie happily got out, gave Giles a quick hug, and ignored the stale sweat and dirty clothes smell coming from him. She lifted the seat forward, and Giles tossed his bag in and climbed into the back, which was a tight squeeze for such a big guy.

They took off down the road, past the Three Squirrels Pub, LeeRoy enjoying the new Mini, and before long, they were on the M2. LeeRoy suddenly remembered he was supposed to be heading the opposite direction while Giles was still in the car.

"Fuck it!" LeeRoy said, shaking his head. "I'll have to drive all the way to Faversham before I can turn around."

"Don't worry," Giles said. "Faversham is just as good a place as any. I'm sure I can find somewhere to stay without too much trouble."

"Alright mate, sorry, I missed that turn."

"No problem," Giles said. "I just go where the work is if I can find any."

"So, tell me, Giles," LeeRoy said, glancing at him through the rearview mirror. "What did you do for a living?"

"You wouldn't believe it, but I used to be a farmhand, and I'm pretty handy at most things. The job I just lost was in a loading bay, but business slowed down and they let me go."

"That's too bad," Julie said. "Yeah, it was. I had a room in the warehouse where I lived rent-free."

Julie and Giles had a conversation all the way to Faversham, where they took the turnoff for Ashford Road. Since LeeRoy's house was to the right, he decided to drop Giles off in town or as close as he wanted, so he turned left.

Julie realised why LeeRoy had made the left turn, but she didn't say anything, figuring that was just LeeRoy being kind.

"Where would you like me to drop you off? Sorry, I forgot your name."

"Giles," Julie quickly reminded LeeRoy.

"Sorry, Giles, I have trouble remembering names. Would the town centre work for you?"

"Yes, LeeRoy, anywhere works for me. Thank you, it would have been a long walk if you hadn't stopped."

"Thank Julie, she made me stop."

Thanks, Julie, that means a lot to me." "No problem, Giles," Julie said, happy to help.

They stopped outside the café where they first met and let Giles out.

"They make a good cup of coffee in there," LeeRoy told Giles.

"Thanks, LeeRoy, but I need to find a job first. They didn't pay me when I was let go, so I need to be careful. That's my problem, and I appreciate both of you — Julie for making you stop, and you, LeeRoy, for stopping and giving me a ride. "Not a problem, Giles, and good luck in finding a job."

They drove off and only got a hundred yards, and LeeRoy stopped the car. "What's up?" Julie asked.

"That guy was good to you Julie, and I feel sorry for him. We just dumped him in the middle of Faversham with no job, no money, and no idea where he is. The least I can do is give him a few shillings to get something to eat and drink." He reached into his pocket and pulled out a ten-pound note. He gave it to Julie and said, "Run back and give him this."

Julie exclaimed, "That's really kind of you. I'm sure he'll appreciate it."

She dashed out and caught up with Giles, who was heading to the town centre.

"Giles," she called out, "Hang on a minute."

Her calling out startled him; he thought he'd seen the last of them.

"You made me jump," Giles told her.

"Sorry, Giles, LeeRoy asked me to run back and give you this," she said, handing him the tenner.

"What's that for?" he asked, not taking it.

"No reason, LeeRoy thought you could use it."

"That I could, but I can't accept that without a reason. I earn my money and don't take from strangers."

"Hey, Giles, I'm no stranger. Consider this rent for the night in the pillbox," she said, chuckling at her speedy response.

"Sorry, Julie, I can't accept charity."

"Yes, you can," she said, dropping the tenner into his open coat pocket and running back to the car, leaving Giles a bit puzzled but extremely grateful for such a kind gesture.

She got back in the car and told LeeRoy what had happened. "Ah, well, at least he has it."

As they drove away, LeeRoy saw Giles going into the café through the rear-view mirror. "Well, that worked," he said. "What worked?" she asked.

"Just saw Giles go into the café."

"Brilliant," Julie said, feeling relieved that he could at least get a hot drink and something to eat.

LeeRoy took them back to their home and parked next to the towering Rolls-Royce, which overshadowed the small Mini "Tinky Winky."

After turning off the engine, he circled around and opened the door for Julie. He assisted her out, saying, "Welcome to your new home," then picked her up and carried her to the front door. He intended to carry her inside, but couldn't find the keys and had to put her down. While fumbling for his keys, he noticed the garden needed attention. He paused, lost in thought. "What's up?" Julie asked. "I was looking over the lawns and gardens. Usually, I have a contractor come once a week with three workers to keep things in order," he replied.

"Why are you thinking about that right now when I'm about to step into my new home for the first time?"

He was still off somewhere else. "Are you OK, LeeRoy?" Julie asked, a little concerned.

"Sorry, yes, yes, I was just thinking." "Thinking about what?" she asked. "About Giles." "Giles, what's he got to do with your garden?" Then she thought she got it. "Do you think he would be interested in looking after the garden?" he asked questioningly while looking at Julie.

"I have no idea, but I'd guess he'd be happy with anything, don't you think?" She replied. "I have no idea; I know nothing about the man except that he said he could put his hand to most things." He seems like a nice guy, and if I'm right probably honest too, but you never know."

"Anyway, I'm getting cold standing out here. Would you like to show me my new home?"

"Yes, sorry," he said as he found the keys and opened the front door, joking, "Welcome to your new home. What's for dinner?" She slapped him playfully.

"Wow, LeeRoy, it seems even more amazing now that I will be living here. I love you; I can't believe it."

LeeRoy went back outside to retrieve her things from the car and looked again at the garden; *I wonder,* he thought to himself.

She made her way to the kitchen, and the first thing that caught her eye was a massive bouquet and a bottle of champagne. LeeRoy thinks of everything, she thought to herself. What a sweetheart!

He joined Julie, who was now making coffee.

"Looks like you're taking over already," he joked. "Someone needs to get you organised," she joked back. "Come here," he said, opening his arms to her. They hugged and told each other they loved one another, Julie thanking him for the flowers and champagne. "I'll look forward to drinking that tonight," she said.

Julie poured the coffee while they continued to chat. Suddenly, LeeRoy changed the subject, looked at Julie, and said, "Why don't we finish our coffee and head back to Faversham to see if we can track down Giles and ask if he's interested in a job?"

"Really, now?" she asked. "Yes, why not? He could be anywhere tomorrow." "You're so impulsive, but okay, if you're sure, let's go," she responded.

They headed back to Faversham, and luckily, they ran into Giles as he was leaving the café. He'd already had a meal and a couple of cups of tea, making the most of the warmth of the café.

They pulled up alongside him, but this time they were in the Rolls-Royce and Giles just kept walking as they stopped next to him.

Julie wound down the window as LeeRoy crept forward, "Hey, Giles, it's Julie." Giles looked at her through the window, across to LeeRoy, then the Rolls. "Wow," he responded, "nice car, I thought you had gone home, I didn't realise you were still in town, then I guess you must have to swap cars."

As LeeRoy opened the driver's door, he got out and said to Giles, "Come and have a seat in the back for a minute. I'd like to have a chat with you."

"OK, sure," said Giles, feeling slightly apprehensive.

"How was the café? Did you grab a bite?" "Yeah, I did, and I had two cups of tea too. It's a nice, friendly place."

"Alright, Giles, I'll cut to the chase. We were discussing something at home and came up with an idea that might catch your attention."

"I'm all ears," replied Giles.

"I could use a handyman around my place if you're interested?" "Really?" Giles exclaimed. "Wow! That would be great, LeeRoy, but I wouldn't want to impose on you." "You won't. I have a little cabin at the bottom of the garden, and you can live in there if you like." Julie turned around, delighted by LeeRoy's kindness. He winked at her. He hadn't mentioned that at home.

"Well," Giles said, amazed. "That sounds too good to be true! Why would you do that for an old tramp?" "Because I've been down on my luck myself before, and I know how hard it is to get back on your feet."

Julie smiled warmly, admiring and loving LeeRoy more each day. She squeezed his knee appreciatively as he continued talking. "Besides," LeeRoy went on, "you can't be that bad, considering how you treated Julie."

"Thanks, LeeRoy."

"Alright then, Giles, I'll take you at your word. But don't ever betray that trust."

"I won't, LeeRoy. I've never been the type to cheat or stab people in the back." Giles's mind drifted for a moment, his thoughts reliving memories. "That's why I'm where I am today – I should have been more careful. But what can you do? – You live and learn."

"That you sure do, Giles, so, okay, it looks like you have a job. Let's go and show you where you'll be working and your new home." "Can't wait," replied Giles.

LeeRoy started the engine, and they kept going up Court Street. LeeRoy cracked his window slightly, trying to ignore the smell.

They pulled up at LeeRoy's house, and Giles was thoroughly impressed. He gaped up at the massive building, amazed. He hadn't expected anything like this place. "Wow LeeRoy! What do you do for a living?" "This and that." Replied LeeRoy non-committedly. Giles let it drop, knowing better than to push him for more information. They parked next to Tinky Winky and all got out.

"Awesome, this!" said LeeRoy. "Started the day yesterday, living here alone, and the next day we're already full!" He laughed, tossing the house keys to Julie. "I'll just show Giles his hotel, and I'll be back soon. This way, Giles."

LeeRoy's so-called garden appeared to stretch endlessly, and Giles could only follow him in a daze. They walked along a winding path near what seemed to be a small lake, leading to a log-style cabin. Giles had expected a garden shed, but it was actually as large as a house. LeeRoy opened the door and flipped the switch.

"Holy cow!" said Giles, looking around at the neat, fully furnished space that even included a small kitchen-diner at one end. "You weren't kidding when you said 'hotel. Is this really where I'll be staying?"

"Yes, it is," LeeRoy said, guiding him through the bedroom and pointing out the small bathroom. "Don't worry, you'll earn the rent. By the way, can you drive?"

"Yeah, I can do that. I still have my licence somewhere. Why's that?"

"Simple, you'll need to run some errands for me – and even drive me around if necessary."

"That's alright, LeeRoy," Giles said. But then he felt a pang of self-consciousness. "I don't think you'll be too thrilled with me looking like this." He looked down at his grubby trousers, the hems frayed to threads, and his grimy gym shoes on his feet.

"Even that won't be a problem," LeeRoy said. "We'll get you all taken care of. Now, feel free to make yourself at home, and we'll sort out your jobs tomorrow. You can take a couple of days to settle in first."

"LeeRoy," Giles' forehead creased in disbelief at his luck. "I can't thank you enough."

"Thank Julie," LeeRoy said. "She made me stop."

"I will, I will. You're a very lucky guy, LeeRoy. Not only is she beautiful, but she's also a kind-hearted person."

"Yeah, I know," LeeRoy said, chuckling as he walked away. "Just don't piss her off (remembering the ashtray), and you'll be fine."

Giles dropped his bag, which held all his possessions. The cabin had three rooms: a combined kitchen and dining area, a living room, and a bedroom with an en-suite bathroom and shower. Though it lacked a bathtub, he wasn't bothered. It felt like living in a dream. The kitchen had a few cans of food in the cupboard but the fridge was empty. He turned it on, and the interior light revealed it was unstocked. Having a refrigerator for the first time in years thrilled him. The cabin also included a gas stove, which he lit with ease, and admired his luck as the flame ignited immediately.

He figured it had to be bottled gas—unlikely there was a main gas line out here. Back in the lounge, there was even a portable TV. Nobody owned a portable TV! That was futuristic! He chuckled, shaking his head in disbelief. He was about to sit down, but then hesitated, standing over the seat.

I can't sit on this nice furniture in these dirty old clothes.

He spun around, wondering what to do next.

There was a bathrobe hanging on the back of the bedroom door. He thought he might take a shower and put on his clothes. *Maybe I could wash my clothes in the sink.*

Giles was just about to change out of his dirty old clothes when there was a knock on the door.

"Just me!" called LeeRoy, opening the door.

Julie was with him and thrust a shopping bag forward: "Thought you could use some milk, bread, and a few other things."

"Thanks!" Giles was still shaking his head. "I don't believe this is happening to me."

"Well, it is," LeeRoy said. "Make the most of it, do your job, and it'll be good for all of us." LeeRoy also handed him a small suitcase. "There are a few clothes in there, Giles. I think you'll agree that what you're wearing is ready for the bin."

Giles nodded and took the bag. "Thanks. Yeah, LeeRoy, they are." He looked up shyly and cleared his throat. "I'm not proud of the way I am, but I appreciate what you're doing for me, and I promise I'll never forget or let you down. Thanks."

"I don't think you will. Come on, Julie. I'm sure Giles would like to have a shower and try on his new clothes. In private!"

"Thanks again, LeeRoy."

"Don't keep thanking me, Giles. I'll get embarrassed," he laughed. "See you in the morning."

"Thaaa," Giles stopped himself.

"I had your first night here all planned out," LeeRoy told Julie at the house. "It was supposed to be super romantic. I was going to carry you over the threshold like a bride and cook you a nice dinner with candles and all the works. But I guess it's too late for that now. I'll make it up to you tomorrow. How about I drive into town and get us a bag of fish and chips?"

"LeeRoy, just being with you is all the romance I need," Julie said with a smile, squeezing his hand. "I'll come with you. We'll grab some fish and chips and go to the creek to eat. To me, that's just as romantic. It doesn't have to be fancy food every time, you know."

LeeRoy was surprised to meet such a genuine girl. Most women were after his money, but he could see right through them. Julie was a breath of fresh air. She knew what she wanted. And those beautiful shoulders of hers were a bonus!

"As always, Julie, you're right. That sounds like a plan to me. Let's go for it, baby."

They went to the fish and chip shop in Ospringe, ordered two bags of cod and chips, and made their way to the creek. LeeRoy had brought the bottle of champagne and two glasses, so they sat on the creek's banks and enjoyed a lovely evening, even though it was quite different from what he'd planned.

After putting the groceries in the fridge, Giles opened the suitcase to find it packed with brand-new clothes. He thought to himself, *that guy has everything.* He stripped off his worn-out, grimy clothes and threw them straight into the trash. In the bathroom, he tested the shower and was excited to find it delivered almost instant hot water. He couldn't wait to enjoy this. *Fuck, this is going to feel amazing* – and it did. It had been ages since his last shower. Giles wasn't a dirty person, just really down on his luck. The room he'd been staying in at the warehouse had a sink, but that was it.

He lathered himself up multiple times; it felt so good that he started singing. He grabbed the shampoo, thinking, *"Shampoo, I haven't had any of this in years. I've only had soap for ages."* He washed his hair three times, deciding to get out before his skin got waterlogged. Another luxury: clean towels. He dried himself off, found some shaving gear, and shaved off all of his old, matted beard. He had a clean shave – something he hadn't had in years. *"Boy, does this feel good!"* He rubbed the fresh skin around his chin, marvelling at himself in the mirror. He was clean-shaven and felt like himself again, as if he were forty-two, not a hundred years old.

He came across a can of baked beans and made some beans on toast, along with a warm cup of tea. It felt like he was staying at the Ritz. After dinner, he cleaned the dishes, dried them, and put everything back where it belonged, just like it was before he used them. He was determined to take good care of this place.

He poured himself another cup of tea and flipped on the TV, but before long, he was fast asleep in his chair.

CHAPTER SEVENTEEN — *Ghosts and Beginnings*

Giles woke up just after 2 a.m., unsure of his surroundings. He stumbled into the bedroom and crawled into a real bed for the first time in five years. It felt so cozy that he couldn't fall asleep, so he eventually got up and crashed on the armchair instead. He wasn't too worried, though – he knew he'd get used to a real bed again soon enough. One step at a time, though. It was all a bit overwhelming.

He woke up again at 6:10, his neck stiff from sleeping in an awkward position. Still, he had to double-check that it wasn't all just a dream. He made himself a cup of tea, finished it, and decided to take a stroll around the garden, which resembled more of a country park. The big pond was more like a small lake, he thought as he walked the perimeter.

He felt a sense of relief for the first time in ages.

At the end of the garden, he came to a small woodland that he strolled through. After turning right at the other side of it, he turned a corner and was greeted with stunning views of the countryside, the Swale Estuary, and the Isle of Sheppey, although he had no idea what he was looking at.

He drew in a deep, refreshing breath and enjoyed the view. Rabbits hopped across the grass, and the occasional pheasant soared low in the sky or strutted across the land as if it owned the place. As far as Giles could see, there was endless green, rolling countryside and farmland to where the Swale merged with the Thames Estuary. The vast stretches of farmland caught his attention.

It brought back memories of the good old days for Giles, who once had something similar in Sussex until things went downhill. He sat down on an old log, lost in thought, and started reflecting on his bad luck.

He had once owned a 125-acre farm on the South Downs and was married, but they didn't have any children. Giles and his wife, Samantha, managed the farm together with a couple of farmhands. Life was going smoothly: they were making a living and didn't owe anyone. Everything seemed perfect, and they were getting by without any significant issues.

Life was perfect, that is, until—Heaven forbid—that fateful day. If only he hadn't come back early from the cattle sale!

It seemed strange to Giles that his wife wasn't home when he arrived, but he assumed she was out working in the fields. Still, he wasn't too worried—he had work to do.

He went to fetch his trusty old Massey Ferguson to bring feed to the cattle in the upper field. The old barn was only a few hundred yards from the house, and as he strolled casually, he didn't suspect anything until he heard sounds. Perhaps an animal had gotten inside?

He slowly opened the barn door and saw his wife bent face-down over a large bale of hay, her skirt pulled up to her waist and her underwear around her ankles, while Tony, one of his so-called trusted farmhands, was mounting her like an animal.

Giles couldn't believe what he was looking at and froze for a second.

They were so intent, they didn't even hear him enter the barn, but they soon knew he was there when a two-pronged pitchfork was stabbed into Tony's back. Tony and Samantha both screamed in pain. Tony jumped off and rolled on the floor. Giles had pulled out the pitchfork, but Tony was still screaming like the Devil himself possessed him. As Samantha scrambled to her feet, Giles hit her in the face, stunning her for a moment, and she tumbled onto the hay bale, her underwear still around her ankles.

Giles stormed over to Tony, consumed by rage, and kicked him repeatedly until he was out cold. Samantha came to, disoriented, and as she took in the scene before her, she cried out to him, "What are you doing?"

"Doing?" he snarled, his fury unchecked. "That's nothing compared to what I'm going to do!"

Giles grabbed her by the neck and began to choke her; his mind clouded with anger.

But first, his mind drifted back to what had gotten him into this mess, and he replayed the whole thing again.

Tony, regaining consciousness, saw what was happening and, despite his injuries, kicked Giles in the back of the legs. As Giles's knees buckled, he stumbled backward, losing his grip and releasing Samantha. She limped towards the house as fast as she could.

As Giles stumbled back to his feet, he flew at Tony again, roaring and wrestling him to the ground.

Samantha got to the house and called the police, sobbing and struggling to recite her address. They assured her they would be there in ten minutes.

"That might be too late!" she screamed, consumed by fear. She hurried upstairs and hid, pushing a chest of drawers in front of the bedroom door. Dropping to the floor, she struggled to hold back her sobs. With shaking hands, she covered her mouth, paralysed with fear and the terror of what might happen if the police didn't arrive before Giles returned to the house.

Back in the barn, Giles crouched down, pulling Tony to his feet, and punched him in the face again.

"You fucking cunt!" he snarled through gritted teeth, repeatedly raining punches down on him. "I'm going to knock your teeth so far down your throat you'll have to put a toothbrush up your arse to clean them!" He continued to hit him relentlessly, eventually flinging him on the floor, unconscious, kicking him three more times for good measure.

Still overwhelmed with rage, Giles rushed back to the house to his gun cabinet, loaded his shotgun, and set back out to find Samantha. He was convinced she was still in the barn, hiding, and was making his way back there just as the police showed up.

To hell with the police, he thought. He didn't care. *How could she do this to me? If he were going to lose her, no one else would get her.* She was dead to him.

The police spotted him with a loaded shotgun and backed off. One of them called for the armed response unit.

 Giles stood frozen, his eyes locked on the police officers hiding behind their car and van. He stopped in the doorway of the barn, his gaze landing on Tony, still motionless and bloodied where Giles had left him. He wasn't sure if Tony was alive or dead. *What am I doing*? He thought to himself.

He spun around, a surge of desperation flooding him. *My beautiful wife*! He almost broke down in tears.

By the time the armed police arrived, their guns aimed at him, Giles had regained his calm and dropped the gun, raising his hands in surrender.

They approached him slowly, ordering him to lie on the ground and cuffed him.

Samantha appeared from her hiding place in the house, her screams piercing the air: "Tony, Tony."

An officer intercepted her and tried to calm her down, but she was hysterical, screaming, "Tony, Tony, he's in the barn! "Oh, God! Has he killed him?" By this time, an ambulance had arrived, and the police officer led her over to it, saying, "We'll check in the barn right now."

Blood was pouring from her mouth from her badly bruised and swollen lips as the paramedics met her.

Armed police approached the barn door with caution and found Tony unconscious on the floor. "There's a severely injured man here!" one officer shouted to the medics who rushed into the barn.

Within five minutes, another ambulance arrived. By this time, Tony had regained consciousness, but his badly swollen mouth prevented him from speaking. The officers and medic were working on stopping the bleeding from Tony's wounds as the second medic arrived in the barn.

They did what they could to stabilise him, then took him to the ambulance on a stretcher. With blue lights flashing, they sped to the hospital, fearing internal injuries from the pitchfork.

The medic treating Samantha patched her up as best he could before she was also taken to the hospital. Samantha sustained a broken tooth, a split lip, a swollen tongue, and a severe headache, but would survive.

When they reached the hospital, it was discovered that one of the pitchfork prongs had punctured Tony's liver, and the other had been stopped from causing serious harm by hitting one of his ribs. He required dental surgery and twenty stitches in his mouth and cheek.

It wasn't necessary to operate on the liver as the doctors were confident it would repair itself, as it was only a small puncture wound.

After Tony and Samantha were interviewed by the police, Giles was eventually charged with attempted murder, grievous bodily harm, and possession of a firearm with intent to endanger life. He had no choice but to plead guilty and was sentenced to 15 years in prison.

During the years he spent in prison, he had ample time to reflect on his actions and underwent a significant transformation.

Samantha tried to keep the farm running with Tony, but the relationship ended after less than a year. It was too much for Samantha to manage on her own, and she quickly fell into debt. The bank eventually took over the farm and sold it.

Giles had lost everything.
Giles was a model prisoner and was released on parole after serving seven years in prison. He had nothing but the clothes on his back when he left.

His wife had squandered everything. After her relationship with Tony failed, she had multiple affairs and was now living on Social Security in a council house.

When he first got out, Giles felt tempted to reach out to her, but he knew that if he did, he'd probably end up back in prison. He couldn't forgive her, not on many levels. With nothing and no place to stay, he hit the streets in Uckfield and lived rough, which wasn't easy for a man like Giles. He had wandered from town to town and ended up in the old pillbox in Detling for a long time before his stay in the nearby warehouse. And now he was here.

Back in the present, Giles shook his head at the memory, wiping away a tear. He was embarrassed by his reaction and had spent the time since then beating himself up for what he'd done. He figured he deserved to live rough – that's what he'd thought.

Maybe not any longer, though. Perhaps he'd finally paid the price. Maybe his luck was turning around.

Now, I've got a second chance. Don't screw it up.

He was walking back to his chalet just as LeeRoy was heading over to check if he was okay. "Morning, LeeRoy." LeeRoy stopped in his tracks, his eyebrows lifting in confusion. He didn't recognise Giles, all clean and tidy. "Holy shit!" LeeRoy said, when he finally realised. "Where the fuck is Giles?"

Giles chuckled. "Amazing what a bit of soap and water and a good night's sleep can do." "You're not kidding!" said LeeRoy. "Bloody amazing. Anyway, come up to the house and we'll talk about how you can make a living." "No problem," said Giles, and they walked together up to the house and through the back door into the kitchen.

LeeRoy's kitchen was enormous, with a large black Aga at one end and kitchen cabinets that must have been worth a pretty penny. Giles was still curious about what LeeRoy did for a living, but decided to ask about it later. "Take a seat, Giles. Want some coffee?"

LeeRoy was already pouring coffee into two cups when Julie walked in. She stopped in her tracks as LeeRoy had, and burst out laughing. "Holy cow! The magic fairy must have cast a spell on you last night! You look twenty years younger – and smell a great deal better too, I guess." "Hope so," Giles shrugged. "How was your sleep?" she enquired. He chuckled. "It was a bit rough! I'm not used to a soft bed. I tried and ended up in the armchair; then the bed." "Like a game of musical chairs!" Julie laughed. LeeRoy sat down with them. "So Giles, what kind of work can you do?"

Giles cleared his throat, eager to make a good impression on his new boss and feeling as if this were an informal job interview. "I'm pretty versatile. As I mentioned in the car, I used to work on a farm years ago, so I'm pretty handy. What's on your mind?"

"The garden needs some work. I have a contractor come in to tidy it up and keep it neat, but I can get rid of them soon enough if you shape up."

"Well, that's them out of a job then, gardening's no problem for me," Giles said. "I actually enjoy it. I've even been a farmhand before." He didn't want to get into the details of how he'd had his own farm and lost it.

LeeRoy nodded with a winning smile. "That's a good start, then. You'll find all the tools you need, including a ride-on mower, in that shed down by the lake."

"Okay. I'll start on it today. Anything else?"

"Yes, there is," LeeRoy scrutinised him, as if weighing him up.

"General maintenance. That is, painting, minor repairs, and so on, but you don't need to start now. Take a day or two to rest up. "

"No problem, I think I can handle that okay, and I'm happy to start today. I'd get bored just sitting around doing nothing; I've had too many days like that."

"That's great, I'll also need you to drive Julie into town occasionally. Until she gets her licence, that is."

"Can I drive Tinky Winky with 'L' plates?" piped up Julie, all excited.

"Yes, you can," LeeRoy said slowly. "But you'll need a qualified driver with you. I've arranged some lessons with a professional instructor to get you started. Before I let you take to the road, you need to be confident in what you're doing."

Julie's eyes lit up. "When's the first one?" "This afternoon at 1 p.m.," LeeRoy replied.

Julie's face lit up with delight. "You think of everything, LeeRoy, don't you?"

"Alright, Giles. I'll leave you to find your way around, and yeah, I should probably let you know what I'll be paying you. I expect you to work Monday through Friday, 9:00 a.m. to 5:00 p.m., with a lunch break. For this, I'll pay you £35 in cash. For any overtime, such as driving or waiting, I'll pay you £2 per hour."

"Wow, thanks, LeeRoy!" Giles's eyes widened with surprise. This was unbelievable. "That's way more than I expected, especially with the chalet too. Do you want some rent out of that?"

"That's no problem," LeeRoy said, shaking his head. "I think of it as a security hut. See, I'm often out, and if you have the lights on and someone's seen moving around the place, it'll be safer." He glanced at Julie and continued. "Besides, I feel better about Julie being here alone if you're on the grounds. By the way, here are the keys to that Toyota pickup over there in case you need to go anywhere."

He tossed Giles the keys and nodded toward a brand-new Hilux parked a few hundred yards away near an outhouse. Giles had never seen anything like it before. "Thanks, LeeRoy." He quickly added, "I'll only use it for work." "That's okay," LeeRoy replied. "As long as you don't take the piss, I don't mind you using it to go into town and stuff." "Thanks again, LeeRoy," Giles said, shaking his head in astonishment, his eyes wide. "I'm sure I'll wake up from this dream soon." "Go on," LeeRoy laughed. "Get on, and I'll see you later."

With a grin, Giles took off, overjoyed and eager to run through the garden, jumping up and clicking his heels together in pure happiness.

LeeRoy turned to Julie, smiling fondly. "Okay, little lady, how did you like your first night in your new home?" Julie replied, "LeeRoy, I haven't had a chance to take it all in yet. I mean, bloody hell, not long ago I was being beaten up by a crazy matron. Now I'm living in a mansion with a handsome black guy who's doing everything for me – and with a new car parked outside! How do you think I feel? Absolutely freaking out – that's how I feel!"

LeeRoy laughed. "You're worth it, **Julie**. I love you a lot, and you make me feel great."

"Is that all?" she asked.

"Plus, you're good in bed."

"Get lost, you jerk!" She threw a tea towel at him.

LeeRoy grinned. "Only kidding, sweetheart. If I had to list all your qualities, I'd be here all day."

"You're a smooth bastard!" she laughed.

LeeRoy stood up and rubbed his hands together briskly.

"Right, it's 11:30. I have things to do, and you need to make yourself gorgeous for your driving instructor."

"Won't need to do anything then – I'm already gorgeous."

"And big-headed," he lightly touched the end of her nose affectionately. "Give me a kiss before I go."

She snuggled up to the big man, and he kissed her on the top of her head, which she loved. So did he – especially the sweet smell of her hair.

"Right! That's enough! Piss off before I carry you up those stairs."

"Promises, promises," she laughed.

"Bye babe. I'll leave the gates open this once so that the instructor can get in without any hassle. They'll close once he breaks the beam, so you'll need to open them on the way out. Enjoy your lesson, and I'll be back around 5 p.m."

"Okay, love you."

"You too!" And he left.

Julie suddenly thought, Shit! I don't have a licence – I can't believe LeeRoy didn't think of that.

She ran out of the front door and just caught LeeRoy as the gates were opening.

"What's wrong?" he asked, rolling down the Rolls-Royce window.

"Old Mr. Perfect – I don't have a licence! We'll have to cancel my lesson. "I thought you thought of everything," she said, sarcasm dripping.

"It's in the kitchen, top drawer by the Aga."

"Do what?" she asked, repeating her words.

"A licence?" she asked, her eyes narrowing. "I just don't believe you. How could you have gotten that? I don't even have a birth certificate."

"Ah, yes. That's in the top drawer, too."

Julie stood there, mouth agape. "How?"

"Don't ask questions, Julie. Just get your documents, they're all there, including your passport."

"Passport!" she exclaimed.

"Yep – all in there."

"Bollocks," she exclaimed. "Is there anything you can't do or get?"

"Not much. Now get out of here, before these gates close on me."

She hurried to the kitchen, pulled open the drawer, and found them inside. How did he manage that? she wondered, flipping through the official-looking booklet and papers. She opened the birth certificate, eager to read its details. Her hands trembled as she examined it. It looked authentic, but had LeeRoy just obtained a fake document? She knew he had been involved in shady dealings, though she chose not to ask about it. Otherwise, how was this possible? The certificate listed her as a female baby and included her real birth date. So far, everything seemed in order.

Mother… Julie Barnes. Julie's heart was pounding as she read the document. She let out a small gasp, her throat suddenly as dry as dust. The birth certificate looked official, but she had no idea what it should look like. She didn't want to get her hopes up only to find out she'd been tricked. As she kept reading, her eyes landed on the address:

An unfamiliar location in London.

Her father's name was listed as "unknown."

Julie gulped, feeling a surge of emotion. LeeRoy had a lot to answer for. She had no idea what was true and what was fabricated.

This person might be her mother. Julie's heart sank at the thought of never having memories of her mother. On the other hand, LeeRoy could have used his connections to get a fake set of documents, all while helping her get a temporary driver's licence so she could learn to drive. *Maybe it was just easier to buy a package deal,* Julie thought cynically.

She held the birth certificate up to the light, wondering if it was real.

She wouldn't find out the truth until LeeRoy came back.

She opened the passport, examining the watermarked paper. There was even a photo of her face! LeeRoy had taken some pictures of her with his camera a few weeks ago—he said he wanted one for his wallet. So, her picture was genuine. But nothing explained the signature, which closely resembled hers. Still, it had to be fake. That realization left a bitter taste in her mouth when she thought about the birth certificate. Didn't LeeRoy understand how it would make her feel, as an orphan who never knew her parents, being taken advantage of like this? The only word that came to mind was "cruel." And LeeRoy wasn't like that, at least not with her.

She tried to shake off her anger and disappointment. After all, he had been doing her a big favour. He bought her a car, arranged lessons, and helped her get a licence—all as a surprise. The birth certificate was necessary. The passport was just a bonus. She needed those ID pieces to get her licence and start her life.

She pondered on it, and after giving it some thought, she forgave LeeRoy. He meant well. Everything he did was to please her, so she couldn't hold a grudge just because she'd been silly enough to think he'd found her birth certificate – with her mother's name on it. He just did what he had to do to get her the licence. That's all.

She gazed out the kitchen window and saw Giles riding the lawnmower, clearly having a great time. He looks happy, she thought. And he should be – he's landed on his feet. She watched, thinking, just like me. Giles waved as he started another lap, and she waved back through the window. But good luck to him. He's a nice guy, and he deserves a break. She headed upstairs to get ready for her lesson. She put on a pair of tight red pants – *to match Tinky Winky*, she thought.

Right on time, the doorbell rang, and she pulled back the nylon curtain to look out of the front window. There was a brand-new Hillman Imp parked outside. *Not as cute as Tinky Winky,* she thought.

She opened the door, and the man introduced himself as John Marks. "And you must be Miss Barnes. Nice to meet you, Miss Barnes. I'll need to take down a few details. Want to sit in the car and fill out the forms?"

"Yes, that's fine," she said, and went to get in the passenger side.

"No, no, Miss Barnes. I need you on the driver's side."

"Oh yes," she giggled, feeling embarrassed. "I'm so used to being the passenger!"

They got in, and John continued: "OK, I have your name and address. All I need is your licence details."

Julie's face flushed bright red, and she felt a little nervous, thinking the document might be fake. She hesitantly handed it to the instructor, who copied a few details, said "OK, that's all I need," and handed it back to her.

She started breathing again.

"Before we begin, you'll notice there are pedals on each side," John said, pointing down to their feet. "This is called dual control, which means I can take over if we encounter any trouble. The pedals on my side will be used less and less as you improve. You see, there are three pedals; the left one is the clutch."

"Clutch?" Julie said, starting to panic. "What's that?"

"I'll explain in a moment," John said calmly. "Don't worry, it's perfectly normal to be nervous."

"OK, sorry," Julie said, beginning to sweat.

"Don't worry, it's quite common," John said reassuringly. "OK, the middle pedal is the most important - that's the brake."

"That's self-explanatory," she interrupted.

"Yes indeed," he said, "and the one on the right is the throttle or accelerator."

"Yeah, I know that one too," she said, feeling proud of herself.

"This lever here controls the indicators. The switch over there, which you don't need to worry about now, is for the headlights."

"Okay," she said. "This lever here is the gear shift, and this one is the hand brake."

"Alright, I think I've got it," Julie said, letting out a sigh of relief.

"Right, we're lucky here. You've got a nice long driveway, so if you're ready, we'll do a quick practice run before heading out onto the road."

Julie gripped the steering wheel, her knuckles turning white, and stared straight ahead through the windshield. "Yep, I'm all set and ready to go."

John guided her through everything, then they gradually moved off. Julie jerked away, quickly stalling the car, and became flustered. "Don't worry," the instructor said, "most first-timers make that mistake. It happened because you let the clutch come up too fast. Now, pull on the handbrake and try again."

Julie took a deep breath and restarted the engine.

"OK, now ease off the clutch and gently press the accelerator pedal."

She did stall it again, but on the third attempt, she figured it out.

Julie drove past the front of the house and then circled back around. After a few laps, the instructor decided she was ready to head out onto the road.

"Do the gates open automatically?" John asked.

"Yes," she said, "just pull up by that tree."

"Julie, you're driving, so you stop there."

"Okay," she said, and she headed towards the gate, which swung open, where Giles was standing by them, looking impressed. They waved to each other as she drove off.

An hour later, as Giles rounded the corner, he saw them returning and was excited to hear about her day.

Julie parked the Imp and thanked John as Giles opened the door for her.

"Hey Julie, how did your day go?"

"It was alright, thanks, Giles – I have another lesson tomorrow, and I've got one every day for the next two weeks."

"That guy's spoiling you."

"Yeah, I know, but I'm worth it," she laughed.

"How was your day, Giles?" she asked in return.

"Fine, just getting settled. I managed to mow all the lawns, which took me three hours to complete. This place is massive."

"I'll take your word for it. I haven't explored the whole garden yet."

"Well, wait until I get everything in order before you do."

Julie took the house keys out of her handbag and went straight into the kitchen, where she opened the drawer to put her license away. She then picked up the birth certificate and passport again. As she slid them back into the drawer, she wondered, "What was he thinking?"

CHAPTER EIGHTEEN — *Oysters, Rings, and Knives*

LeeRoy arrived home at 6 p.m. "You didn't wreck John's new little Hillman then?"

"No, I didn't, and I'll crash you if you keep on," she laughed. "LeeRoy, I still can't believe all this. I keep thinking I'll wake up and it'll all have been a

dream."

"No worries, my little darling. Go make me a nice cup of coffee, and I'll give you another surprise."

"Another one? How many more?" "That depends on you," he said with a sparkle in his eye.

"Aha." "Go make the coffee. I'll step out and see Giles while you do, OK?" "Yes, sir. Right away, sir!" she said, saluting.

As LeeRoy stepped out the back door, he noticed the well-maintained lawns and realized Giles had invested a lot of effort. He felt proud of his choice, trusting his instincts. Although he was initially cautious when Julie mentioned the old tramp, he quickly sensed that Giles was a good person. Julie clearly had a soft spot for him, and Giles displayed genuine care and affection for her, along with a respectful demeanour toward LeeRoy. The garden further confirmed that Giles was a hardworking man, trustworthy, and the kind of person LeeRoy wanted in his life.

LeeRoy knocked on the door of the chalet, and Giles opened it almost immediately. "Hi LeeRoy, come in." "Hey Giles, looks like you've been busy today. Everything okay?"

"Yeah, yeah, LeeRoy, and even if it weren't, it would've been okay." Giles was beaming. "Yesterday I was out on the streets, and now look where I am."

"Don't keep bringing it up, Giles. You'll earn your keep, don't worry." LeeRoy gave him a look, as if he was deciding whether to share something, but just said, "I've got a driving job for you tomorrow – just a quick trip to London to pick up a small box, is that okay?"

"Absolutely," Giles said, feeling like he'd do anything for this guy. "It'll be awesome to get behind the wheel – I've been waiting a while."

"Yeah, be careful, okay? I don't want the merchandise getting damaged – and don't go over the speed limit either!" he joked, only half serious. "Hey, Julie's making coffee – want some?"

"Yeah, thanks, but I don't want to put you out."

"Listen, Giles, if it was a problem, I wouldn't be asking you, would I?"

They wandered back to the big house, with LeeRoy praising Giles's work on the lawns.

"Need another mug, Julie. We have a guest. Sit yourself down, Giles. You make the place look untidy," LeeRoy said jokingly.

"Thanks, LeeRoy."

"Don't keep thanking me."

They all listened eagerly as Julie shared her experience from her driving lesson, with LeeRoy playfully teasing her now and then. As the conversation began to slow down and Giles finished his coffee, he turned to LeeRoy and asked, "So, where's my destination for tomorrow?"

"East London, Plaistow. I'll give you the address in the morning. "Okay, no problem, looking forward to driving again."

Giles finished his coffee, thanked Julie, and added, "I'll be heading out now. What time do you want me to leave in the morning, LeeRoy?"

"You just need to be there by around ten," LeeRoy said. "Okay, I'll leave at half past seven. It's not that far," Giles said. "Alright, mate. See you in the morning – don't do anything I wouldn't do," LeeRoy said.

"That leaves it wide open," Julie joked. After Giles left, closing the door behind him, LeeRoy turned to Julie and said, "He's a nice guy. I wonder what happened to him." "No idea," Julie said, her eyes narrowing in thought. "Maybe one day he'll open up to us."

"Maybe," LeeRoy said, thinking out loud. "He's clearly educated. Strange, but that's just how it goes. It takes all kinds. What do you want to do tonight?"

"For me, I'm completely content in my new little place – well, it's not that little, but I have no plans to leave."

"Don't start being a homebody!" LeeRoy laughed.

LeeRoy, you need to understand that I spent my life in an orphanage, then on a broken-down bus, and later in a pub. Julie rolled her eyes. "Don't get me wrong—the room at the pub was great, as was living in the bus, and in a way I'll miss all of it. Chas has been good to me, as have all my friends on the bus. In fact, everyone I've met—except those two jerks—has been friendly. I can't understand it."

"Julie, it's because you're a nice person," LeeRoy said, smiling fondly at her. "That makes it easy for people to be nice to you."

"Aw shucks." Julie pursed her lips and stuck out her finger, striking a Betty Boop pose. "Thanks, LeeRoy."

"Come here, you silly cow, and give me a hug!" He pulled her into his strong, muscular arms and gave her a tight squeeze.

"Easy, you big oaf. You're gonna crush me to death."

"I could eat you up," he said, loosening his grip a bit. "I love you to pieces."

"It will be death if you squeeze me much harder!"

He chuckled. "How about I take you out for dinner tonight? Then we can grab a beer with Chas."

"Oh, okay," she said with a big sigh. "If I have to leave this awesome spot! Where are we headed?"

"I'm still undecided. What about that seafood place in Whitstable? You have to bring your own wine, but the food is great."

"That sounds perfect to me," she said, "but make me one promise."

"What?"

"You stay off the oysters. You're enough of a fucking animal without any help from them!"

"Ah ha – can't promise, they do say they are an amazing aphrodisiac, and with you sitting opposite me looking gorgeous and a few glasses of wine. Might just fuck you under the table, there and then, without any oysters!"

"Promises, promises!" She wagged a finger at him, a teasing smile on her lips. "I'm heading for a bath and you're locked out!" "No problem. I'll go get the chainsaw." "You behave or I'll put you on rations!" With that, she took off up the stairs, laughing like a little schoolgirl. He loved that girl.

Julie didn't realise it, but he'd already been to Whitstable and booked a table for 7:30 p.m. LeeRoy made a few calls to ensure everything was set for the morning pickup. Everything was in order. He went upstairs to one of the five bathrooms in the house, took a shower, and got ready while Julie was still in the tub. He was tempted to surprise her but decided against it; he went back downstairs and turned on the TV. He was one of the first people in Faversham to own a colour TV, and he enjoyed sitting back and watching the news on the BBC.

Julie walked in at 6:45 p.m., and LeeRoy caught his breath when he saw her coming down the stairs. She was breathtaking.

"Wow," LeeRoy said, "you must've been the first one off the line when God made your batch. You look stunning. I might have to keep you on a ball and chain." "I might like that!" she laughed.

LeeRoy caught his breath and said, "Let's go. I'm starving, and if we stay here another second, you'll be heading back up those stairs." "Behave, you big animal. Can we ride in Tinky Winky, LeeRoy?" "Ugh, Tinky Winky – where did that stupid name come from?" "I have no idea," she said. "She just looks like a Tinky Winky." "What's a Tinky Winky, anyway?"

"I have no idea if such a thing exists. From what I know, I've got the only Tinky Winky in the whole world. Make that two Tinky Winkies, if you count yours!" she erupted into laughter.

"Ha-ha," he said sarcastically, then added, "but I don't want to show up at that nice restaurant in a Mini. Later, when you've had a few more lessons and we go out, you'll be able to drive. But until then, we'll stick with the Roller."

"Okay," she shrugged. "No problem. I'm getting hungry now. For food, before you say anything else!"

He chuckled. He always laughed a lot when Julie was around.

They arrived in Whitstable, parked by the Pearsons' Arms, and walked back to Wheelers Oyster Bar in the high street.

LeeRoy was holding a bottle of Chablis, which he handed over to the lady at the reception desk. She'd put it on ice and serve it up shortly. Once shown to their table, they sat down and looked at the menu.

LeeRoy couldn't resist. "Hey, I think I'm going to order a dozen oysters to start with, no matter what. It's their specialty."

"Oh, I hope they don't all work tonight," Julie said with a laugh. "You might just get drunk and fall asleep."

"Yeah, yeah, yeah," he smiled. "What are you having? Why not get a dozen oysters too? We could party all night!"

"I'll be happy with just half the night," she muttered, scanning the menu. She looked a bit uneasy as she admitted, "I might try the scallops since I've never had them before."

"Have you ever had oysters?" he asked.

She glanced around, as if worried someone might overhear, then whispered, "Honestly, LeeRoy, I've never even seen one, except in a magazine."

He raised an eyebrow, about to protest, but she kept going: "I'll try one of yours when they come out. Then hopefully, you won't be on top of your game tonight," she chuckled.

"OK, what are you having for the main meal?"

She glanced down at the menu again, fidgeting with a strand of her blonde hair.

"I'm not sure," she said softly.

"Not sure why?"

"LeeRoy," she whispered, blushing, "I've never been to a nice restaurant. I have no idea what most of it is."

His heart melted. He spoke to her in a gentle tone,

"Don't worry, I'll order for you. Do you like fish?"

"Yes, but I don't like the water they swim in!"

The wine arrived, and the waitress poured it for them.

"Alright, let me spoil my little lady," LeeRoy said with a grin.

"About time," she replied, with a bit of a smirk on her face. He raised an eyebrow, pretending to be disappointed. "I know, I think I'll order the monkfish for you. I'm sure you'll like it."

"Yeah, I'm sure I will. I trust your choice. What are you getting?" "Well, I'm going to treat myself and order the lobster."

"I've never tried that either," looking around the room again.

LeeRoy threw up his hands in mock frustration. "There goes more of my dinner!"

They ordered and drank their wine, chatting until the starters arrived.

Julie slipped an oyster into her mouth and almost spat it right out. She retched, forcing herself to swallow it, her eyes welling up with tears from the strain of not vomiting.

"Fuck!" she said out loud. "They taste like snot."

LeeRoy burst out laughing, as did a couple on the table next to them. "They're an acquired taste."

"Acquired taste? How can you eat them? They're disgusting!"

LeeRoy snickered. "Well, I like them, and they give me a hard-on. In fact, I can feel the first one working already!"

"Well, I can assure you – the one I had won't work for me. It might make me sick, but that's all."

"Well, let's hope you like your scallops," he nodded at her scallops cooked in a white wine sauce.

Julie sliced a scallop and cautiously tasted it, fearing it would taste like the oysters, but she nodded enthusiastically to show she enjoyed it.

"Takes the horrible taste of those oysters away," she said. "Make sure you wash your mouth out with Dettol before you kiss me again."

They finished the starters, had some more wine, and the main course arrived. "

"That looks good," said Julie, smiling from one plate to the other.

"Sure does," he agreed. "Well, let's hope you like the fish."

She tasted it, and her face lit up. "Wow, yes! Beautiful!"

"Would you like to try a piece of my lobster?"

"I hope it's better than those oysters," she said cautiously.

"It will be!" He picked up his fork, dipped a generous piece into his garlic butter, and reached out to offer a piece to her rosy lips. She opened her mouth like a baby bird, and he felt a warm thrill watching her delight as she chewed, her eyes closed.

"Ah, yes, that is nice," she announced, smiling warmly at LeeRoy. He was utterly enchanted.

He watched her, prettily eating, smiling, and chattering. He couldn't get enough of her.

Halfway through the meal, just as Julie was about to take a bite of fish, LeeRoy casually asked, "Will you marry me?" She nearly choked, her hand flying to her mouth as she mumbled through a chunk of fish, "What? Did you just ask me to marry you?"

Yes, I did.

"Fucking hell!" she exclaimed out loud, and a few people glanced back. She didn't care. "Marry you? Oh LeeRoy! Absolutely, yes, yes, yes, yes, yes, yes!"

"I'll take that as a yes, then?"

"Yes," she gasped, her eyes glittering with tears. "I will marry you!"

Two groups of people who overheard the conversation erupted into loud applause. Julie blushed bright red and let out a snort of embarrassed laughter through tears of joy. All the other customers at the remaining tables turned to look as LeeRoy pulled out a small box and handed it to Julie. She stared at him in complete surprise. She had thought he was proposing right then, but this made it even more serious – he had planned it all along!

She opened the little hinged leather box, and inside was an engagement ring with the biggest diamond she had ever seen.

She was now in tears, and the whole restaurant was cheering and congratulating them. She took the ring out of the box and handed it to LeeRoy, saying shyly, "Please put it on for me."

"With pleasure!" he said, slipping the ring onto her finger.

She looked at the ring, looked at LeeRoy, and then looked around at all the people watching with tears in her eyes. This was the happiest day of her short life. LeeRoy handed her his hanky, and she dried her eyes.

"Oh, LeeRoy, I'm overwhelmed! It's a lovely ring, but a bit too big. I'm afraid it will fall off and I will lose it."

"That's no problem. The jeweller mentioned he could resize it within a couple of days if it didn't fit. Before we leave, put it back in the box, and I'll take it back tomorrow and get it sorted." "OK, but I don't ever want to take it off."

Two staff members came up, smiling broadly; one carried a huge bouquet, and the other a bottle of champagne.

Unbeknown to Julie, when LeeRoy stopped by Whitstable earlier that day to reserve the table, he had also arranged for champagne and flowers to be brought out if she said yes, which he was sure she would. This was just too much for poor Julie – she wanted nothing more than to hide under the table.

He had left four bottles earlier and said, "Bring out a couple more, please," waving his hand. "For everyone. Let's all have a drink." The champagne was poured, and LeeRoy made a toast to their future.

"I'll drink to that," Julie said softly, while the other customers in the room raised their glasses and cheered. Julie's face turned bright red as she giggled.

They finished their meal since Julie was too excited to eat more. They had coffee, and when LeeRoy paid the bill, he left a massive tip for all the help the staff had given him that day.

Hugging her flowers close, Julie and LeeRoy walked back to the Rolls-Royce.

As always, LeeRoy was a gentleman, opening the door for Julie. But before they knew what was happening, LeeRoy was attacked by three muggers. They all had knives and threatened to use them on LeeRoy.

Julie was paralysed with fear, too afraid to move or speak up for fear of what might happen to LeeRoy.

One of them said, "It's easy, buddy – turn around and face that wall, or I'll put this knife in the back of your head–or your girlfriend's."

LeeRoy wasn't stupid, so he did as he was told, all the while waiting for his chance to fight back. One of them held a knife to his throat while the other two went through his pockets, stealing all they could find – almost £120 in cash. They were amazed at their good luck, swearing as they took his watch and gold chain.

"Get down on the floor," they said.

LeeRoy followed the instructions. One person stood over him while the other two went to Julie, whose legs had turned to jelly, and she was crying and in shock.

"You fucking hurt her, you bastards, and I'll not rest until you are all dead," grunted LeeRoy, his eyes wild. He would kill them with his bare hands if they touched her.

"Shut the fuck up!" said the one leaning over him, pressing the knife against his throat. "We don't hurt girls. But you're no girl, so keep quiet."

They snatched Julie's handbag, watch, and the new ring before the three of them took off like lightning. They were gone before LeeRoy could even get to his feet.

He began to chase after them, but he cared more about Julie than the jewellery or the money, so he stopped and rushed back to where she was sobbing.

"They took my ring, LeeRoy."

"Bastards. But don't worry, sweetheart. Are you ok?"

"Yes, they didn't hurt me."

"They took your ring. That's fucking well hurt me! I promise I'll get it back or die trying. Scumbags!"

"You'd better call the police," Julie said.

Just as LeeRoy was about to speak, a kid appeared at his shoulder. LeeRoy instantly reacted as if he was about to attack, but the kid raised his hands and said, "Whoa, hold on! I just saw what happened."

LeeRoy relaxed a bit, but he was still on edge.

"I'll never admit I saw anything to the cops," the kid said, "but if you promise to keep me out of it, I'll tell you who they are—they're wankers anyway and nobody likes them, but if they find out I grassed them up, well, you can imagine what they'd do to me."

"That would be nothing compared to what I'll do when I get my hands on them, and get my hands on them, I will. Anyway, I give you my word that they'll never find out from me that you even talked to me, so don't worry. You know who they are, then?"

"Yeah, the Fenton brothers - John, Pete, and Steve. They live up in Baddlesmere Road."

"What's the door number?"

"Dunno. Police will know."

"Fuck the police," snarled LeeRoy, his eyes blazing. "I'll deal with them myself. What's your name, son?"

"Robert."

"Ok, Robert, here's the deal. I want you to find out what number they live at, then keep your mouth shut."

Robert's eyes went wide as he realised he was getting into something he didn't want to be a part of. He started to feel scared and wished he had just walked away without saying anything.

He took a deep breath. "Look, Mister, if you're not going to the police, I think I should just let it go."

"Do that if you want," LeeRoy said. "Or – you can find out that house number, and I'll give you a hundred quid."

"A hundred quid?" gasped Robert, his mind quickly turning over. "But how do I know you'll pay up?"

"Robert, my son, I'm not like those three jerks. Just get me that house number and you'll see!" He went to his car and pulled out a business card with his number on it. "Call me when you have it, and I'll be right here to pay you before you even give it to me. Got it?"

"Yeah, yeah," Robert said uneasily, starting to freak out. "Go ahead. Just leave me alone and call me as soon as you get it." Robert didn't need to be told twice.

LeeRoy got into the car, leaned across, and hugged Julie, who was still crying.

"What a night!" she sniffled. "I only had that beautiful ring on for an hour."

"Don't worry Julie. I promise you'll have it back soon."

He was confident she would, one way or another. Even if those guys had gotten rid of it before he caught up, he'd buy her another one just like it. She wouldn't notice the difference.

Or he hoped she wouldn't.

As they drove home, LeeRoy said, "I was going to take you to the pub so you could tell Chas and the others your news, but I guess we'll skip that now."

"I think so," sniffled Julie. "I must be a mess after all that crying – happy and sad tears, all in one night."

When they got home, LeeRoy said, "Sit down, and I'll make you a cuppa."

He was filling the kettle with water when the phone rang.

"Hello," he listened for a few seconds. "That was fast. You have it already? Great. Good job. I won't ask you what it is now.

Can I meet you at the harbour at ten tomorrow morning? Yeah, okay. See you then."

"Was that Robert?" asked Julie.

"Yes, it was."

She looked at him, her face serious. "Please don't do anything that will get you in trouble LeeRoy."

LeeRoy's eyes sparkled. "I promise you darling, it's not me who's going to be in trouble."

He made the tea, and they took it up to bed with them. "And I had plans for you tonight!" he said.

"I'm sure you did," Julie said, her voice filled with sadness, all the life drained from her. "But you can forget about all that tonight."

"Don't worry, I'm not feeling up to it right now," he said grimly. He drew her close, wrapping an arm protectively around her, and they eventually drifted off to sleep.

CHAPTER NINETEEN — *Dawn, Promises and Schemes*

Around 6 a.m., LeeRoy woke up and quietly slipped out of bed, not wanting to wake Julie. He looked at her sleeping form, one slender arm stretched above her head, and her golden hair spread out like a fan. Her features were delicate, like a porcelain doll, but she was so much more. She breathed softly through her slightly parted pink lips, her life and vitality shining through.

She sure is beautiful, he thought. God, I love her.

He stepped into one of the other bathrooms, took a shower, headed downstairs, and made a cup of tea.

He caught a glimpse of movement out of the corner of his eye and jumped up, fists clenched, his heart racing with adrenaline and fear. What the hell was that?

It was just Giles walking outside.

That scared the crap out of me.

He called out from the back door, "Want a cuppa, Giles?"

"Never turn down a good old cup of tea, especially at this hour." He said, strolling over.

As they sat at the table sipping their tea, Giles couldn't help but notice LeeRoy's brooding expression. "You alright, LeeRoy?"

"Yeah, just had a minor issue last night." He brought Giles up to speed on the whole story, including his engagement to Julie.

"Fucking hell!" said Giles. "And congratulations... So, you're heading back down there later to meet the guy with the house number?"

"Yeah, meeting him at ten."

"Want me to come with you? Instead of the Plaistow trip?"

"No, Giles. Best you steer clear – you don't want trouble with the cops if things go south."

"Oh, I've had my fair share of that," Giles muttered into his cup, taking a sip.

"Yeah, I guess you would have been living rough."

"No, I don't mean that," murmured Giles.

LeeRoy looked up at him with a puzzled expression. "What do you mean then?"

"Oh," he said, pausing to think. "I had some issues years ago, but it's all in the past now I hope."

"Is there something you want to talk about, Giles?"

"I wasn't going to." Giles fiddled with the handle of his cup, debating whether to share his secret. He let out a sigh and looked LeeRoy straight in the eye. "I was trying to keep it behind me, but you've been good to me." He let out another sigh. "I guess you have a right to know who you're living with."

Giles told LeeRoy the whole story. LeeRoy listened without interrupting.

"Well, well," said LeeRoy when Giles had finished. "That's a real surprise. I never would've guessed that. Anyway, that's no problem for me. If I'd been you, his balls would've been fed to the pigs."

Giles laughed. "Thanks, LeeRoy. It's funny, but I feel a lot better now that I've talked about it. I'll never do anything like that again. And I'd never done that to anyone before. Please don't tell Julie."

"Don't tell Julie what?" Julie said, standing in the doorway. They both spun around.

"Nothing," said LeeRoy.

"How can you not tell me nothing? Come on out with it."

"Don't be nosey," said LeeRoy. "It's a secret, so come and sit down and I'll pour you a cuppa."

"I don't like secrets."

"Well, this is one you'll just have to forget about. Boys talk." LeeRoy said firmly and quickly changed the subject. "I just told Giles what happened last night."

"I'm sorry, Julie," Giles said. "I feel for you."

She sank down, looking downcast. "Yes, not the best engagement party, was it?"

"Giles, why don't you take Julie into Faversham this afternoon when you get back from Plaistow? No second thoughts, take her to Canterbury instead. Here, Julie, go get some shopping therapy!" he handed her a stack of twenties, totalling a hundred pounds. "Oh, LeeRoy, you don't have to do that!" she exclaimed. "That's a lot of money."

"Easy come, easy go!" he chuckled. "You won't want to be dragged around girlie shops with her, Giles, so go do a bit yourself," and he handed him £20.

Giles whistled. "Are you sure, LeeRoy?"

"If I weren't sure, I wouldn't have given it to you. Now get out of here!" he joked. "Head to Plaistow and make sure you're back by around one o'clock or milady won't get enough shopping done."

"Alright, one o'clock it is. See ya later," Giles said, standing up.

"Shit," Julie said after the door slammed shut behind Giles. "I forgot – I've got a driving lesson later."

"Don't worry, I'll call him and cancel it for today."

"Yeah, okay. Not feeling it anyway. Can Giles drive Tinky Winky?"

"Yeah, he can," LeeRoy said, laughing.

"Great, we'll take her instead of that old truck."

"Her?" LeeRoy burst out laughing. "Her!"

LeeRoy drove into Whitstable and straight to the harbour. He was only there for two minutes before Robert arrived.

"Get in," LeeRoy said, opening the door, and Robert entered cautiously. "This is fancy," Robert said, settling into the leather seat. "I've never been in a Roller before."

"Forget that. Do you have the number?"

"Yes, I do. Did you get my money?"

LeeRoy gave him £100. "You're very trusting. What if I just ran off?"

"Robert, my son, if you try to run off, you'll have a hard time walking, let alone running."

"Just kidding," he muttered, sweat forming on his upper lip.

"The number?" Robert handed LeeRoy a piece of paper with the number on it.

"Thanks, Robert, by accepting that hundred quid from me, you've entered into an unspoken agreement with me." Robert's face drained of colour. "Break it by talking to anybody at all, and you'll face the same fate as those three wankers. Do you understand?"

Robert grasped the message and promised to remain silent under any circumstances. "Sorry," he said softly, the glint on his upper lip now apparent. "I don't know your name and prefer not to, but if you're interested, I know where they'll be on Friday night."

"Where?"

"Just down there," he said, pointing toward the bowling alley. "They usually turn up around half nine on a Friday. They do some deals with a guy there. I think he's a fence, so if they have anything of yours to sell, that's where they'll be."

"That's great, Robert." LeeRoy handed him another twenty quid.

"Thanks mate," Robert said, surprised but feeling relieved and more confident. "For this kind of money, just ask if you want any more info."

"I might do. Write your phone number on that piece of paper. And remember – keep quiet!"

"Don't worry, mate. I've got it," he said as he scribbled down his number.

"OK, now piss off and make sure you're nowhere near that bowling alley on Friday." "Alright. Thanks for the cash. Can I ask your name?" "No, you can't – piss off!" "Alright, I'm going." And he left.

As LeeRoy drove out of the harbour car park, turned left, and slowly headed down the road, he thought, 'I should check it out after dark.' Then he drove back to Faversham.

Once home, LeeRoy immediately picked up the phone. "Sam, I have a job for you and the boys this Friday."

"No problem, LeeRoy. What are you doing down there, starting a war?" Sam asked with a smirk. LeeRoy explained the situation. "Those bastards!" Sam growled, voice rising. "They chose the wrong guy, that's for sure!" LeeRoy agreed. "You still have that warehouse in Plaistow?"

"Yeah, why?" What are you planning?"

"Something real nasty for those wankers," LeeRoy said through gritted teeth. "Is that nutter Sid still around, Sam?" "Yeah, he is," he replied hesitantly, "are you going to use him?" "I think so," LeeRoy said. "After what they did to Julie – and had me on the end of a knife – they deserve it." "Haha," said Sam. "I haven't seen that nutcase at work for ages."

"Make sure you bring a camera with you. I'll call you later with the details."

"OK. I'll get the boys organised."

LeeRoy put the phone down and stared out of the window, thinking. He was having second thoughts about using Sid.

He's a total nutcase and would do anything for a fiver.

He gazed off into space for a moment, ignoring the birds hopping around on the lawn below. His mind flashed back to the sight of his own face on the ground, the knife at his throat. He recalled Julie's horrified expression, tears streaming down her face.

Screw it, he thought bitterly. They deserved everything coming to them, and they would indeed get it.

Later that afternoon, Julie walked in, dropping her shopping bags on the carpet. "I'm exhausted!" she gasped and flopped down into a chair. "It's hard work, shopping."

"That's something I'll never find out. What did you get?"

"What didn't I get?" she sniggered. "I spent all your money. I bought a lot of things, mostly clothes, along with some other bits and pieces."

"You sound like the Dave Clark Five."

"What?"

LeeRoy started singing the pop group's hit: "I'm in pieces, bits and pieces."

"Oh – that's funny!" she said, playfully tapping him on the arm with the back of her hand. "But the highlight of my day was cruising in Tinky Winky. I really love that car. I can't wait to pass my driving test." She stood up and went to look inside the fridge. "What shall we have for dinner tonight?"

"I don't care. Listen, I must nip down to Whitstable around nine, so let's have an early dinner. I'll drop you off at the pub. You're working tonight, right?" Julie turned around, frowning. "Yeah, I told Chas I'd be in for the rest of the week. Why do you have to go to Whitstable? Or should I not ask?"

"Best if you don't."

"LeeRoy," she said softly, coming over and lightly resting her hands on his chest, looking into his eyes. "I don't like this. Please don't do anything reckless." He looked back at her steadily. "I won't. Don't worry."

LeeRoy drove Julie to work.

"I'm not going to mention us getting engaged yet," Julie said sadly, involuntarily glancing at her empty finger.

"No, don't worry, sweetheart. Wait until you get your ring back," LeeRoy said, kissing her. "Love you."

Julie rested her hand on his cheek and smiled softly. "Love you. Future husband."

Julie went upstairs to get ready for her shift. She was running late but knew she could get away with anything with Chas since he had a thing for her. Still, she was safe—he knew it would be instant death if he tried anything with her and LeeRoy found out.

CHAPTER TWENTY — *Dark Lanes and Quiet Hands*

LeeRoy drove to Whitstable. It was October, and it was dark outside. He parked in the bowling alley car park and waited for a few minutes, turning off his headlights but leaving the engine running as he looked out into the darkness. No streetlights were close enough to cast their glow this far, and the only light was the faint neon sign of the bowling alley. Even when the front door opened, its narrow strip of light only illuminated the step and didn't reach any farther.

Perfect! he thought. Nice and dark. Just have to make sure that we get them out here.

He drove out of the car park, satisfied.

At home, LeeRoy called Robert and asked how the Fenton brothers got to the bowling alley.

Robert mentioned, "They have an old red Thames van with seats in the back." Then he asked, "What time do they arrive?"

"I'm not certain, but since they're typically there by 9:30, I would guess around 9, maybe earlier."

"OK, Robert. You've done well, but remember, keep your mouth shut."

"I will. Don't worry."

"I'm not worried," said LeeRoy. "It's you that should worry if you gob off."

"I won't. I won't!"

"Good. See you soon."

Robert hoped not.

LeeRoy parked on Preston Street and entered the pub. It was a relatively quiet evening, and Julie was talking with another barmaid when she noticed LeeRoy coming in.

"Hiya, darling," she greeted, smiling warmly. With a grin, LeeRoy pulled out his wallet from his inside pocket. "Hello, sweetie. Are you okay?" He studied her face meaningfully.

She brushed off his concern with a wave of her hand. "Yeah, I'm fine."

"You been busy?" He asked. "Nah, been quiet tonight. Want a Guinness?"

"Yes, please." Always keeping his wits about him, he scanned the bar.

"Were you a long time in Whitstable?" she asked suspiciously, holding the pint glass under the foaming tap.

"No, I wasn't – I've been home."

"Everything okay?"

"Yes — no problems."

She set the creamy-headed pint on the bar counter and scrutinised his face, but could read nothing from his expression.

LeeRoy was sitting at the bar, chatting with Julie and the other barmaid, when the door opened, and the two scumbags walked in. They froze when they saw LeeRoy, spun around, and went straight back out, the door closing behind them.

Julie and the other barmaid burst into laughter. "Obviously not very thirsty tonight!"

Chas walked through from the back. "Hey LeeRoy. Julie, get us a gin and tonic, please." As she quickly poured him his drink, he joined LeeRoy at the bar. "How's it going?"

"Just fine," LeeRoy said tightly.

"Now, now," Chas said. "What's up?"

The bar was getting crowded, and Julie and the others were too busy to notice much, but LeeRoy leaned in and tilted his head, indicating to Chas that he should move closer so he could hear what he had to say. LeeRoy quietly said, "You won't believe this, but last night I took Julie to Whitstable for dinner and asked her to marry me." "You did? No wonder you're looking down," Chas joked. "She said no?" "Nah, quite the opposite. She said yes."

Chas frowned. "Changed your mind?"

LeeRoy snorted. "Fuck off. I love her to bits."

"So, what's up then?"

"We were only fucking mugged when we left, by three young guys with knives. They cleaned me out and then stole Julie's new ring! She'd only worn it for about an hour."

"Fuck, LeeRoy! I'm guessing neither of you was hurt." He shot a glance at Julie, who was chatting with a customer, clueless.

"No, we're okay," LeeRoy said, his eyes narrowing. "But they're not fucking gonna be."

"Do you know who they are then?"

"Yeah, I do now and fuck their luck, Chas – they're gonna pay dearly for what they did." He took a sip of his beer. "It's not so much the mugging," LeeRoy shook his head in disbelief. "I could walk away from that, but the bastards robbed Julie." He looked fondly over at Julie, serving customers politely, hiding her hurt. She was terrified. But let me tell you, Chas, not as fucking terrified as those three assholes are gonna be on Friday.

"I don't blame you, LeeRoy, but I don't want to hear any more." He raised his hand. "Good luck." He paused for a moment.

"Julie's working on Friday."

"Yes, but I'll get Giles to bring her in and pick her up again later."

"Giles? Who's Giles?"

LeeRoy told him the story, ending, "And he seems like a nice guy."

"Right old softy you are," said Chas.

"Not really," said an embarrassed LeeRoy. "He'll earn his keep."

Friday evening came around, and Giles was taking Julie to work at 7 p.m.

"Don't wait up, love," LeeRoy said, kissing her on the driveway before she got in the car. "I'm not even sure I'll be back tonight, so don't worry." That was all it took for Julie to start worrying. She looked at him in the dim light from the open car door, his dark features barely visible in the darkness.

"LeeRoy," she said, with a warning tone in her voice. "Be careful."

He flashed a grin. "Julie, I can take care of myself and you. Have a good night." He opened the passenger door and guided her inside.

Giles, ever discreet, acted like he wasn't there and waited patiently, his hands resting lightly on the steering wheel, ready to go.

Julie grasped LeeRoy's hand. "Please be careful, whatever you're doing, I love you!"

"Same here, my little angel." He winked, then stood tall and stepped back from the car, raising his hand in a wave of goodbye. "Very much. Everything I do is to make our life together even better. Just remember that."

"I love our life just as it is," Julie's voice trailed off helplessly.

She reluctantly closed the door, and LeeRoy turned to head back into the house, a determined look on his face.

LeeRoy's boys arrived at the house a few minutes later, having been waiting up the road until they saw Julie leave.

"What's the plan?" Sam asked.

LeeRoy described the car park layout and said, "We wait here for them to arrive. Once they do, get them into the van swiftly and quietly. Knock the fuckers out if necessary."

"Sounds like a pleasure," Sam said.

"Disable them with duct tape, drive them up to your warehouse, I'll meet you there, and with Sid's help we'll sort the fuckers."

"Sid will love his part." Replied Sam.

"Bet he will, the dirty bastard!"

They arrived at the bowling alley at 8:30 p.m. and found the darkest part of the car park to wait.

"What are we looking for?" Sam asked, scanning the parked cars.

"An old Thames van," LeeRoy said. "But remember, they all carry knives."

"Fuck the knives, they won't get a chance to get them out, let alone use them." He focused on the area outside the door.

"Lads – check out those bins." Three of LeeRoy's boys jumped out of the back of the van and stealthily moved in, hiding behind some large industrial rubbish bins.

They had been patiently waiting when a police car drove into the car park, with headlights shining on their van and the bins. LeeRoy and Sam quickly crouched down to stay hidden and avoid detection by the police. The three guys behind the bins did the same. The patrol car then circled the car park before driving away. Sam took a deep breath and spoke first. "Fucking hell, that was close and a bit scary—no idea what excuse we could have given if they had spotted us, but luckily they didn't."

The three men near the bins were growing cold and bored when, at 9:04 p.m., an old red Thames van pulled into the car park.

Sam tapped LeeRoy on the arm, but LeeRoy was already nodding, eyes locked into the occupants of the van, a rush of adrenaline flowing through him. The van was parked a little way from their location, but they had to pass the bins to reach the bowling alley. The brothers got out, locked the van, and chatted and laughed as they walked past the bins.

Sam started the van and drove swiftly towards the bins. One of the brothers, mistakenly thinking the van was leaving the car park, stopped and extended his arm to hold back the other two, allowing it to pass safely.

LeeRoy's boys pounced. The brothers had no chance against these three huge men and were on the ground before they knew it. Their muffled shouts were instantly cut off by a cloth soaked in chloroform.

LeeRoy had already jumped out of the van to open the back doors, and the three brothers were quickly pushed inside before the doors were slammed shut. The whole process took less than a few seconds, and impressively, by the time the next group of visitors entered the car park, Sam's van was already pulling away as if nothing unusual had happened. They moved with practiced ease.

They headed out and drove through Whitstable town, passing Wheelers, where the mugging had taken place. The same police car was parked opposite, but, as before, they saw nothing, and everyone started breathing easier again.

They quickly joined the Thanet Way, headed onto the M2, and continued through the Dartford Tunnel. They hurried past Dagenham and arrived at Sam's warehouse in Plaistow in about ninety minutes. Throughout the journey, the three brothers remained unconscious thanks to more chloroform.

CHAPTER TWENTY-ONE — *The Warehouse Reckoning*

After a while, the first brother opened his heavy, blurry eyes and looked around, struggling to recognise his surroundings. A harsh, focused light impeded his vision after being shut for so long, yet he faintly sensed the darkness surrounding him. He blinked slowly, feeling dull and unable to focus. His tongue was fuzzy, his jaw ached, and his mouth was tightly shut.

As the other brothers regained consciousness one by one, only seconds apart, what they were experiencing terrified them to the core.

They realised that they were all naked, their feet duct-taped to the legs of three separate chairs, arms taped behind their backs, and gagged by tape across their mouths. Their pelvises had been positioned to be thrust forward by the tape around their thighs, binding them to the chairs, spreading their legs apart so that their testicles hung down vulnerably over the front edge of the seats.

What scared them even more was the three huge black men sitting right in front of them with loaded sawn-off shotguns trained on their chests.

The lads' eyes widened in terror, and they emitted various whimpering sounds. One struggled against his bindings, but the others were too weak with horror to move.

They heard a strange, echoing sound of footsteps behind them across the concrete floor, which was even more unsettling than seeing the gangsters in front of them.

LeeRoy emerged from behind the brothers, his heels clicking as he strode across the floor with his hands relaxed behind his back.

He paused before them, maintaining direct, steady eye contact with each.

"Do you remember me?" he asked.

They didn't quite recognise him since it was dark when they robbed him, but because he was black, they had a pretty good idea of who he was.

LeeRoy stepped up to one of the brothers, Pete, and ripped the duct tape off his mouth. The boy gasped. "Who are you?" he asked, his voice trembling with fear.

"I'm the fucker you mugged in Whitstable the other night," LeeRoy said, holding up the engagement ring box that one of Sam's men had found in Pete's pocket during their search. Luckily, the ring was still inside. "Now you're gonna pay for it big time." Pete swallowed, but his throat was so dry he almost choked. "What are you going to do to us?"

"I don't know yet," LeeRoy said casually. "But I can guarantee you're not going to like it. Not one FUCKING little bit."

The three brothers stared at him, their eyes bulging in horror, but LeeRoy continued: "Now, you took a hundred quid from me. I want it back, naturally. And you took my watch, which is nowhere to be found. But the biggest mistake you made was taking my lady's ring. Big, big, big fucking mistake!"

Just then, Pete rallied, making one last desperate attempt to save face. "We just found the ring. Who said it was us?"

LeeRoy leaned in, getting right in the brother's face, his eyes blazing. "A little fairy told me. There's no point in you trying to act like it wasn't you, because I know it was."

The youngest brother, John, was crying, tears streaming down his face and dripping onto his bare testicles. "Shut the fuck up!" shouted LeeRoy. "You fucking baby!" He couldn't help it, and he started pissing himself.

"Baby needs a nappy, does he? Not so fucking brave now, are you?" LeeRoy slapped him across the face, yelling, "Shut the fuck up!"

This only made him cry harder, snivelling and whimpering, but with his mouth taped shut, he wasn't making much noise.

"Right, you," LeeRoy said, pointing at Pete. "Where's my money?"

"We spent most of the money," Pete said, trying to be obedient. "But there's still some at home."

"Is there?" LeeRoy asked. "Well, how do you suggest I get it back?"

"Let us go, and I promise to get it for you."

LeeRoy burst out laughing. "No fucking way, you wanker! You robbed me and terrified my girl, and for that, you're going to regret it forever."

Sam stepped out from the shadows, holding something metallic in his hand that looked like a pair of pliers.

"Do you know what that is?" LeeRoy asked.

"No," a frightened voice said.

"Well, I'll tell you what it is. It's what they use on lambs' tails – to cut them off. Show them, Sam."

Sam inserted an elastic band into the contraption and fully opened it. The brothers' eyes were all bulging.

"No!" cried Pete, the only boy who could speak. "Please no!"

"See, now, they don't want lambs' tails dangling down, like they do. So, they're CUT OFF!" It's called 'tail docking', in case you're interested," and laughed out loud. "So, we thought we'd do the world a favour and make sure you wankers don't breed."

"Please! Don't! We'll do anything to make it up to you!" the lad pleaded; his face twisted with upset and fear.

"It's way too fucking late. You're a fucking tosser!"

Now, all the brothers were panicking, frantically mumbling or silently screaming behind their tape, tears and sweat pouring down; their bodies were writhing and struggling, but they were firmly taped in place.

"We're going to put one of these bands around your bollocks."

"No!" shrieked Pete, his face collapsing in on itself, like a toddler in tears, as he wailed, "Please! Please!"

"Shut him up!"

One of Sam's men shoved the business end of a sawn-off shotgun in the lad's unwilling mouth. The lad fainted. Another big guy ripped off a length of tape and stuck it over the unconscious lad's mouth. He was only out for a few seconds, but came round wishing he was dead already.

Sam and one of the others held down the chair of the other brother, Steve, who was the oldest and the ringleader. Sam opened the contraption, slipped it over the boy's genitals, and let it close. He made a high-pitched whimpering sound through the tape, his eyes wild with fear. Even though he was strapped down, he fought and struggled like a man possessed by the devil himself. He would have been heard all the way over at Bow if he weren't gagged.

The other two guys were hyperventilating with fear when LeeRoy said, "Put one over his prick too; hopefully it will stop him pissing, and his balls will explode," laughing at the thought.

"Brilliant idea," laughed Sam. "A double docking".

They were about to do the same to the other two brothers when they heard the sound of a key rattling and a door opening filling the air.

They all turned around – even LeeRoy and his crew.

It was Sid. He had a key and had let himself in.

"Hello, boys," he said with a grin. He was a stocky, pale man with facial tattoos, a thick beard, and greasy greying hair.

"Looks like a good party. Can I join in?"

He had a sickening laugh, which did nothing to calm the brothers.

"Come in, Sid," LeeRoy said. "It wouldn't be a party without you."

Sid went over to the other two younger brothers, a wild grin on his maniacal face.

"Nice." He looked them both over and said again, "Nice! Lovely little boys."

He approached John, the youngest one, leaned in close and exhaled heavily into his ear, his moist breath reminiscent of a lover's sigh. John could smell whisky and the nauseating funk of old, stale sweat. Sid licked John's ear with a slow, wet tongue.

"Like that, do you, sonny?" Then he put his hand down on the lad's limp, icy-cold penis. "Lovely! But I bet that won't go hard tonight, will it?"

The crazed young lad was shaking his head from side to side, as if trying to get rid of him, but Sid was going nowhere.

This was Sid. 'Sick Sid, the pervert', who would fuck a frog if he could stop it jumping.

Sid looked like the main character of the kids' show Catweazle – a scruffy 11th-century wizard with wild, matted hair and a grey beard – and he smelled like a skunk. He was repulsive, but he didn't care. He didn't have to please anyone: he was going to get laid tonight, and he didn't need anyone's permission.

"I'm ready," said Sid, dropping his grimy pants, revealing his thick, stiffening member.

The brothers understood what was coming, but they couldn't prevent it. Their shouts and sobs were silenced, yet tears flowed down their contorted faces.

Sam and one of the others cut the duct tape from the youngest one's legs, dragged his scrawny body up from the chair, and forced him face down over an old oil drum, holding him there.

Sid stepped forward, slapped a handful of Vaseline over the brother's arse and his now-erect penis. He thrust it into the lad and violently raped him, taking his time, enjoying not just the sex but also the fear and pain of his victim while his brothers watched, terrified.

They ripped off the boy's duct-tape gag for identification, and Sam took pictures with their Polaroid camera. They wanted some insurance and believed that the photographs would prevent the brothers from going to the police out of shame and humiliation.

Sid withdrew with a grunt, leaving the boy torn open and almost choking on tears and snot.

Sid was an animal. He wanted another chance, so they brought up the other brother and did the same to him, even though he was struggling so much that it took four of them to hold him down. But Sid had his way.

Both brothers lay on the floor, bleeding and crying, but who cared? No one was there to help, and those present certainly didn't care.

They put the two raped brothers back down on the chairs and taped them to the legs again. They were soon sitting in pools of blood and semen.

LeeRoy said, "I'm guessing you're all wishing you hadn't robbed me, eh?"

They were both sobbing, but didn't say a word.

"OK, let's decide what we do next."

Both cried, "No, please!" and "Nothing else! We'll do whatever you want."

LeeRoy sneered, "We could get Sid to bring a few of his friends to the party. Would you like that?"

"No! No!" They shrieked. "Pleeeeease! Let us go! Please."

"Let you go? Why?" LeeRoy barked. "So you can run to the police? No way! The party's only just begun."

"We won't go to the police! We promise."

"Funny," said LeeRoy. "I know you won't, because we are going to bury you in the foundations of the new motorway bridge on the M2."

"Please! No. Please!" Sobbing even louder, they said, "We'll get your money back to you. Please don't do anything else to us."

LeeRoy turned to Sam, "What do you think?"

"It's getting late and I'm tired," Sam shrugged. "I think we should just top them now and fuck off home to bed."

The brothers looked horrified, too stunned to protest. "Well, there you go, boys. Sam wants his beauty sleep. You know what? That ring you wanker's stole was my fiancée's engagement ring. We just got engaged an hour before, and you fuckers took it. Do you understand why I'm upset?"

"Yes," one of them snivelled. "We're sorry."

"No, you ain't sorry. The only thing you're sorry about is, what do they say? Ah, yeah, you're only sorry that you got caught. Anyway, at least you ain't bum virgins anymore and that wanker over there," he nodded toward Steve, "won't be deflowering any virgins when that band does its job or his balls explode, and he'll be the only eunuch in the village." They all laughed out loud at that, except the brothers, of course.

LeeRoy paused, stroking his chin like a pantomime villain. I need to consider this carefully. There's a chance you might approach the old Bill.

"We......"

"Shhh!" LeeRoy hissed. "I'm thinking aloud, so shut up. As I said, you could go to the old Bill, so if we buried you all in concrete, you wouldn't be able to."

"We won't!" shouted one of the brothers. "Please let us go, we promise, please!"

"Shut up! And stop squealing like a little girl. I have an idea. I'm heading to a nice, warm hotel for the night to think about it. Will they be okay here, Sam? "

"Sure, no problem. I have a nice, cold cellar where I can lock them up."

"Alright, do that, and we'll meet here at ten in the morning to decide what to do with them."

"I don't know why you don't just shoot the fuckers," said Sam.

LeeRoy clicked his tongue, like he was considering it. "We'll see in the morning. Let them sweat it out."

Steve, with the lamb band around his testicles and penis, had passed out and was silent.

"Chuck some water over him, Sam, and bring him around." Sam obeyed, pouring a bucket of icy water over Steve, who woke up with a look of terror and shock. For a moment, he was confused about his location, but then everything came back to him quickly.

He was trembling with fear and the icy water, but remained silent.

LeeRoy looked over at Steve with hate in his eyes and said, "Right, you bastard, you're the oldest and ringleader." He then looked over at Sid, who was getting ready to leave. He'd had a good time; now he was off to the pub to get pissed. "Fancy one for the road, Sid, before you go?"

Sid didn't need to be asked twice; he quickly approached Steve, who was frantically struggling to escape, but the duct tape held firm.

Sid touched his nipples, which were hard, not from sexual excitement but from the freezing water. He tried desperately again to get away, all the time knowing it was not going to happen.

LeeRoy beckoned to Sam to remove his gag. "Let's hear him scream," said LeeRoy.

They forcibly removed the duct tape from him, but his struggle was so intense that LeeRoy had to intervene and assist. In the end, they managed to force him into position, and Sid was getting ready. "Hurry up," LeeRoy said. "Sorry, boys, I don't think it's going to work again. I'm getting old; things aren't what they used to be! "

Steve, still struggling, was thrown into a corner of the warehouse and told not to move an inch, or else. His testicles were hurting so bad he didn't want to move anyway.

"It's your lucky day," LeeRoy barked at Steve as they retaped him to his chair.

"I don't feel too lucky," he snarled back, aware he was nearly out of Sid's reach. "OK, I'm bored now. Stick 'em down the hole and let's get out of here," suggested LeeRoy.

They were pulled down a few stairs, still bound to the chairs, into a damp, musty basement. The cold October night and underground air made it bitterly cold, so Pete asked if they could have their clothes back. "I doubt the boss will let that happen," Sam said, "but I'll ask. If it were up to me, I'd let you freeze to death." He headed upstairs to LeeRoy and asked the question. LeeRoy thought about it. "Can they escape from that cellar?"

"No way," Sam replied. "There are no windows. It's been soundproofed with the door closed for this very purpose, and they wouldn't be able to break it down, not even with a sledgehammer."

"Alright, let them loose and give them their clothes."

"You're getting soft in your old age, LeeRoy."

"No," he replied, smiling and speaking more softly. "I've already decided to let them go, but let the fuckers suffer overnight."

Sam grabbed the clothes and threw them onto the wet floor, while another person cut them free. The older brother, Steve, was now awake and in agony. "See you at ten!"

Sam then slammed the door shut, locked it, and wedged a piece of wood against it for added security. They locked the warehouse and left.

Julie's shift felt like it was dragging on forever. Even a busy night couldn't keep her from wondering what LeeRoy might be planning. She knew he was organising something and seeking revenge, but she hoped he wouldn't do anything dangerous that could get him hurt—or worse, killed. She also didn't want him to hurt anyone and end up in trouble. If he were smart and played it safe, he might just scare those guys and get her ring back.

She knew that had really pissed him off.

She didn't even care about the ring. All she wanted was LeeRoy.

Those guys had a knife, and she was scared of what they might do if LeeRoy tried to face them alone. *He wouldn't, would he?*

He had what he called "business associates," and he knew how to take care of himself. That was all she could rely on to make her feel better.

He wasn't a violent man at all. She knew that, or at least she believed or wanted to believe it. He was a gentle giant, but Julie understood that he was angry with those guys for ruining a beautiful moment, stealing from both of them, and scaring her. If there was one thing she knew about LeeRoy, it was that he was a proud man, very protective of his family. And that's what she was now: family—almost his wife. Even a mild-mannered man could act out of character if his loved ones were under threat.

Even if the guys didn't hurt LeeRoy, what if he did something terrible to them? What about the police?

These unwanted thoughts kept creeping into her mind, despite the noise of the bar and the pouring of pints.

"You all right, Ju?" asked Chas.

He wasn't generally a sensitive person, but he could tell Julie was upset that night. Her usual radiant smile appeared strained, and when she wasn't occupied with a customer or engaging in cheerful conversation, her expression was etched with concern.

"Yeah. Yeah!" she responded cheerfully, but her smile was forced and didn't reach her eyes, which remained troubled. After she answered his question, he noticed her face fall.

Damn that girl, Chas thought. *She's still beautiful, even when she frowns. A guy could easily get into trouble over her.*

CHAPTER TWENTY-TWO — *The Morning After*

The two younger brothers quickly got dressed. "For fuck's sake, get these things off my balls and prick!" moaned Steve, panicking, picking at the tight rubber bands hopelessly. Frozen, he gave up and began wrestling his arms into his shirt and jacket with painful effort. His testicles were swollen, and his penis was throbbing and feeling like it was about to fall off, but he had to get the bands off before he needed a piss – too sore for him to bear clothes on his bottom half, he left his pants and trousers off.

"They've swiped our knives. How are we supposed to do that?" asked Pete. "I ain't got no idea, but you've got to think of something."

There was no light in the cellar, but they'd left one on in the warehouse, and a small, toughened glass panel in the door let in a bit of light.

"Can you put my socks on for me, John?" Steve asked the youngest. "I'm in too much pain to bend over, and my feet are fucking freezing."

Pete felt around on the floor and found a small piece of stone, no bigger than a brick shard.

"I can try to cut them off with this," he said.

Steve couldn't see what he had found, but he didn't care as long as whatever it was worked. "If it works, I don't give a fuck what it is," he cried out, sweating from the pain of both bands.

You're lucky you're my brother; I wouldn't mess with anyone else's bits!

"Shut up and get it off before they fall off."

Pete scratched at the first rubber band around his testicles, but it was so tight that the stone slipped and cut into Steve's sack.

"Shit!" he dropped the stone, worried about how his brother would react.

"Just fucking do it!" snarled his brother. He didn't care – he just wanted the bands off, and the sooner, the better.

It took over ten minutes, but eventually, there was a snap, and the band broke. The lad's testicles were very, very sore, bruised and bleeding, but saved – or, at least, he hoped they were.

"Now get the other one off," he demanded.

"Fuck off, you can reach that one yourself," handing Steve the piece of brick or whatever it was.

Steve mumbled but took the piece and, as gently as possible, hacked at the second band, which again eventually freed his manhood with a loud snap.

He was still in pain, but the relief was incredible; however, he was panicking about the potential damage that might have occurred.

He was desperate for a pee and hobbled over to a corner in the room and screamed as he tried to piss; the pain was like razor blades passing along his penis. He stopped, sobbing in pain, and had to let it out a little at a time.

Pete hugged himself, gazing into the blackness. "Do you think they'll kill us in the morning?"

"How the fucking hell do I know?" said his older brother, easing himself into his Y-fronts, trying to avoid touching any delicate parts.

The younger brother was crying; he was very sore and still bleeding. "It's all right for you," he sobbed. "That fucking weirdo fucked both of us. He's probably given us some disease as well. How the fuck can we live with that? And they took fucking pictures too. What the bloody hell are they going to do with them?"

"No idea," the older brother said, hesitantly pulling up his trousers. "Probably nothing. If they don't do us in, they'll keep them as insurance against us going to the cops."

"Fucking hell! This is your fault!" said the little brother, John, jabbing his finger at his big brother.

"How's it my fault?"

"I told you he was too big to tackle."

"Well, that's a load of bollocks, because we done him, didn't we?"

"We did, for sure; but by fuck, he's getting his own back."

"Fuck knows what he'll do in the morning."

The three of them sat, shivering and wondering what the future held for them.

"I need a crap," said Pete.

"Well, you'll just have to wait," said the eldest brother.

"I can't!"

"Fucking hell! Get over in that corner, and I'll kill you myself if you stink the place out."

Pete crouched in the corner and started to scream.

"Ow, ow! That fucking weirdo has ripped my insides out. Fucking hell! That hurts!"

"Shut the fuck up," snarled Steve. "We don't want to know, get on with it."

"It's all right for you!"

"All right for me? My bollocks feel like they've been slammed in a car door, and they're probably all black by now, and my prick will probably fall off, so shut up!"

John was traumatised and slunk off into the opposite corner, weeping quietly and feeling very sorry for himself.

The night was cold and dragged on. The lads huddled together but got no sleep.

Julie, exhausted from a stressful night, barely moved as LeeRoy slipped into bed beside her. "Are you okay?" she murmured, sensing his presence and feeling the warmth of his body as he curled around her, relieved that he was with her. She sighed, comforted that he was safe, and snuggled into him; he wrapped a strong, warm arm around her, pulling her close.

"I can sleep now," she said, as if she had already fallen asleep. Feeling secure and comforted, she immediately drifted back into her dreams, happier now that LeeRoy was home.

LeeRoy could have stayed in Plaistow, but he was sick of that place and those little shits who left a bad taste in his mouth. Like a homing pigeon, he felt the urge to return to Julie—to lie close to her, partly to comfort her, and partly to comfort himself.

His mind was completely clear of guilt, knowing those bastards got what they deserved. But the adrenaline rush and his plans for the next day kept him up, even though he had to get up early anyway. He figured he could slip out before dawn without waking Julie and tackle the unfinished business.

Just after ten in the morning, the lads in the cellar heard the door being opened and started to panic.

Sam came in with a loaded sawn-off shotgun and bawled, "Lie face down on the floor!"

They did so silently, their clothes absorbing the cold, muddy water on the floor. They hesitated to push their luck further if they still had any chance left. Another person entered the cellar and bound their hands individually using duct tape.

"Get up and don't be stupid enough to try anything funny. Upstairs."

LeeRoy sat in the warehouse, fingers intertwined as if meditating. He smirked. "Had a good night? I had a great night. Justice is a wonderful thing."

The brothers didn't say a word.

"Right, you wankers. You're lucky. I'm in a good mood. I'm engaged to a beautiful woman, even though she hasn't had anything to show for it for a while. Whose fault was that?"

He paused, casting a cool glance across all three of them. "Here's what's going to happen: you can find your own way home – how you do that, I don't give a fuck. I'll give you a couple of days to get there. Then, on Tuesday next week, I'll be at Faversham Station at 10:00 a.m. One of you, and I don't care which one, will also be there. And you'll bring everything you stole from me, and I mean everything. Do you understand?"

"Yes," they mumbled.

"Louder. I didn't hear that."

"Yes," they all barked.

"One other thing. If you go to the police, I've already paid these guys to cut you up into little pieces. Understand?"

"Yes, we do," Steve, the older brother, said. "Don't worry. We know when we're beaten."

"You should consider yourselves very lucky. Sam here wanted to torture you all until the end. Don't try to avoid me – I know where you live." He gave them the address to prove it. "Cut them loose, Sam. So, fuck off and be there Tuesday or hide forever."

They just wanted to run, but Steve's testicles were hurting like crazy, and the other two were suffering just as much from the rape.

CHAPTER TWENTY-THREE — *The Debt That Wouldn't Die*

Julie was in the kitchen when LeeRoy returned, and she greeted him with a big smile.

"Hi, darling! Didn't expect you back so soon. Good thing my new boyfriend just left!" she laughed.

"That I don't worry about," LeeRoy replied, wrapping his arms around Julie and pulling her close. "No one could satisfy you like I do."

"Old Mr Bighead again, huh?" she patted his chest firmly.

"Nope, just know I have some special powers over you."

"Yeah, I'll just let you keep thinking that. Anyway," she asked, "what brings you home at this time?"

"I have something for you," he said, pulling the stolen engagement ring from his pocket.

Julie threw her arms up and yelled, "You got it back!"

"Yep."

She took the ring and placed it on her finger. "Oh, LeeRoy it's more beautiful than I remember!"

"Don't doubt it. You only had it on for an hour."

Her mood shifted from happiness to worry. "How did you get it back?"

"You don't need to know, Julie."

She frowned. "LeeRoy, I hope you haven't gotten into trouble."

"Who?" He pointed at himself, eyes wide. "Me?"

"Yes, you. What have you done?"

"Nothing to worry about," he smiled.

"Why don't I believe you?"

"No idea," said LeeRoy innocently.

Julie looked into his eyes for signs she should worry, but he seemed completely calm.

"Well, whatever," she said, deciding to drop it. "I have my lovely ring back,

and I'm engaged again—twice in one week!"

"Lucky girl, and both times to the best-looking guy in town."

"Oh, that head's getting bigger," she laughed.

"Right, little lady, now that we're officially engaged, everyone's going to ask when the wedding will be."

"Oh my gosh, I hadn't thought about that," she said, eyes wide with wonder.

"When do you think? This is so exciting, I'm getting goosebumps!" LeeRoy laughed and shook his head. "Classy! How about next May?"

"Yeah!" she exclaimed.

"That's it then. My freedom ends in six months!" she laughed. "Your freedom was over the moment we got engaged," LeeRoy said. "You're such a goofball." She wrapped her arms around him. "I love you, LeeRoy."

"Do you really? I wouldn't have guessed. I love you too, baby, so much." "Where should we go for our honeymoon?" she asked, growing even more excited. She was imagining—did she even dare? —Paris.

"I thought I'd take you to the Caribbean and then down to Peru for a few days before we head home."

Julie drew in a sharp breath, overwhelmed. "Wow, that sounds incredible! I've never travelled abroad before." She was in awe and couldn't picture it. "I've heard of the Caribbean, and I know your family are from there, but I know nothing about Peru. Why Peru, wherever that is?"

"I have friends in Cusco, and we can hike up to Machu Picchu if you're feeling adventurous."

"Whoa, hold on," she said, "slow down. The Caribbean, I can understand. But Peru, Cusco, and what did you say?"

"Machu Picchu."

"Ma-chu Pi-cch-u," she said slowly. "What the hell is that?"

He laughed. "It's an ancient Inca site and popular tourist destination, dating back to the 15th century as far as I recall. The Spanish destroyed many Inca settlements, but never located Machu Picchu. It remained hidden in the jungle for centuries and was rediscovered by Hiram Bingham about 50 years ago. You follow parts of the old, paved Inca Trail up to 13,500ft."

"What!! Hang on, 13,000 feet? That's nearly up to the moon," she gasped.

"Not quite," he laughed, but close. If you want, we can book a guide and hike up there."

"What?" Her voice sharpens into a screech. "Walk up a mountain? I'm not very eager to climb a hill, let alone a mountain."

LeeRoy chuckled. "It's not that bad. The porters carry all your gear. All you do is walk, like taking a Sunday stroll."

"Well, it doesn't seem like a relaxing stroll to me," she said doubtfully. "I need to look into it before I commit to anything like that." She shook her head gently. "I love you and trust you with other women, but that's as far as I go," she joked.

Back in Plaistow, the brothers tried to hitch a ride but had no luck. Nobody wanted to pick up three young guys looking like vagrants on the run. They had no money left – LeeRoy had seen to that. So they walked across town, and once they got off the main road, they took a direct route through some fields and farmland. They were fucked (two of them literally) and hungry, but they had been lucky. They spent the night in an old barn, which had a few boxes of sour apples, but it served their needs. Outside, there was a tap where they could also get water.

"How do you think he found us?" John asked, wincing as he ate the bitter cider apple. "I have no idea," Steve replied, "but if I find out someone ratted on us, they'll regret it more than this. Still, we'll probably never find out."

Around 5 am, the barn door suddenly swung open, startling a farmhand who saw three men lying on a hay pile. Scared, he hurried back to the farmhouse to tell the farmer and others what he had witnessed.

The farmer and two other men accompanied him back to the barn. When they arrived, the three brothers had left, and they were already on their way up the farm track. The farmer shouted for them to stop, but they ignored him and ran. However, because of their injuries, the farmer and his helpers soon caught up with them.

When the farmer caught up with them, slightly out of breath, he asked, "What the hell were you up to in my barn?"

The brothers were in no condition to put up a fight, so they stopped and sat on the grass verge.

"I can see you haven't stolen anything, so what's the score?"

"Nothing, mister," said Steve. "We're trying to get to Whitstable and only slept there for the night. We don't have any money, so we can't buy a train ticket. I assure you, we didn't cause any damage; we just slept."

The farmer looked around at the hand that had discovered them and confirmed they were all asleep on the hay when he arrived.

The farmer, uncertain about how to proceed, said, "OK, give me your names and addresses and then go on your way."

"OK, OK," said Steve, who gave their names but provided a false address and quickly made off.

They had no idea where they were, so they kept walking until they came to a crossroad with a sign pointing to Dartford, which they knew was on the way home.

But what they hadn't expected was the River Thames. "How the hell are we going to get across the river?" Steve moaned. "The only way is the tunnel, and we're not allowed to walk through that. The nearest bridge we can walk over is Tower Bridge, and that's in the wrong direction and miles away. Fuck, fuck, fuck. We're screwed. If we keep walking in this direction, we'll end up in Southend, and we'll be able to see Whitstable," he quipped.

"Very funny, I don't think." Said the youngest brother sarcastically.

The middle brother was nearly in tears and blurted out, "We're fucking miles away. How the hell are we supposed to walk fifty-odd miles with no money, food, or drink? I'm already starving and a fucking river in the way."

"No idea," replied Steve, "I could kill that bastard for doing this to us."

"Oh yeah, Mr. Billy big bollocks, aren't ya when he's not around? Say that to his face next time you see him," said his little brother, stepping back from Steve and bracing for a slap.

They walked three miles before it started to rain. Their lightweight clothes, which had dried after being wet and muddy from the warehouse, were about to get wet again. There wasn't much shelter available; they tried to hide under a tree, but the rain grew heavier and the tree offered little protection.

"Fucking hell," Steve shouted, "what the hell have we done to deserve this?" Then he remembered what they had done and fell silent.

"We're already soaked, so no point in standing here," Steve told the other two. "Let's just keep walking and find some shelter. I'm bloody freezing."

After another three miles, they reached the edge of a small gathering near Woolwich. They caught sight of an old, seemingly abandoned barn inside a field. Climbing over a gate, they found the door was open. Wet and miserable, they stepped inside to escape the rain.

Unlike the previous barn, this one was empty, but at least it was dry.

They found some old boxes to sit on, but that was all the comfort they got tonight; they were wet, cold, and downright pissed off.

"What the hell are we going to do?" the youngest brother asked. "I'm bloody cold and wet, and I need food."

Steve hesitated briefly before saying, "It'll be dark soon. We're near some houses; I'm not sure where we are, but there must be a place where we can break in and find some grub, anything, I'd eat a raw onion right now. I'm completely knackered and out of energy."

They settled in and attempted to make themselves as comfortable as possible while sitting on the wooden boxes that leaned against the old barn wall.

They were desperate and decided to check out the neighbouring houses. They felt so hungry and hopeless.

It was past midnight; the rain had ceased, and under a clear, moonlit sky they looked across the fields to find a way to avoid the road.

They noticed a row of dark cottages and assumed everyone was asleep, so they decided to climb over the fence and try to break into the back of one of the buildings.

It was a simple walk up the garden path to the back door, where they checked the window to see if they could get in quietly. While Steve was looking around the window, Pete tried the door. To his surprise, like many folks, they had left it unlocked.

He signalled to the others, who paused what they were doing and followed Pete toward the kitchen. Even without torches or any light source, the moonlight was enough to see everything around them. Their first stop was the fridge; it was almost empty, but they took whatever was edible and ate as much as they could.

They then continued to search the kitchen and found some small currant buns, along with a few bottles of milk. Pete quietly searched drawers for valuables and found 12/6p (Twelve Shillings and Sixpence), which he pocketed, and a couple of packets of Woodbines; at least they could now have a fag.

They left as quietly as they arrived, eating the remaining buns and drinking all the milk on their way back to the barn, when Pete suddenly stopped. "What's up?" asked John. "Think about it—if we return to that barn, we'll have to walk through this place in the morning, and I bet the house owner would have realised someone broke in. The place will be full of police," Pete said. "So what are we going to do?"

"We'll just have to keep walking and get as far away from here as possible before morning." "No way, scoffed John. "I'm knackered." "Up to you, you can stay here and hope the old Bill doesn't find you in the morning." "At least I'll get a lift home." He again scoffed. "But I guess you're right, fuck, let's go."

They continued to walk through the night, and when they were about 6 miles from Plaistow, 6 miles from that warehouse they'll never forget, they saw a sign that said 'Woolwich Ferry' with an arrow pointing to the right.

"What's that?" asked John. "A ferry, does that go across the river?"

"How the fuck should I know?" replied Steve, "I have no bloody idea where we are, let alone where that goes. But it's worth a look — if it does cross the river, we could maybe sneak on it."

They trundled on for half a mile and found the terminal, along with a sign pointing to the Woolwich Free Ferry.

Steve looked at the others and said, "Surely, we can't be that lucky." But as it turned out, they were. There was an early morning boat waiting, and they walked on; it left forty minutes later.

They disembarked on the opposite side, unaware of which way to go next. They were talking amongst themselves, trying to figure out which way to go when John interrupted, saying, "I saw a sign pointing to Welling at the crossroads. If we get there before morning, we can catch a train to Whitstable, or as close as the twelve and six will take us." "Good idea, John. Well done, let's do that," and off they went, jumping off the road to hide whenever an odd vehicle came along.

They were not quite right about the place they had stolen from the previous evening crawling with police when the break-in was reported. Just a lone copper on a bike had turned up.

Arriving at Welling station at around 6 am, they were ecstatic that they had enough cash to get home with 9d (Nine old pennies) left over.

The train arrived at Whitstable at 9:10 am, and they had never been happier to see that station.

By the time they finally arrived home, their parents were luckily at work. Since they often disappeared for days, they hadn't been missed. They raided the fridge, ate everything available, and drank plenty of water. Afterwards, they took turns in the bathroom—John went first, while the others kept eating.

John ran the bath, since they didn't have a shower. When there was enough water in it, he stripped off his dirty, blood-encrusted clothes and climbed in. The hot water stung badly, but he persevered, and his lower half was soon completely submerged.

He had time to think, alone for the first time, and he started to cry. What if everybody in Whitstable found out he had been fucked up the arse? He didn't care about what had happened to the others; he was only worried about himself. What if their parents found out?

Fuck, what a mess!

John was abruptly pulled out of his daydream by a loud bang on the door. "What the fuck are you doing in there?" Steve yelled. "Hurry up! We need to get in before Mother and Dad get home."

John quickly washed himself from head to toe, paying special attention to his buttocks. After drying off, he took some antiseptic cream from the bathroom cabinet, carefully applied it to his butt, and then got dressed. He cleaned the bath and turned on the water, setting aside the antiseptic cream for Pete, knowing he would need it too.

It was finally Steve's turn, and he knew this was going to hurt his testicles, but it had to be done. He made sure the water wasn't too hot, stepped into the bath, and gently lowered himself down, but as soon as his testicles touched the water, he let out a loud scream.

"Fuck, fuck, fuck! That's fucking painful!"

He added more cold water to the bath and tried again. It was a little better, but it still hurt like a bitch, and it got worse as the parts where the ring had been, along with the grazes and cuts, entered the water. Tears filled his eyes, but he knew he had to do it or they'd get infected. Try explaining that to the doctor!

He started thinking of ways to get back at LeeRoy, but quickly decided it wasn't a good idea. What if it went wrong? They wouldn't survive another session in Plaistow, so he promptly dismissed the idea.

Once he was done and the area was dry, he found some disinfectant and poured it on the cuts, wincing as the excruciating pain hit, his tears filling his eyes. He imagined his bruised testicles turning completely black with infection and felt terrified they might fall off if too much damage had been done. Just to be safe, he also grabbed some antiseptic cream. His mother would notice the missing supplies, especially when his two younger brothers used up a lot of it over the next few days.

The three of them were in the kitchen when John said,

"How are we going to pay the money back?"

"No fucking idea," said Steve.

"We only have until Tuesday to get the money," he reminded them. "I know, I know. Give me a moment to think," their older brother replied. "He's not going to forgive us easily on this. He didn't even bring up his watch and chain."

"Fuck!"

They had amassed large gambling debts, but fortunately, they were able to take a significant amount from LeeRoy. They paid Jonno, a loan shark, with interest by giving him cash, the watch, and LeeRoy's chain—no questions asked.

They spent the remaining money on alcohol, gambling, records, clothes, women, and a new engine for the van—none of which they could trade in. The engagement ring, clearly valuable and eye-catching, was meant to be sold to their contact at the bowling alley that evening. "How much do we have left?" Steve asked. "About ten pounds," John replied. "Fucking hell!" John exclaimed. "Where are we going to get ninety pounds by Tuesday?" "Fuck knows!" Steve responded, running his hand through his hair.

"Ask Jonno to return the money?" Pete suggested. "You must be joking," snorted Steve. "What if we give him the ten pounds back and ask for some time to arrange the rest?"

"Yeah, I can see him going for that option, I don't think."

"Well, what other choice do we have? One of us needs to be at Faversham Station in two days, so who will be the lucky one?" Pete said.

"We'll have to draw straws for it," Steve replied, "but before that, we need to make a pact."

"A pact?" asked young John. "Yes, a pact that what happened in London stays in London – and we never tell anybody." The brothers looked at each other. "Well, I don't have a problem with that," said John. "I want nobody ever to find out what happened."

"Nor me," said Pete, "but it wasn't so bad for you." "Not so fucking bad?" shouted Steve. "I nearly lost my balls and knob, I still don't know if I have any permanent injury, and I'm not going to the doctors to find out. And you can guess what stick I would get if anybody found out. How are "ewe" today, ma-a-a-a-ah? What a little lamb—and crap like that! Believe me, I'll stay very quiet!"

"OK, that's settled then," muttered Pete. "Nothing more will ever be said about it."

"But who'll go back to meet him again on Tuesday?"

"Why don't we all go?" John suggested. "There's safety in numbers."

"No," Steve responded, "he said only one, and he's not the kind of guy you mess with."

"There's a deck of cards over there, so why don't we cut for it? The highest card wins," Pete said, walking across the room and opening a drawer in the sideboard. "It doesn't matter how we do it, but one of us has to go." He took out the cards, shuffled them, and placed them face down on the table.

"Youngest first," he said, as John took a cut of the cards and kept his pile face down until the others had cut. "Okay," Steve nodded to John. "Flip yours over. High card wins." John revealed his cards: a nine of spades. Steve showed a seven of hearts. Pete turned over a joker. John burst out laughing.

"Fucking hell! I'll have to cut again!" Pete did and showed the king of hearts.

"Looks like it's you then," Steve announced. "Never been very lucky at cards!" said Pete, staring at the accusing king as if he hoped it would change before his eyes. He swallowed. "So, what am I gonna tell him about the money being short?"

"No idea," said Steve, "but you've got all day tomorrow to think of something."

"Me? Thanks a lot for nothing!" he spat and thought for a moment. "Could ask Dad to lend us the money."

"Dad?" Steve snorted. "Fuck off! He ain't got a pot to piss in, and even if he did have, he sure wouldn't lend it to us."

"Yeah, I know," Pete ran his hand over his pale face. "I'm just grasping at straws! Fucking hell, that's the last time I con anybody."

Steve chimed in, "Might be an idea to go out tonight and con somebody else to raise the cash!"

"Fuck off," said John. "No fucking way!"

They all jumped at the sound of somebody opening the front door.

Their parents walked in.

"Oh, so you decided to come home then," said Mother, through tight lips clamped down on a Woodbine.

"Well, we do live here," said Steve.

"When it fucking suits you!" she said, whipping out the fag and jabbing it in the air to emphasise her words. "It's about time you lazy bastards got real jobs and your own homes. I'm not feeding you forever."

"Calm down, Mother," muttered Pete. "You know what it's like in Whitstable. Unless you're a fisherman or a millionaire, you're stuck in the middle with fuck all."

"And you'll always have fuck all if you don't put yourselves out," said Dad, switching on the TV and settling into his armchair, waiting for the set to warm up.

"Ah, come on," said Steve, "let's have a walk down to the harbour. I'm not in the mood to argue."

"Never fucking bothered you before," said Mother.

At the harbour, they sat on a bench looking at the fishing boats being unloaded.

"I wouldn't do that crappy job anyway," said Steve. "Stinky damn fish!" The other two muttered their agreement. John angrily threw a pebble into the sea. "There must be something we can do to get that £90."

"What, genius?" sneered Steve. "I don't know, but there's gotta be a way." "Well, when you find out what it is, let us know." Steve stood up, adjusting the crotch of his trousers to ease his discomfort. "Let's walk into town. It stinks here."

They walked past the Pearson's Arms and the alleyway where they had mugged LeeRoy; "Wished we'd never seen that poxy alleyway," scoffed Steve. The others grunted in agreement and walked on. They passed the restaurant and wandered across the road. The arcades were busy, and John stopped abruptly.

"What's up now?" said Steve.

"Look."

"Yeah, arcades. So what?"

"Look at all that money. Do you think they leave it in the machines at night?"

Steve and Pete latched onto what John was thinking.

"They may do," said Steve, "but what the fuck would we do with half a ton of pennies?"

"There might be pennies in the machines," John said, "but they must have notes, from when they give change for the machines."

"Hey, he might be onto something," Pete said.

"You could be right," Steve said, "but how do we get in? The main street is too brightly lit at night. Let's look around the back instead."

They walked as casually as possible around the block, where there was a car park. The back of the arcade buildings was nearby, separated by only a six-foot wooden fence.

"What do you think?" John asked, trying to hide his excitement.

"Well," Steve said, peering through a gap in the slats, "it seems straightforward to reach the building, but gaining entry might be another story. We won't know until we get there, and I highly doubt they'll leave the door unlocked like they did the other night."

Pete joined him, scanning the few windows and doors. "It's worth a try, though. Could solve our problem for sure."

"Alright, we'll come back tonight and see if we can get in. I'm going home to catch some sleep, I'm knackered," Steve said.

"Let's walk up to the bowling alley and get the van," Steve said. "That's if the damn animal didn't torch it, but I guess we'll soon find out."

Upon arrival, the van was in good condition. Although the engine spluttered from sitting cold for a few days, they drove it home and went to bed without saying a word to their parents, who were in the kitchen.

They woke up at 9 p.m. and drove down to the bowling alley, their usual hangout.

When they entered, Robert was by the bar. He noticed them approaching and panicked briefly, but he could only stand his ground, hoping they wouldn't realise he was the one who had informed on them. They recognised Robert but didn't like him, so they acknowledged him with a grunt and moved to the other end of the bar.

Robert took a deep breath, allowing his heart to slow down a bit.

Fuck! That was scary! he thought. *But they obviously don't know – and thank God for that.*

After several games of bowls, the brothers stayed until closing at 2 a.m. They drove to a shady spot behind the arcades and quickly climbed the fence. At the back door, they checked for alarms but found none.

"Give me that crowbar," Steve muttered, and he soon had the window by the door open. Being the smallest, John was hoisted inside first, then he opened the door for the others. Inside the office, a safe in the corner made their hearts sink.

"Fuck!" Steve gasped.

Unable to open the safe, they searched the office for other cash. Suddenly, a shout came from upstairs: "Who's down there? I've called the police!"

'Shit.' The brothers scurried to the door but were blocked by a large man in the doorway.

Steve punched him in the face before he could react, knocking him down. The brothers jumped over his sprawled body and ran, but the man grabbed Pete's ankle, tripping him.

"Fuck!"

Pete yelled, panicking, and stomped on the man's head with his other foot. The man let go immediately, groaning, and Pete caught up with the others.

The brothers ran like the wind, and when Steve jumped over the fence this time, he didn't think about his safety. The arcade owner was too shocked to chase after them, so they reached the van and drove away quickly before the owner could see their vehicle or describe it.

"Fucking hell!" Steve panted as they sped away. "That was close. I didn't think anyone was living there. We should hide the van in case he recognises it." As they turned onto Cromwell Road, a police car with flashing blue lights appeared right in front of them, heading straight at them. The police lights flashed, and the car swerved to the side, blocking the road. "Reverse!" Pete shouted.

But as Steve shifted into reverse, he noticed a dark sedan—probably another cop car—had pulled up right behind them. With no way out and dark figures already looming outside their van doors, they couldn't even run away.

"Fuck it," Steve breathed.

Two officers opened the van doors, one on the driver's side and one on the passenger side. "Turn off that engine and get out!" they ordered the lads. "Keys!" the largest cop demanded. Steve handed over the keys, and the officer went to check the back of the van where John was sitting, just as another police car arrived. "Get out!" he told John. All three were ordered to place their hands on the van's roof and spread their legs. They had no choice but to comply.

Lights were starting to come on in some of the nearby houses, and people were pulling back their curtains or opening their windows to see what was going on.

"What's the problem?" Steve asked the cop innocently.

"Shut up! We'll ask the questions!"

Police were searching the van, looking for any incriminating evidence.

Steve's eyes flicked nervously towards them because he knew they had stolen seat cushions in the back that they had nicked from a train. But the cops didn't seem to notice.

The police found nothing since the brothers had dropped the crowbar and left it behind when they were disturbed.

"Where have you just come from?" the cop asked.

"Timbuktu," Steve said.

The cop slapped him on the head. "Don't get smart with me, sonny – where the hell have you just come from?" "Faversham," Steve muttered.

"And what were you doing in Faversham?" "Shagging," Steve replied.

"Now I know you're lying," said the cop. "There aren't any girls in Faversham who are that desperate. I'll ask you one more time, or you're going to be arrested for obstruction."

"Who am I obstructing?" snapped Steve.

"Me, you fucking arsehole," the officer seethed. "Now – last chance – where have you just come from?"

"OK, OK. Nowhere specific. We've just been out driving." "Oh, I see. Just a country drive at three in the morning. Were you anywhere near Gladstone Road?"

"Fuck knows. Where's that?"

"Don't be a smart arse, you know exactly where it is. Just off the high street, back of the arcades."

"No, I haven't been anywhere near there tonight. Why?"

"Well, I think you have," the big cop leered in Steve's face. "And I think you just tried to rob the place."

"No way!" Steve shot back, outraged. "Where's your proof?"

"Don't worry. We'll get that soon enough. You're all under arrest for suspicion of breaking and entering. "Caution them, Constable."

All three were loudly protesting and were handcuffed, then placed in separate police cars to prevent them from making up stories on the way to Whitstable police station.

They were kept in separate cells for the same reason they arrived in separate cars: to prevent them from collaborating on a story. However, the two younger brothers understood that it was best to remain quiet and let Steve manage the situation.

They were held for a maximum of 24 hours without charge, interviewed one at a time, and all responded with "no comment" to every question, frustrating the police.

They were brought to an identity parade within those 24 hours, but the arcade owner, whose face was swollen and bruised, couldn't identify any of them with one eye completely closed.

They were released on police bail while awaiting further investigation. "Don't get too comfortable," the charge sergeant warned them as they departed. "It's only a matter of time." Since the police had driven their van to the station to impound it, the brothers reluctantly received their keys and personal belongings that had been confiscated before being locked up.

Once they were safely inside the van, Steve commented, "All we need to do is keep our mouths shut. They have no proof, and that tosser didn't ID us, so everything looks fine."

"Maybe it looks fine on that side," John replied, "but we still have a problem paying that guy back tomorrow morning."

"Yeah, I get it," Steve sighed. "All we can do is give him the cash we have and ask for more time to settle the rest—no other option. You can only ask," he told Pete. "He's not going to do anything at ten in the morning in broad daylight."

"I fucking well hope not," Pete responded.

They stayed indoors Monday night, too afraid to go out.

CHAPTER TWENTY-FOUR — *The Cost of Crossing LeeRoy*

On Monday morning, Julie was in the library with an atlas open, tracing the coast of South America. After LeeRoy shared his honeymoon plans, she went to the library to pick up books and learn more about them. She hadn't realised Peru was in South America, and she was unclear about the Caribbean's location.

They never covered this in school! She knew she wasn't unintelligent, but there was a lot she didn't understand, and she aimed to impress LeeRoy. She was much younger and less experienced than he was, especially since he was more street-smart and worldly.

One day, she dreamed of being as clever as LeeRoy and becoming the wife he truly deserved. While she knew she was enough for him and felt secure in his love, she still longed to please him. She aimed to better herself, not only for him but also for her own growth.

LeeRoy had restored her confidence. All the confidence that had been knocked out of her at the children's home and taken away by the attempted rapes, he had helped her rebuild herself and made her feel whole. She wanted to do something for him in return.

As the initial excitement of wedding planning faded, she began researching their honeymoon destinations. Learning about Jamaica brought her closer to LeeRoy and his family's heritage. She also wanted to know about Machu Picchu and Peru. By the end of her research, she might even surprise him with her new knowledge of Mayan culture - or was it the Inca culture? She wasn't entirely sure. Clearly, she had some catching up to do.

She went to the library desk, beaming with anticipation, and eagerly waited for her stack of books to be stamped. Her eyes sparkled with joy. The librarian watched her, amused. She had never seen a teenager so excited to check out a few history and geography books.

Maybe there was hope for the younger generation, after all.

The next morning, Pete reluctantly boarded the train from Whitstable and arrived at Faversham station at 9:55 a.m. Worried about being late and missing LeeRoy, Pete quickly headed for the exit and looked around outside. LeeRoy was waiting in his Rolls-Royce, with the window down, signalling toward Pete. After a brief pause, Pete thought about his next move, then approached, feeling uneasy.

"Get in," LeeRoy commanded.

Pete thought, fuck it, I didn't expect to be forced into a car. Fuck.

He quickly looked for an excuse to refuse, but nothing came to mind, so he opened the passenger door and got inside. LeeRoy started the engine. "Where are you taking me?" Pete's voice trembled.

Don't worry, scumbag. Just around the corner."

Pete felt no more reassured. LeeRoy was alone now, but he could easily meet up with his thugs at any moment. Pete's glance darted to the car door handle, estimating how quickly he could jump out of the Rolls while it was moving.

LeeRoy drove to the recreation park and pulled into a parking bay. He glanced at Pete. "Well?"

Pete handed LeeRoy a brown paper bag. As soon as LeeRoy took it, he noticed it was light. He balanced it in his hand, feeling its weight, and looked directly at Pete.

"I don't think all my money is here," LeeRoy said calmly.

We need some time to get it," Pete gulped, dread in his voice about what might happen next.

LeeRoy said nothing, locking eyes with him, and said, "Looks like you're in a bit of trouble, doesn't it? You clearly liked our Sid."

"Please, mister," Pete started to beg. "We'll get it for you, but it's not easy."

"Not fucking easy?" LeeRoy yelled. "You found it easy to steal it from me!"

Pete could see that LeeRoy was getting very angry. "I'm sorry, we promise to get it. We won't let you down."

"That, my friend, I can guarantee." He stood up. "Let me think—wait here." LeeRoy stepped out and strolled across the park. Pete sat, his knee bouncing nervously, contemplating leaving a dozen times. But since LeeRoy knew where they lived and could find them anywhere, Pete stayed in the car, watching LeeRoy's muscular figure pacing the grass and lost in thought. His mouth was dry as he waited for what was to come.

LeeRoy returned, climbed back into the Roller, and asked, "Do you boys have passports?"

"No, why?"

"Because you're going on a little trip."

"Trip?" Pete's mind jumped to a submarine ride in a concrete suit.

"Right, listen." LeeRoy jabbed a finger into Pete's chest. "This is what you're gonna do. You go to the post office and get yourselves a one-year passport. I assume you low lives have got birth certificates?"

"I guess so," Pete replied, wondering if his mother had a hiding place for such things. He didn't have a clue.

"Get them, then go to a travel agent and book a day trip to France."

"France?" Pete asked, confused. "We've never travelled abroad." "I don't care. You're going now." "Why?" "I'll explain later. Get the passports and arrange a day trip to Calais for next Saturday." "How can we do that?" Pete asked, puzzled. "You've got every last penny we had."

LeeRoy reached into the paper bag, tossed the remaining £10 back at Pete, and handed him another £20. "There. You owe me even more now until I say it's paid off. Now, get out and get lost. You can walk back to the station. I'll be in touch. I've got your phone number, your address, and everything else I need to find you."

Pete took off, relieved to get away unscathed.

"Well?" asked Steve when Pete got back home.

"He gave me the ten quid back and another £20."

"What?" Steve said in disbelief. "Why?"

"Coz he likes me."

"Don't be a tosser."

Pete told them about the deal and how they had to get passports and day tickets to Calais.

"What does he have in store for us out there?" John asked nervously. "We'll likely vanish and never be seen again." "No, I don't think it's that," Pete said. "I suspect he wants us to bring something back—probably drugs."

John reacted sharply: "Fucking hell! If we're caught with drugs, we'll spend ten years in prison." "If we don't follow his orders, that freak will mess us up badly and bury us somewhere on a construction site. I'd rather take the chance." "Me too," Steve agreed.

"Why?" said John. "He didn't fuck you."

"That perv tried, but I was just lucky (if you can call what they did to my nuts lucky) that he couldn't get it up again. He didn't bury me under a building either. But whatever he wants, we have no choice."

They went to the post office the next day and picked up their passports, then bought day tickets.

That evening, the phone rang, and their mother answered, "Ello."

The voice on the other end said. " Can I speak to Pete, please? "

"Who's that?" "Just a friend," LeeRoy replied. "Didn't know he had any friends," she said, smirking as she looked down at Pete sprawled across the couch as if it were his own.

"It's for you. When did I become your secretary? About time you useless lumps of flesh got jobs and paid something to help with the phone bill and slammed the phone down on the table."

Pete staggered off the couch and grabbed the phone, dread filling him. "Hello."

It was LeeRoy's unmistakable voice. "I want you on the train to Faversham, getting in at nine o'clock tonight."

"We're going bowling tonight," Pete explained.

"Get on that fucking train!" LeeRoy yelled. "I'll be waiting for you," he added before slamming the receiver down.

Pete spoke quietly to his brothers, out of their parents' hearing, and they all agreed they had no other option.

Their train arrived at Faversham station at 8:55 p.m., and they quickly headed outside.

LeeRoy was leaning out of his Rolls-Royce's window. "I hope you're clean. Get in the back."

They didn't dare disobey or question him, sitting in the back like naughty little children.

He drove to the fishing lakes near Bysing Woods and pulled over. It was dark and eerie, and the three boys shifted nervously in their seats, frightened of the unknown. They feared this man. Steve noticed that his younger brothers were paralyzed by fear. Their wide eyes reflected the moonlight, and they were gasping quickly, their breathing loud enough to be heard.

LeeRoy sat quietly in the darkness, the tension around him palpable. Steve couldn't bear the suspense anymore. "Why did you bring us out here?"

"Just wanted to show you something," said LeeRoy quietly. "What?"

"That fishing lake." He nodded toward the distant, dark, shimmering expanse. "It has so many pike that they must eat each other to survive." "So?" said Steve.

"So," LeeRoy said, "if you fuck up on Saturday, that's where you'll end up – as fish food. They'll strip you clean in thirty minutes." The guys said nothing, staring out into the darkness, each lost in his own fear. LeeRoy kept going, restarting the engine. "Or there's one more option."

He drove again, climbing the hill, turning right onto Bysing Wood Road, and entering Oare. The brothers exchanged nervous glances, too tense to speak. They passed the Three Mariners and the Castle Inn silently. Crossing the creek, LeeRoy turned left, following it for nearly a mile, then slowed as they approached a long, low building surrounded by a fence.

"What the fuck?" John whispered.

They drove through the gates at less than walking pace, and the lads couldn't help but be aware of the disturbing stench of rotting flesh that seeped into the car. It stank like hell. A single dim security light cast a ghostly glow over a horrifying sight silhouetted against the sky. It took their breath away in more ways than one. They sat there, mouths agape in horror, as they covered their noses to block the overpowering, foul smell. John began retching, while LeeRoy stopped the car. "Get out." They complied without hesitation.

Ahead of them stretched a mountain of corpses: stiff, spindly limbs jaggedly protruding from the heap. The faint light revealed details that only disgusted them more: dead, dull, film-covered eyes; filthy, tangled hair; and fragile bodies with bony ribs. John bent over to vomit, his stomach rebelling against the stench and horrifying sight. Hooves, fur, ears, tails, muzzles, and snouts completed the scene in an otherwise grey, oozing jumble of dead animals.

"Do you know what this factory does?" asked LeeRoy, standing with his hands on his hips, as if surveying his estate.

"No," said one of them.

Well, I'll tell you. They take all those dead animals, put them in those big ovens," he pointed to them, "and cook them until all the fat drains out into containers and the flesh melts away. The bones are then sent through that crusher over there and made into bone meal."

The brothers didn't need to be told why they were being shown this place. They were certain that a few people had already been processed here. "So," said LeeRoy, "fuck up, or cross me, and it's the lake or this place. You'll hope it's the lake because we'll top you first – in this place, you go in the cooker alive."

"Mister," Steve cleared his throat. "We'll do what you want us to."

"I am confident about that, but remember, I don't tolerate failure," LeeRoy warned. "So tomorrow morning, you'll catch the 8:30 ferry from Dover to Calais. You'll explore Calais, visit a few bars, and have some drinks—just enough to avoid getting drunk or attracting too much attention. At 2:30, you'll be sitting outside Bar Carousel on Rue du Four à Chaux, drinking a beer." "What is that?" asked Steve.

"Shut up. It's a café that serves beer. I've written it down, but I thought you all couldn't read." He continued, "You'll receive three shopping bags filled with duty-free bottles. When passing through Customs in France, act a little tipsy — but not too much. They'll be glad to see the back of you, so you shouldn't have any issues. Do the same when returning to England. If you get stopped, that's on you. Snitch, and you're dead. Understand?"

"Yeah, yeah, don't worry," the guys nodded and agreed.

"I'm not concerned," LeeRoy said, "but you three should be. When you return, take the A2 heading toward Lydden, and there's a lay-by just before the turn-off. A dark blue Jag will be waiting there."

This was blowing Pete's mind. He hoped his brothers were paying attention because to him, it seemed like a lot to take in.

LeeRoy kept explaining. "Make sure no one's watching, then take the three bags and put them in the Jag's boot, which will be open. Shut it firmly, then get back in your van and drive off. Got it?"

"Yeah, then we're good, right?" Steve asked.

"No!" LeeRoy laughed, as if he were joking. "Not until I'm paid back – and with interest too."

"What do you mean?" John muttered. "We have to do it again?"

"Yes, you do," LeeRoy said. "Over and over, until I say otherwise, or until you get caught." He got back into the car. "Now get lost, and I'll contact you—unless you're locked up in a French jail," he laughed.

"Hey!" Pete said, startled at the thought of being left with this mess, in the dark, miles from anywhere. "Can't you give us a ride back to the station, please?"

LeeRoy glared at him, his eyes piercing. "Maybe I could, this time. Get in and make sure you wipe any dirt off your shoes first. You need to be fresh for your big overseas trip, don't you?" As the guys settled into the Rolls, he added, "Now shut up. I don't like the sound of your voices."

Nor yours, thought Steve, but he wasn't brave enough to say it out loud.

Despite feeling hesitant, the brothers were excited about traveling abroad for the first time, especially on a ship! As they boarded the ferry, they marvelled at its size. They quickly found the bar, happy it was open and serving drinks, and they ordered three beers, even though it was only 8 a.m.

As the ferry set off on schedule, the sea was initially calm, but after about thirty minutes, a sudden gust of wind caused the ship to lurch. John was already feeling queasy from the gentle sway and the disorienting feeling of being at sea.

Before long, he was seasick. With no way to reach the side of the ship or the toilets, he threw up all over the bar floor, splattering his boots and his brothers. The smell and sight of that, along with the unpredictable swaying of the ship, quickly caused his brothers to do the same.

They spent the remainder of the journey in the ship's bathrooms, slumped over cubicles, toilet bowls, or sinks, groaning and occasionally lifting their heads with dazed eyes, mucus and vomit hanging from their chins as they moved with the ship's rocking.

By the time they reached France and the calm waters of Calais harbour, they were still in bad shape. On land, they still felt as if the ground was swaying beneath them, and they moved carefully, their sense of balance completely off. "Fuck that," Pete said. "I just wanted to die." "I understand how you feel," Steve responded. "That was horrible!" They felt somewhat better but were already dreading the return journey.

They breezed through Customs without any issues, found the bus station, and arrived in Calais by 11:45 am, local time. However, they had no idea that France was an hour ahead of British time and thought it was only 10:45 am. Of course, they went out drinking. They didn't realise the French beer was stronger than what they were used to, and they soon became completely drunk. They remembered to stop by the Bar Carousel, but, naturally, they were an hour late. Luckily, they didn't miss the messenger: the owner, Michel, was the one with their bags. He gave them a stern talking-to in French, which they didn't understand at all. Luckily, he spoke good English and managed to explain that there was a time difference, and they hadn't adjusted their watches.

Pete immediately started mocking Michel's accent, "Ah, this we did not know. Murky buckets, Mon sewer!"

Michel looked annoyed. When he introduced himself and told them his name, Steve remarked, "Michelle? That's a girl's name!" John then began singing the Beatles' song "Michelle," and the others joined in loudly, singing, "Michelle – ma belle! Hon-hee-hon-heehon!"

Michel was furious and gripped Steve by the lapels, pulling him up, staring directly into his eyes, and saying, while breathing garlic-scented breath all over him. "You'd better sober up before going through Customs," he told them. "You don't want to draw too much attention, YOU FUCKING UNDERSTAND?" Then, he pushed him back down into his chair.

Pissed and overconfident now, they ignored him and tried to order three more beers.

Michel could tell this was all going to go downhill quickly, so he said, "I'm giving you only one drink: a shandy. And you'll sit here until it's time to go. L told me you were idiots."

"Ah, thanks very much," winked Pete. "At least we know the mystery man's name starts with L, now."

"Maybe," Michel warned. "But if you know what's good for you, you'll forget it quickly. What time does your ferry leave?" "5:15," Steve answered. "Alright," Michel replied. "I'll arrange a taxi to pick you up at 4 p.m. Just stay put."

"Can't we have another beer?" John said sulkily.

"No, you can't. I've changed my mind. You're not even getting a Panache."

"A what?" asked Steve. "What's a whatever you said?"

He repeated, "Panache, shandy to you ignoramuses."

"You can have a sandwich and coffee to help you sober up. If you mess this up, you know what'll happen. I've been told to mention 'Sid.'"

"Fuck off," said Steve under his breath, not wanting to piss him off more. "Don't worry," Steve tried to straighten up. "We'll be OK."

"I'm not so sure about that."

Michel brought out the sandwiches and coffee for them, then made them pay. Steve, surprised, took out some francs that LeeRoy had given him and reluctantly handed them over. They had thought they were special and would get them for free. They were wrong again!

They sat smoking, eating, and drinking coffee, their wooziness and volume fading.

"What's in the bags?" John asked finally, taking a look into the carrier bag at the duty-free bottles. "We could definitely have a drink!"

"That might not be a good idea," Steve cautioned, realising things were getting out of control. As the older brother, he knew he had to get the guys under control before they ended up in trouble–or worse. "Save it for later. This is fucking—" he shook his head, unable to find the words to describe what this was. His younger brothers exchanged nervous glances, stunned into silence. They then ordered more coffee and spoke quietly about football, their earlier bravado fading. As time passed and the alcohol's effects wore off, they became more subdued. The taxi arrived promptly.

They would also need to cover the cost. In the cab, Steve fiddled with the franc notes in his wallet, running his fingers over them.

"There won't be much left of what L gave us," he said sceptically, "I thought we would have enough to get some duty-free fags, but it's not looking promising.

"L? Getting to know him, huh?"

"Well, we don't know his full name. We only know it starts with 'L.'"

"It should start with 'C,' John interjected. 'Cunt!'"

"Mr. Brave, aren't we?" Pete snorted. "Next time you see him, call him that."

They were dropped off by the taxi driver who, unknowingly to them, ripped them off. It was France, and they were using francs, which were completely unfamiliar to them.

They proceeded to Passport Control and then Customs.

"Just walk straight through," Steve whispered.

"Piece of cake."

"Let's say that once we're on the other side," he replied.

They had enough Francs left to buy a pack of 200 cigarettes.

The ferry pulled into port right on time at 5:40 p.m. UK time, and this time, the others knew to adjust their watches accordingly. They went through passport control, acting a little pissed, but not overacting.

Then came customs. If something had gone wrong, it would have been there. Each brother was carrying his duty-free bags, and to their surprise, the customs officers didn't even glance at them. They were in the clear and stepped out into the fresh English air, finally able to breathe. "Told you!" laughed Steve, starting to feel cocky again. "Easy peasy!" "Sure was," said John, relieved. They walked to the car park, got into the van, and drove out of the harbour, up the steep hill, and onto the lay-by. This had been way too easy. They spotted the Jag, parked behind it, and without even speaking to the driver, who didn't even turn around, they tossed the bags in the boot. As soon as they slammed it shut, the car was gone.

"Well," said Steve, "how fucking easy was all that?" "Too easy," said John.

They drove home.

Over the next five months, LeeRoy organised five more trips to France and Belgium for the brothers, and each trip went smoothly. The brothers enjoyed their days traveling freely and the duty-free cigarettes. On their sixth trip, they drank too much, and at French customs, Pete accidentally dropped his duty-free items next to a Customs officer. A bottle of wine broke, and the plastic bag burst open.

The Customs officer wasn't too worried until the younger brother lunged for the bag, slipped, and spilled both his and Pete's belongings on the floor. The officer quickly noticed the suspicious brown paper packages spilling out. There was a lot of shouting in French, and within seconds, several armed gendarmes had the three brothers on the ground and handcuffed. They were taken to a back room where they were strip-searched and their bags emptied. Each bag contained one kilogram of cocaine. The brothers realized they were in serious trouble, as they were officially arrested, charged, and held in custody.

When LeeRoy found out, he was more upset about losing his stuff than anything else. He didn't give a shit about the brothers. But they'd paid back what they'd taken and even added thousands on top of that.

The brothers eventually went to trial for drug trafficking. They were found guilty and each was sentenced to 10 years in prison.

LeeRoy heard the news and thought. *Too bad, but that's just how it is*. He never bothered to think about them again.

Besides, he and Julie had other things on their minds as the wedding drew near.

CHAPTER TWENTY-FIVE *From Wedding Bells to Prison Cells*

The big day finally arrived. It was shaping up to be an extravagant event. As LeeRoy had promised, it would be top hat and tails—the whole traditional setup. He was determined to make it unforgettable for Julie. The wedding was scheduled for 2:30 p.m. at St. Mary's Church of Charity. Sadly, neither LeeRoy's sister nor his mother could attend from Jamaica—his mother was too ill to travel, and Rosina stayed behind to care for her. The church was filled with over 150 guests, all from LeeRoy's side, since Julie had no known relatives. LeeRoy made sure everyone knew this, so the guests comfortably filled both sides of the aisle.

Julie wasn't bothered by it; she was marrying the man she loved deeply. She now saw Giles as family because of how close they'd become, and he was giving her away that day. The other three barmaids were her bridesmaids.

She had considered contacting the orphanage and inviting some of her friends there, but decided not to in case the horrible matron insisted on accompanying them.

As Julie walked downstairs, surrounded by the other girls, it was as if a bolt of lightning had struck Giles.

His ears seemed to buzz, and his focus narrowed to the dazzling vision before him.

Julie's blonde hair was adorned with tiny glass crystals, piled on top of her head beneath a delicate lace veil, making her beautiful face appear small and elfin. Her wide blue eyes looked larger and more expressive than ever. The girls had wanted to go all out with her makeup, but Julie had restrained them. Still, she was stunningly beautiful, and in her elegant white gown, she looked radiant, like a model in a magazine, sophisticated.

Giles had always seen her as a pretty teenager, but now she was a stunning adult woman. Her presence took his breath away. She smiled brightly, and to Giles, it was like the sun shining on the first day of spring.

"Will I do?" she asked.

Giles was momentarily speechless, his throat tightening and tears welling in his eyes. His mouth gaped, but no sound emerged.

He felt foolish and humiliated, though he couldn't understand why. Julie suddenly burst into laughter, her voice ringing in his ears like tinkling bells.

Although it was initially overcast, the sun now shone brightly. Chas, as LeeRoy's best man, was there when LeeRoy arrived at the church in his white Rolls-Royce, thirty minutes early. They stood outside, soaking up the sunshine, as LeeRoy tried to hide his nerves. Chas stood beside him, offering reassurance. "Hey, she might not show up," Chas joked. LeeRoy frowned, but they both headed into the church.

Julie arrived in a stunning white carriage pulled by four gleaming white horses, with Giles beside her. "Are you okay?" he asked. She smiled, feeling better than fine. The bad weather earlier hadn't bothered her. They arrived at the church five minutes past the scheduled time, exactly as planned.

As the Wedding March began playing, Julie entered the church. She looked stunning in her elegant white gown, her long train carried by three bridesmaids dressed in pink, as she walked down the aisle, arm in arm with Giles. He felt a surge of pride, his chest swelling with emotion. His love for her was as deep as LeeRoy's.

LeeRoy remained facing forward, noticing only the gasps of admiration behind him as Julie approached. When they reached him, he glanced at Julie and felt his heart skip a beat. She looked stunning—completely his. He felt fortunate. When the vicar asked if he took this woman as his wife, he couldn't wait to say, "I do," and as they were declared "man and wife," LeeRoy almost shouted with happiness.

The young photographer from Universal Photo Services, next door to The Hole in the Wall, was busy organising the groups and taking all the photos.

He asked Julie to tell him when she would toss her bouquet, as tradition required, but she kept it and asked LeeRoy, "Can you walk with me to Barrie's grave, please?" with tears in her eyes, then paused all the photo-taking.

Leaving the guests to talk on the church lawn, they moved to the back of the church, where Barrie's grave was. The grass looked fresh, with a few new blades sprouting, and the wooden cross marking the headstone was still bright in the sunlight.

Julie stood silently in prayer, then placed her bouquet on the grave, close to the base of the simple cross. She was crying, and this sad moment was a stark contrast to the joyful day.

"Will his family ever find him?" she asked LeeRoy softly.

LeeRoy thoughtfully pressed his lips together. "I have no idea, but I promise that when we get back from our honeymoon, I'll arrange for a better headstone for him. If you'd like, I can even hire a private detective to try and find them."

"That would be so nice, LeeRoy," her tear-filled eyes shining with gratitude and love. "You're a softy on the inside." She only knew one side of him.

LeeRoy handed Julie his hanky, and she dried her eyes.

She cleared her throat, shook out a shudder of her shoulders, and said more brightly, "We'd better get back to our guests."

The only suitable venue in town for the reception was the Ship Inn on Court Street, a sixteenth-century establishment that served as a key stop for coaches traveling between London and Dover. Julie's horse-drawn carriage fit right in as it entered the courtyard through the archway, a place once frequented by thousands of travellers, military personnel, merchants, and many others over the centuries.

"This spread's fit for Henry the Eighth!" Chas exclaimed, clearly impressed by the sight of tables laden with an array of dishes – from lobster and caviar to chicken drumsticks and sausage rolls.

"Since when did Henry the Eighth eat sausage rolls?" Val said dismissively. "Well, that Marie Antoinette bird ate cake, didn't she?" he responded, surprising Julie with his unexpected knowledge of history.

Julie couldn't help but smile at LeeRoy's arrangement for lobster to be served. It took her back to the first time she tasted it, with LeeRoy's encouragement—the same night he proposed.

He truly thinks of everything!

They all had a fantastic time, with plenty of drinks and no trouble, although there were going to be some massive hangovers the next morning. LeeRoy and Julie left the reception at 11 p.m. and were driven home in LeeRoy's Rolls-Royce by Giles, who stayed sober just for that occasion.

They had decided to stay at home that night and the following day because they were leaving for Jamaica on Monday, giving them time to relax and recover from their long day.

They had both been eagerly anticipating consummating their marriage that night, but since they were both utterly exhausted, they embraced and fell asleep. They made up for it the next morning.

Monday morning arrived. Check-in was quick and easy since they were, of course, travelling first class with British Airways to Kingston, Jamaica.

Julie had never experienced anything like it. Besides it being her first plane trip, the ten-hour flight was pure luxury. They ate, drank, and slept on the long journey, and several hours later, they arrived, cleared customs, and where LeeRoy had another surprise waiting outside for Julie.

He had arranged for them to be flown to Montego Bay by helicopter after a sightseeing tour of the island.

Julie was so excited that she was speechless.

Bexhill to Montego Bay, I must be dreaming! She looked out of the helicopter window, smiling so much her face hurt. To LeeRoy's surprise, she knew a lot about the island.

"They must be the Blue Mountains!" she exclaimed, pointing. "Did you know they stretch for over forty miles through Surrey and part of Middlesex? It's funny to think we're all this way, and we're in Surrey! Is that the Rio Grande River?"

LeeRoy laughed in disbelief. Julie never failed to surprise and delight him.

"Hey! Who is giving this guided tour?" the pilot complained good-humouredly over his microphone.

They reached the hotel in just over an hour, thanks to its own helipad.

They checked in and had a wonderful week, mostly lounging around, but also enjoying some downtime and dining out.

Julie still refused to go for a swim in the ocean, despite LeeRoy's promise to teach her. She was tempted to try paddleboarding but backed out at the last second.

They visited LeeRoy's mother, who was feeling much better after her illness, and also caught up with Rosina. LeeRoy's mother was delighted with this charming girl, who seemed to have softened her handsome son.

Julie was just as happy to meet his warm, down-to-earth mother, even if only briefly.

It all passed by way too fast.

Next, they planned to go to Peru, where LeeRoy was set to meet his friend Tino. After some hesitation, Julie finally agreed to attempt the hike up to Machu Picchu.

In for a penny, in for a pound, she had thought. Besides, from what she'd read, it was an incredible sight – once in a lifetime, and it just had to be done.

Little did Julie know, LeeRoy had booked them an extra week at a hotel there after the hike.

He told her the news while flying back to Kingston in the helicopter. "LeeRoy, you're insane! I can't even imagine how much this must have cost!" She shook her head, aware that LeeRoy was wealthy but acting like a millionaire, and she didn't feel she needed all of that.

"Don't worry your pretty little head about it, Julie," he laughed. "This is my one and only shot at getting married, so why not? Just enjoy and make the most of it. Besides, you'll need a break after climbing that mountain!"

"You told me it was going to be easy," she said, playfully punching him.

It was a short four-hour flight to Lima, followed by another hour and a half to Cusco. At the airport, they were greeted by a chauffeur in a brand-new Rolls-Royce.

"Seems like all your friends drive Rollers," Julie said. "Who is this guy, anyway, and how do you know him?"

"LeeRoy shrugged. "Business."

"What kind of business?"

"Nothing you need to worry about," LeeRoy said, leaving it at that. Julie raised an eyebrow.

They reached a mansion on the outskirts of Cusco, with towering stone walls and guarded by armed guards at the large steel gates.

Julie's eyes widened as she looked at LeeRoy, but he stayed calm. This was just another day. The gates opened when they arrived, and they continued down a long, curved driveway lined with trees.

The Rolls-Royce rolled into a spacious courtyard and stopped in front of the grand double-polished mahogany doors guarded by two men. One door swung open, revealing a tall, copper-skinned man dressed perfectly.

He had small, dark eyes, a sloping nose, and a high forehead that gave him a regal appearance. He resembled an Inca from the books Julie had read. The man opened Julie's car door and offered his hand to help her out. She was impressed.

"You must be Julie," he said flawlessly in English. "And I have to mention, LeeRoy's description of you was completely inaccurate. You're more stunning than an angel," he told her, as he kissed her hand. Julie blushed, yet a surge of pride welled up inside her.

"May I introduce myself? My name is Agustino Montana, Tino to my friends, at your service."

"Hello, Agustino, sorry, Tino," she said, charmed. "That's an unusual name. Is it Peruvian?" "No, my dear. It's a Spanish name that means majestic and dignified, which I hope you'll find me to be," he said with a teasing smile.

She laughed. "I'm sure I won't be disappointed."

LeeRoy looked at her with admiration. He appreciated that he could take Julie anywhere, and despite her youth, she seemed unfazed by anything she faced. She was confident but never arrogant. She was beautiful but humble, with a natural demeanour that allowed her to handle any situation. While he wanted to protect and care for her, he recognised her inner strength. He felt lucky and knew he was fortunate.

Agustino walked around to the other side of the car and hugged his old pal, LeeRoy. "It's good to see you again, my friend.

It's been too long."

"Yes, I know. But you know how it is," LeeRoy shrugged.

"Time flies, and you have no idea where it's gone."

"That, my friend, I agree," Agustino said, raising an elegant finger toward LeeRoy before motioning them to come closer. "Now, come on in. We have a lot of catching up to do."

Two of Agustino's armed guards opened one heavy mahogany door each, and they stepped inside.

Julie was mesmerised by the spectacular entrance hall. A large chandelier hung in the centre, while on each side, a mahogany staircase curved up alongside walls adorned with very expensive-looking oil paintings. If these are original artworks, Julie thought, staring in awe, they must be worth millions!

She noticed that the double staircase connected at the top and led into a spacious minstrel gallery that overlooked the hall. Once more, Julie was quite impressed with LeeRoy's friend.

They proceeded along the hallway and entered a spacious reception area through a large mahogany door.

"Please, take a seat, and we'll mark your arrival with a bottle of champagne."

Julie couldn't help but stare in amazement. On one side of the room, large glass doors opened to a spacious indoor swimming pool, with a view that extended to the distant mountains.

This guy must have found the Inca gold! she thought to herself.

They settled into plush leather sofas, and as the massive doors swung open again, two servants entered with champagne and glasses. They poured four glasses, and Julie wondered who the fourth was for.

Then the door opened, and a striking woman of Spanish appearance entered. She was not only beautiful but also remarkably graceful in her well-fitted designer attire and high heels.

"Ah, may I introduce my wife, Lucia?" Agustino said, turning to her. "Lucia, this is Julie. And you know LeeRoy, of course."
"Hello, Julie. Nice to meet you," Lucia said with a perfect, yet distinctly Spanish-English accent. "It's about time someone managed to tame LeeRoy," she laughed.

"That remains to be seen," Julie replied. "But it's a pleasure to meet you, Lucia. You have a lovely home!" Her eyes swept around the room. "I'm enjoying what I've seen so far." "Come with me, and I'll give you a tour," Lucia said with a smile, extending her slender hand to Julie. "Bring your drink. I'm sure the boys have plenty to talk about, which we're not interested in anyway."

"Sounds great," Julie said, and they began the tour.

Agostino's gaze followed the girls as they departed, but he kept talking to LeeRoy. "Since you're only here for two days, LeeRoy, we need to go over a few things."

"Sure. Fire away."

"OK," said Agustino. "When you get back from your wild hike, you'll stay here for a few days, and I'll update you on everything then."

"Sounds like a plan to me, my friend."

Augustino shook hands with LeeRoy and said, "I believe you'd like to freshen up before dinner. I'll show you to your room, and I'll ask Lucia to bring Julie up once they finish their tour and have had a long talk, I'd assume, and see you at dinner at 8 p.m.."

When Lucia showed Julie to their room, ten minutes later, she entered and immediately exclaimed to LeeRoy, "What a house! I've never seen anything like it. I thought your house was a palace. Did he find the Inca gold?"

"Something like that, and it's our house now, not mine anymore," grinned LeeRoy.

They showered and rested before a king's dinner. Afterwards, they moved to the luxurious lounge for coffee, then enjoyed more champagne while chatting, before retiring early. They faced five challenging days ahead.

Early the next morning, Agustino personally took them to the meeting point for their trek. He found the guide and three others, all from the United States, who were with the same guide. Among them were two girls, Tansy and Lilac, whose names Julie found unusual but didn't mention. The man's name was also unusual to Julie—Ajax. He later explained that it originates from Greek mythology and means "of the earth." Ajax is a hero mentioned in Homer's Iliad, also known as "Ajax the Great." Julie was curious but not particularly interested. The guide's name was Mateo.

They gathered in a small clearing, surrounded by several small buildings, buses, and many other trekkers with their guides.

A young girl was selling bamboo poles decorated with ribbons and fabrics. She knew a little English and said they were for good luck, and they would help people climb steep slopes. LeeRoy bought two, and since they only cost about one pound in English money, he gave her twice that amount. The girl was very grateful and followed them until they boarded the coach, then waved goodbye as they headed toward the mountains and the starting point.

Julie was both excited and nervous; her only previous adventure was walking away from the orphanage.

The scenery was breathtaking, the weather perfect, and she was celebrating her honeymoon. As she jostled along the rough mountain trail, she closed her eyes, thinking about what had happened to her shortly after her escape. Her thoughts were broken when LeeRoy tapped her on the knee and pointed across a small river to a herd of llamas grazing on the hillside.

"Oh, wow," she exclaimed excitedly. "They sure look unusual, like tiny giraffes. Before I started researching Peru, I hadn't heard of llamas. They are lovely—can we bring one home? It would love your garden," she giggled.

"I doubt Giles would be happy if it started eating all the plants, so I think it's best not to, don't you?" Before she could answer, he took her hand and squeezed it gently; they were deeply in love and enjoying their getaway.

They approached a left turn, and in front of them was a bridge that LeeRoy thought would definitely not support a person crossing it, let alone a bus.

The bus stopped behind three other buses, and he noticed people getting off. Mateo spoke over the dilapidated intercom system. "We need to get off here. Although the bridge is safe, we are not allowed to cross with passengers on board, so you will need to get off, and once the bus has crossed, you can walk across and get back on." They did as they were told and watched the three other buses cross one by one, with the passengers following successfully. Julie was very hesitant when it came to their turn to cross. The bus had gone over okay, but she wasn't happy.

They started crossing a shaky wooden plank walkway with cracks and gaps, watching the fast-moving river below. She sighed in relief once she stepped onto solid ground again.

"I hope we don't encounter much more of that on the rest of the trip," she said as she cuddled up to LeeRoy after they got back on the bus and settled in again. "Well, this is Peru, not Faversham. Anyway, I thought you would be used to an old bus." He suddenly stopped, realising what he had just said and noticing the sadness and horror on Julie's face. LeeRoy quickly apologised for speaking impulsively. She nodded and said nothing, gazing out the bus window in hopes of spotting more llamas or even alpacas.

After two more hours on perilous, bone-jarring, narrow cliffside paths—barely roads—the group reached a small settlement. Mateo announced they would stop there for a break and mentioned that food and drinks were available if they wanted them.

Everyone was eager to get outside and stretch their legs. LeeRoy, Julie, and the other three group members found a small café, or more like someone's living room. The space seemed clean, so they took a look at the minimal menu, although none of them could understand anything on it.

Mateo was close by, so they asked him if he could translate it for them.

"Yes, of course," and he started to read from the top.

Ceviche is very tasty, it's considered our national dish and has a variety of local ingredients, including raw fish marinated in lime juice." Julie immediately decided against that one.

The second option is Lomo Saltado, a stir-fry with marinated beef, onions, tomatoes, and soy sauce. Julie was interested in that choice but wanted to wait and see what the final option would be.

"This dish is called 'Cuy,' a traditional Peruvian dish made from guinea pig." He was about to keep explaining when Julie and the other two girls all cut him off at once, saying, "No way, how can you eat a pet?"

Mateo clarified that guinea pigs are not traditionally kept as pets in Peru. They are not pigs, nor do they live in the wild; instead, they are bred specifically for food by the people of the Andes.

"I don't care," Julie said. "I'm not eating a little furry pet." The other two girls agreed. LeeRoy and Mateo found the situation amusing and were laughing at them. "It's not funny," Tansy snapped.

They all ordered the other two dishes; the guinea pig tempted LeeRoy, but he didn't dare try it, fearing he would upset Julie and the other girls. Everyone ordered Inca Kola to go with their lunch.

The next part of their journey was just 45 minutes away. They reached what was essentially the base camp, where they met the eight porters and handed over their luggage for the trip, which was limited to twenty kilos; all they carried was a backpack with water and other essentials.

"OK, are we all ready?" Mateo asked. They confirmed they were. "It's just an hour to our first night stop — nothing too demanding for your first day. OK, follow me."

They set off up a gentle incline, with stunning scenery as they looked down into a steep valley where a small river meandered into the distance.

The hour passed quietly as they reached a small plateau. To their surprise, the porters had somehow arrived ahead of them, and the camp was already set up with tea and coffee ready, as the sun was setting behind the distant mountains. It was warm and calm, with no wind at all.

They all found their tents and dropped off their backpacks before returning to the main tent for tea, coffee, and some locally made cakes.

They all gathered around, casually chatting since it was their first chance to get to know each other. The girls, a couple from Texas, were joined by Ajax from Maine, on the other side of the USA. They exchanged polite

conversation.

LeeRoy and Julie decided to go to their tent and rest until dinner, which was scheduled for 7 p.m.

Dinner was a meat stew, and Julie hesitated to ask about the meat, fearing the worst. Mateo saw her picking it over and reassured her it wasn't a guinea pig. Relieved, she enjoyed her meal.

That evening, Mateo told them to grab a blanket, lie down, and look up at the stars. They were all amazed by how clear and numerous the stars were—something none of them had ever seen before.

He went on to explain, "In the high, mystical peaks of the Andes, beneath the vast, shimmering night sky, an ancient science was practiced and perfected. The Inca civilization, whose empire once stretched across most of western South America, was skilled in architecture and talented in astronomy. In Inca astronomy, stars and constellations were not just celestial objects, but symbols with spiritual and practical meaning."

"I suggest that when you're ready, you get an early night. We'll be leaving at 7 am. You'll receive a call at 6:00 a.m., breakfast will be served at 6:30 a.m., and you'll be on the trail by 7:00 a.m."

"I didn't think we'd have to wake up that early," Julie whispered to LeeRoy.

"Three more mornings like that," he replied, and they headed to bed. The tent was small, but they were exhausted and fell asleep quickly. Soon after 6 am, there was a tap on the tent. LeeRoy unzipped it, revealing a bowl of hot water and two coffees outside. "There ya go," he said to Julie. Room service—what more could you want? "I want my bed and bathroom," quipped Julie. "You're going to have to wait a while for that," replied LeeRoy. (Little did she know how long it was going to be)

Backpacks on, they started their first full-day hike at 7:15. The weather was enjoyable and not too tricky, and they reached their lunch spot by 11:45. Once again, they were happily surprised to see the food tent set up with tea and coffee ready.

They spent an hour and a half having lunch before continuing their journey. They saw some porters far ahead on the trail, and it seemed like it would take forever to catch up. However, they were surprised to arrive at the same spot later, realising it was probably just an optical illusion.

"How are you finding it, Julie?" LeeRoy asked. "Yeah, okay. I had no idea what to expect, but so far, it's been fun, especially meeting people from America, even though they speak funny. Well, the two girls do, anyway—a real drawl."

They reached the next camp, which was once again all set up and ready, just as it had been the night before, and the morning was expected to be the same.

When they were ready to leave the next morning, Mateo warned them that the next part would be more difficult because they were now at 8,000 feet and the climb would be a little steeper. He handed everyone some coca leaves and told them to chew on them, as it would help ease altitude sickness. LeeRoy knew precisely what they were, but Julie had no idea and didn't like the taste, so she decided to skip them.

He wasn't joking about this getting hard, was he?" Julie said to LeeRoy, taking deep breaths in between. "Just think how fit you will be when we get there." He replied, also struggling to catch his breath.

They eventually reached lunch, camp tea, and coffee, all of which were ready again. "The porters are amazing," she said to LeeRoy, "When we left this morning, I was convinced we would get here before them, as they hadn't even started to pack things up, then they came running past us as though they were on flat ground at sea level."

"I guess they are acclimatised, and of course, they do this every day, but rather them than me, it's bad enough carrying this backpack up those steps. It's incredible how they carved so many over the mountains."

Each step, although only 3-4 inches high, feels like it's ten feet. I know it's the altitude, but I never expected it to be this hard."

"Matio mentioned that after we leave, we have roughly an hour, and then the rest of the day will be downhill and pass through a forest."

"Thank goodness for that," Julie responded. "This really is challenging, but I am genuinely enjoying it. The highlight so far has been those stars—absolutely incredible."

They reached the top, which flattened out for a while, with many small stones piled one on top of the other. Julie asked Mateo what they were.

"Native people in Peru have used specific stacked rocks to communicate a variety of messages to passers-by. Indicating a threat or deep snow is one example."

However, stacked rocks are used as a symbol of reverence for gods and goddesses in many cultures. Stacking rocks can also represent helping others. If you see stacks of stones in an area, it indicates someone has been there before. So, they want you to follow their trail for those times when you're lost on the trail and can't find your way out. Most of these have been built by tourists just like you."

"That's so interesting, isn't it, LeeRoy?"

"Very," he replied casually, not showing much interest. "Can we build one, please?"

"Really? If you want to put a rock on a rock, go ahead, I'll watch."

She struggled getting them to balance, but managed to get three on top of each other and was very proud of it.

They began descending, but then wished they were climbing again because going downhill was much harder on their knees.

They reached camp excited about arriving at Machu Picchu the next day and got a good night's sleep.

The following morning, they set out on an arduous trek to the lunch stop, but they arrived safely.

Lilac spotted some llamas about a hundred yards away and decided to see if she could get close enough to pet one. She slowly approached, but the stud llama was uneasy, snorting as she got closer. She should have heeded the warning but continued.

She was within ten feet when the stud llama charged at her. He stopped short, reared up, and flailed his front legs with dangerous-looking hooves.

She managed to duck as he kicked out, then turned and ran back, feeling lucky she hadn't gotten seriously injured or worse.

They didn't realise that Machu Picchu was just over the next ridge, only about a mile away.

Mateo encouraged them to climb the final mile and see the ruins as they reached the top.

They reached the top, planning to move forward, when Machu Picchu suddenly appeared before them. All of them were awestruck by the sight of this legendary place, just below their vantage point.

"Wow," Julie said, gripping LeeRoy tightly. "This is incredible, way more breathtaking than all the pictures I've seen. It was tough getting here, but it was worth it. Thank you."

LeeRoy and Julie said their goodbyes to Mateo, giving him a generous tip that made him very happy. They bid farewell to the others in the group, exchanged addresses, knowing deep down they probably wouldn't contact each other again. They spent the rest of the day walking around the ruins, amazed at how tightly the massive stones fit together and how the hell they managed to get them up there in the first place; they'd probably never know.

The porters had dropped off their things at the hotel, the "Tierra Viva Machu Picchu." The hotel was a 3-star establishment, clean, and had friendly staff.

Their one-night stay wasn't quite what they expected, even though they had a stunning view from the balcony of a rock-strewn river rushing down the mountain toward the Pacific Ocean.

When Julie flushed the toilet, the water wouldn't stop and overflowed. In a panic, she called LeeRoy as the water flooded the bathroom floor and started spreading into the bedroom. LeeRoy quickly tried to contact reception, but the phone was out of order. He ran down seven flights of stairs to reach reception, repeatedly banged the bell on the counter, and finally, someone responded. They seemed indifferent, casually picking up the phone and speaking to someone he guessed was a maintenance worker. "OK, Sir, the plumber will arrive soon," LeeRoy said. "He needs to be quick, as the water is in the room too."

LeeRoy returned to the room, where water was now near the bed. They could only sit on the balcony and wait for help to arrive and fix the problem. When help finally arrived, the bedroom floor was completely submerged. The plumber took two minutes to stop the water, but the room was still uninhabitable, so they had to move to another room. "Well, that was exciting," joked LeeRoy, "Another story to tell Chas when we get back," he laughed.

In the morning, they returned to Cusco with ten others in an old Yak-24 Russian twin-bladed helicopter, which was more of a bone shaker than the bus had been four days earlier.

They were picked up by Agustino and driven back to his home.

They had dinner that evening and looked forward to a few days of rest before returning home.

Julie was awakened at 2 a.m. by someone softly knocking at the door. She shook LeeRoy's shoulder to wake him. His eyes snapped open, and he quickly got out of bed to open the door, surprised but relieved to see Agustino standing there. Julie sat up straight in bed, straining to see what was happening.

"What's the problem?" LeeRoy muttered, squinting against the corridor light.

"Can we talk privately?" Agustino asked urgently.

LeeRoy nodded, exited the bedroom, quietly closed the door, and then followed Agustino down the corridor.

They headed down to Agustino's office and shut the door.

"What's up?" LeeRoy asked.

"I just got a call from the Customs Office commander-in-chief. He said that the police are gathering evidence and plan to arrest two of our Customs contacts next week. So, you'll need to leave tomorrow instead."

"OK, I understand," replied LeeRoy. "What's the plan?"

"I'll book a hotel in Lima for you, and you will find a suitcase in the wardrobe. You'll stay there tomorrow night and leave the next morning."

"Okay. Are you sure your guys in Lima will be okay?"

"Yeah, yeah. The police here don't act swiftly, and it's likely just a formality. They'll accept a bribe, and the case will be wrapped up. That's how things go around here."

LeeRoy went back to his room to find Julie still sitting up in bed, her eyes filled with alarm. She asked, "What's wrong?"

"Business," LeeRoy said. "But we need to head home the day after tomorrow, and we will stay in Lima tomorrow night."

Julie was surprised and worried, but she knew she shouldn't push the issue. She loved LeeRoy and appreciated everything he'd done for her. If it weren't for him, she might be living somewhere like that old pillbox at the top of Detling Hill. She patted his hand. "Don't worry, LeeRoy. I've had a wonderful honeymoon, and you're right. We can always come back."

The next morning, Agustino dropped them off at the airport, and they said their goodbyes. "Good luck," said Agustino.

A short flight to Lima and a taxi to the Hotel de Palma, and they checked in. The room had been paid for in advance by Agustino.

When they got to the room and LeeRoy opened the wardrobe, the suitcase was there.

Julie noticed it. "LeeRoy, someone left a suitcase here." "No, sweetheart. That's ours. We're bringing it with us." She glanced at him. "Why? What's inside?" "Nothing for you to worry about." "Are you certain?" Julie's voice trembled, showing her worry. "I'm guessing what's inside, and I don't like it. What if we get caught?"

"Don't worry. It's all under control. Agustino has friends at the airport." "I'm sure he does," Julie replied, "but I still feel uneasy." LeeRoy wanted to avoid the topic. "Let's go out for dinner tonight and get an early start. Tomorrow will be a long day." "Hmmm," she pondered. There was no convincing him otherwise; she just had to trust him. "Sounds good to me." The next morning, they checked out at 8 a.m., took a taxi to Lima airport, and approached the check-in counter. They handed their tickets and passports to the check-in agent. LeeRoy felt a bit nervous, knowing the police were about to arrest corrupt customs officers. Meanwhile, Julie remained unfazed—she was unaware of the issues and trusted that LeeRoy and Agustino had everything under control. She felt relieved when their bags were tagged and placed on the conveyor belt.

"See, I told you there wouldn't be any problems," LeeRoy said, visibly relieved.

Julie smiled and squeezed his hand. *"I should know by now - LeeRoy takes care of everything."*

They approached Passport Control, quickly went through, then moved through the X-ray, Customs, and arrived in the departure lounge. They headed to the café, ordered two coffees, and relaxed for an hour before their flight was announced.

Unknown to LeeRoy, the conveyor belt carrying suitcases to the loading bay broke down, causing several suitcases to get stuck and spill their contents onto the floor. Staff hurried to gather the clothes and personal items that had fallen out. Unfortunately, among them was the case with the cocaine—its ripped lining made the heavy, flat bags easily recognisable as suspicious. Police whistles sounded, and police and military officers swiftly arrived at the scene.

LeeRoy, being the only Caribbean in the airport, was easily identified as a prime suspect, and before he had even touched his coffee, he and Julie were surrounded by police with their guns drawn.

"Down!" they cried angrily, waving their guns.

"What are they saying?" Julie's voice trembled.

"Down! Down!" yelled an officer. LeeRoy and Julie swiftly dropped to their knees, face down on the floor, as officers pushed them into position, guns pointed at their heads. Their pockets were searched, and Julie's handbag was emptied. An officer scrutinized their passports, muttering something in Spanish to his colleagues.

No one spoke to Julie and LeeRoy as their wrists were cuffed, and they were forced to stand, then marched out of the airport and loaded into an old army truck. Julie, frightened and tearful, asked LeeRoy, "What's happening?"

"No speak!" a soldier shouted,

She looked at LeeRoy, and he could see in her wild eyes that she was terrified.

What had he done wrong? How had they discovered the drugs? He felt the worst for Julie, but he had already decided to tell everyone she was unaware of everything.

Though he knew he was in serious trouble, he still believed they would free her once her innocence was proven. The truck stopped, and they were forced out and taken to a dilapidated police station, where they were held in separate cells. Julie, whimpering, was led there, trembling with shock and fear. Above her, a slow-moving ceiling fan stirred the heavy air but offered no relief. Three hours later, LeeRoy was brought into another room, handcuffed to a bolted-down table, with two armed guards standing on either side.

A few minutes later, the door opened and a large, intimidating National Police officer introduced himself in English as "General Don José Rufino Echenique Benavente".

"Why am I here?" LeeRoy asked, keeping his cool even though his stomach was twisted with worry about Julie.

"I believe you're fully aware of why you're here, my friend," the General said sarcastically. "But just in case you're too stupid to realise, I'll clarify. We found a suitcase with your name on it filled with cocaine at the airport. Do you claim it's not yours?"

"I'm not saying anything until I have a lawyer."

Don José burst into laughter. "Lawyer! This is Peru, not England. I decide whether you see anyone and when." He sneered at LeeRoy. "Now, before we resort to other measures, I'll ask you again: is the suitcase yours?"

"No comment," said LeeRoy, then winced as he was struck in the back with a rifle butt by one of the guards. The pain was intense, and he dropped to his knees under the table. The handcuffs pulled him back, digging into his wrists.

"I'll ask you for the last time," said Don José, "is that suitcase yours?"

"No comment," said LeeRoy, bracing himself for another rifle butt.

He wasn't disappointed – but this time, it was rammed with force into the side of his head, and he was knocked unconscious, a gash on his temple bleeding profusely.

If only the two scumbags and three brothers could see him now. He was dragged, bleeding, back to his cell, still unconscious.

Don José shouted at the guards to bring the girl in: "¡Traigan a la chica!"

They went to Julie's cell and found her sitting on the bunk, hugging her knees tightly to her chest.

She looked up in terror as the door swung open. The two guards approached her, hauling her off the bunk without a word.

"Hey!" she shouted, her fear evident.

They led her to the interview room and sat her down at the same table LeeRoy had been chained to, but they didn't bother cuffing her. She was a petite figure and no match for the towering guards. She wasn't going anywhere.

The sight of all the fresh blood on the floor made her nearly faint.

What have they done?

"¡Consigan un vaso de agua!" Don José demanded that they get her a glass of water before introducing himself to Julie.

"Where's my husband?" Julie's eyes widened, staring uneasily at the blood smears on the floor.

"Don't worry about him. He's fine," Don José said with a smile that was more unsettling than his previous stern glare.

Her throat was dry. "When can I see him?"

"That depends on you." Don José raised a quizzical eyebrow and pressed his fingertips together into a steeple shape.

"You do realise you're in serious trouble, don't you?"

"Why – what have I done?" Julie asked, her voice trembling with emotion. "Why am I here?"

"What have you done?" Don José snorted. "Attempting to smuggle nearly two kilograms of a controlled substance, specifically cocaine, out of the country. How does that sound for a reason?"

Julie began sobbing loudly, but Don José was unaffected. He slapped her face and yelled, "Shut up!"

It didn't succeed; instead, it exacerbated her state. She was hysterical, screaming, and through the muffled cries, she sobbed, "I want my husband!" That still didn't persuade this hardened Peruvian, who slapped her once more.

Back in his holding cell, LeeRoy had regained consciousness and could hear Julie screaming. Frantic and furious, he started banging on the cell door and shouting, "Leave her alone!"

Don José stood up, walked out, and went along to LeeRoy's cell.

"What are you doing to her?" LeeRoy shouted at Don José through the observation slit, pressing his face against the door as if trying to squeeze through to help Julie.

"Back away from the door!" Don José ordered LeeRoy to the back of the cell, threatening to shoot him. LeeRoy obeyed, and Don José ordered two armed guards to open the door. "Abrir la puerta!"

The guards entered and told LeeRoy to sit on the bunk, with two submachine guns pointed at him. LeeRoy did as he was told.

As Don José entered, LeeRoy roared and attempted to leap, but he was pushed back onto the bunk before lifting an inch.

"Calm down, my friend," Don José smiled eerily.

"You're no friend of mine."

"I'm more of a friend than you think."

LeeRoy's lip curled. "And just how do you figure that?"

"Simple," Don José said. "Keep denying it, and we may need to hurt her again. Admit the truth, and your lady will be free." He smirked. "See how good a friend I am?"

LeeRoy simmered with anger. His only thought was to take the blame to protect Julie. After three hours in the cell, he reflected on their dire situation. Seeing that they were clearly harming Julie, he felt unbearable guilt. He understood they were in serious trouble with no clear escape. Although caught red-handed, he would rather die than allow Julie to be harmed or implicated.

"OK," LeeRoy said finally. "You give me your word that you'll send my wife back to England, and I'll admit to it."

"Good," Don José smirked. "You see, I am your friend."

He turned to one of the guards. Lleva a la mujer de regreso a su celda y tráelo de vuelta a la sala de entrevistas. ("Take the lady back to her cell and bring him back to the interview room.")

After taking Julie back to her cell, the two guards leered at her, with one even touching her as she walked past.

"Bastard!" She tried to slap him, but was knocked onto the bunk.

The guards both left, laughing.

Minutes later, LeeRoy was handcuffed to the interview table again, his previously spilled blood now a brown stain.

"OK," said Don José. "First question – where did you get the cocaine from? Who is your contact here?"

"Whoa!" exclaimed LeeRoy, clearly surprised. "I only confessed to attempting to smuggle it out of Peru—nothing more. I would be dead within two days, and you know that."

"That would save us a lot of trouble," said Don José. He sniffed.

"Anyway, we're reasonably sure who it is, but as you're well aware, he's well protected. So, I guess we'll have to settle for you."

Don José handed LeeRoy a handwritten statement and a pen, expecting him to sign. LeeRoy glanced at the sheet and immediately noticed it was entirely in Spanish.

"No way," he said. "Not until I know my wife is safe and the document is translated into English. Additionally, I want to see a lawyer," he added, his tone tinged with anger.

"You're pretty demanding, aren't you?" Don José sneered.

"Especially since you're not in a good position to demand anything." "That's the deal."

Don José looked at him, lost in thought. "Okay," he finally said. "This will be finished tomorrow." He ordered the guards, "Take him back!"

They shoved LeeRoy back into his cell, slamming the door so hard that he crashed into the back wall and hit his head, which nearly knocked him out again. More blood was now pouring from his previous head wound, but there was no chance of getting any medical help.

Feeling disoriented, he slowly shook his head and attempted to collect himself. On the rough bunk, he found a worn and dirty sheet, but he used it as best as he could. A jug of water was placed on a nearby ledge, and he dipped the corner of the sheet into it, trying to clean himself up.

He couldn't stop thinking about Julie and the trouble he'd gotten them into. He shouldn't have tried this with her along for the ride.

Stupid, stupid bastard!

He might curse himself now, but dwelling on it was useless. His priority was to find a way to escape this situation. He hardly slept that night, and they didn't bring him any food until 6 a.m.— only a bowl of something like porridge that tasted terrible, but he had no option but to eat.

At 10 a.m., LeeRoy's cell door opened, and he was led to the interview room, where he was chained to the table once more.

A sharp-looking young guy walked in with Don José.

Don José introduced the man, saying, "This is your attorney, Jordi Gine Aragones."

"Pleased to meet you," he said to LeeRoy, who said nothing.

"I understand you want to make a full confession. Is that right?"

"Yes, that's right," LeeRoy said, "as long as my wife goes free and the statement is in English."

"That's not a problem. I understand General Echenique Benavente has given you his word on that."

"Yes, he has," LeeRoy said warily. "But how can I be sure he'll keep it?"

The young lawyer shrugged. "You'll just have to trust him." He gave him a translated copy of the statement. LeeRoy couldn't argue; he saw the statement was in English and read it—nothing unexpected, nothing to dispute.

"What can I expect to get?"

"Well, it's quite a serious offence, and you will most likely be sentenced to fifteen to twenty years, I'm afraid."

"Fuck," LeeRoy's head dropped. He'd had it all and blown it. He couldn't believe it! He should've left it to his mules, but no – he thought he knew better, trusting Tino's professionalism. He figured he'd kill two birds with one stone by taking Julie to exotic places and showing off. He'd thought he might as well do a drug run while he was there and cut out the middleman to make some extra cash. He didn't even need the money!

Stupid! Stupid! His greed and complacency led to his downfall. However, he hoped Julie would be released and worried about her, wishing to see her. He asked his lawyer the question.

The lawyer glanced over at Don José.

"It's not possible," the man said firmly, shaking his head.

LeeRoy felt crushed.

CHAPTER TWENTY-SIX — *Prisoners of Peru*

It turned out that things were much worse than LeeRoy had thought.

Don José wasn't a man of his word.

Rather than being released, Julie was already being transferred to the infamous women's prison in San Juan de Lurigancho, Lima, called Miguel Castro.

It was a hellhole, and Julie would be entirely out of her depth in that situation here.

She'd been shoved into a van, protesting, but no one appeared to speak English, and she had no idea where they were taking her.

Upon arrival, she was roughly stripped and thoroughly searched.

Julie stood in fear, trembling from shock rather than the humid, suffocating air in the prison processing room, tears flowing down her face. The hardest part was not knowing what was happening or what had happened to LeeRoy.

Then, she was handed some old, roughly woven clothes that resembled sacks and marched through the prison amid jeers and catcalls from the tough-looking female inmates and some male guards. Julie was filled with terror.

She was shoved into a dirty cell already crowded with fifteen other women. The door slammed shut, locking her inside.

The other women stared at her—the blonde stranger—before whispering urgently, which increased Julie's unease.

One of them eventually approached and began babbling in Spanish. Julie had no clue what she was saying and made that obvious.

One of the other women spoke a little English, but not enough. "What are you in for?" she asked coldly.

Julie attempted to explain, but they frowned and stopped listening. Lacking enough English to understand, they left her alone in the corner, where she cried softly.

LeeRoy was taken to Sarita Colonia Prison in Lima, which was far worse than the women's prison. Although it was designed to hold 500 inmates, it was overcrowded with over 2,500 prisoners, most of whom were detained for drug offenses.

LeeRoy would later discover there were more than fifty Brits inside, but at that time, he was still undergoing the entry process and only saw Spanish-speaking individuals.

Stripped naked and searched, he, like Julie, was given old sackcloth clothing to wear.

He was taken to a cell meant for thirty prisoners, but over 100 were crammed inside. It was cramped and smelled of male sweat, dirt, and urine. In those tight spaces, scuffles often broke out, and violence was widespread.

LeeRoy moved through the bodies, found a small space to sit, and planned to stay quiet until he understood how things operated inside.

Once it became evident that LeeRoy was English, the news quickly circulated within the cell. Two other British prisoners in the same cell then introduced themselves: Jim Bower, also called "Jimbo," a red-haired man with a bushy beard, and Steve Stein.

They shook hands before sitting beside LeeRoy in the crowded cell to chat.

LeeRoy appreciated having someone to speak English with, especially as they exchanged survival tips for this hellhole.

Jimbo told him, "The Prisoners Abroad Organization will send you about £60 every three months through the British Embassy in Lima."

"Yeah?" LeeRoy raised an eyebrow, surprised by the news.

"Don't get your hopes up," Jimbo warned. "You won't be able to keep much of it." He looked around the cell, where the other prisoners' scowling faces underscored his warning. They all knew when the money came, and they would demand most of it as "protection money."

"Fuck that!" said LeeRoy, who was accustomed to leading the mob. Steve Stein shook his head. "You have to understand, LeeRoy — the prisoners control the jail."

LeeRoy frowned, but Jimbo continued from where his friend stopped: "The prison is run by two gangs, the Mistrals and Los Aztecs." A few prisoners looked over, tense at the mention of the gangs amid their otherwise unclear chatter. Nonetheless, Jimbo and Steve continued speaking softly and urgently, revealing that the prison guards were also involved in corruption, allegedly accepting bribes to maintain order.

Over the following hours, LeeRoy paid close attention. He gained more insight from his new friends as they talked about their "alleged" crimes. Drawing from Jimbo and Steve's experiences and their knowledge of the legal system in that country, LeeRoy was informed that he could face a sentence of six to seven years for his type of crime.

Christ! That's better than the fifteen to twenty years my lawyer mentioned! LeeRoy thought. He suspected his lawyer had been exaggerating to make himself look good, especially since LeeRoy received only half the sentence he had anticipated.

That was still too long to be without Julie.

Jimbo told him that most foreign prisoners are released early on probation. The only conditions are that you can't leave Peru, and you can't work.

LeeRoy's mind worked fast. That wasn't so bad for him, at least. Sam could send him money over, and Tino would surely help him out.

However, it still didn't ease his feelings of missing Julie.

"Oh, and the food isn't fit for rodents to eat, let alone humans," said Steve.

"And the water's polluted," added Jimbo.

It truly felt like hell, but it functioned more like a protection racket than a prison.

LeeRoy's first night was unbearable. The foul smell of stale sweat, urine, and excrement assaulted his senses, and with the cots packed tightly together, there was hardly any room to move. The constant sounds of coughing, sneezing, farting, and fighting made it impossible for him to get any sleep.

As dawn arrived and sunlight filtered through the narrow window slits, LeeRoy understood there was no fixed wake-up time. The stories he heard from the Brits were accurate: the prisoners managed the situation, and everyone mostly did as they wished. The rule of survival was in place, with guards keeping out of the way.

Breakfast was inedible—a black, grey mess that resembled wet cardboard in both look and taste, yet they had no choice but to eat it or go hungry. The small amount of water LeeRoy managed to gather in a plastic cup appeared murky and had a foul taste, as if it had come directly from the sewer.

Fuck! He had to get out of that place.

"Has anyone ever escaped from here?" he asked one of his new friends, Steve.

"All the time," Steve replied, "but they shoot first and ask questions later if they catch you.

"Listen, Steve," LeeRoy said quietly. "I need your help. I can't stay in this shithole. I'd prefer being dead than remaining here for six years." Steve nodded, prompting LeeRoy to go on. "They've agreed to drop all charges against my wife. As soon as I know she's safe, I'm leaving. Who should I speak to?"

"It's not as straightforward as it seems, LeeRoy," Steve said softly, glancing around anxiously as if fearing someone might overhear. "You'll need to bribe at least three guards, and you'll have to go through Jesús to do it. Not the Jesús up there," he pointed to the sky, "but the one who leads the Mistrals—he has the most sway here."

"Do you know him?"

"Yeah, of course I know him. Everyone knows him. But have I ever spoken to him? Not a chance," Steve said urgently, his expression serious. "He's a dangerous man, and it's best to keep a low profile around him. He'd cut your throat for just looking at him."

"Ow!" LeeRoy jumped.

Two prisoners walked past, and one of them stepped on LeeRoy's foot. LeeRoy knew it was intentional, but as a new arrival, he didn't want to cause trouble.

Unfortunately, it wasn't his decision. The man turned and kicked LeeRoy in the leg, shouting in Spanish. LeeRoy tried to stay calm and apologise, but they didn't understand—and clearly didn't care.

The guy kicked LeeRoy again while yelling a barrage of harsh words in Spanish, angering LeeRoy. Without thinking, he quickly stood up, filled with rage.

"Whoa!" Steve shouted, trying to step in, but there was no stopping LeeRoy. LeeRoy was like a machine. He grabbed the guy by the throat and then punched him right in the face. The man fell, and his friend charged at LeeRoy, swinging a shank made from a sharpened piece of welding rod. He wasn't quick enough, though, and LeeRoy knocked him out cold.

The first guy lunged at LeeRoy once more, charging in low with a roar. LeeRoy swiftly brought his knee up, connecting solidly under the guy's chin with a dull crack, and he collapsed, unable to get back up.

There was loud applause and cheering from around the cell. LeeRoy had been noticed.

Loud applause and cheers erupted from the crowd around them. LeeRoy finally grabbed their attention.

"For fuck's sake, LeeRoy!" Steve hissed, his eyes darting around the room in search of more danger. "You know how to make friends!"

LeeRoy just stared at him, but Steve continued, "They won't let this go. You'll need eyes in your arse, now."

"What was I supposed to do? Let that tosser stick me?" LeeRoy shook his head, frustrated. "No chance." He paused and muttered, "Steve, I want to talk with this Jesús."

Steve let out a frustrated sigh and rolled his eyes. "You have a better chance of talking to the real one than him." "We'll see," LeeRoy replied.

After being knocked out, the two thugs regained consciousness, quickly got up, and exchanged a look of pure hatred toward LeeRoy before walking away peacefully.

"They'll be back," Steve warned. "Looking forward to it," LeeRoy said, still riding high on adrenaline and almost smirking.

"You need to be careful in here, LeeRoy."

"Yeah, I know. So, how do I get to Jesús?"

"By just keeping on like that, I suppose," Steve joked.

"You know what I mean," LeeRoy muttered. "There's got to be a way." He paused briefly. "You know what, Steve? I'm just going to walk up to him. Does he speak English?" Steve burst out laughing, unable to believe it. "I think he does speak English, LeeRoy, but I doubt you'll even get within twenty feet of him. Armed guards surround him— and I don't mean the prison type."

"I don't care," LeeRoy said grimly. "There has to be a way."

Early in the morning, Julie's cell door swung open, and a bucket of foul, rotten waste was dumped onto the floor. The other inmates hurried over, using their hands to scoop out pieces of the mess, since they had no plates or utensils.

Julie was horrified to realise this was breakfast and lingered nearby, waiting for a gap in the crowd. She carefully dipped a finger in, lifting a lump of the grey-brown porridge, then withdrew, her lip curling in disgust. It tasted like pig manure, and

Julie couldn't bring herself to eat any of it, much to the others' pleasure, who then received more.

Julie withdrew to her corner, crying softly, but no one noticed, and they let her handle it on her own.

Julie wondered if the lack of food all day was the reason everyone was so eager for breakfast. In the evening, they were herded into an exercise yard for half an hour before being allowed into a dirty canteen.

The prisoners handled all the prep, cooking, and serving tasks. Julie quickly realised that having money meant getting food—no money, no dinner. It was as simple as that. Since she had no money, she went hungry. But she wasn't too worried—she was already feeling sick and scared. No one had explained what was happening, leaving her in a state of shock and confusion. She had no idea if she'd stay for a few days or forever. They were herded back into the communal cell, where the door was locked again. Julie started crying again. She was told in Spanish to shut the fuck up, which she mostly understood from the threatening tone and the angry looks from the other women. She bit her lip and wiped her eyes on the rough fabric of her prison smock, trying to hold back her sobs. About an hour later, the door opened, and two male guards entered, pointing at Julie and signalling for her to follow.

A woman prisoner suddenly stepped forward, positioning herself between the guards and Julie, and held her ground. Recognising what was about to occur, she urgently confronted them. They pushed her aside, seized Julie's arm, and forced her out.

They took her to the shower room, locked the door, and made her strip and shower in front of them. She tried to turn her back and cover herself with her hands, but they shouted and waved her hands down. They leered and sniggered amongst themselves, chattering animatedly together and occasionally catcalling in Spanish. Julie had never felt so vulnerable and humiliated.

She looked at them for permission to leave, and they nodded, smirking. She grabbed the thin towel folded on the bench and tried to cover herself immediately.

As soon as she dried off, there was a knock at the door. The guards spoke in Spanish and opened it. Two more guards walked in, smiling and sneering, looking her up and down as she stood there, feeling tiny and even more exposed in her thin bath towel.

Julie could tell from the look in their eyes what was coming. She tried to take off, but two guards grabbed her. They tore off her towel as she screamed, then threw her to the tile floor.

The men completely overpowered her, and in the end, after taking a backhand across the cheek, she didn't fight back because she knew she'd just get beaten anyway.

She was held down and raped in turn by each of the guards, and then the first guard raped her again.

They finished with her, then dragged her back to her cell, still naked, opened the door, and shoved her inside.

Other prisoners sat in silence, feeling uneasy and watching intently. Julie curled up on the floor, sobbing.

The guards threw her clothes in after her and slammed the door shut. The other women weren't surprised; it had happened to many of them before, and they knew it would happen again.

One of the women softly rested her hand on Julie's back and whispered in Spanish. Another gave Julie her prison clothes and helped her put them on.

They felt somewhat sympathetic towards her, but it didn't do much to help Julie in her current situation. She wanted to give up and die.

LeeRoy had had enough. He managed to grab a piece of paper and a stub of a pencil and wrote a note. He asked Steve to point him toward Jesús. Reluctantly, Steve took him on a walk around the prison, searching for Jesús among the hundreds of inmates. Outside in the exercise yard, Steve stopped short and nodded towards a group of heavy-set men. If LeeRoy had been alone, without Steve's guidance, he might have already guessed that Jesús was the leader sitting in the middle of his bodyguards, who chatted and deferred to him. Jesús was about forty years old, a big man who looked like he could handle himself, even without his henchmen around.

Steve warned LeeRoy not to go, but he was already walking across the exercise yard toward Jesús. Steve shook his head in despair. As expected, before LeeRoy reached Jesús, the bodyguards pushed through, surrounding him quickly. LeeRoy raised his hands in surrender, palms open, and showed the note between two fingers.

"Por Jesús," he said.

Before he could even figure out where he was, LeeRoy was grabbed and slammed to the ground, his face pressed against the dusty earth, and the note snatched from his hand. A boot pressed into the back of his neck kept him from seeing what was happening. The note was handed to Jesús, who could read and speak English.

It said: "My name is LeeRoy. I have good contacts in the UK, and I'd like to discuss with you the possibility of getting out of here. I've been told you're the right person to speak to."

Jesús read the note and signalled to his men to bring LeeRoy over. They checked him for weapons before allowing him to approach their leader. Then, they pushed him forward. As LeeRoy drew closer, Jesús indicated a seat across from him, and LeeRoy took a seat.

"So, my friend, you have some nerve," Jesús said, eyeing LeeRoy with his piercing black eyes. "Not many get this close to me. Now, please tell me what I can do for you in exchange for what you can do for me. But first, why are you here?"

LeeRoy explained the situation to him, and when he mentioned Cusco and Tino, Jesús became more interested, interrupting LeeRoy.

"I've heard of this Agustino. Agustino Montana."

"Yes," said LeeRoy, "the same."

"So why isn't he helping you?" asked Jesús.

"Because we have a pact that if any one of us is compromised, we don't, under any circumstances, contact the other."

Jesús nodded in approval. "I can understand that," he said. "So, if I can help you, what can you offer me for my trouble?"

"I can pay you, and I can put you in touch with big people in England. It could be very lucrative for you."

He sighed, nodding again. "That might be quite helpful, I suppose, but we should settle on my compensation. What are you thinking?"

"I can set up a payment of £5,000 to any account you choose – and another £5,000 if I make a successful escape."

Jesús narrowed his eyes. "And if it isn't?"

"If that happens, you've failed, so you won't get the second five grand."

Jesús nodded again, relaxed. "Alright, that seems fair. But how do I know I'll get the second payment if you succeed?"

"You don't," LeeRoy said. "But trust me, if I get out, I'll be happy to pay you. Plus, I'm sure you've got plenty of connections that would find me quickly, and I wouldn't feel safe owing a lot of money to you."

"That, my friend, is completely correct, so remember that," Jesús said, narrowing his eyes and pursing his lips in thought. Then he added, "Alright, leave it with me, and I will get back to you."

"Thank you, Jesús."

"You'll be paying, of course. By the way, I hear you had a problem this morning." "Nothing I can't handle," LeeRoy said.

"Watch out, my friend. Some of these desperate people in here would kill you just for a biscuit."

"I understand."

"I don't believe you do," Jesús cautioned. "However, I'll inform others that you're under my protection—at least until you settle your debt," he said with a smile. "That should keep you safe from most dangers, but not all." LeeRoy gave a brief nod.

Everyone across the yard was curious about how a black Brit managed to connect with the main guy.

This had earned him some respect, but not from everyone.

LeeRoy got back to Steve and said, "See? Easy."

Steve chuckled nervously. "I can't believe you pulled that off – what exactly did you say to him?"

"Not much. I just made him an offer he couldn't turn down." "So, will he help you now?" "I hope so," LeeRoy replied.

Julie woke up to her usual breakfast routine the next morning. The door opened, and a bucket of slop was delivered into her cell. Her hunger was so intense that she had to eat, even though it made her feel sick. The water she received was only slightly better. Throughout the day, doubts and accusations swirled in her mind. She began to resent LeeRoy for what he had done to her, but she desperately wanted to see him.

That evening, a girl in the cell sat beside Julie. Julie looked up cautiously, but the young woman stayed silent—she knew Julie didn't speak Spanish. Instead, she reached out and took Julie's hand. After a brief hesitation, Julie responded to her kind gesture, letting her stroke her hand. It was the first real sign of kindness she'd received.

But then the girl placed her hand on Julie's leg and ran it up her thigh, beneath her threadbare skirt. Julie pushed her away, disgusted. The girl snapped at her and started throwing insults in Spanish, but at least she got up and left Julie alone.

Later that evening, two guards came back to take Julie away, and she was once again forced into the shower - this time by six guards, including a woman. Julie started to cry, fearing another tough day like the previous one, but she still clung to a small hope that having the woman there might change things for the better.

However, when she was clean, the men grabbed her again and pinned Julie down whilst the female guard kneaded her breasts, messing about with her, then finger-fucked Julie before sitting on her face, forcing Julie to have oral sex with her. When she was finished, the five male guards raped Julie again.

She was unresponsive and had a vacant stare, barely able to squeeze out a tear.

Worried sick about Julie, LeeRoy was trying to understand what had occurred. He thought she had been released, but perhaps she also considered contacting Giles or Sam and found a way to return to England. He wished he knew for sure. He didn't want to ask Jesús for too many favours—his primary focus was on getting out of there. He would have to wait and see if Julie or someone else reached out.

They still had some vacation time remaining, so everyone at home wouldn't suspect anything was amiss just yet. However, in a few days, Sam would start to notice he was missing. News will circulate that there was a problem at the airport, and Tino may already have heard. LeeRoy couldn't afford to wait idly; he needed to step up and devise his plans.

Early the next morning, two guards came to take Julie away. She had been expecting to be raped again, but they took her to the interview room, where she met her lawyer, Adrianna Madigan, for the first time. Julie nearly broke down with relief. The woman was slightly overweight, with a neat bun of dyed-blonde hair that had a reddish tint. It seemed out of place, set against her otherwise Spanish appearance: olive skin and dark brown eyes.

Julie thought the solicitor, being a woman, would at least understand what had happened to her and take action. But she was terribly mistaken! After Julie finished telling her about the abuse in prison, the solicitor shrugged. "It is just one of those things that happen in Peruvian jails," Adrianna told her, her accent clearly American. "There is nothing anybody can do."

"What?" Julie sucked in a breath. "That can't be right!" "Nobody will admit to knowing anything. It's your word against theirs."

Julie was speechless, but as a victim, she was no longer surprised by anything. Exhausted, she abandoned her pursuit of justice and focused on the urgent matter at hand. "Can't you get me out of here?"

"I think I can get you out on bail," the lawyer told Julie, "But you'd have to show up at the local police station every Thursday until the trial."

Julie's heart leapt at the idea of escaping that terrible place. "That would be great," she said, her thoughts occupied by the possibilities. "But I don't have anywhere to stay." "That's no problem," Adrianna replied casually. "There's a hostel nearby where you can stay quite cheaply. The items and money taken at the airport will be returned to you, and I assume you had some cash on hand?" "Yeah, I did," Julie nodded, feeling more hopeful. "About £100." Luckily, she had managed to keep some money of her own!

"Good," Adrianna nodded stiffly. "That should keep you going until you can get more sent over."

"When will I know if I can get bail?" Julie asked eagerly. "This afternoon, I hope," Adrianna replied, closing the file and placing it in her briefcase. "I've scheduled a court session for this afternoon." She stood up, snapped the case shut, and added, "Just doing my job." "Thank you, Miss!" Julie exclaimed, almost tearful with relief. "I really appreciate it." "Oh!" Julie held up her hand. "Is it possible for me to see my husband?" "Once you're bailed out, you might be able to visit him with a visitor's pass, but you'll need to check with the prison." Julie's heart leapt.

That afternoon, they spent only a few minutes in court. Fortunately for Julie, she was granted bail, provided she didn't seek employment and reported to the local police once a week as required.

Her lawyer explained that they didn't want to incur costs for holding foreign prisoners on remand. However, she had to report weekly or face immediate return to prison.

Julie had already collected her clothes for court, and a guard returned her other belongings to her. She signed for everything, except her passport and credit cards, which the authorities retained. When she checked her purse, only £40 of the £100 she expected was there. When she voiced her concern, the guard said, "No te entiendo."

She beckoned Adrianna over and explained what had happened. Her only words were, "This is Peru, I'm afraid." Julie realised arguing was pointless, and she was fortunate to have the forty pounds still.

"Come with me, and I'll drop you off at the hostel," Adrianna told Julie. "I've arranged for Prisoners Abroad, the charity, to cover the first two weeks. After that, you'll need to reapply if you can't come up with the money. And it has to be cash."

After ten minutes, they arrived at the hostel. Julie was initially hesitant because it looked somewhat dilapidated, but she quickly recalled the prison conditions and said nothing.

Julie was led to her room, which felt like a luxury compared to the prison. There was a shared bathroom and shower down the hall, so her first task was to take a shower. Still traumatized from her recent ordeal, she locked the door carefully and wedged a chair under the handle. Her eyes kept nervously glancing at the door every few seconds, even when the water was running and she was standing under the shower. It would have been nice if the water had been hot, but this was an improvement over the prison, and she appreciated that.

After dressing, Julie took a quick walk and came across a café. She eagerly ate her first real meal in days. As it was getting late, she decided to go back to her room and get a good night's sleep in the comfort of her new home.

Adrianna suggested that taking a taxi was the easiest way to reach the male prison, but Julie needed to conserve her money. The hostel manager, who spoke some English, offered several public transportation options and gave clear directions.

The following morning, she visited a nearby bank to exchange her forty pounds for U.S. dollars, which are more widely accepted than the local currency. She finally received a little over sixty dollars.

Julie finally reached the prison by bus. She approached the reception desk to inquire about LeeRoy, but the staff didn't speak English and were unsure of her request. She wrote his name down and handed it to the guard, who then checked the records. When he returned, he said, "Diez dólares." Julie understood that he wanted ten dollars but wasn't sure what for. "Por qué?" was one phrase she had learned in Spanish. "Diez dólares," he repeated. With no alternatives left, she gave him $10. He handed her a visitor's permit for 2:30 that afternoon, which was just under two hours away. She waited in the office, sensing the staff's resentment.

Around 2 p.m., people started arriving and lining up outside. Julie guessed this was the visitor line and joined it. Most of the waiting crowd were women, all with Peruvian Indian or Spanish features, and they eyed Julie with suspicion. The sun shone brightly overhead.

At 2:45 p.m., the prison gates opened to admit visitors. Everyone had to undergo a detailed search before entering.

The visiting room was large, filled with numerous tables securely bolted to the floor, on which prisoners were chained. Julie noticed LeeRoy as soon as he saw her. Although he was expecting to meet his attorney, he was more excited to see Julie.

Don José had kept his promise, as far as he believed. She was now free! However, he couldn't stand when she approached because he was chained to the table. Julie hurried over and hugged him tightly before someone shouted at her. Even though she didn't understand Spanish, she knew it meant "no touching."

"Are you okay?" LeeRoy asked her urgently.

"Yes," she replied, choosing not to share all the details – she didn't want him to freak out – but it was clear she had been through a tough time.

"Don José kept his word then," he said with a grin. "Which is more than I expected."

She cut him off. "No, he didn't!" she exclaimed. "I ended up in the worst prison, and I'm only here now because my lawyer got bail for me."

"The fucking bastard!" LeeRoy snarled. "I should have known better than to trust the shithead." He glared into space, seething at what he'd do to him if he ever got his hands on him! "Where are you staying? Do you still have the money I gave you?"

"I'm staying in a hostel. It's not luxurious like the Ritz, but it's much better than a prison, and I only have sixty dollars left. The guards took the rest—about forty dollars, since I paid ten dollars to get in here, not counting the bus fare." "Bloody hell!" exclaimed LeeRoy. "Listen," he said softly, leaning in. "I plan to escape in the next few days." "That's fantastic, LeeRoy!" Julie said, her face lighting up. "They've even granted you bail?" "No, darling, they haven't," he replied, glancing around the room at the guards. "I've made a plan to escape and run for it."

"How?" Julie was in shock. "How can you manage that?" She nervously licked her lips. "And even if you do, how will we return to England?" "I don't have an answer right now." LeeRoy's gaze remained on the guards watching them. "Our main goal is to escape first, then we'll sort out the rest. I refuse to spend six years in this crappy place. It can be done, but I need your help."

"What can I do?" Julie asked earnestly.

"I need you to call Giles, tell him what happened, and ask him to call Big Sam. You can find his number in the study's phone book. Have him explain the situation and transfer £5,000 to this

Swiss bank account." LeeRoy, with his eyes fixed on the guards, handed her a tightly rolled scrap of paper, roughly the size of a matchstick, taken from inside the hem of his prison shirt. "And when I return, we'll need another £5,000 transferred." Julie shivered as she slipped the note into her pocket. "I don't like this, LeeRoy. What if you get caught? You'll be in even more trouble than now."

"I'll take my chances," he said. "Now listen carefully. You'll need to stay at that hostel, and once I'm out, I'll find it and see what we can do about booking a first-class flight back to London." Julie almost couldn't contain her laughter. "First class? I'd be happy with a bike ride. Anything but returning to that place. It's horrible inside." "I understand, darling. It's no better here, I promise you." A loud bell sounded suddenly, signalling the end of visiting time.

"I love you, Julie."

"Love you too, LeeRoy," Julie said sadly. "I shouldn't, after all this, but I just can't help it." She gave a wry smile. "You're going to pay when we get home, that's for sure." And she walked away.

Near the hostel, Julie discovered a phone box outside and made a collect call to Giles, which took almost 25 minutes to connect.

Once she'd explained everything, Giles couldn't believe what he was hearing.

"I know LeeRoy has been kind to me, Julie, and I don't want to criticise him, but that was simply foolish."

"I know," she sighed. "But please do what I asked you – and do it now."

"Alright, Julie," he hesitated. "Are you alright?"

"Yes, as good as I can be. It was rough in there."

Giles sounded just as worried as she was. "Promise me you'll call if there's anything I can do, okay?" "Yes, I promise. Don't worry." Her voice trembled, "God, this is a mess."

CHAPTER TWENTY-SEVEN — *Bullet at the Gate*

The next morning, LeeRoy was summoned to meet Jesús, who sat in his usual spot in the yard. One of his henchmen frisked him and allowed him to pass.

"Welcome, friend. You've kept your side of the deal. I just received word that the deposit has arrived."

"Great," LeeRoy said. "When can I leave?"

"Whenever you're ready," Jesús smiled, showing a gold tooth. "Does tonight work for you?"

"Absolutely, LeeRoy agreed. The sooner, the better. What's the plan, and how easy or difficult is it going to be?"

"It'll be a piece of cake."

"If it's that easy," LeeRoy said suspiciously, "why are you still here?"

"I'm still here by choice. I've got everything I need. Women, booze, and everything else," he swept his hands through the air, indicating as far as the eye could see. "I call the shots outside. And it's safer for me in here."

"Fair enough," said LeeRoy. "Now, how do I get out?"

"Please wait in the shower room tonight at 9:30. You will be escorted to the kitchens, where a garbage truck departs every evening at 10:00. It will be searched, but somehow, the guards won't notice you on the cabin's floor."

"I hope so," said LeeRoy. "And if I am, the other £5,000 will be in your account tomorrow night."

"Nice doing business with you, LeeRoy," Jesús said as he extended his tattooed hand for a handshake. "And I look forward to doing even more business when you're back in London."

LeeRoy pumped his hand enthusiastically. "You got it, Jesús. And thanks for everything."

Julie had no idea what awaited LeeRoy's escape. All she knew now was that she had done her part, and if Giles and Sam handled their side, she just had to wait. The corruption in Peru was so evident that she believed the prison chief was probably bribed to let LeeRoy walk out the front door. She just needed to stay at the hostel and wait for LeeRoy to arrive once he was free.

And then life could get back to normal, she had to admit; she had no idea what normal was anymore.

At 9:30, LeeRoy waited in the shower room as instructed. When a guard entered, LeeRoy held his breath, but it was fine since he had already been paid. The guard signalled him to follow, and they moved into the kitchen, passing three other guards who ignored them.

Jesús was definitely a miracle worker! LeeRoy almost couldn't help but smile.

The guard opened the door to the compound behind the kitchen, and the truck was right there.

The driver had already opened the passenger door, and LeeRoy quietly got in. He attempted to squeeze onto the floor, but his long, muscular limbs made it challenging to fit in the confined space.

They passed through all three checkpoints without any trouble and were free, well, free from the prison, but not yet Peru.

They travelled roughly 2 miles before stopping. The driver turned to LeeRoy and said, "Fuera, Fuera," meaning to get out. LeeRoy hesitated, checked for safety, and then jumped down. He was unsure of his location or next moves; all he knew was that he had to find Julie and then figure out the next step.

He planned to hide, contact Sam, and devise an escape plan for getting out of Peru.

The truck driver had left him in a quiet area of Lima. He had a rough idea of how to get to where Julie was, but it was several miles away and late at night. He had no money and reflected that he should have stayed longer to organise things better. However, he decided it was too late and started walking toward what he believed was the way to Julie.

He kept walking, conscious that the prison might have realised he was missing by now. However, Jesus told him they wouldn't notice until morning's roll call, so he felt somewhat reassured for the time being.

He noticed a bike leaning against a fence and cautiously looked around. With no one in sight, he approached the bike. Since it wasn't locked and had no lights, he quickly checked his surroundings, then jumped on and pedalled as fast as he could through the darkness toward the woman he loved so deeply.

He got completely lost and had no idea where he was again. He realised he was never going to find the hostel; he had no way of finding out where it was, as he had forgotten the name Julie had told him when she visited him.

He discovered a quiet back road and a nearby park with a bench. Sitting there, he thought about his choices. There weren't many options, and he started to realise how foolish he had been. He had everything—ample money, a lovely wife, and a wonderful house. A perfect life—yet he managed to ruin it all.

He had to keep moving, but to where? he couldn't stop thinking about Julie. He had no way of finding her. *Fuck, you fucking idiot, I can't escape back to England and leave Julie here on her own. I have no option; I'll have to give myself up, make a better plan, and try to escape again. What if I do, and they put me in solitary confinement, and I can't contact Jesus? Even if they do, I'm sure he will be able to reach me — in fact, I'm sure he will. He'll want the rest of his money.*

I was too eager to get out and didn't think it through. What else can I do? If I run, I have no money, no Julie, I'm fucked, idiot.

He was somewhere in the middle of Lima, looking and feeling sorry for himself. The sun rose above the rooftops, and he sat in a bit of a daze. *There must be something I can sort, but I have no idea what.* He knew the police would now be searching for him, and as a Black Englishman, he understood it wouldn't be difficult to identify him. He wasn't mistaken—he was spotted by a lone officer who called for backup. Within minutes, multiple police cars arrived almost simultaneously. Several cops had their guns drawn and aimed at LeeRoy, shouting "Bajar, Bajar." He didn't need to understand the meaning, so he raised his hands. They were not happy with that and repeated, "Bajar Bajar," while gesturing to the ground.

LeeRoy lay on the ground, instinctively knowing what to do by placing his hands behind his back. He was quickly handcuffed, though not before receiving a solid kick to the ribs.

The officers were excited, but LeeRoy didn't understand what was happening; he was pulled to his feet, thrown into a van, and soon returned to prison. He was taken underground, where a big wooden door opened, and he was pushed inside while still handcuffed. The cell was dark, damp, and smelled like a sewer, and then the door slammed shut behind him.

He stayed inside, still in handcuffs, without food or water for more than three hours. When the door opened, two guards entered quietly, seized him, and led him up three flights of stairs to a room with a steel table in the centre. They sat him in a chair behind the table, unlocked one cuff, but then relocked it to the table.

He stayed there for thirty minutes until the door opened, and a familiar voice said, "Good afternoon." It was Don José. LeeRoy shot daggers at him. "What do you want, you lying bastard?" he snapped. "Now, now, that's no way to greet a friend," Don José replied with a smile. "You are no friend of mine," LeeRoy barked. "You lied to me, promising to free my wife if I signed a confession." "Well, things don't always go as planned, I'm sure you agree. Your escape didn't go to plan either, or you wouldn't be sitting here now."

"Fuck off," snapped LeeRoy.

"This is just a formality," Don José said. "I need to ask about your escape and who helped you, but I doubt you'll say anything. My presence here shows I have done my duty." Don José then rose silently and departed. The guards freed LeeRoy from the table, led him back to the room he had just left, opened the door, removed the handcuffs this time, and pushed him inside again.

It was after 8 p.m. when the hatch in the door opened, and a mess they called food was handed through, along with a mug of water. Despite the food's foul smell, LeeRoy, who was starving and dehydrated, appreciated anything he received.

He was left there for five days without a shower, with a bucket in the corner that wasn't emptied during those five days and nights he was there.

Julie had tried to visit again but was told she couldn't, and no one explained why; she asked Adrianna if she could find out why she couldn't see him.

Two days later, Adrianna visited Julie and explained why she couldn't see him. "Why?" Julie asked sharply. "I'm about to tell you. Your husband escaped from prison."

"He got away?" Julie exclaimed.

"No, unfortunately not. He was recaptured the next morning and is now in solitary confinement." Julie lowered her head and started to cry. "Does that mean I won't see him again?" "No, I've been told he should be transferred back to the main prison in two days, but this is Peru, so expect it may not happen."

LeeRoy was let back into the general population in three days. The first thing he did was shower and shave.

After stepping out of the shower, he was approached by two of Jesus's henchmen who simply said, "You're wanted." LeeRoy understood where he was being taken.

He approached Jesus, who appeared somewhat puzzled. "What happened? You were only out overnight — how the fuck did you get caught so quickly?"

LeeRoy first assured him, "Don't worry, you'll still get your second payment." Jesus responded, "Please, to hear that." He then asked, "Now, what went wrong?" LeeRoy explained his decision, admitting he shouldn't have been in such a rush. He mentioned that they need to plan differently and try again next week if possible.

"Anything is possible, but it will be on the same terms. Are you okay with that?" "Yes, yes, of course. The money is not the problem, but I will need some cash before I leave again. Can you arrange $1,000 for me? Of course, I will ensure it is repaid with interest before I leave."

"That, my friend, will not be an issue. Let me know when you're ready to leave, and I'll take care of everything once more." LeeRoy shook his hand, as many other prisoners watched, curious about how he had become part of Jesus's inner circle so quickly.

Two days later, Adrianna visited Julie and gave her the good news that she could now see her husband, which made Julie very happy. "Great," she said, "I'll go this afternoon."

She arrived at the prison slightly late but still managed to enter and see LeeRoy. As always, he was sitting at a table, chained with both hands.

She attempted to hug him, but noticing a guard watching, she sat down opposite LeeRoy instead. The first thing she said was, "Adrianna told me you escaped, but they caught you the very next morning. What happened?"

He recounted the story once more and told her he planned to leave again on Friday. "Remind me of the hostel's name and keep repeating it until you leave, so I don't forget." She did so multiple times. "Are you sure this is a good idea? If they caught you before, they might do so again." "Don't worry, I'm sure Jesus is bunging every cop in Lima; they only caught me last time because I let it happen." "If you're certain," she replied, "I'll be ready this time. At least I know you're coming and will be prepared. I might have been out dancing last time and missed you." She smiled, excited by the thought of them being free and together again.

The bell rang, signalling her to leave. She repeated the hostel's name once more, and LeeRoy mouthed it back, quietly saying, 'See you Friday.'

LeeRoy made a collect call to Sam and had the money sent to the Swiss bank account, along with the additional $1000, as he had done before. Jesus sent one of his henchmen, who gave LeeRoy the $1000 and said, "Be ready just as last time."

As before, LeeRoy was in the shower room, and it felt like déjà vu as he was in the truck, ready to escape once again.

They had to go through the three checkpoints again before LeeRoy was free. They quickly passed the first two, but at the third, the barrier remained closed, and the guard signalled for the truck to pull into a lay-by. The driver muttered curses under his breath as he followed the order, sweat beading on his forehead as he looked around, clearly upset.

This wasn't supposed to happen. They were meant to drive straight out.

LeeRoy, crouching on the floor, immediately sensed the tension and braced himself.

A guard armed with an automatic rifle approached the driver, motioning for him to roll down the window and asking for his ID, which he handed over. LeeRoy tried to curl into the corner, but being a large man, he didn't fit comfortably in the tight space. Luckily, the guard couldn't see the passenger side foot-well because it was too high for him to see over the door.

As the guard returned the pass to the driver, he started searching under the truck and opened the back. The driver's panic grew. This wasn't what he had been told to expect. He looked at LeeRoy, gesturing him to leave with a wave and saying, "Fuera! Fuera!"

However, there was no way LeeRoy could escape. The guard, hearing the driver's cry, immediately became suspicious. He circled to the passenger side and opened the door. As he did, LeeRoy quickly kicked him in the head with one leg. The guard fell, but in the process, with his finger already on the trigger, he fired the rifle, spraying the cabin with bullets.

LeeRoy was shot in several places and gasped in shock. He looked down in surprise, watching the blood bloom out across his prison shirt.

It all happened too quickly for the pain to set in.

All he felt was shock and amazement as the large red stain on his chest spread wider, darkened, and became wetter.

Wow, I never thought.

Then he coughed up blood into his mouth, tasting the bitter metallic flavour, and watched it drip out in thick strings, drooping from his chin and splattering into his lap.

That's a surprise!

Again, he felt only slightly amazed, staring down in wonder as his entire world closed in and everything went black.

………Julie?

CHAPTER TWENTY-EIGHT — *Northbound Without a Passport*

Julie remained awake all night, staring out the window, wishing LeeRoy would emerge from the darkness and take her away from this terrible country. As dawn broke, she understood that he had either been caught again or chosen to stay. She planned to visit later and discover what was wrong and finally fell asleep.

Later that evening, Adrianna Madigan, Julie's lawyer, knocked on her bedroom door. Julie, mistaking her for LeeRoy, jumped up excitedly.

"Oh, hi, Adrianna," Julie said, surprised and upset. "I wasn't expecting to see you for a while."

"Sit down, Julie."

"Why? Is something wrong?" Julie asked, surprised by her lawyer's serious face. "Do I need to return to that dreadful prison?"

"No, Julie, not until after your trial," she said, pausing and meeting Julie's gaze. "But I'm sorry to say I have some terrible news for you."

"What?" A tight breath escaped Julie.

Adrianna cleared her throat and nervously patted Julie's hand. "There's no easy way to say this, Julie, so I'll just say it. Your husband is dead."

Julie stared at her, unable to believe what she had just heard.

"No," she even laughed, dismissing it as a ridiculous idea. She had just seen him recently. Then it hit her, and she burst into tears. "What do you mean by dead? I saw him just the other day! How? Why?" Her face fell in grief and disbelief. "Oh my God! You must be wrong!"

"I'm sorry, Julie, but I'm not mistaken. He was shot while trying to escape from prison."

"No, no, no!" Julie cried hysterically.

Adrianna tried to comfort her, but nothing seemed to help. Julie's whole world had just shattered, and she didn't know what to do.

Adrianna stayed with Julie for an hour until her tears slowed down a bit, but eventually, she had to leave.

"Are you going to be okay?"

"How am I going to be, okay?" Julie groaned. "My husband's dead, and I'm going to end up in prison thousands of miles from home. I wish I had died with him."

Adrianna's lips twisted, uncertain of what to say. After a brief silence, she reached out and touched Julie's shoulder. "I'll come to see you tomorrow morning, Julie, but I need to leave now."

Julie attempted a comforting smile. "That's okay, Adrianna. I understand it's not your fault. Thanks for sitting with me."

"Not a problem, Julie," Adrianna replied softly. "See you in the morning."

As the door closed, Julie buried her head into the pillow, tears falling as she drifted into a restless sleep.

Julie woke up at 2:20 a.m., feeling lost, confused, and alone. The memory of the terrible news she'd received and the fact that she'd never feel LeeRoy's strong arms around her again brought her to tears. She cried until exhaustion took over, then fell asleep again.

A knock at the door at 9:30 a.m. the next morning woke her. It was Adrianna asking, "How are you, Julie?"

"I don't know, Adrianna," Julie said, her voice flat, her eyes red and swollen. "I'm devastated, but also numb, exhausted, and sore from crying all night. I hoped I would wake up and discover it was just a bad dream. But it's real." She shook her head, exhausted, and her thoughts drifted to what the future held.

"Will I still have to go to court?"

"Yes, Julie," Adrianna said. "I'm afraid you will. You won't find any sympathy here. They probably won't even know what happened, and they definitely won't care, especially since you're a foreigner."

Julie bowed her head sadly, tracing her fingers along the frayed edge of a blanket. "What will happen to LeeRoy?" she asked. "His body will probably be sent back to England after an autopsy," was the answer. "Will I be able to see him?" Her voice quivered at the thought of seeing her beloved LeeRoy, who was always so lively, now lying cold on a slab, his smooth black skin pale and lifeless.

"I doubt that, Julie. Not in Peru, at least." "Well, it won't be in England, will it?" Julie snapped angrily.

"Look, Julie," Adrianna said softly, "I'm sorry for your loss, but now we need to focus on you and how we can help you move past this." Her voice faded slightly. "Though I don't think we'll get you fully off. Are you supposed to report to the police today?"

"If it's Thursday, then yes," Julie replied vaguely. "I have no idea what day it is."

"Yes, Julie, it is Thursday. Come on, get ready, and I'll drive you down there."

Julie felt unwell and exhausted, yet she understood she needed to visit the police to avoid returning to jail, something she desperately wanted to prevent. She followed her usual routine of washing, dressing, and brushing her hair. After twenty minutes, she was ready, and Adrianna took her to the police station.

She was in and out in two minutes – they weren't interested. Neither was she.

"I'll drop you back at the hostel, Julie," Adrianna said, leading her back to the car.

"That's okay, Adrianna. I'll walk back," Julie's voice was flat, all emotion drained from her. "I have all the time in the world."

Adrianna looked closely at her. "Are you certain?"

"Yes, I'm sure," she said quietly, then lifted her gaze to Adrianna's face, attempting a reassuring smile. "I want to walk. I need some time to think."

"Alright, then," Adrianna said, still uncertain. "Bye for now. I'll contact you as soon as I have any updates."

"Thank you."

Julie was overwhelmed with a flood of thoughts. Stranded in Peru with a drug smuggling charge and her beloved husband gone, she thought, 'What a disaster!' Her mind was filled with worry and grief. She understood she couldn't endure ten years in that awful place; she wouldn't last a year, let alone a decade. She needed to find a way out of the country, but with almost no money and no passport, it seemed impossible. Still, she was determined to try, even if it meant risking her life. Staying felt like being dead, and attempting an escape seemed just as lethal—but she had no choice but to take the risk. Returning to that terrible place was unimaginable.

Three weeks passed, and she reported to the police every Thursday.

When she returned from deep in her thoughts to the hostel, she barely noticed three American guys at the reception. One of them greeted her with a "Hi" as she approached.

She barely acknowledged with a mumble of hello, but as she passed by, she suddenly paused. Overcome by desperation, she hesitated briefly before turning around. All three men now watched her as she quickly looked down the hallway to confirm no one else was nearby.

The guys were confused – she was standing there, staring at them.

"Are you okay?" one of them asked.

She started crying uncontrollably.

Another guy dropped his backpack on the ground and approached her, asking again, "Are you okay? Oh, God – what a stupid question. If you were okay, you wouldn't be crying."

She couldn't even respond.

"Come over here and sit down," he told her.

She sat in a chair just inside the door, trembling despite the hot day and the lack of air conditioning in the hallway.

"My name's Harry," he said, sitting beside her. "And those two friends are Mike and Mike. Yes," he smiled. "It can be confusing at times. Now, what's wrong? Is there something we can help you with?"

Julie, overwhelmed with emotion and unable to hide it, felt she had nothing to lose. She chose to disclose everything – even that she was contemplating fleeing the country, whether legally or illegally, if it came to that.

Harry said, "Wow, that's tough. So, you're planning to try escaping from Peru?"

"Yes, I am," she said, nodding firmly. "But it won't be easy. I don't have much money, and I don't have a passport, but I can't stay here. I'll die in prison." Her voice faltered, and she broke down again.

"Can you give us a minute? I want to talk to the Mikes."

"Yes," she said, wiping her nose on her sleeve and trying to compose herself. "Of course. I need to go to my room to collect what few belongings I have. I'm leaving now."

She stood up, her eyes glassy and vacant like a zombie, and walked toward the stairway.

"But if we get caught helping her, we'll also end up in prison!" the older Mike warned after Harry explained the situation.

The younger Mike shrugged, saying, "Yeah. It wouldn't be safe for her to travel with us."

Harry sighed and paused to consider. "You're right, of course," he admitted reluctantly. "So, what should we do? We have to help her. We can't just walk away and leave her to face that prison alone."

The two Mikes agreed, but the older Mike said, "All we can do is give her some money and wish her luck. I'm not taking any chances. And if we're seen with her," he made a throat-slitting motion.

The other two agreed, but they didn't have much spare cash. They needed what they had for the rest of their trip in South America.

"C'mon," Harry encouraged, opening his wallet. "Let's see what we can spare."

"I guess we can always ask our parents for more," Mike said with a slight smile, his eyes filling up.

They scraped together sixty-five dollars from their pockets and wallets. It wasn't much, but it would help Julie.

Julie returned calmer, having made her decision. She carried her bag and approached the boys with a hopeful expression. She was now receptive to any help they could provide.

Harry glanced at her and said, "We've discussed your situation, and we can offer you sixty-five dollars to help you out." He took a deep breath and added, "I wish we could do more, but we believe it's too risky."

"I understand," Julie interrupted, avoiding further embarrassment for him. "I wouldn't want to put you in a difficult position like I've experienced." She aimed to sound cheerful, though it was just an act. "Sixty-five dollars would be a big help, and I truly appreciate it. However, please note that this is a loan, correct? Can I get your addresses? If I manage to succeed, I'll return the money to you."

"That won't be necessary," Harry said with a smile, trying to reassure. He coughed awkwardly. "And I don't think it's a good idea to give you our address, just in case you get caught."

"You're right, of course," she said, shaking her head. She had almost forgotten she was a fugitive.

"We'd love to hear if you make it," little Mike said shyly.

"Hang on," she said, then approached the empty reception desk, took a pen and paper, and wrote her Faversham phone number before handing it to Harry. "Call this number. Giles will let you know if he's heard anything."

"I feel bad just letting you walk away," said Harry, "but we just can't take the chance."

"It's not a problem," said Julie, smiling bravely. "I'll probably handle it better on my own." She didn't honestly believe what she was saying. "Thanks again to all of you. You might have just saved my life. Now, I need to go. I have six days before I have to report again."

"Good luck, Julie," the Mikes said. "We'll call you in a couple of weeks and hope you answer," Harry added with a reassuring smile. "You're a courageous girl." Brave? she thought. *No, not courageous—terrified and desperate, more accurate.*

Fuck, what the hell am I doing?

Outside the front door, it suddenly hit her—she had no idea where she was headed. Her plan was simple: find a bus station and board any bus going north.

Why north? She had no particular reason, just felt the need to go somewhere. Maybe she could find a map and figure it out, but for now, escaping Lima was her priority.

After an hour of walking, she finally found a bus station at Commercial Centre Plaza Norte.

Repeating the same process she had in Hastings—now a distant memory—she randomly chose a destination that sounded appealing: Huacho. Although it was only about 100 miles away, it was enough distance for now.

Julie's trip would take two to three hours, arriving in daylight with enough time to pick up a map and find a place to stay.

The ticket agent didn't speak English, but through gestures, facial expressions, tone of voice, and images in a brochure, Julie understood she had two bus options to Huacho: a cheap one for $2 that took longer, or a faster, more expensive, and safer one for $10. She would have preferred the pricier bus, but as she wanted to save her limited funds, she chose the cheaper option.

However, in Peru, that wasn't the best decision! The cheap buses were old and poorly maintained, frequently breaking down. When they did, they simply did what was necessary to get started again. Many fatal accidents involving these buses were primarily due to poor maintenance and overworked, underpaid drivers working long shifts without adequate rest. Mugging was another issue, though less frequent during the day; overnight buses were often held up by bandits in the mountains.

Julie, of course, was unaware of these risks and had no clue about the dangers. The bus arrived: a very old Leyland, spewing black smoke from its exhaust.

Julie quickly realised she should have paid the extra fee, but it was too late. The bus pulled over, and the driver kept the engine running, probably worried it wouldn't start again. Julie showed her ticket and got on, moving to the back so no one had to walk past her. She sat down and soon started choking on the diesel fumes and thick black smoke from the exhaust, but she had no choice but to endure it. Seven more passengers boarded — she counted them and scrutinized each one, feeling nervous and paranoid, yet confident that the police wouldn't be looking for her for another six days as long as she checked in. She was foolishly hopeful she'd be home by then.

Surprisingly, the bus departed on time. It made several stops at different bus stops before leaving Lima, and eight additional passengers boarded along the way. None of these new passengers sat in the back with Julie, which she was pretty pleased about.

After approximately thirty minutes, the bus pulled over at Alfredo Mendiola, and about twenty additional passengers boarded. However, no one took the seats in the back. Julie assumed it was because she was a white girl, and she probably was correct.

They continued through several towns, with people boarding and leaving the bus. Finally, they arrived in Santa Rosa and travelled along the coast road through Chancay. At that point, Julie started admiring the ocean view, but they soon stopped at Huaral, where several families got on, carrying small cages with live chickens. The bus quickly filled up, including all the seats around Julie. A woman with thick arms sat beside her, her rolls of fat spilling into Julie's space as she held a rusty cage with three chickens crammed inside. The unpleasant smell of sweaty bodies and chicken waste almost made Julie gag. It was nearly as bad as being in prison.

The bus was now crowded, hot, and filled with fumes, unwashed bodies, and animal waste, but Julie had no choice. She had to accept whatever came. The rest of the bumpy ride was very uncomfortable, but they eventually arrived in Huacho.

Julie was happy to get off that bus. She could see the ocean and decided to head that way. She didn't know why—it was just a gut feeling, but she went anyway. Passing an old gas station, she went inside to look for a map. Luckily, it only cost a dollar. She also bought two chocolate bars for fifty cents more. They would keep her fuelled for a while.

She couldn't shake a strong sense of déjà vu as she left with her belongings. Here she was again, as if destined to keep running away, walking toward the sea, as if it were calling her.

Julie finally arrived at the shoreline at 5:10 p.m. To her surprise, a long pier extended in front of her, bringing back memories of Hastings and her first adventure after leaving the children's home. She gazed at the vibrant blue ocean and reminisced sadly about everything that had happened since then. These were bittersweet memories. She had been so happy since meeting LeeRoy! Now she shed another tear, letting the sunshine dry her face. She understood she had to stay strong and was resolved to survive.

She wandered around, adjusting to her surroundings while thinking about where to sleep later and trying to avoid drawing attention to herself. She found an old, discarded straw hat near the pier and tucked her tousled blonde hair into it. This helped hide her face, making her less noticeable as the only pale-skinned blonde woman in town.

By 8 p.m., Julie was worn out and searching for a place to rest. The pier was a solid structure, so she knew she couldn't find shelter beneath it. She walked along the beach, where she had noticed some small, overturned rowing boats. She scanned her surroundings for passersby and, when no one was watching, crouched down to slip beneath one of the boats. It was dark inside the coffin-like structure, but she didn't linger on dark thoughts—she was too exhausted. Soon, she drifted into a deep sleep.

Just after 6 a.m., Julie was abruptly awakened by a loud noise and bright daylight as the small boat she hid under was overturned, exposing her. The shock hit Julie, the elderly fisherman, and his son. At first, they believed she was dead, but they soon saw she was alive when she jumped up and ran away. Her legs, exhausted from deep sleep, shock, and shifting sand, couldn't outrun the son, who quickly caught her.

"Let me go, let me go!" she yelled, but he held her firmly as she struggled against him with all her might, unable to break free.

Realising resistance was futile, she stopped fighting. The son held her close and guided her back to his father, speaking gently in Spanish, a language she didn't understand.

The father said something to the son and walked off at a brisk pace, which sent Julie into a panic, thinking he was going to get the police. She started to struggle again, but she was no match for him. *This guy's as strong as LeeRoy.*

That thought caused her to break down in tears. The son appeared worried, unfamiliar with seeing white girls in that area. He was frightened by the fact that he had a crying white girl in his grasp.

Just then, the father returned with a young girl, barely a teenager, who could see that Julie was terrified.

"Are you American?" she asked. Julie was surprised to hear English but also pleased that she could communicate. "No, I'm English," she answered. "Please relax," the girl said. "Nobody's going to hurt you. I'm Lina," she added, patting her chest.

The young man said something to her, and she nodded, then told Julie, "My brother, Marco, will let you go. But..." She raised a finger. "Please don't run away. We won't harm you."

"I won't," Julie replied, her fear and despair making her feel too weak. The girl then asked, "Why were you beneath my father's boat?"

Julie started panicking again. If she told them the truth, they'd probably call the police. "I lost my passport. I lost everything. I was mugged two nights ago in Lima. I'm trying to get to Ecuador because I have friends there," she said, pointing to the map she bought at the gas station.

"Ecuador!" the girl exclaimed. "That's a long way."

"I know," Julie said, though she wasn't sure about the distance or the exact location of Ecuador. It had seemed near on the map. "How will you get there?" Lina asked.

"I have no idea," Julie shrugged. "I guess by bus."

The girl translated everything for her father and brother, who, judging by their sympathetic expressions, felt sorry for her, but there wasn't much they could do. They had a long conversation in Spanish, which ended with the man telling his daughter, "Breakfast!"

"Our father says you should come home and eat," Lina told Julie.

"That's very kind of him," Julie replied. "Please tell him thank you very much, but I don't want to trouble you, as I think they were just going fishing, and I would hate to hold them up." Julie was concerned about being seen by others and possibly attracting the police's attention.

"It's not a problem. They were preparing the boat to go out later and returning home for breakfast beforehand, so it's no bother at all. You are very welcome. It's also good for me to practise my English," Lina said.

"If you're sure it's not a problem, I'd really appreciate it."

The father smiled and said something, but Julie didn't catch what it was—only that it was kind.

The family brought Julie to their modest home, where they set out bread, jam, ham, olives, and sliced avocado on the table and encouraged her to eat.

"Avena," the man said with a smile, spooning some oatmeal for her.

"Quaker," Lina explained, pronouncing the brand name clearly to show they had Quaker oats.

Their kindness touched Julie, and grateful

After finishing, Lina gestured to the wash basin and asked, "Want to wash up?"

Julie eagerly accepted. The bathroom was a small tin structure beside the house, with a sink and a cold-water tap, but she didn't mind. She was moved by their kindness despite their hardships and felt grateful. When she returned inside to say goodbye and thank them, she saw Lina packing a school bag. She initially thought Lina was headed to school, but then Lina buckled the straps and handed the bag to Julie.

"There is some food and water, enough for a couple of days."

Julie began to cry.

"What's wrong?" Lina asked, concerned.

"It's nothing. I've encountered some terrible people in Peru, but also very kind ones, and you are definitely among the nicest."

"Kind ones?" the girl asked, her young brow furrowed in confusion.

"You are very kind," smiled Julie, wiping away a tear. "Oh, thank you."

"I mean it," said Julie. "You've been exceptionally kind to me, and I can't thank you enough."

"As Americans often say," Lina said with a smile, "You're very welcome." The two men remained stiff in the background, offering shy smiles. Julie kissed both of them on the cheek, making them grin and blush intensely.

"I have to leave now," Julie said. "But if I ever return to this country, I will make sure to visit you." She knew this would never actually happen; she only wanted to leave and never return.

"That's nice," Lina said. "Goodbye and good luck."

"Thank you," Julie said, giving Lina a quick hug before heading back to the bus station, still moved by the family's kindness.

While in the waiting room, Julie examined the map and located Ecuador. It seemed as good a destination as any, as long as she could leave Peru first. Then she might dare to call Giles.

The bus timetable showed only a single bus that morning, heading to Barranca about fifty miles away. She would have preferred a longer trip, but this was the only option available, so she paid $7 for a ticket.

The bus left on schedule, and she arrived at Barranca by noon without incident. Though somewhat confident, she still felt nervous about crossing into Ecuador without a passport. She decided to put those worries aside for now.

In Barranca, she checked the schedule and found a 3 p.m. departure for Chiclayo, over 400 miles away, with an expected arrival time of around 1 a.m. She wasn't eager to spend the night on a bus, but believed she had no other choice.

She spent fifteen dollars on a ticket, her anxiety mounting as her limited funds trickled away like water. Fortunately, she had some food and water, provided by the kind fisherman and his daughter.

Once again, Julie was surprised when the bus left on time. It was slightly better than the first two she had ridden, but not significantly. Fortunately, she had the back seat all to herself again.

There were about thirty people, including five kids, on the bus as it departed. The first stop was Tarapaca, where a few people got off and a few more boarded, and the bus was soon on its way again. The next stop was La Gramita, before they headed over the mountains to another place with the same confusing name: Tarapaca. For a moment, Julie panicked, thinking the bus had somehow driven her back again, but she noticed the terrain looked different. As she traced the route on the map with her finger, she realised it was in an entirely different location, even though it had the same name.

Four backpackers and four suspicious-looking men boarded the bus, but Julie ducked down, hiding her face with her hat and shrinking into the corner. She decided it was safest to stay hidden. The less she was seen, the better, particularly since the police might start questioning people later when they realised she was missing.

The bus was filling up, and two elderly women sat beside Julie. They didn't say a word, and Julie leaned against the window, trying to sleep despite the bus's rattling and swaying.

The bus was climbing the mountain and nearing a crossroads when one of the suspicious-looking men stood up, prompting the other three also to rise.

The first one walked directly up to the driver and pressed a gun to his head, while the other two positioned back-to-back—one facing the back of the bus and the other facing forward. Both had handguns and were yelling at the passengers in Spanish, their voices rising above the gasps of some of the passengers.

Julie immediately knew what was happening, so she quickly pulled out most of the money she had left and stuffed the bills down her sock.

The bus halted at the crossroads, and from what Julie could see, the robbers instructed everyone to leave their bags on the seats and exit the bus. Meanwhile, a truck arrived at the intersection.

One by one, passengers were allowed to leave the bus. Tourists were frisked beforehand, but the Peruvian nationals were let go without losing their dignity, even if their bags on the seats were fair game. As the four backpackers tried to disembark, a gangster held a gun to them, while another ordered them to remove their watches and searched their pockets.

Julie was the third from last to step off. The gang noticed she was a white girl and searched her thoroughly, even finding the money in her sock.

Julie began to cry in despair, having lost everything. Once everyone was off, two hijackers watched over the crowd with guns, while others searched the bus and emptied the luggage on the seats for money and valuables.

After they finished, the men quickly ran to the waiting truck, climbed in, and disappeared. The Peruvian passengers and the driver got back on the bus as if nothing had happened. Julie believed this was common, and since the Peruvians had nothing, they had nothing to lose. The gang's main target was the backpackers, and Julie's few remaining dollars were just a bonus. She was surprised they hadn't found the $10 hidden in her satchel as bait, meant to distract them from her sock stash. She guessed they thought it was a kid's bag and didn't bother checking inside.

I should have left the other money there.

After that detour, the bus arrived in Chiclayo at 2 a.m. The smooth and efficient hijacking only delayed them by 25 minutes. Julie was feeling very anxious, worried that the driver might have alerted the authorities and that the police were waiting to take statements. But she didn't need to worry – it seemed like a regular occurrence, and the bus company didn't bother reporting it to the police.

Julie and the backpackers each received a printed card stating that they must visit the local police station to file a report to make an insurance claim.

One of the backpackers asked Julie, who was trying to stay out of the way, if she spoke English.

"I am English," she said. "So are we." He introduced himself as John. The other three joined them. "Where are you from?" John asked. "Faversham," Julie said. "And you?"

"We all live in London. We were enjoying this trip – until now."

His friend, Gerry, added, "But we were warned this sort of thing could happen, so we hid most of our money, cameras, and passports in our backpacks, which were in the hold. Bandits rarely go there because there isn't enough time to search everything, and they're afraid of getting caught." "You're lucky—they took all my money, just a small amount of what I had left, except for ten dollars."

"Are you insured?" John asked.

Julie almost cried again but ended up bursting into laughter. "What's so funny?" he inquired. "Oh, it's a long story," she replied.

"We have plenty of time," Gerry added. "Let's grab a drink or something." They headed toward a bar as Gerry continued talking,

"We need to report to the police station in the morning, and the next bus isn't until ten tomorrow."

Once they had ordered some drinks and snacks, insisting that they pay and Julie join them, Gerry smiled expectantly, eager for her story. "Go on, then. We're all sitting comfortably, so you can begin."

"Look, you seem like a nice bunch of guys," Julie sighed, "but you don't want to get involved with me."

"Why? Are the police after you?" John asked with a joke.

"In fact, yes, they are," she responded casually.

"Really?" John exclaimed, surprised. "No way! You're joking, right?"

"I wish I were," she replied sadly. "I wish I were."

"Why? What did you do?"

She scrutinised them, made her judgment, and chose to take a risk. They were English and appeared to be sincere, decent men. These days, she often relies on the kindness of strangers, a recurring theme in her life. Despite facing hardships, she trusts her ability to read people well.

Although she might have faced difficulties, she was not stupid. Taking a deep breath, she retold her story, becoming emotional as she shared about LeeRoy and her time in prison, while they listened quietly.

"Holy crap, Julie!" Gerry exclaimed.

John asked seriously, "What are you trying to do?"

"Where are you going?" The other two asked, "Do you have your passport?"

Julie shook her head. "No, I don't, and I only have $10, so I'm in a bit more trouble than I was already. I'm trying to get to Ecuador."

"Ecuador? Why Ecuador?"

"I have no bloody idea," she shrugged, feeling silly to admit it. "It seemed like the most straightforward country to get to. I need to get out of Peru, find a British Embassy, and get home, hopefully."

Gerry nodded. "I'm guessing you won't be going to the police station later?"

"No chance. I'd be sent straight back to Lima, and I'd rather be dead than go back to that shithole of a prison."

John paused briefly, glanced questioningly at his friends, who nodded, then told Julie, "We're heading north for a while. Feel free to join us if you'd like."

"Thanks, John," Julie said earnestly, "but if you're caught helping me, you might end up in prison yourself—and trust me, you wouldn't want to see a Peruvian jail." She sighed, feeling like she was going in circles, repeating the same story without making any progress.

John shrugged his shoulders, appearing uncertain. "I suppose you're right, but I would feel guilty not helping you."

One of his other friends, Tom, proposed, "Why not ride the same bus as us so we can watch over you, but you sit alone and act as if you're not with us?"

Julie shrugged and said, "I don't see a problem with that," then added, "I only have $10 left, and that won't get me far." Hoping they would assist again and feeling guilty about assuming that, but in desperation, she had to put her feelings aside.

Gerry chimed in, "We're heading up to Piura and then hiking across the mountains to Chulucanas. I think we'd be more than happy to chip in and pay for you to get there."

A couple of his friends nodded in agreement, and Keith added, "Yeah, it's only about $15—that's under $4 each, so it won't break the bank if we all pitch in."

She was about to speak, but Gerry interrupted her. "I know you don't want charity, but you're in a tough spot, and we genuinely want to help you."

Gerry added, "But we need to watch out for ourselves, so we'll do what we can and stay careful, okay?"

Julie drew in a sharp breath and smiled in relief. "Thank you. You have no idea how much that means to me. This is only my second time meeting trekkers, and each one has been incredibly kind."

"Come on, Julie, what kind of people would we be if we left you here? We couldn't bear to live with ourselves."

"I understand and would do the same, but I don't want to cause you trouble, so I'll act as if I didn't see you when others are present."

"Ah, forget about the money," John said, waving his hand dismissively. "You're a brave girl, Julie. I don't think I'd do as well in your position." The others agreed.

"Let's try to rest before morning," Gerry suggested. "After that, we can go to the police station. Oh, wait," he paused. "Actually, I don't think we should file any reports," he said, glancing at the others. "We didn't lose much, and with the insurance excess, we won't get much anyway."

"Then we don't need to go to the police station!" John snapped his fingers in agreement. "What do you all think?" he asked the others. They all agreed and selected spots at the bus station to settle down and try to sleep.

Back in the UK, Giles was overwhelmed with worry. He busied himself keeping the gardens and house immaculate while LeeRoy and Julie were gone, hoping to distract himself. Still, he was deeply unsettled by what Julie had told him, sensing that what she shared on the phone was only the beginning.

If only he knew what was going on!

He almost thought about reaching out to the British Embassy in Peru, but he understood it was wiser not to alert the authorities. If LeeRoy and Julie managed to escape, he would have to wait for news.

He had completed what Julie asked for and what LeeRoy wanted. Giles and Sam collaborated to deposit £5000 into the bank account Julie provided over the phone. The remaining £5000, which LeeRoy wanted them to set aside and have ready, was still sitting there, waiting for his instructions to transfer it. However, they were still waiting.

Giles felt frustrated and angry. No matter what LeeRoy's motives were, he shouldn't have brought Julie into it. Julie was sweet and innocent, having done nothing wrong, and she trusted LeeRoy with her life.

Every time Giles thought about it, his fingers clenched into knuckles, and he imagined himself punching LeeRoy hard to teach him a lesson. Although he respected LeeRoy and appreciated his help, he wasn't sure he could forgive him for risking Julie's safety. If anything happened to her, his jaw tightened, and his fists clenched.

CHAPTER TWENTY-NINE — *Water, Dust, and the Road to Freedom*

At around 8 a.m., one of the guys suggested grabbing some breakfast at a small food stall just outside the bus station.

"Come on, Julie," John urged her. "We'll treat you to breakfast. That won't break the bank either."

"I feel bad about all this," Julie said. "You've been so kind."

"That's no problem," one of the guys said. "It's all part of our adventure. Just imagine the story we can tell when we get home! Ambushed by bandits, helped a beautiful English fugitive escape from Peru, and by the time we spice it up, who knows what the story will be? I could even write a book about it," he laughed and opened the door for Julie.

They walked over to the small stall and ordered a kind of breakfast. There were eggs, scrambled with who knows what — it was spicy, but it tasted okay. There were also thin slices of ham, spicy sausage, and hot coffee.

They had just arrived when a police car pulled up and parked nearby. Two officers stepped out and sat at the table next to them.

Julie's heart was pounding, as was the guy's, but the police paid them no attention, just ordering coffees and chatting, assuming they were all backpackers together.

The guys and Julie finished their breakfast so quickly that they probably would get indigestion later, but they just wanted to get away from the police.

At the bus station, Julie said, "That's why you must stay away from me. If they had recognised me or even suspected anything, you all would have been in trouble."

"You're right," Gerry muttered, sweat falling from his wrinkled forehead. "Here's $15. It might be better if you buy your own ticket."

"It will be," she said, taking the money gratefully. "And from now on, if anyone is near us, I'll just ignore you. Okay?"

"Yes, Julie." John ran his hand through his floppy fringe. "God, this is not real!"

Surprisingly, the next bus left on time once again. Julie had become so accustomed to the laid-back vibe of British transportation that she couldn't believe a relatively poor country like Peru could be so efficient. Still, it suited her needs just fine.

This part of the journey covered nearly 180 miles and took over five hours along the smooth Panamericana Norte Highway. After dozing off most of the way, Julie reached Piura without any issues.

When they disembarked, John quickly shared a brief history, mentioning that Piura was founded in 1532 by the Spanish and is Peru's oldest city.

Julie tried to sound interested, but she was mainly eager to get started as soon as possible.

Piura was the site where the Spanish exported stolen Inca gold to Spain.

"Right," Julie muttered, distracted.

As they exited the bus station, one of the men noticed a poster for a carnival that evening. "That seems like a lot of fun."

A nearby bus driver, who spoke English, joined in, saying, "Yes, this month is Inti Raymi in Peru — a time of celebration, romance, and a bit of chaos." He smiled and continued.

"Be prepared to get quite wet if you're out in the streets, as Peruvians love to throw water at each other and anyone nearby during carnival season. Also, watch out for pickpockets."

Keith recommended they stay and experience the carnival, and everyone agreed.

John then suggested to Julie that she join them that evening. "One night won't make much difference, and you might even enjoy it." Julie's foot bobbed nervously, feeling frustrated about not being able to distance herself further from Lima. "I really should move on," she said, gazing into the distance.

But John insisted, saying, "Come on, we'll treat you and find the hostel so you can share a room with us." He added sincerely, "Don't worry, we're all safe."

"You're the last thing on my mind," Julie replied.

She paused for a moment, knowing they needed a break. Some fun amidst all this chaos would be good.

However, with any luck, her disappearance wouldn't be noticed for a few more days, when she failed to check in with the police, so she decided to stay. She needed a bed and a shower, and it would be good for her to try to unwind, at least for one night, and clear her mind of LeeRoy and the fear of being caught and returned to prison. She shuddered at the thought.

They took a local bus to the hostel and checked in. John, ever the good Samaritan, booked and paid for Julie's room. Julie was so thankful that she gave him a big hug and a kiss on the cheek, making him blush deeply. The other three felt a bit envious.

They arranged to meet at 6 p.m. in the lobby, and Julie headed to her room.

The bathroom was down the hall, but she didn't mind; her priority was to get clean. Luckily, it was empty, so she locked the door and turned on the lukewarm water. This brought tremendous relief. She finally relaxed after days of stress.

She leaned over and washed her underwear in the bathwater as best she could.

Hearing someone try the door — she froze in alarm, flashes of prison guards invading her privacy and worse rushing through her mind. She pushed away those traumatic memories and quickly steadied herself.

It's a shared bathroom, after all. Other people need to use it too.

"She decided she had stayed long enough, and swiftly dried herself before putting on her dirty outer clothes again. She wrapped her wet underwear in the towel and carried it under her arm.

She opened the door and jumped in alarm at the sight of the tall figure behind it. Almost too late, she realised it was just John, waiting for his turn.

"Sorry!" he exclaimed upon seeing her shock and then stepped back.

"Didn't mean to scare you."

"Oh!" she laughed, her hand fluttering to her chest. "Silly me!"

He smiled and nodded towards the bath. "Bet that feels better now."

"Yes, John, it does!" she laughed. "I can't thank you enough."

John puffed out his chest, feeling quite proud. "I'll tell you what, Julie. I'll take a quick shower first, then take you to town to buy some new clothes. Yours look a bit worn, and you'll feel more comfortable in some fresh ones."

Julie flinched and blushed with embarrassment. "No, John. You've done enough."

"Don't be silly," he said, wagging a finger at her. "Clothes here are very affordable. Don't argue."

She nodded quietly before returning to her room and breaking down again. Everyone was so kind! She missed LeeRoy terribly, feeling fear once more as she thought about everything that had happened, still uncertain about what was to come.

She lay on the bed and was asleep within seconds, but was awakened twenty minutes later by a knock on the door. All four guys were waiting for her. "Come on, wakey wakey. Let's go shopping.

"Julie stood at the open door and said, "As much as I need new clothes and appreciate what you're doing, you don't have to do this. I feel terrible about it."

"OK," John said, with a serious tone. "If the roles were reversed and I needed help, would you help me?"

She looked at each of them in turn, and they offered encouraging smiles. She shut her eyes, shook her head slowly, and let out a heavy sigh like a deflating balloon.

"Okay, I give up," Julie said, closing the door. "Let's go."

The town was nearby and lively, with preparations for the festival underway. They quickly found a women's clothing store, where Julie chose the most affordable clothes and only the essentials, feeling guilty but knowing they all contributed to the $19 for her outfit. These were just kids, and she knew they didn't have much money to spare. She didn't want to take advantage. She appreciated their help and would repay them when possible.

Back at the hostel, Julie was excited to change into clean clothes and smiled for the first time in ages. She had also bought some new underwear.

"I'll knock on your door at eight," John said.

"Thanks again, you guys," Julie said, her voice firm. "I'll repay your kindness someday."

"That won't be necessary, Julie," Tom reassured her. "We're just glad we could help."

Precisely at 8 p.m., they knocked on her door and left. They discovered a cozy café with outdoor seating and sat down at a table. They ordered five Piscos, Peru's national drink, and a few plates of Juanes: seasoned rice bundles wrapped in green bijao leaves. Juanes is named after Saint John, possibly due to their resemblance to the saint's severed head, which was displayed on a platter.

They laughed and chatted, and although Julie joined in, she still battled a deep sense of grief she tried to hide while with them.

After a couple more beers, they decided to walk through the streets and join in the festivities.

Crowds filled every area, smiling and chatting, with music echoing from every corner—a vibrant carnival scene. Soon, the first bucket of water was thrown, marking the start of many that night. Fortunately, despite the excitement, it was a warm evening, making the water feel quite refreshing.

Encouraged by the cheerful mood and drinks, Julie nearly forgot she was a fugitive and a recent widow. With a few beers and the lively atmosphere, she began to enjoy the night, watching the street dancers and sipping more Pisco sours. As she drank more, her relaxation grew, and so did that of the men around her.

It felt so good to numb her pain and escape her thoughts and memories temporarily.

By 1 a.m., John decided he had had enough and said he was heading back to the hostel because they had a long day ahead. Julie and the other three guys agreed, and they began walking back.

They retraced their steps, but over time, the wandering crowds caused disorientation, and they lost track of their route. After asking some confused, non-English-speaking partygoers for directions, they finally made it back to the hostel around three o'clock, utterly exhausted.

Julie, still intoxicated, couldn't stop thinking about LeeRoy during the walk back to the hostel. She grabbed onto the guys to keep her steady after a slight stumble. The alcohol gave her a warm, fuzzy feeling that dulled her senses, leaving her only feeling drunk. Even hours after they stopped drinking, she remained in a haze.

"I'll see you to your room, Julie, to make sure you get in safely," John said.

Gerry raised an eyebrow, while the other two looked at John, thinking, *"You lucky bastard!"*

However, John wasn't focused on that. He was drawn to Julie – who wouldn't be? — But he genuinely cared for her. He knew she was vulnerable even before she got drunk, and he would never try to exploit her. It wouldn't be right, and he'd hate himself forever if he did, just as she would think it unthinkable.

Julie was still a bit unsteady from the alcohol, stress, and exhaustion, so John held her arm to stop her from falling back down the stairs. They unlocked her room door, and John helped her into bed, though he didn't want to risk undressing her, so she stayed fully clothed. Afterwards, he left. As he closed the door behind him, he suddenly realised the latch was on the inside, meaning he'd left the door unlocked.

He thought, *"God, I can't leave her in bed asleep with the door unlocked. It's too risky. I'll have to wake her up to lock the door behind me!"*

He quietly opened the door, but Julie was deeply asleep, snoring loudly. "Damn," he thought, trying to find a solution. Should he take her key to lock her in? What if she needs the bathroom after drinking and can't open the door? She'd panic. What's next?

He hesitated. No choice.

He slipped back into her bedroom, locked the door, crept across the room, and fell asleep next to Julie, exhausted.

Julie was the first to wake, groggy and slightly tipsy. She was shocked to see John lying next to her, unsure of what had happened. She freaked out, her memories of the prison rapes flashing through her head, and instinctively shoved John off the bed.

He jolted up, eyes wide with alarm, exclaiming,

"What's going on? You scared me half to death."

In a panic, she reassured herself that she would remember if anything happened. Seeing that both were fully dressed, she felt a sense of calm. During a brief moment of anxiety, she discreetly checked herself; everything was dry, and she experienced no discomfort.

"I just need to know what you're doing in my bed!" Julie asked, feeling worried. After John explained everything, she was so relieved that she smiled sincerely. "Thanks again, John. First, for caring for me, and second, for not taking advantage of me while I was drunk. Thanks."

"No problem, Julie."

John returned to the room he shared with his three friends. As he entered, they were all lying in bed, chatting.

"Hey, you're a lucky bastard," Keith said.

"Shut up," John responded, blushing. "Nothing happened. I was helping her out."

"Helping her out," Gerry echoed. "Come on, John. That's what I call getting lucky."

"I told you nothing happened," John replied.

Gerry snorted. "I don't believe you."

"Well, you should," Julie said as she walked into the room. "John was a complete gentleman and didn't try anything. He was just worried because I couldn't lock the door." The guy reddened and apologised to Julie.

"What about apologising to me?" John said.

"Come on, man," Gerry laughed, and John joined in.

As the laughter faded, John turned to Julie, showing signs of awkwardness. "I hate to do this, Julie, but we need to leave soon to catch our bus. Are you sure you won't come with us?"

Julie shook her head. "I have to head north and leave this country. We've spent too much time together already. I need to keep my distance from you to prevent any trouble for you, too."

John looked at her, concern evident on his face. "Are you going to be okay?"

Julie couldn't say yes. "I'll let you know when I'm back in England," she murmured, head down. Then she straightened and said with more confidence than she felt, "I'm aiming to reach Huangala today and then we'll see what comes next."

"I feel terrible leaving you," John said, "but I think we have no choice."

They hugged, and John pushed another ten dollars into her hand, refusing to accept a refusal.

As she exited the bedroom, she told them, "Try calling me when you get back. If I'm not there, at least I should have contacted Giles, and he'll know what's happening." The guys were very sad and frustrated to leave her, but they had already said their goodbyes.

Julie decided to try hitchhiking that day, because it was only about forty miles, and she was low on cash. So, she started walking toward the Panamericana Norte Highway. She reached the roundabout just north of San Sebastian and then continued along the road.

After walking for over an hour, an old truck pulled up. She casually approached, peering into the cab. She had already decided that if a younger man with a rugged appearance offered her a ride, she would decline. Tired of being exploited and aware of the risks, she was cautious. The driver, an older man, seemed harmless enough. She held a piece of paper with "Huangala" written on it and showed it to him.

He nodded and said, "Sí, sí. No hay problema."

She decided it was all right, so she got into the truck. It was a battered, old, rust bucket, but it was going in the right direction.

They drove for an hour at speeds no higher than 30 mph, but Julie didn't mind because it was faster than walking. The old man turned on the radio, tried some small talk, and smiled at her from time to time, but otherwise stayed silent once he realised she couldn't speak a word of Spanish.

Finally, he turned to her and asked, "¿Quieres un café?" she didn't understand him entirely, but caught the word "coffee" and his gesture, so she guessed his question.

"Sí. Thank you," she replied, expecting him to pull out a flask, but he didn't. After about 200 more yards, he turned off the main road. Julie felt a little worried but tried to stay calm. He seemed okay, and she thought she could probably take him in a fight. Though wiry, he was small and likely in his seventies.

They reached a small village with a central square featuring a tiny café on one side. He parked right next to it, got out, circled, and opened Julie's door, offering her his hand to help her down.

Julie was encouraged by the old man's kindness and began to think that the only unpleasant people she encountered in Peru were in Lima. Besides the bandits, everyone else she met since leaving Lima was friendly. They sat at the table, and two coffees arrived. Julie tried hers, but it was awful—despite being very sweet, it still had a bitter, harsh taste. She had no choice but to act as if she enjoyed it.

Two bowls of a thick soup made of potato, corn, and barley were placed before them. Although it looked unappetising and reminded Julie of prison food, it turned out to be much better than she'd expected. As she ate, she found it delicious. The old man declined her offer to pay, which was a relief for Julie. After finishing, he signalled to get her another coffee, but she politely refused, not wanting to offend him.

The old man finished his drink and spoke to her in Spanish. When he stood up and opened the truck door for her, she realised they were leaving once more.

They kept a steady 30 mph pace, finally reaching Huangala at 4 p.m. It was a long drive, but at least it didn't cost her anything.

The old man dropped Julie off on the outskirts of town at an old bus shelter, where she thanked him, and he drove off at his steady 30 mph.

Julie pulled out her map and estimated it was only about fifty miles to the border.

Should I attempt to find another ride tonight or wait until morning? she pondered. She examined the map more closely. She planned to cross the border at El Alamor. But how could she do that without a passport? She couldn't imagine, especially without first seeing how the crossing was set up. She concluded she'd concentrate on reaching the location first and deal with the border crossing afterward, once she had seen it.

I'll try to bluff my way across.

As it was getting dark, she chose to find a place to sleep so she could wake up feeling refreshed in the morning.

While walking about a mile, she noticed some old, abandoned barns on the right side of the road. She quietly approached them, wishing LeeRoy were with her, hoping to go unnoticed. Though she felt scared, she knew she had to continue.

Four empty buildings stood nearby, with no signs of life around. She entered the first one, completely abandoned, lacking a roof or shelter. The second building looked decent from the outside. She found an open door and entered. It seemed to be an old hay barn, though it hadn't been used in a while. Moonlight streamed through holes in the roof at one end, revealing parts of the sky, but that didn't matter since the weather was warm and clear, and the roof appeared intact and safe enough to the left of the doorway. *This will* do, she thought.

She settled in comfortably and unwrapped the package the young girl had given her in Huacho. Inside, she discovered five pieces of something resembling cake, which tasted reasonably good. She devoured two pieces because she was starving, then drank some water provided by the lovely young girl and soon fell asleep, still worn out from the all-night carnival.

She slept soundly but was awakened just after 5 a.m. by the birds' noisy chirping outside.

She stood up and stretched, feeling tired and stiff, but knew she had to stay strong and keep moving. After having one more piece of cake and some water, she started walking back to the main road. Although tempted to take a bus to El Alamor, she chose to save money and decided to try hitchhiking once more.

Two hours later, a pick-up truck stopped next to her with two young men inside. She paused, recalling her promise to herself.

One of them stepped out and signalled for her to get in, but she disliked his appearance and declined, saying, "No, thanks," as she kept walking. The man returned to the truck, and they then drove alongside her with their window down; they gestured and spoke urgently in Spanish. She tried to ignore them, but they persisted, the truck matching her walking speed and looming like a predator.

She looked around for an escape route, but the area was empty, and the road was clear. Panic began to rise. What could she do? There was no place to run or hide.

As the pickup stopped right in front of her, the man in the passenger seat quickly got out. Julie immediately ran in the opposite direction, but he was faster and soon caught up. Stronger, he grabbed her and dragged her back to the pickup while she screamed. She fought fiercely, forcing the driver to come out and help his friend push her into the cab. She was caught between them, aware of what was about to happen but scared that if she fought too hard, they wouldn't just rape her – they might even kill her. Who would care out here?

They shouted at each other across her and then turned off the road into a wooded area. They stopped and dragged Julie out. One of them had a gun and pointed it at her. The other went through her backpack, but when he found nothing of value, he shouted at Julie, "Passport? Money?" In broken English.

"I don't have a passport or money," she sobbed, but they didn't understand and just threw the satchel on the ground, furious.

One of them held her, while the other ripped her clothes off and threw her to the ground and dragged her through the gravel onto a grass verge, grazing her back and arms, where she fought to get free to no avail. The one with the gun held it to her head, while the other raped her. When he'd finished, he took the gun from his friend, who also raped her.

Afterwards, the first mean-looking man aimed the gun at Julie, and her heart almost stopped. As she squeezed her eyes shut, unable to bear it, the man pulled the trigger, and the breath caught in her throat.

Nothing happened. Julie heard a click and opened her eyes, shocked to find herself still alive.

He pulled the trigger and tried again, cursing out loud two or three more times. Each time, Julie stared in horror, bracing for the searing pain that would come before she died. But the gun wouldn't fire. In a panic, his friend shouted, and they sped away in the pickup, leaving Julie to cry on the ground, battered and traumatised.

She stood frozen for a moment, struggling to process what had just happened. The attack had occurred so quickly, and she was terrified her attackers would return and finish the job. They had no idea she wouldn't be able to go to the police. She was a mess, overwhelmed by fear and confusion.

She managed to stand with the help of a nearby tree, her limbs trembling violently. In a daze, she slowly gathered her scattered clothes and the remaining food from her bag. Still shaken from the shock, she poured most of the water over her to soothe her raw pain and wash away the filth. She checked her torn clothes, which were in rough shape but still wearable, and got dressed.

She had no choice; she had to keep walking, but she felt numb.

CHAPTER THIRTY — *Fifty Miles from Freedom*

It was nearly two miles to the main road, but she stopped at an old tree and collapsed to the ground. She had given up and just wanted to close her eyes and be with LeeRoy in heaven, though that's probably not where he ended up.

She sat there sobbing, her head spinning with confusion about what to do next. For an hour, she remained numb, crying, cursing, and experiencing a whirlwind of emotions—loving LeeRoy, hating him, then loving him again. She felt unsure, angry, and overwhelmed, even wishing she could disappear.

She drank the last of her water and understood she had to leave; she couldn't merely sit and wait for a taxi. Summoning her strength, she got up and somehow continued onward. She had to get back to the main highway, and she eventually made it.

Now she had no idea what to do next. Where was LeeRoy when she needed him? He would've protected her from those two bastards. She sat on the roadside, sobbing uncontrollably, unaware of a car stopping behind her.

"¿Estás bien?" a woman's voice asked.

Julie didn't hear or understand initially, but the voice repeated, "Are you okay?" She looked around and saw a woman leaning toward her from the front of the car, but her attention was caught by a man in the driver's seat, causing her to panic. Frightened, Julie tried to stand and run, but her legs felt so weak she collapsed, crying hysterically. The woman hurried toward her.

"Estás bien?" she asked again, then, noticing her blond hair, "Are you American?"

"No," Julie sobbed, "I'm English."

"What happened to you?" the woman asked softly.

Julie looked up at the woman, tears blurring her vision. Through the mist, she saw the woman's gentle, worried face. Julie knew she wouldn't hurt her, so she let the woman help her sit up in the dirt, still crying. "I've just been raped by two men in a white pick-up truck," she managed to say between gasps.

"Oh my God!" the woman exclaimed, her husband already dialling the police. "We'll take you to the hospital."

"No, no!" Julie cried out. "Please, no police. I don't want to deal with that right now."

"Okay, okay," the woman waved to her husband, saying, "No llames a la policía." She was puzzled but realised she had to calm Julie down. "Try to relax." She gently brushed the dirty blonde hair away from Julie's face and asked, "What were you doing out here?"

"I was on my way to Ecuador," Julie sobbed.

"You've got to be crazy – traveling alone? Are you hurt?"

"No, no, I don't think so. I'm fine. I'm fine, just a graze, please. I need to get to Ecuador."

"I don't think you're in any shape to travel. Why won't you report this to the police?"

"I simply don't want to," Julie said, her voice trembling. "I want to go home. I want LeeRoy." She was so distressed that she wasn't even sure what she was saying.

"Who's LeeRoy?" the woman asked.

"My husband," she cried.

"Where is he?"

"He's dead!" she shouted, collapsing to the ground and crying uncontrollably.

"Dead!" the woman exclaimed, clutching Julie tightly and trying to calm her down.

After a while, Julie's sobs began to slow, and she eventually quieted down.

"Can you talk now?" the woman asked gently.

"Yes, yes, I'm OK."

"Was your husband killed by the people who attacked you?"

"No, no," Julie said, panting with exhaustion. "He was killed in Lima."

She told her that her husband had been mugged, but she couldn't bring herself to reveal the truth. She desperately needed to escape, but fear and confusion were clouding her judgment.

"I have friends in Ecuador, and I just need to make it there."

The woman paused for a moment, and her husband, who had been standing outside the car, approached her cautiously. He spoke to her in Spanish, and she replied. Julie watched quietly, confused, unable to understand their conversation.

"Don't worry," the woman said softly with a smile. "He was just asking what happened. He doesn't speak English, but like me, he's worried about you being out here alone. We live nearby and are heading home. Would you like us to take you there so you can relax and freshen up?"

Julie hesitated briefly. She wanted to leave the country but found herself in a difficult situation. The woman appeared kind, so Julie thought, "If you don't mind – yes, please."

"Okay," she said.

The woman helped Julie up, walked her to the car, and opened the back door. Julie got in and collapsed on the back seat, flinching at the pain from the grazing on her back and arms, and crying again.

The woman got in with her. "It's not far – about ten minutes," she said.

Julie just sniffled.

They arrived at the house, which was perched on the side of a hill overlooking the Pacific Ocean, with the Andes in the background. It was a stunning location, but it was utterly lost on Julie at that moment.

The woman stepped out and walked around to the other side of the car, opening the door for Julie, who carefully shambled out, trying to avoid rubbing her injuries.

"By the way," she said, "my name is Rose, and my husband is Fredrick."

"Thanks for helping me, Rose," Julie said, her gratitude so overwhelming that it brought tears to her eyes again. "I really appreciate it."

"That's okay, Julie," Rose said gently. "We couldn't just leave you there." She took Julie's arm and led her into the house.

It was a classic Peruvian chalet-style home for the upper class, featuring a spacious kitchen that connected to the rest of the house.

Rose sat Julie at the large, old wooden table in the centre of the room and asked if she wanted a drink. "Yes, please. A glass of water would be great, thanks." She brought the water over and sat down with her.

"Feeling any better?" she asked just as her husband entered. "Yes, thank you so much. I don't know what might have happened if you hadn't stopped."

"I hate to think about it," Rose said, "but you're safe now."

Fredrick spoke to her, and she translated his words for Julie. "My husband believes we should call the police. This is a grave crime, even in Peru."

"No, please don't," Julie urged, fighting to hold back her rising hysteria. "I don't want any trouble." She had not even told her that they had attempted to shoot her, fearing that, despite Julie's protests, these people would still call the police.

Rose translated for her husband, who just raised his hand in the air, shook his head, and walked away, mumbling.

"He thinks you're stupid: first, for being out here on your own, and secondly, for not reporting those animals."

"He's probably right," Julie said, "but I just want to get to Ecuador and find my friends." "Why don't they come get you?" Julie thought fast. "Because they don't know I'm on my way there."

"Have you not called them?"

"No, I lost the number," Julie bluffed.

"Do you have the address?" "No," Julie said vaguely, hoping to buy herself time.

"Then how will you find them?" Rose asked, frowning.

"I know the town," Julie said, surprised at how easily the lies rolled off her tongue. "I'll just ask around when I get there." "Which town is it?"

Luckily, Julie had noticed that the British Embassy was in Quito. She told Rose that was where they lived.

Rose burst into laughter, incredulous. "Julie, do you understand that Quito is more than 1,700 kilometres away? That's nearly 1,000 miles. How are you planning to get there?"

"I don't know," Julie said, "but I have to figure it out somehow."

"Do you have any money?" Rose asked, already expecting the answer.

"No, I only have $10."

"You won't get very far on $10, will you? You're crazy if you think you can travel through Peru and Ecuador, which is way more dangerous than here, with just $10. Don't you have any family who could send you some money?"

"No," Julie said, "and I'd have to show my passport to get it, but I don't have one."

"You don't have a passport? How on earth do you expect to get into Ecuador without one?"

"I don't know." Julie's tears started to fall again. "I don't know."

"What happened to it?"

"I lost it."

"Have you reported it to the police?"

"No!" Julie's voice cracked. She felt terrorised, even by this patient woman's interrogation. "I can't."

"Why not?" Rose asked more insistently. "I doubt you're being completely honest with me. Are you in some trouble?" Julie began to cry again, feeling overwhelmed.

"Julie, I want to help you, if possible, but I need honesty. I suspect you're in some trouble, and I need to understand for my peace of mind."

"Nothing. I'm fine."

"Julie, you're not fine. Your husband is dead, you've been raped, and you don't have a passport or any money. That's not even close to being fine."

Julie could tell Rose was getting annoyed and decided she had to come clean, risking that they wouldn't call the police.

"I'm sorry, I'm just scared. I don't have anyone to turn to or help me."

"Unless you tell me what's going on, I won't be able to help you. Just come clean now."

"Okay," Julie said hesitantly. "I will, but promise me you won't call the police."

"Unless you have murdered somebody, I promise."

Rose looked at Julie, her eyes searching hers, her lips tight in thought. Finally, Julie started sharing her story.

Julie took a deep breath, her hand reaching for her throat. "To keep it simple, my husband was caught with cocaine in his suitcase, and since I was with him, I got arrested as well. But I swear, I had no idea!" She looked at Rose, who showed no sign of judgment, so Julie continued. "I ended up in Miguel Castro Prison in Lima – and it was a nightmare. I was raped by the guards, even a woman guard joined in."

Julie continued, "They took everything from me. The food was inedible, and the water was undrinkable. I was terrified inside. But I was lucky, if you can call any of this luck – I got bail. My lawyer arranged for me to stay at a hostel. She was the one who told me that LeeRoy had been shot trying to escape from prison." Julie broke down, sobbing, and said that she loved the man who had been so good to her.

Rose gently squeezed her hand. Julie took a deep breath and resumed. "After that, I decided to try to escape and return to England, but I didn't know how. I've decided to try to leave the country and seek help at a British Embassy. I took a northbound bus, bought a map, saw Ecuador, and decided to try to get there. This is as far as I've managed to go. You know the rest." Julie stopped, letting out a deep sigh.

"My God, Julie, that's terrible!" Rose said quietly. "You poor girl." Then she adopted a more practical tone. "You can't leave here without any money. Could you contact your family and ask them to send some funds? If they can, I will go to the bank and retrieve it for you."

"Would you do that for me?" sniffled Julie, gazing at her through red-rimmed eyes.

"Yes, I would. Drug smuggling is wrong, but I couldn't be responsible if you went back to that prison. That's something I couldn't live with."

"The issue is, I don't have any family in England. I was an orphan, and LeeRoy was my only family." Julie shrugged and then said, "There's one person who might be able to help me, but I need to call him."

"That's okay, Julie. You can use our phone."

"Thank you, Rose, you are very kind, thank you."

"It's okay, Julie. I'm just glad it was us who discovered you. God alone knows what might have occurred if we hadn't—I'm afraid to imagine."

She showed Julie the phone, provided her with the bank details to transfer the money, and told her she'd leave her to it and left the room.

Giles picked up her call. "Julie! Thank goodness, I've been so worried. Are you both alright?"

That set Julie off crying.

"Julie? Julie, speak to me. What's wrong?"

She steadied herself as much as possible. "Giles, LeeRoy's dead."

The line fell silent for a moment as Giles's mind hurried to grasp what she was saying.

"Dead? What are you talking about? How? What the hell's happening out there?"

She was alone, miles away. Giles's jaw clenched in anger and frustration.

Julie explained everything to Giles, urgently needing money to travel to Ecuador and get an emergency passport. She spoke so quickly that Giles had trouble keeping up.

"Whoa, slow down! Take one step at a time. Just breathe deeply. We'll have you sorted out soon."

Julie took a few deep breaths and said, "Listen, I need to tell you something. Giles, I've been raped in prison and again this morning on the road."

His heart pounded. Giles's fists tightened. "My God, Julie! Are you okay?"

"As well as I can be," she replied. Sharing what happened was a relief. It eased the pain in her heart by putting it out in the open, where it felt less intense. "A kind lady and her husband rescued me, and I'm now staying at their home."

"Where exactly are you?"

"Around fifty miles from the Ecuador border, near a town called Huangala."

"Julie, let me think for a minute – what a fucking mess!"

Giles's mind was overwhelmed with anger, confusion, and bewilderment. "OK," he said calmly, attempting to reassure Julie. "Let's handle one thing at a time. I'll have Sam transfer some money to you, which shouldn't be an issue. He'll be devastated to hear about LeeRoy, but our top priority is ensuring your safe return. Can you give me the woman's bank account details?"

Julie provided Giles with all the required information.

"Alright, how much should I send out?" "Just £200, I think, since I might get robbed, but it should cover a bus to Quito."

"Quito? Where the hell is Quito?"

"It's the capital of Ecuador—the only place where I can get an emergency passport. But it's over a thousand miles away, assuming they don't send me back to Peru."

"Bloody hell, Julie! This is madness."

"I know, Giles, but I have no choice. What else can I do? I'm not going back to that crappy prison. I'd rather die. Or kill myself."

"Don't talk like that, Julie," Giles snapped, with concern. "You need to stay positive."

"But this is a nightmare, and I'm struggling with losing LeeRoy," her voice broke again.

"I know, Julie, but he would want you to be strong and get back here safely."

At that moment, Rose quietly entered the room and silently mouthed, "Is everything okay?"

"Yes," Julie responded, covering the receiver with her hand. "My friend is going to arrange for £200 to be transferred to your account—hopefully today."

"I'll ask my bank to call me when it arrives." Rose discreetly exited the room, gesturing, "Want some coffee?" "That would be nice, thanks." Julie then spoke again into the phone. "Sorry, Giles. That was the lady helping me."

"You're fortunate she came by, Julie. I'll ask Sam to send an extra £100 so she can treat herself to something nice."

"That's a great idea, Giles. Thanks." "Now listen carefully, Julie," Giles said sternly. "I need you to keep me updated on your location as often as you can call. Do you understand?"

He was going crazy, imagining the horrors she had faced and what might still happen, but he knew he had to remain calm and reassuring. His genuine desire was to fly out there and rescue her himself. Somehow, it had to be possible. He considered asking Sam or doing anything he could think of. Julie was in danger!

"Yes, Giles. I'll do what I can."

"The first thing I need to know is the time of the bus you're getting to the capital in Ecuador."

"Quito. OK, Giles. I'll call you just before I leave."

"One last thing, Julie. I'll call you once the transfer is complete. Do you have the number where you'll be?" She read the number written on the dial to Giles.

"What's the time out there, Julie?"

She looked around and saw a wall clock. "It's just after 2 p.m."

"OK, that makes you five hours behind us, so I'll make sure I don't call in the middle of the night."

"Thanks, Giles."

"No problem. Just be very careful, alright?" he said, his voice trembling. "Please."

After her call, Julie went to the kitchen where Rose was pouring coffee.

"Julie," Rose said, "by the time the money arrives, I won't be able to collect any until tomorrow, so you can stay with us tonight." At least you'll be safe."

"Are you sure?"

"Yes. There's no way I'm letting you go out alone tonight. Come on, I'll show you to your room, and you can take a bath or shower—whichever you prefer. Are you sure you're okay and don't need a doctor?"

"Yes, I'm fine," Julie sighed, then added, "and thank you, Rose. I appreciate your help. Giles is sending an extra £100, just for you, as a token of appreciation. We want you to get something nice for all your help."

Rose looked surprised.

"That's not necessary. I'll give it all to you when I withdraw it from the bank."

"No, Rose, it's for you. I won't accept it."

"We'll see," Rose replied.

The room was tidy yet straightforward, offering a stunning view of the ocean. Julie found the bathroom, filled the tub, and then removed her clothes to step in. The sensation of getting clean was terrific, particularly washing away the dirt and grime from her skin, but the grazes on her back were worse than she thought and stung like hell as she lowered herself into the bath and let out a silent squeal in pain.

She sank into the bath and began thinking about LeeRoy again, and tears started to well up once more. She had managed to hold herself together for so long, pushing her grief aside to get through, but it had taken a heavy toll.

It feels like all I do is cry. She couldn't believe how much of a mess she was in. She couldn't accept that LeeRoy was gone and that she'd never see him again.

What would happen to his body? Would they return it or bury him in an unmarked grave somewhere? She had no answers. Tears slowly rolled down her face.

She returned to the present and washed her hair, which felt refreshingly clean. She remained in the tub until she felt completely clean and nearly her old self again. As she got out, she picked up her underwear, intending to wash them in the tub water, but then she noticed that they were stained with dry semen.

She screamed, reliving her trauma, nearly vomiting, and then broke down in tears once more. Rose heard her and hurried into the bathroom, followed closely by her husband, who was right behind her. Seeing that Julie was still naked, Rose gently pushed her husband back out of the room.

"What's wrong?" Rose asked, wrapping a towel around Julie's shivering body and slipping her arm around her shoulders, she then noticed the injuries to her back and was horrified. "What happened here?" she asked.

Julie, sobbing, shared what had happened. "It was when they dragged me across a dirt track to the grass, I think, I'm not too sure, I just..." she waved her hand uselessly in the air, "freaked out at the thought of what they did to me."

Rose went to the cupboard and took some antiseptic cream and a plastic bag. "Here, Julie, pack all your clothes into this, and I'll dispose of them. I'm about your size, and I have plenty of clothes, including new, unused underwear."

She then removed the towel from Julie and gently applied the cream. It eased her physical pain but couldn't alleviate her mental anguish, which would linger for a long time.

"Thanks, Rose. I can still wear the clothes, but I'd appreciate the underwear, though. I don't think I could put those back on. Thank you."

"Julie, just put everything here," Rose said gently but with authority. "Let me get you some fresh, clean clothes."

Julie looked into her eyes. "I can't believe this country, Rose." Rose seemed puzzled, prompting her to clarify, "Well, people here are either incredibly kind or complete bastards. Sorry for the language, but they frustrate me."

"That's alright, Julie. I understand," Rose said soothingly. "Just a few minutes, and I'll get you some fresh clothes." Soon after, the kitchen door swung open, and when Fredrick looked up, he was stunned.

Standing right there in his doorway was a vision. Julie looked stunning, with her nearly white-blonde hair and a healthy tan, wearing clean clothes that highlighted her curves. She'd lost a bit of weight recently, but she was breathtaking. Fredrick said something to his wife, who playfully slapped him on the arm - pretty hard.

"I think my husband is going to have a heart attack," Rose said.

"I'm sorry," Julie replied, looking concerned.

"No, no. You're a beautiful young lady, especially now that half the dust from Peru has been washed off you," she joked.

"Thanks, Rose," Julie smiled, a little hesitantly. "I feel so much better now."

They had dinner at eight, and Rose was an excellent cook. Julie realised she was pretty hungry after all. The only thing that bothered her was that Fredrick occasionally glanced her way when she wasn't looking. She felt a bit uneasy but tried to ignore it. After dinner, they sat outside on the patio, chatting and sipping drinks, and finally went to bed around 11 p.m.

Four hours later, Julie was suddenly awakened by a feeling that someone was watching her. She thought she could hear breathing nearby as she lay on her side. When she opened her eyes, she saw a shadowy face in front of her, staring at her, and it instantly brought back the terrible memories of the rapes she had suffered.

She let out a loud scream.

Fredrick was kneeling beside her bed, waving his hands, trying to calm her down, but she was already screaming. In a panic, he covered her mouth to silence her, but she bit him and broke free, yelling even louder.

Fredrick gave up trying to quiet her and ran out of the room, only to run into Rose.

She guessed what had happened and also shouted at him in Spanish, hitting him with both fists. He pushed her away and disappeared.

She rushed in to see if Julie was alright, but she was shaking badly.

"Julie, I'm sorry. He hasn't done this in years. He didn't mean to cause harm, I'm sure. He likes to watch, but he should know better given the circumstances. I have no idea what got into that stupid bastard."

"It's okay," Julie said hurriedly, gathering her belongings. "I have to leave now. I can't stay here. I'm sorry." She began crying again. Rose moved to comfort her, but Julie pulled back. "Please, Rose, you've been kind to me, but I need to go. I'm sorry. Please let me go."

Rose bit her lip, tears filling her eyes, but she left the room. Julie could hear her arguing with her husband.

Julie had just finished getting dressed when Rose returned, begging, "Julie, be sensible. You can't go out so late! I'll tell him to fuck off and find a hotel for the night, and I'll stay here with you."

"No, Rose, I'm leaving now," Julie said firmly, her tears dried. She was working to contain her growing anger. She was sick of being a victim and refused to accept it any longer. "Thank you for everything you've done for me, but I can't stay here anymore. Sorry. Please, just let me go."

Despite Rose's pleas and reassurances, Julie grabbed her satchel and left.

It was completely dark outside, making it hard for her to see the path ahead. She remembered that the main road wasn't too far, since it had only taken ten minutes to reach the spot where they had found her. Finally, she saw the highway and walked for about an hour and a half. By 6 a.m., the sky was starting to brighten, but she knew she needed rest.

The only shelter she found was some large rocks, behind which she hid. She held a heavy rock in her hand, determined to defend herself better in the future. Despite this, she couldn't sleep, staying alert to danger and troubled by restless thoughts. As she sat, her life replayed in her mind—from the attacks she had endured, to LeeRoy, her childhood, prison, the old bus, and her current situation. None of it made sense. She wondered what she had done to deserve such suffering.

Apart from a brief period with LeeRoy when she felt truly happy, her life had been a series of disasters. Still, in that moment, it all seemed even worse.

She shifted from hopelessness to courage, then from determination to despair. She searched for something to live for.

Freedom!

Gazing up at the brightening sky, in a new wave of energy and a desire to live, Julie decided to start walking. The border was only about fifty miles away.

It will take me three days to walk there, but I definitely won't be hitchhiking.

She walked for two hours, keeping close enough to the road to follow it, but far enough away to avoid being pulled into any car. Some vehicles slowed down, but she continued confidently, ignoring them as if she were heading to the next intersection. She didn't rely on them or anyone else.

A car approached on the road ahead, and she briefly panicked when the door opened and someone stepped out. Her hand clenched around the rock she was holding. However, as she squinted through the sunlight at the figure, she paused in surprise.

It was Rose, and she was alone. Julie felt a great sense of relief seeing that Fredrick was not with her.

"Hi, Julie. I've been searching for you," Rose said with a mix of apology and relief. "Listen, I'm sorry about last night. That bastard will be paying for it for a long time—if I even let him come back into the house."

Julie remained silent. Rose then handed her an envelope, explaining, "This is the money your friend sent. I went to the bank first thing this morning and converted it into U.S. dollars. All £300 is in there. I don't want any of it, Julie. You'll need every cent of it."

Julie swallowed hard. "Thank you, Rose," she said, overwhelmed by her kindness. She genuinely believed she had lost all that money and had decided she would have to try contacting Giles once more somehow. "And I know it wasn't your fault, but I just had to get away."

"Yes, Julie, I understand. The bastard. What are you going to do now?"

"I'm going to get to the border to attempt crossing," she shrugged. "There's nothing more I can do."

"I can take you there. It's not too far — at least by car." Julie almost collapsed in relief. "Thanks, Rose. That's very kind of you again."

"Julie," Rose shook her head sadly, "after what happened last night, it's the least I can do."

They were nearing the border in a little over an hour. As they got closer, Julie kept fidgeting in her seat and finally said, "Rose, it's better if you drop me off here so you won't be seen with me."

Noticing Rose's puzzled look, Julie said, "Just in case something goes wrong – and with my luck, it probably will." Rose's expression turned doubtful. "You're right, of course, Julie, but I don't like leaving you here."

"You must, Rose. And thank you again, sincerely. I can't imagine what might have happened to me if you hadn't appeared. Also, don't be too harsh on your husband; he didn't do anything wrong."

Maybe not, but the bastard shouldn't have been in your room. He's going to have a tough time for a very long time, believe me.

"I do, Rose. I do. Bye. Thanks again."

"Make sure to call me when you return to England," she said, handing Julie a card with her phone number. Julie raised her hand to decline it. "I can't accept that, Rose." "Why not?" she asked. "In case I get caught. If they find your phone number on me, they'd go straight to your house. But don't worry — Giles has your number in England." "Yes, of course." She returned the card to her purse, feeling embarrassed, but sincerely added, "Please do let me know."

CHAPTER THIRTY-ONE — *From Fertilizer to Freedom*

There was a bus terminal at the border, with Ecuador just a quick drive over the river bridge. During their car ride, Julie discussed with Rose the possibility of buying a bus ticket and crossing the border without inspection. Rose was sceptical, but neither of them could come up with a better plan, so they decided to try.

Julie went to the ticket office and requested a ticket to Quito.

"Sí," the man said without even looking at her. "Passport, please."

Julie, prepared to tough it out, tried to explain that she had lost her passport. The man acknowledged this and signalled to a police officer. She nodded in response, offering a shy smile.

Leaving the ticket desk with a dry mouth, Julie realised she couldn't get a ticket without a passport.

She entered a bus shelter to gather her thoughts and couldn't hold back silent tears once more.

So close, so close! There had to be a way!

She could see beyond the border, across the river, to El Lalamor in Ecuador and to freedom. It was so close. She gazed longingly at the patch of land that meant freedom.

But how could she cross the river without crossing the bridge and going through Customs on both sides of the border?

Maybe if I walk up the river, I could find a small boat. There had to be another way.

But she couldn't think of anything, so she headed up the riverside, being very careful not to be seen by anyone at the border.

She walked for more than two hours. The terrain became increasingly difficult. She had to scramble over rocky outcrops to keep the river in sight, yet she still found no boats.

There was nothing to help her. She recalled when LeeRoy volunteered to teach her swimming, standing there and gazing across the river. The river was only about 100 yards wide in some places, so she might have been able to swim to Ecuador!

But that was impossible unless she found a life jacket by some miracle. Even then, she doubted she could cross without being swept out to sea.

She walked a bit farther, feeling lost and hopeless.

She saw a built-up area ahead and decided to find a place to sleep before it got dark. She discovered an old shed containing just a few bags of fertilizer, which provided a soft place to rest. She was desperate, exhausted, scared, and hungry.

She heard distant traffic and wondered if she could find the road and sneak into the back of a truck heading across the border, but the sound was faint, and she realised it was miles away, so she pushed that thought out of her mind.

She sat on the plastic bags, wondering how she'd ever cross the river, when a crazy idea came to her. Could she make a makeshift raft or life jacket out of the fertilizer bags?

Her adrenaline was rushing, so she grabbed a bag and spilled the fertilizer onto the floor.

Now what? She held the sturdy plastic sack, scanning the building. She needed something to seal the top.

She looked around and found some baling twine, but needed a knife or scissors to cut it. Outside, she searched around and found a piece of broken glass, hacked off a few pieces, and set them on the floor. Then she focused on the sack. She gathered the open end of the plastic sack, squeezed it into a pouch in her fist, and blew into the narrow neck. She took deep breaths and exhaled into the bag until it started to inflate.

It took some time, and she had to pause and rest several times. But gradually, the fertilizer sack filled with air. When she finished, she felt light-headed, and her cheeks ached. She squeezed the bundle tighter, folded the open ends, and tied it securely with baling twine. She pressed the bag gently, and it stayed inflated. To her surprise and joy, she ended up with a surprisingly sturdy pillow of air.

Julie felt a mix of excitement and fear, as she was scared and hesitant because of her intense dislike and terror of water. She considered that this idea might work, but worried about drowning if they deflated halfway across the water. That fear made her even more anxious.

Throughout the evening, she packed her belongings and inflated three additional sacks, tying them together with twine to resemble giant balloons. She removed her outer clothes, leaving only her underwear, which was all she had left. Julie was excited, despite being terrified of the water. The thought of escaping that prison in Lima overwhelmed her fear. She decided to make her break in the dark. The river was just a quarter mile away, and she would look suspicious, nearly naked, carrying four inflated fertilizer bags across open fields if anyone saw her.

Crossing at night would be more dangerous, but she would at least stay hidden. She looked very odd walking across the ploughed fields with inflated fertilizer bags, but she was indifferent; she sensed freedom and was confident no one could see her in the darkness. She soon reached the river. There was a grassy swamp to cross first, then a muddy bank before she hit the water.

Freedom was right there. She started walking through the swampy grass, but the large sacks, full of air and tied with string, slowed her down.

Soon, she was waist-deep in reedy fronds and water, covering the soft, wet ground. It took all her strength to lift her feet, and the grass jabbed at her bare skin. She couldn't walk through it easily, so she lay flat on her stomach, pulling herself along in the shallow water by grasping the stiff grass and pushing with her feet.

Frozen with fear, she dragged the inflated sacks behind her until she reached the muddy bank. It felt like an eternity. The mud was even more difficult, but she kept on her stomach, pulling herself forward, until she finally reached the water's edge. She sat on the rocky shoreline to catch her breath and looked out at the dark waters. She was utterly terrified. She knew nothing about Peru or what might live in its rivers. She had no idea that the river was home to crocodiles and piranhas; if she had known, she definitely would not have tried to swim across.

She adjusted the bundle of twine holding the bags under her arms, then tied one wrist to it. After a brief hesitation, unsure if the water or whatever was inside was holding her back, she remembered the prison in Lima. Taking a deep breath, she then slid in.

She plunged straight underwater, having no idea how to swim, despite having flotation aids. She swallowed water, panicked, and thrashed around, but eventually managed to lift her head so it stayed above the water surface.

She held the bags tightly and steadied herself. Now, floating downstream, she suddenly realised that if she didn't reach the other side quickly, she would end up back at the crossing she had just come from and would likely get caught.

She began kicking her legs, holding the sacks with one hand and using the other like a paddle, but her progress across the swift river was slow. After roughly ten minutes in the water, she grew exhausted from her struggle. She knew she just needed to hold on a little longer to rest. She had no idea what might be in the river and tried not to dwell on it.

She saw the lights in the distance and realized it was the Customs checkpoint she had seen earlier that day. She knew she wouldn't make it across before encountering it! She had almost reached the middle, but the river's current was strong there.

She had no choice but to hold on tightly and hope she wouldn't be seen. Feeling something brush against her leg and panicked by thoughts of crocodiles, she let out a high-pitched scream. The border guards heard her and shone their torches across the dark river. She kicked and paddled furiously, still trying to reach the Ecuadorian side. Just before she went under the bridge, the guards spotted her, and a loud chaos of shouting erupted on the bridge.

The current was strong and fast where the river narrowed beneath the bridge. Still, Julie quickly moved through and emerged on the other side, disappearing around a left bend where the river widened and slowed. The narrowing and turning of the river had helped Julie, and after one last push and scramble, her feet touched the riverbed on the Ecuadorian side. She felt relief but also fear. She knew she had been seen crossing, which raised the question: would they start searching for her?

What she didn't know was that the officers she saw were merely guards on the Peruvian side. They weren't particularly interested in who was crossing out of their country. Even if the person was a criminal, they considered it no big deal—just an extra piece of paperwork if they got involved. They decided that the Ecuadorians should handle it. The guards resumed their activities: smoking on their side of the bridge and chatting casually like a group of old women.

The bank on the Ecuadorian side was all sand, making it easy to walk on, and Julie quickly reached the solid riverbank, safely in Ecuador. She lay on the cool grass, gasping heavily, feeling like she might burst into hysterical laughter. Cold and exhausted, she was also elated. She had conquered her fear of water and escaped from Peru!

She struggled to untie the string on the bag with her clothes and cash. She was cold, with numb fingers, and couldn't undo the knot.

Unable to undo it, she bit the sack, creating a small hole large enough for two fingers, then ripped it open, spilling everything onto the ground, and quickly dressed. Though everything was slightly damp, it was otherwise intact. Her priority now was to escape as far from the river as possible, convinced they would come looking for her. However, she needn't have worried; in South America, nobody paid attention.

It was pitch-black, and she had no idea which way to walk. She also needed to rest; her limbs were still shaking from the exertion of gripping onto the bags for dear life while thrashing through the heavy water in her desperate bid for freedom. Finding some shelter under an old tree, she tried to sleep, her mind racing and adrenaline still coursing through her. She did manage to get a little sleep, but it was very fitful, as thoughts of reaching Quito kept intruding on her rest.

The sun rose spectacularly above the horizon, but Julie didn't notice—she had other things on her mind. She grabbed her map, figured out which way to walk to find a road or a town, and then located a bus station.

She started walking as the sun rose on her right, assuming she was heading north and away from Peru. Occasionally, she would stop to eat a bit of food, drink water, and attend to her needs.

She continued walking all afternoon and, by 4 p.m., was exhausted. Believing she had walked enough for the day, she took refuge under an overhang near a small rock formation that served as a makeshift cave. Sitting there in silence, she suddenly realised she could hear the sound of running water. Her head instinctively turned, as if a bird had moved, to confirm if she had truly heard it.

She rose and headed toward the source of the sound. It grew louder and clearer, leading her to a lagoon with a towering waterfall.

"That's beautiful!"

Realising it was likely pure mountain water, she dipped her hand in and took a sip. It was cold, clear, and tasted fantastic.

She ran back to get her backpack and took out the water bottle. She emptied the old, stale water and refilled it with fresh mountain spring water.

As she returned to her shelter, she noticed a tree heavy with oranges. She grabbed one, peeled it, and ate the juicy segments.

This was her lucky day – food and water all in one place. After what she'd been through, it seemed like a paradise to her.

What if I just stayed here forever?

Simply being in this spot felt like a dream, but she knew she had to keep moving forward. Her main desire was to get home. She packed her backpack with oranges, returned to the shelter, peeled an orange, ate it, and then ate another. This improved her mood significantly, and she quickly fell asleep.

She was awakened just after 10 p.m. by a fierce thunderstorm and heavy rain, but she was fortunate enough to find enough cover to stay dry. Lightning flashed across the sky, but she somehow felt exhilarated by the energy in the air as she hugged her knees, safely sheltered and alone. She sat listening to the pounding rain for a while, then lay down and eventually fell back asleep.

Early the following morning, she began walking in the same direction and soon reached an old, muddy dirt trail, soaked by the storm overnight. Assuming it must lead somewhere and noticing it headed north, she continued along it, even though she saw nothing for at least three hours. Then, she heard the sound of a vehicle engine chugging nearby.

She was scared again, out in the open with no place to hide.

If it were the police, she had no idea what would happen to her. And even worse, could she get raped again? The thought made her skin crawl.

The sound originated behind her, probably from the same dirt road. She moved off the path and stood still. When the vehicle drew closer, she recognised it as an old tractor towing an empty trailer.

As it approached her, she paused, uncertain whether to try to flag a ride or let it go.

Without hesitation, she decided to try for a lift, as she didn't know how far the next town or bus station was. She waved down the tractor, but the weathered old farmer driving it didn't seem to notice, and it continued on. Julie's shoulders sank in disappointment.

Then, as if the driver had changed his mind, the tractor stopped about a hundred yards in front of her.

She approached hesitantly. The driver stepped out, moved to the back of the trailer, and waited for her to catch up. "¿Qué estás haciendo aquí?" he asked, frowning but not unkindly.

She didn't understand, but she guessed he wanted to know what she was doing all the way out there alone. "No lo entiendo," she shrugged. That was most of the Spanish she had learned during her time out there: "I don't understand."

She pointed to the trailer and then to herself, and he understood that she wanted a ride.

"OK, no hay problema, consíguelo."

She understood it was fine from his waving arm and climbed onto the trailer.

The ride was rough, but she was making progress. She didn't know exactly where she was headed, but she was glad to be out of Peru, for which she was grateful to God.

Eventually, they reached a farm encircled by thousands of trees, where people were harvesting what she later learned were coffee beans.

The old man guided her to a weathered shack that seemed to house several people, and he motioned for her to sit at the table. After saying, "Momento," he left.

Five minutes later, he returned with a young man of European descent. The man greeted Julie with a French accent, which proved to be accurate.

"Hello," she responded.

He was tall, handsome, with dark hair and an athletic physique, though Julie wasn't fully paying attention to his appearance.

He explained that the farmer had asked him to speak with her, believing she was either English or American.

"He said he picked you up miles away, in the middle of nowhere. Where have you come from?" *Fuck,* thought Julie, *here we go again!*

But she figured that since she was no longer in Peru, it shouldn't be a big deal to explain at least some of why she was there and how she got there.

"What's your name?" Julie asked.

"Franco – and yours?"

"Julie."

"Bonjour, Julie. Nice to meet you."

"You too. I'm guessing you're French?"

"Oui, je suis français." He nodded, his dark eyes amused.

"Yes, I'm from a small village near Lyon."

"What are you doing in Ecuador?"

"I come out here with friends, working around the country. That way, we get a cheap backpacking holiday. This week, we're helping with the coffee bean harvest, but that's enough about me. Tell me why you were found out on the plains."

She sighed. "It's a long story, Franco."

She felt like she could confide in him. After all, what was he going to do—call the police? She doubted it.

"I'm trying to get to Quito to get an emergency passport so I can return home."

He looked at her with curiosity. Once more, she shared her story, omitting the rapes. She was trying to keep those memories out of her mind.

"My God! That sounds like a story straight from a book!" he exclaimed. "Listen, Julie. I have an idea. We only have five days left here, then we'll head north — but not all the way to Quito, just most of the way. Why not ask the old man if you can lend a hand here for the rest of the week? That way, you can travel with us, earn some money — though not much — and your food and shelter will be taken care of."

Julie hesitated briefly before deciding, feeling somewhat secure. "Yes, that sounds good. Do you think he'll be okay with that?" "Yes, I'm sure he will," Franco said with a grin. "He's short on pickers as it is."

Franco quickly went out and returned shortly after. "All set," he announced. "You're now officially employed at Farm Bella Rosa."

"Thanks, Franco," Julie said with a grateful smile. "You have no idea how much this means to me, especially since I'm traveling with you too."

She had met many people in Peru, but since she was wanted there, she always had to leave them for their safety. She was excited about the idea of traveling with some companions for a while.

"The others will return in about an hour, so relax, and Sarah will see you when she arrives."

"Sarah? There are six of us: I'm from France, three men, and two women from England. None of them speaks Spanish, only I do. That's why the old farmer called me in to help explain."

"Two girls from England! Wow – that sounds great to me!"

Franco continued to explain about all the people she'd soon meet.

An hour later, everyone, including the workers and backpackers, returned to the shack. Franco introduced each person, and they all seemed very friendly. The blonde girls, Sarah and Angie, were particularly eager to hear Julie's story, with Sarah showing more enthusiasm. She was a bit bigger than Julie, but still about a size 10. Although she seemed somewhat loud, she appeared to be fun to be around.

Angie had short, blonde hair and was a heavy smoker, something the others didn't appreciate, but they tolerated her.

Colin, about 32 years old and approximately 5 feet 8 inches tall, was stocky, balding, and had a somewhat rubbery face. Franco had previously told Julie that Colin was a roofer in England, but lost everything due to gambling and women.

Mark was slightly shorter than Colin and had dark, thinning hair. Franco mentioned that Mark had pissed off so many people in England that he had to stay out of sight for a while.

Johnny was as bald as a badger and about five feet eight inches tall. He used to sell farm equipment, but nobody knew what went wrong because he didn't talk much.

Julie thought it was funny that she already knew so much about these strangers without having met them. Franco had filled her in on their life stories!

Julie eagerly anticipated a warm meal served by the farmer's wife. The group gathered around a large wooden table as she brought out a big pot of stew.

Julie didn't realise what the meat was until she had eaten her fill, but her reaction was priceless when the others revealed it was guinea pig. "That's alright," she said casually. "I was so hungry I would've eaten it raw."

Everyone chuckled at her response. After dinner, the girls showed Julie to her room. Since there were two spare beds, Sarah kindly let her choose her preferred one.

There's a shower over there. Don't take this the wrong way, but you could probably use one.

"No offense taken, Sarah," Julie admitted. "I probably smell like that river. I'll take a shower with all my clothes on to clean them, but since I have nothing else, I'll have to let them dry on me as best I can."

"Nonsense," Sarah said. "Angie and I can find you something to wear for tonight." "Yeah, we can," Angie agreed, already rummaging through her backpack, a cigarette dangling from her lips, and dropping ash. "You go take a shower, and we'll figure something out for you."

When Julie was clean and dressed, they headed back out to join the boys. They all took a second look at Julie – she was stunning. "Alright!" Franco exclaimed, clapping his hands together and standing up. "Let's go!"

They planned to borrow the old farmer's tractor and trailer, then drove to a small village about a mile and a half away. Julie, for the first time in a long while, felt relaxed and looked forward to enjoying a couple of cold beers at the local tavern.

It was a peaceful moment as they sat outside around an old wooden table, ordering seven beers. Sarah, the curious one, was eager to find out everything that had happened to Julie.

"Come on! Spill the beans, mystery girl!"

Julie hesitated, sitting between the two girls, and looking at each one in turn, unsure of how to start. She exhaled a heavy sigh. It didn't matter anymore; she had shared her story many times before, often in far worse situations. Now that she was out of Peru and beginning to trust these people, she decided to start from the beginning, explaining why she fled the orphanage and sharing details up to the day she met them.

She didn't go into too much detail and skipped over many of the painful parts, just covering the main points. She had released most of her emotions during the events themselves and felt relatively detached, so she spoke calmly, as if it were just a story rather than her own heartbreaking life. Yet even this seemingly calm retelling couldn't help but move her audience.

Their mouths hung open in surprise; the girls even shed tears; they all sat silently, listening throughout, and remained that way for a whole minute after Julie finished, absorbing the impact.

Sarah broke the silence first. "Bloody hell, Julie! If that's the truth – and of course, I believe you – then that's amazing. Sad, but amazing, nonetheless. There's no way I could've done what you did."

"Nor me," Angie said, fighting back tears.

The boys all agreed they wouldn't have handled it either.

Franco exclaimed, "I can't believe you crossed that river. Did you know there are anacondas, crocodiles, and piranhas there? Probably many other dangerous creatures, too."

"I had no idea," Julie said, her eyes wide. "If I had known, I might still be in Peru. I just needed to get across."

They treated her with refreshed respect and kindness. Though she appeared delicate like a flower, this woman was remarkably strong, intelligent, and resourceful.

CHAPTER THIRTY-TWO — *Boarding Pass to Freedom*

The week went smoothly, and they were all set to leave for Chimborazo, about 200 miles away. The old farmer had given them a ride into town and dropped them off at the bus station, where they bought tickets for the bus that left at 2 p.m.

Another long bus ride, but this time Julie felt safe, and talking with friends felt almost normal again. She still knew she had a long way to go and wasn't sure if she'd succeed, but her determination kept her moving forward. So far, so good.

They arrived at Chimborazo six hours later. The area was very remote, with only one hostel, but it was clean and well-kept. The main activities involved relaxing and enjoying a lukewarm shower, a rare treat that cost $1 per person. Although food options were scarce, with no cafes or restaurants nearby, they could buy ingredients and cook for themselves.

Julie volunteered, believing it was the least she could do for her new friends. The meal was modest, but they were used to that and made the best of what they had. After dinner, everyone helped with the cleanup and washing the dishes. They played some card games before going to bed. Another calm day went by, and Julie was thankful for it.

The next day, the bus wasn't scheduled to arrive until 3:10 p.m., so they waited and chatted until it showed up, which was ten minutes late, but it wasn't a big deal. Only Julie was in a hurry; the rest of the group was going only as far as Tungurahua, so Julie would be traveling alone again on the way to Machachi, where another hostel was waiting.

That was the furthest she could go during daylight, and then it was just another 40 miles to Quito, which both excited and scared her. She thought it would be better to arrive in Quito in the morning rather than late at night.

Franco also warned her against traveling at night, since bandits in the mountains frequently robbed many overnight buses. Having experienced so much in Peru, she didn't need to be told twice.

They reached Tungurahua after a few hours, and it was time to say goodbye. This was a tough moment for Julie; she was alone once again and felt the weight of that loneliness. If only LeeRoy had been there!

Unfortunately, she had come to accept that he wouldn't be there for her again. Giles was the only true friend she had in the world, and he was still so far away.

They all hugged each other warmly and sincerely, promising to stay in contact once they reached home. As the bus drove away with Julie onboard, she waved goodbye to her new friends through the dusty window, tears streaming down her face. She believed that Sarah and Angie were crying as well. Then, they disappeared.

Julie settled in for the next leg of her journey, which was relatively short—only 70 miles. She was nearing her destination.

The bus stopped at Avenue Pablo Guarderas, where Julie got off. It was dark, and the neighbourhood looked rough. Shadowy figures appeared in the distance, and the streets seemed gloomy and threatening. As her fear grew, she noticed a taxi. Feeling relieved, she signalled for it.

The driver turned around on the road and looked at her through the open window, a cigarette hanging from his lips.

Julie said, "Hostel."

He frowned and grunted something in Spanish. At first, he didn't understand what Julie was saying, but when she repeated herself and made sleeping gestures at him, he finally realised what she meant.

"Sí, sí," he said. "Enter."

Julie felt uneasy but had no choice. She moved into the back seat as the driver started driving. He began speaking in Spanish, but she replied, "No lo entiendo," and he stopped.

She saw his dark eyes in the rearview mirror, watching her, so she shifted to avoid his gaze.

The driver picked up the radio and spoke rapidly and excitedly. Julie's discomfort increased.

After about ten minutes, they reached a neighbourhood she could only describe as a slum. She sat up straight, tense and alert for danger. The taxi stopped, and a sudden wave of fear washed over her.

She was proven right.

Two men yanked open the back door and dragged Julie into the street. She immediately started screaming, kicking, and biting. The taxi door slammed shut, and the vehicle sped off at full speed.

One of the men held his hand over Julie's mouth, and the other one took her thrashing legs, and they carried her into an old garage.

They pushed her into a corner and signalled for her to be quiet. Julie wasn't stupid and followed orders, but what scared her was that this was a developed area, and these guys seemed like they wouldn't hesitate to kill her.

She squeezed into the corner as tightly as possible, watching them search her bag, keep the cash, and scatter the rest on the floor, her belongings now spread out. Her eyes moved quickly around the room, looking for something to use as a weapon. But before she could react, it was already too late.

One of the men, a skinny but muscular guy, grabbed Julie by the throat, pulled her to her feet, and started patting her down, searching for more valuables. He conducted an overly thorough search of her body, including inside her blouse. He squeezed her breasts and took his time, even fingering inside her underwear. She glared at him, her mouth twisted in hatred, but she could see he was getting turned on.

Then, a loud noise outside abruptly broke the tension, followed by shouts. The guy at the door looked out and shouted to his buddy, urgently motioning for him to come over. The skinny guy dropped Julie, hurried to the door, muttering something, and then both men quickly took off, leaving her trembling.

She didn't know what caused the noise or who made it, but she felt some relief that it had happened. However, if those two guys had been frightened away, she wondered what might be outside.

Wary of encountering something worse, she listened for a few minutes. Everything was quiet. She grabbed her satchel and began packing her things. In the darkness, she fumbled and nearly dropped her bus ticket, but she caught it and went to the door, peeking out like the first guy did.

She looked outside cautiously, questioning what she could have done wrong to deserve all this shit in her life. The street was faintly lit, dark, and deserted, bordered by old, rundown buildings. She was clueless about her location or how to get out. Going to a hostel wasn't an option since they had taken all her remaining money, and reporting to the police wasn't possible.

She was lucky she hadn't been raped yet again, but she was still fuck knows where, and it was not impossible that it could happen again.

She grabbed a short iron bar she found leaning against the doorway, tested its weight thoughtfully, then adjusted her grip, holding it like a weapon until her knuckles whitened.

"Enough is enough!" she snapped out loud.

She was ready to fight or die if she was threatened again.

She had no choice but to keep walking and hope she'd find a safe spot. If that were even possible in this country.

Again, wondering *"What the fucking hell have I done to deserve all this shit? she thought."*

She moved toward a spot where the crowded buildings parted, carefully listening to the street noises. Once she left the tangled alleys with towering structures, the area was brighter, making her feel safer. The only people she saw were family groups.

After walking for a couple of hours, she saw a road sign pointing toward the E35, which she knew was the highway to Quito. The iron bar was heavy in her backpack, but it was comforting to know it was there.

Luckily, sticking to the better-lit main streets meant she mostly encountered couples and mixed groups hanging out outside bars and cafes or walking from one place to another.

It was an arduous journey, and Julie took three hours to reach the highway. She was worn out, exhausted, and hungry. She had been walking for over five hours, but she had to keep going. She jumped and grabbed her bag when a startled dog suddenly barked at her.

"Don't mess with me, bitch!" she growled back, pointing the iron bar at the dog.

As she walked away, she couldn't help but laugh at herself. *Bitch! It could've been a male dog, for I know.* She hadn't exactly stopped to check. She snickered, wondering if she was getting hysterical from fatigue.

After another hour and a half, she saw the bus station ahead and felt encouraged by the sight. She began walking faster and arrived there at 2:20 a.m.

The door was open, and she entered. Although the ticket office was closed, several people sat or lay around, dozing as they waited. Julie checked for danger and decided it was safe to stay, noting that the people were grouped into three and appeared harmless. She found an empty seat and sat down, completely drained. Taking a sip from her water bottle, she tried to sleep, clutching her bag and bus ticket tightly.

The bus was supposed to leave at 11 a.m., so she had a lot of waiting to do, but she wasn't going back into the streets of that town.

Nobody bothered her, and she was able to find a bathroom and fill up her bottle with water.

The bus arrived, and she showed her ticket before boarding. It was a roundabout trip, with the bus passing through small towns and obscure parts of the city, but it finally reached downtown Quito at 1:10 p.m.

Julie was nearly trembling with relief — her long-standing goal was finally within reach.

All that remained was to find the British Embassy.

Luckily, as she checked the worn map displayed inside the bus station, she realised the embassy was just a short walk from the city centre, where she had left the bus.

As she entered the embassy, she was immediately struck by the formal atmosphere and the tidy appearance of the receptionist, who was dressed in a crisp, tailored outfit. Julie had been traveling for days without a shower, and her clothes were torn and filthy from constant wear. Despite her dishevelled look, she understood there was little she could do to change it.

At the desk, the woman smiled brightly and asked in English if she could help.

"I hope so," Julie said. "I've been robbed – I've lost my passport and all my money."

"Oh, dear, another one," the receptionist said.

"Pardon?" Julie asked.

"Sorry, nothing," the woman said, waving her perfectly manicured hands dismissively. "This happens all the time. Do you have your police report?"

"No," Julie said, her heart racing. "I didn't go to the police."

"Why not?" the woman asked.

"Because I'm more scared of the police than I am of the robbers," Julie said.

The woman looked at her closely, then said in a low, confidential tone, "I can understand that. Okay, I need you to fill out this form." She handed it to Julie, along with a pen. "We'll see about getting you an emergency passport and a loan to get you by. Do you have any family in England who can arrange a flight for you?"

"Yes, I do!" Julie almost burst into tears in relief. There was light at the end of this tunnel of hell.

Julie's hands trembled as she filled out the form. Handing it back to the receptionist, she was told to wait in the lobby while the woman took the form to another office.

After Julie's initial excitement, her anxiety grew the longer she waited. She wondered if LeeRoy had gotten a fake passport for her and if there was no record of her being a British citizen. She worried about the questions they might ask, such as when and how she arrived in Ecuador, or other difficult questions. She also feared there might be a warrant for her arrest, which could send her back to Lima. Panic set in as she felt overwhelmed.

Twenty-five minutes later, the receptionist came back with an envelope.

Julie's heart was racing, her throat dry. The receptionist handed her the envelope. Julie took it and looked up at the lady, questioning.

"There is one hundred dollars inside, but our system is slow here, and we can't locate your details. You'll need to return in three days, and hopefully, your passport will be ready by then."

Julie's heart missed a beat, and she stood staring at the receptionist in disbelief.

Realising there could be a problem, she thanked the lady and asked, "Do you have a phone number for a safe cab?" "Yes, no problem. I'll call one for you."

"Thank you, and can you ask them to take me to a hostel, please?" "Certainly"

Julie was now panicking, thinking, "What if they discover it's fake? Will they send me back to Peru, or maybe to England, to face the consequences? I'd be happy to face any consequences in England, but there's no way I'm returning to Peru."

She decided to settle into the hostel and call Giles. The taxi arrived, and fifteen minutes later she reached the hostel, checked in, and decided to freshen up before going out to find a phone box.

She found a public phone booth but couldn't work out how to use it and make a collect call to Giles. She noticed a café across the road, went in, and asked if the lady behind the counter spoke English. She didn't, but an older man sitting by the counter said he did and asked if he could help.

"I hope so," Julie said. "I need to make a collect call to England, but I have no idea how to do it." "Ah, okay, no problem. Sit there," he said, pointing to a chair opposite him. "And once I've finished my coffee, I'll take care of it." Julie thanked him and sat down. "Would you like a coffee too while you wait?" he asked.

"That's very kind of you, but no, thank you." They exchanged pleasantries, and when he finished his coffee, he walked across the street with Julie to the phone box. It was in use, but the lady soon finished, and the old man asked if she had the number.

"I don't have it written down," she said, "but I can give it to you when you get through to the operator."

"OK, that will be fine."

He got through to the operator and explained in Spanish what Julie wanted, then asked for the number, which Julie relayed.

After a few minutes, he handed the phone to Julie. She thanked him, and he continued on his way.

She took the phone and said, "Hello."

"Julie," Giles sounded desperate to hear her voice. "I told you to call me and let me know where you were! Why haven't you? Where are you right now?" he asked."

"Quito," she replied.

"Have you been to the embassy and sorted a passport?"

"Yes, I have been to the embassy, and they lent me some money. However, they mentioned an issue with finding my passport details. I'm not sure if that's correct or if LeeRoy might have given me a fake passport, as there is no record of it."

"That doesn't sound good," he replied.

"I know, I'm scared if I go back and find out it was a fake, God knows what could happen." "Let me think for a moment," Giles paused silently, then said, "I need to speak with Sam."

"Give me the number where you are, and I'll call you back as soon as possible." "It's a public phone booth," she advised, "and the number on the dial is 55489654, but I don't know how to dial it from England." "Don't worry about that, I'll handle it," Giles assured her. Julie interrupted before he could hang up, saying, "I need to buy some new clothes. Can you call me in an hour? I'll make sure I'm near the booth."

"Alright, but don't be late." "You sound like a dad," she joked. Giles was surprised to feel his heart sink a little, even though it was nice to hear Julie laugh genuinely and happily for the first time in a while.

Using the money the embassy had loaned her, she found a nearby clothing store, bought the essentials, returned to the hostel, took a quick bath, and changed into new clothes, happy to toss the old, dirty ones in the trash.

The phone booth was close by, and she was waiting there, but no call arrived. She waited another ten minutes, feeling a bit worried, until the phone suddenly rang.

She opened the door and grabbed the phone. "Hello"

Giles suddenly spoke without any greeting. "Listen, I've talked to Sam, and the passport was fake." Julie's heart sank, and she began to cry. "What am I supposed to do now? If I go back to the embassy, they'll probably arrest me, and if they find out about Peru, they'll likely send me back." She sobbed.

"Don't worry, or at least try not to—Sam is arranging another passport for you. Could you let me have the hostel's address? He will send someone to deliver it once he has booked a flight. It should arrive before your next embassy appointment. If it doesn't, they likely won't bother searching for you."

"Another fake, huh? Great. I'll probably end up in prison in Ecuador."

Julie, listen, since you cleared customs in England and Peru with your old one, there shouldn't be any issue there.

"With my luck, I wouldn't bet on it. I can't remember the address off hand; I'll have to go and get it. Could you please call back in ten minutes?" "Yes, no problem."

She got the address, and Giles called back exactly ten minutes later, asking, "Do you have the address? "Yes, it's Hostel L'Auberge, Av. Gran Colombia N° 15-200, Yaguachi, Quito." "OK, I will call this number tomorrow at 10 am your time to confirm what's happening, OK?" "Yes, OK, thanks, Giles. Sorry if I sounded sharp, but dealing with my passport being fake and having to use another fake to get home is freaking me out."

"Yeah, I understand that. Stay positive; it'll all be okay."

"I hope so, but I feel scared. "I know we'll talk tomorrow." Then Giles hung up.

Feeling hungry, she found a small café near her hostel. She ordered a sandwich and coffee. Although she was starving, she had a hard time finishing the sandwich. She then ordered another coffee to go, paid the bill, and headed back to the hostel.

She had trouble sleeping, tossing and turning all night, worried about the fake passport and the risk of getting caught and sent back to Peru.

The next morning, she returned to the same café and ordered only coffee; she wasn't in the mood to eat.

At 10 am, she was waiting by the phone booth when it rang exactly on time.

"Hi Giles, do you have any news?"

"Yes, a friend of Sam's will be with you tonight, though I'm not sure of the exact time since it depends on how long it takes to clear the airport and get a taxi to you. He has your passport and will travel back with you. He also has a spare suitcase filled with ladies' clothes and items, so it won't appear suspicious if you arrive at the airport empty-handed."

"Thanks, I was worried that they would question why I had no luggage."

"OK," said Giles. "You're booked on an overnight flight, direct to Heathrow." The flight, BA254, leaves at 4:45 p.m. tomorrow and arrives in London at 6:10 a.m. I'll be there to meet you."

Julie could have wept. Her knees felt like jelly, and she placed her hand on the wall of the telephone booth to support herself.

Giles finished, "You need to go to the BA check-in and give them this number: 17523. Can you remember it? 17523." "I can remember that." She repeated the number. "Thanks, Giles, and please thank Sam for me, too." "I will, Julie. Good luck. 17523," he repeated, with a worried tone.

She wandered the streets of Quito for a few hours, anxiously passing the time and worrying about what lay ahead.

She went back to the hostel, lay down, and dozed for a couple of hours, waking up around 5:30 in the evening.

Back to the café for more coffee, and this time she managed to eat a plate of Bolon de Verde, considered a national dish of the country. Then, she returned to the hostel to wait for Sam's friend.

He arrived at 11:20 p.m., knocked on her door, and Julie opened it with caution until she saw a black Caribbean face and knew immediately who it was; she let him in.

He introduced himself as Josef, with no last name.

"OK," he said almost immediately. "When you arrive at the airport, you'll need to check in yourself. I'll be watching in case there are any problems, not that there will be much I can do if there are, but we'll worry about that if it happens."

That statement didn't fill Julie with much hope, but she understood the reasons and the fact that she had gotten this far. Surely, nothing can go wrong. She didn't feel too confident, though.

"Thank you, Josef, I do appreciate you helping me."

"That's OK, and I'm very sorry for what has happened to you and, of course, the loss of LeeRoy. He was a great friend and will be missed."

Leaving one suitcase with Julie, he said, "There are probably things in there you could use. I'll go down to reception and book a room for tonight. Try to get as much sleep as you can, as it's a long flight tomorrow." "If I get on it," she replied. "You'll be OK," he tried to reassure her.

Josef knocked on Julie's door at 10:00 AM and asked what she did for breakfast. "There's a little café just down the road a bit, give me five minutes and I'll come down with you. I need something to settle my churning stomach."

"OK, I'll wait in the reception for you."

After breakfast, it was 11:30, and Josef suggested, "We should leave for the airport now to ensure we have enough time in case of any issues."

Julie felt much happier now that she had someone watching out for her, but she was still afraid of what might happen at the airport.

Julie went to the check-in desk and quoted the booking number.

The lady at the desk rifled through some papers. "Ah, yes. Here we are, a one-way ticket to Heathrow. May I see your passport, please?"

Julie handed it over, barely able to breathe.

"Do you have any luggage to check in?"

"Yes, just one suitcase," she was still panicking inside.

"OK, that all seems in order. Here's your boarding pass and ticket."

Julie took them, and she was relieved. That was it, now. Nothing could go wrong now. She'd be in the air in a few hours.

She showed her boarding pass at Customs and put her worn-out satchel through the X-ray machine. She was going to keep that satchel forever! She walked over to Passport Control. The officer opened her passport and asked, "When did you arrive here?"

Julie panicked. "About two weeks ago."

"What airport did you arrive at?"

Still panicking, Julie said, "This one."

"That's impossible," he said. "We would have a record of you arriving."

"I have no idea," Julie said, her voice rising in pitch.

"Please follow me," he said, guiding her to an interview room. She attempted to steady her nerves, realising she was hyperventilating, and sweat was streaming down her body.

"Sit down."

He left the room with her passport. A thousand thoughts rushed through Julie's mind. Would they lock her up here? Would they send her back to Peru? She was terrified.

He returned ten minutes later and handed Julie the passport, open to one page. She took it, puzzled, and looked inside. There, right in front of her, was an exit stamp.

"You may go now," he said.

Julie hurried out of the room and dashed to the departure lounge, where she saw Josef waiting and signalled to him that everything was fine. The next thirty-five minutes felt like an eternity as she sat waiting, her fingers twisting.

Her eyes constantly scanned for anyone in an airport uniform, even from afar, and she held her breath, worried they'd approach. Then it happened. First in Spanish, then:

"All passengers for flight BA254 to Heathrow, please proceed to the boarding gate." Julie broke into a sweat. Her head bowed, she avoided eye contact, desperately wanting to push past everyone and board the plane. She still believed someone would come to take her away, thinking her luck was about to run out again.

But no! Unbelievably, she was on the plane, walking up the aisle, and found seat 52A - a window seat. She sat down quickly and buckled herself in, feeling safer now that she was secured. She thought to herself that they'd need an army to get her off the plane. She gripped the metal buckle, staring out the tiny window, her knee bouncing with impatience as she prayed for take-off. She was on edge, expecting police guards to storm the plane and drag her away at any moment. *Just let's take off, and I'll be okay.*

There weren't many passengers on the flight, and Julie had three seats to herself. With everyone on board, the doors closed, and the plane began taxiing down the runway.

As the plane took off, Julie's apprehension started to fade. She still felt uneasy, even at 30,000 feet, wondering how long it would be before they left Ecuadorean airspace and were out of reach.

Nothing could go wrong now, could it?

She was right. After half an hour of the flight, dinner arrived, and the tight feeling in Julie's stomach started to ease. She found herself enjoying her in-flight meal, feeling safe and secure for the first time in what seemed like weeks.

After the dinner was cleared away, Julie was able to stretch out across all three seats and quickly fell into a deep sleep. She rested peacefully, feeling warm and safe, and genuinely hopeful for the first time in a long while, but still had to get through British customs.

She woke up completely refreshed, just two hours from Heathrow. Then she headed to the tiny plane bathroom, doing her best to freshen up. She grinned as she made her way back to her seat, surprising fellow passengers with her radiant smile. Then, she buckled her seatbelt and sat up straight, alert and ready for the rest of the trip.

As the plane touched down on the runway, Julie burst into tears of relief and didn't stop until they'd parked at the terminal.

CHAPTER THIRTY-THREE — *Home, Not Whole*

Julie faced a lengthy walk to customs and was tempted to run, but she resisted the urge. She queued up, and when her turn came, she thought, "This will probably be fine."

It was! A glance at her passport, and she was permitted to re-enter England.

She left the corridor and stepped into the airport's arrivals area, her heart racing with excitement and lingering anxiety.

Her eyes scanned the crowds of happy people waiting for their friends and family, searching.

There were Giles and Sam, waiting for her! She pushed through the crowded gateway, ran to hug them, and burst into tears. They were crying too.

"I'm so sorry, Julie," Sam said gruffly, yet with compassion. He shared LeeRoy's loss almost as intensely as she did and was trying to be brave.

"Are you okay?" Giles asked, his hands gently cupping her face, his concerned eyes searching hers.

"Yeah, Giles," Julie swallowed hard, trembling with relief. "I am now. I can't believe I'm home." She shook her head, struggling to find the words to express everything. Whatever she said wouldn't be enough.

"That was a real nightmare!"

"I can't imagine what you went through out there," Giles said softly, placing his arm around her gently as she trembled with emotion and relief. "Come on. Let's get you to the car and back home."

As they were leaving, Josef approached to say farewell. Julie hugged him and said, "Thank you so much, Josef. I don't think I could have managed that without your assistance. I will always remember what you did for me," then gently kissed his cheek. If he weren't Black, he might have blushed.

Sam was behind the wheel, and Giles sat in the back with Julie.

"Do you want to talk about it?" He squeezed her hand.

"Later. I want to get home and have a real bath. I must look a mess."

"Don't be silly, Julie," he said softly. "You always look a million dollars."

They drove the rest of the way home in almost silence. Julie snuggled up to Giles and finally felt safe.

They went back to the house in Faversham and parked the car in front. Sam was the first to get out and opened the passenger side for Julie. She stepped out, glancing up at the big house with a mix of nerves and resolve. She took a deep breath.

As Sam opened the front door, Julie stepped up to it but stopped in her tracks. She couldn't bring herself to walk through it.

"Are you okay?" asked Sam.

"No. I can't walk into the house, knowing LeeRoy's never going to be there again," she cried.

Sam, with his arm around Julie, softly whispered—an impressive feat for such a big guy—"LeeRoy would have wanted you to be happy. He loved you so much."

She smiled gratefully through her tears, knowing Sam was right. She owed it to LeeRoy to make the most of her life, so she took a deep breath and slowly walked into the house.

They all headed into the kitchen, and Giles put the kettle on to make them all coffee.

Julie felt like she couldn't settle down just yet. "I'd like to go take a bath now. Please excuse me. I'll come back down and explain everything to you – if I can, without falling apart."

"You take your time, Julie. We can wait."

While Julie was in the bath, Giles called Chas and told him Julie was home.

"I'm coming right up," he told Giles firmly.

"I'm sure that'll be fine, Chas, although she's still quite fragile. She needs all the support we can give her. I only know a little about what happened out there, but I think she's had a tough time."

"Okay, don't worry. See you in ten."

Chas arrived in eight minutes, and Giles prepared a cup of coffee for him while they waited for Julie. She returned about forty-five minutes later, and Chas stood up and hugged her.

"Are you okay, Julie?"

"Yes, Chas. It will take a long time to move past what happened. I'll never forget it, but hopefully someday I can push it out of my mind," she said with doubt. "LeeRoy, though, will always stay at the front."

Giles had made a fresh pot of coffee and poured Julie a cup.

She wrapped her small fingers around the mug and sighed, "It feels like a bad dream even though I know it isn't. Now that I'm home and safe, it doesn't seem real. I'm sure you all want to hear exactly what happened."

"Yes," Giles said. "We'd all like to make sense of it all, if possible. But only if you're ready."

"I think it helps me to get it out of my system," she explained. "Talking about it, it releases the pain."

They sat silently while Julie recounted, step by step, what had occurred. It took her an hour, and once she finished, all four were in tears — even Sam.

Giles moved closer to Julie, gripping her firmly. Through her tears, he said, "You're incredibly brave, Julie. I can't believe you didn't break down completely out there."

"Believe me, Giles, I nearly did, a few times," she said, shaking off the terrible memories from her mind. "My main priority now is to find out if we can get LeeRoy's body back home."

"Leave that to me," Sam said. "I'll handle it and make all the necessary arrangements." He cleared his throat. "There's one more thing I need to tell you, Julie."

She looked up at him, her eyes filling with fear, unable to hear any more bad news. He continued, "LeeRoy has left everything he has to you." Julie let out a tiny sound. "How do you know that?"

"I know because the day he married you, he signed his will while we were still at the reception. His solicitor was there, and I was a witness, if you remember."

Julie frowned, recalling, "Yes, I do remember him there." Her expression then fell again, tears beginning to roll down her cheeks. She gasped, saying, "Oh, LeeRoy!" Tears welled up as she continued, "That man was so kind. I don't know how I'll manage without him. I miss him so much, especially now that I'm home."

She looked around the spacious kitchen, a worried look tightening her brow. "It was very kind of him, but I just can't afford to run this place alone."

"Julie," Sam said, holding back a laugh, "once you discover what he's left you, you'll never have any trouble. Trust me."

Julie dismissively waved the suggestion, still frowning. "Well, Sam, that's not a priority for me right now. I want to bring him back here," she said, biting her lip. She wanted him alive, but that wasn't going to happen. The best she could do was return his body and give him a proper funeral to honour his memory. "Once he's here and I've laid him to rest, I'll focus on sorting out my life."

Sam nodded. "As you mentioned, the priority is recovering his body and ensuring you're alright." He paused briefly before adding sheepishly, "Do you think you should see a doctor, um, after everything that happened to you?"

"Yes, Sam, maybe." Julie had been through a lot, and she didn't want to think about it. The thought of pregnancy or disease had crossed her mind after every rape she'd suffered. "That's a good idea. I'll call him tomorrow." She let out a sigh, gazing blankly at Giles and Chas, and said, "I'm thankful to all of you, and please don't take this the wrong way, but would you mind if I had some time alone for the rest of the day?"

Sam and Chas nodded and shifted in their seats, preparing to head out.

"Of course, we don't mind, Julie," Sam said. "I need to get back to London anyway. I'll stay in touch, especially about getting LeeRoy back." He stood up and nodded toward the dresser. "By the way, I've left two thousand pounds in that drawer over there to help you out until everything is settled."

Julie's eyes widened. "Thanks, Sam. I promise I'll pay you back as soon as I can."

Sam smiled sadly. "Julie, you owe me nothing."

Chas left, patting her on the arm and saying, "You know where I am." She thanked him.

"I'll be in the chalet if you need anything," Giles said, hugging Julie again. "It's wonderful to have you back, Julie, but I still can't believe what's happened to you and especially LeeRoy."

Julie gave him a watery smile. "You have no idea how it feels to be back, Giles, but I'm drained."

"Yep, I understand. See you later, or in the morning."

"Thanks. I do appreciate everything you've done for me."

Julie was alone in the silence, so deep she felt deafened. Hesitating, she went upstairs, slowly opened the bedroom door, and suddenly burst into tears again.

She had been there earlier, before her bath, standing alone in the middle of the room, feeling the pain again. She opened LeeRoy's closet, gazing at the empty suits. She lifted the sleeve of one of his shirts and pressed it to her cheek, tears soaking it, her throat sore from crying.

It kept worsening instead of improving. Each time she entered the room without LeeRoy, she felt on the verge of tears.

She lay down on the bed, moved to LeeRoy's pillow, and buried her face in it, taking deep breaths through her nose.

She still thought she could smell him, which both hurt and provided some comfort. She realised she might never be able to wash that pillowcase again.

She rolled over, clutching the pillow to her chest with her face pressed into it. She tried to sleep, but the nightmare kept repeating in her mind, making rest impossible. Eventually, she fell into a restless sleep, only to wake up again, screaming and covered in sweat.

Where was LeeRoy?

She took a few seconds to realise where she was. Looking at the bedside clock, she noted it was 2:10 a.m.

Wondering if she would ever get over this, she thought she needed to talk to the doctor.

Feeling jetlagged and unable to sleep, she went to the kitchen and made a cup of coffee.

Almost immediately, there was a knock on the door. Though it was a gentle knock, it startled her. She spun around and saw Giles pressing his hand against the door's glass and watching her with concern. She unlocked the door and let him in. "You scared me, Giles."

"Sorry. I tried to knock softly."

She poured some coffee into a mug. "What are you doing awake at this hour?"

"I could ask you the same," he responded. "I couldn't sleep," she explained. "I'm exhausted but just can't fall asleep." "Me neither," he admitted. "I was sitting on the veranda and noticed your light turn on, so I wanted to check if you're alright."

They sat down with a cup of coffee each and fell silent for a moment, lost in their thoughts. Then Giles said, "I can't even imagine what you've been through or how you're feeling or how it will affect you down the line."

Julie looked at him, biting her lip. He noticed the blood rushing to her mouth, resembling a smear of lipstick. Despite her sun-tanned skin from days of walking outdoors, she appeared somewhat pale and unwell.

He added, "What I can say is that both you and LeeRoy have been very supportive of me, and I will always be there for you. "Just ask, and if it's possible, it'll get done."

Julie's red lips pressed into a tight smile. "Thanks. You're a kind man, and I truly appreciate that." He nearly blushed. "I'll need you to drive me to Faversham in the morning to see the doctor." She looked up at him, her expression thoughtful, as if she was trying to come to terms with something. "Can I confide in you, Giles?" She bit her lip once more. "Stupid question. I know I can."

"Yes, of course you can," he said, worry etched on his face. "What's going on?"

"It's difficult, but I need to be honest," she said, meeting his anxious gaze. "I've missed a period, and I suspect I might be pregnant." Julie noticed it was a sensitive topic for him, and Giles seemed uncertain about how to reply.

He had a good idea what she was worried about.

"Do you think it's LeeRoy's? Or one of the bastards that raped you?"

"Sorry, I'm stuttering, you get the idea."

Julie picked at the side of her coffee cup, where a blob of coffee stained the whiteness.

"That's the problem, Giles. I have no idea, and there's no way to find out. I'll talk to the doctor tomorrow and see what he suggests."

"My God, Julie," he murmured, shaking his head slowly. "What else can happen to you?" She gazed into the depths of her cup, finding no answers. "No idea, Giles, but I expect it will get worse before it improves." They sat talking about trivial matters when Julie remembered she had promised to call someone once she was home safely.

Giles, do you still have the number for Rose in Ecuador?"

"Sure."

He returned a few minutes later and gave the number to Julie.

"I'm going to try to call Rose and then go to bed and get some sleep. You should do the same. I'll let you know in the morning what time I get an appointment with the doctor."

As Giles went to leave, she suddenly said,

"Oh my God! Has anyone told LeeRoy's family?"

"Yes, Sam called his sister yesterday morning. I know they took it pretty hard, and I think they'll be coming over, but Sam will fill you in on that."

Julie sighed in relief. "Thank goodness for that. I wouldn't have wanted to be the one to call them. It's unfortunate she was so ill and couldn't attend the wedding...," she said mournfully, reminiscing about their happiness. "Or Rosina, having to look after his mother."

"Yes, it was a shame," Giles said, patting her hand before heading out the back door. "You know where I'll be in the morning. Try to get some rest."

Julie dialled the number in Ecuador, and a man answered in Spanish.

She knew who it was. She just said bluntly, "Rose, por favor."

The man guessed who it was, too, and she heard him call out to Rose, mentioning Julie's name.

Rose's voice came next, breathless. "Julie! Are you okay?"

"Yes, Rose. I got back okay. I'm safe now. It was a terrifying experience, and I appreciate everything you did for me. Please, if you ever come to England, you must let me know."

"I will, Julie."

They talked for over half an hour, then Julie said, "I'm sorry, Rose. I'm exhausted and need to get some sleep. I promise to stay in touch. Thanks again."

The next morning, Julie called the doctor's office and made an appointment for 11:20. After showering and dressing, she went to Giles and told him the appointment time.

Giles dropped her off, and she eventually saw the doctor, recounting most of what happened. After examining her, he concluded that she was in good condition, given the circumstances.

He requested a urine sample from her to be sent to a lab for confirmation. From what she told him and his findings during the exam, he was pretty sure it would simply confirm her pregnancy.

"My God! What should I do?" Julie exclaimed. "How can I tell if it's LeeRoy's or one of the others?" She had barely avoided swearing in the surgery.

The doctor shrugged. "That's a tough decision you have to make, Julie. But think about this: even if it's not LeeRoy's, do you still want to end a life? A baby's life that has the chance to live, through no fault of its own?" The doctor raised an eyebrow. "You have to ask yourself a question, it's straightforward, Julie. There's a reasonable probability that LeeRoy is the father, but it's not certain. How would you feel if you decided to abort? You wouldn't know exactly who the father is, but you'd constantly wonder."

She had been wondering for days.

"You have a living human inside you. Can you destroy it? I don't mean to sound harsh, Julie, but the facts are the facts. It's going to be tough for you to decide, but I'm sure whatever you choose will be the right one."

Julie swallowed hard. "How long do I have to decide, doctor? Do I have a week or two?"

"Yes, that's not a problem. Come and see me again if you need to."

Giles was outside, leaning against the car and waiting for Julie. As soon as he saw her, he stood up, attempting to gauge her mood. He had made up his mind not to question Julie until she was prepared to talk.

Julie asked him if he would take her to the café where she first met LeeRoy, just thirty yards from the doctor's surgery. Giles locked the pickup, and they went inside. This was another sad moment in her brief life, but she accepted it as it came.

They sat at the same table where LeeRoy had first spoken to her. Tears shimmered in her eyes, though she wasn't sobbing. Giles ordered two coffees and brought them to the table. He had all the time she needed and was willing to listen if she wanted to talk.

Julie gave a sheepish smile. "Did I mention that this is where I met LeeRoy for the first time?"

"No," Giles said, frowning with concern. "I had no idea that was the case."

"Are you okay?"

"Yes, I'm fine."

Julie sat there, lost in thought, gazing out the window.

Incredibly, at that very moment, the two scumbags walked by, and one of them noticed Julie, stopping the other to point and laugh.

They had a brief chat before entering the café. Giles, facing away from the door, didn't see them arrive but soon heard their voices. Since Faversham was a small town, everyone familiar with LeeRoy was aware of the rumours about his supposed death.

Gary walked up to them, all hyped up and talking a big game. "Not so tough now that your big black man's not around to back you up!" he said, with the other one egging him on.

When the two guys spoke up, Giles stayed quiet. Instead, he stood, looked over at the café owner, and said, "Sorry, Len." Then he faced the two men again, still silent. The café was crowded, so the two men stepped back and taunted Giles, saying, "Come on! Try it if you've got the guts!"

He did.

They stood side by side, mocking with sneers and catcalls. Giles, forgetting his record and that he could be in serious trouble if ever prosecuted for any violence, kicked Gary in the groin with his left foot, then immediately kicked Paul in the groin as well. Paul didn't have time to react before Giles punched him right on the bridge of his nose, breaking it instantly.

Paul was knocked out cold, and Giles grabbed Gary, yanking him to his feet by his jacket lapels. His face was a mask of anger, his nose just inches from Gary's, his sweat and spit splattering Gary's face as he snarled, "You fucking losers will never talk to that lady like that again! You'll never speak to her again, not after you've gone in to apologise to her." He tightened his grip on Gary's throat, shouting, "Do you understand? If you don't, LeeRoy's friends will pay you another visit. Do you get that? Now tell me you understand."

Gary's eyes widened in shock, but he couldn't speak and just nodded his head.

Giles grabbed Paul by the throat, too, and now he was choking one of them in each hand. "Do you understand?"

Paul croaked. "Yes."

Giles released them both, leaving them gasping for air. Gary grasped his neck, and his voice was hoarse as he croaked, "You've done some damage, you bastard."

"That's nothing, you pricks," Giles snapped. "You're so clueless you'll never learn, but for your own sake, I hope you do eventually. Now, go inside and apologise."

Gary and Paul quietly walked in, looking down, and mumbled an apology to Julie, who pretended not to notice.

"Better head to the Cottage Hospital. It looks like he might need a bandage," Giles said.

The guys slinked off, muttering under their breath.

Giles went back inside and said, "Sorry, Len."

Len shrugged. "Don't apologise – serves those pricks right. They're nothing but trouble."

"You didn't have to do that, Giles," Julie said with a wry smile. "But I'm sure LeeRoy would have been proud of you. You're full of surprises, aren't you?"

"I surprised myself, Julie."

Julie set down her coffee cup. "Would you mind taking me to the pub to see Chas and Val, please?"

"Sure, no problem. You're my boss now," he added quickly. "As long as you want me around, that is."

"Don't worry, Giles," she smiled gratefully. "You're not going anywhere."

They walked into the bar and found themselves surrounded by well-wishers, who offered condolences and expressed their sympathy. Julie had become quite popular while working there.

They headed to the back room and found Chas and Val. Val wrapped her arms around Julie, and they both started crying as they greeted each other and chatted seriously.

As Giles filled Chas in on what had just happened at the café, he kept a close eye on Julie.

Chas fumed, "That's it. They're never coming back to this pub again – the wankers. I wish I'd been there. I would've given them a fucking good beating myself." He turned to Giles, his voice dropping to a confidential tone, "How's she doing?"

"She's holding up. Just took her to the doctor, but I haven't asked her how it went yet."

"Well, I'm confident she'll be fine. She's a resilient little girl," Chas said.

"I hope so," Giles said.

"Yeah, but what a lousy thing to happen! I can't believe it," Chas said, swinging his arm toward the door of the bar. "Come on, Giles. Let's get a beer and let the girls talk."

"Good idea."

Val listened with a mixture of sadness, anger, sympathy, and concern as Julie shared her experiences of rape and the resulting pregnancy.

"What will you do, Julie?"

"I don't know, Val." Julie looked up at the ceiling and let out a deep sigh. "But at the moment, I think I'll keep it." Val squeezed her hand as she added, "After all, it might belong to LeeRoy. And if it doesn't, I believe I could still love it."

Val took a deep breath and let it out through her lips. "It's not a decision I'd want to make. I don't envy you one bit."

A few weeks passed, and Sam then called with good news: "Julie, I've arranged for LeeRoy to come home." Julie sighed with relief and began to cry, saying, "Thanks, Sam. When will he arrive?"

"Next Wednesday. I've set up for the funeral home to collect the body and handle the funeral arrangements. I'll confirm the date as soon as I get it. I'm assuming you'd like him buried in St. Mary's, where you got married?"

"Yes, Sam, that would be great. If possible, I'd like him to be buried next to Barrie."

"I'll see what I can do. Will LeeRoy's mother and sister be here?"

"Yes, Sam. Oddly enough, they're arriving next Wednesday as well. I hope they don't see the coffin being unloaded."

"That won't happen, Julie. It won't be visible to the public."

"Thanks, Sam. You're a good friend. LeeRoy would have been proud of you."

"No problem, Julie. He would have done the same for me."

CHAPTER THIRTY-FOUR — *Inheritance and Aftermath*

There was much to consider and organise. Julie was led into the solicitor's office, recognising him from the wedding.

"Please take a seat," he told her. "Would you like some tea or coffee?" She declined, and he continued, "Julie, I asked you to come in because I need to review LeeRoy's will with you. I'll keep it brief. You're a very lucky girl, Julie."

"My husband is dead!" she snapped back. "How does that make me lucky?"

"Julie, I'm sorry. I only meant regarding what LeeRoy left you in his will." "Yes, I understand, but it still hurts—and it always will."

"Yes, I understand that."

"Can you really? I seriously doubt it," she snapped, then settled herself. "Anyway, apologies. I'm a bit sensitive."

"That's understandable. Alright, I'll go on. As mentioned, I'll keep this brief for now. LeeRoy has left you all his possessions, including all investments and bank balances. As of two days ago, the estimated value of his investments is one million, two hundred and twenty thousand pounds."

Julie flinched sharply. She looked at the solicitor's calm, expressionless face. "Are you serious? Did I hear that right?"

"Yes, Julie, you did," the lawyer said with a slight smile. "Additionally, there are another nine hundred thousand pounds in two accounts at National Westminster Bank in Market Place. I also know he has an account in Jersey, but you'll be contacted about that separately."

Julie was speechless for a moment, absorbing the sheer size of everything. Her mind was racing. Then she asked with concern, "What about his mother and sister?"

"They're taken care of. He also has money in Bermuda, which hasn't been left to you."

Julie let out a relieved breath. "That's okay. As long as his family is okay."

"Yes, they are, Julie." The lawyer continued: "I've arranged for the money to be transferred into your account."

"I don't have a bank account," she interrupted, as if searching for a reason why this couldn't be true. It was all too much to take in. She had no experience with banks.

"You do now, Julie," the lawyer explained. "A cheque book will be sent to you later this week. Here are all the details of your account. LeeRoy's accountant will be in touch, but not until after the funeral and you've had time to process everything."

Julie couldn't see how that could happen. "Oh, and LeeRoy also had a life insurance policy, so I notified them in a letter yesterday. They'll need a copy of the death certificate before releasing the final payment, but I'll handle all of that for you."

Julie's mind seemed to shut down, overwhelmed by everything. She shook her head faintly and muttered, "I'm stunned."

The solicitor nodded and folded his hands on the desk, patiently waiting for any questions.

Julie waved her hand vaguely and absentmindedly. "If that's all, I'd like to leave now, if I may?"

"Yes, indeed, you can. My secretary will contact you once all the necessary documents are prepared for your signature."

Julie was in a daze as she left the solicitor's office, accidentally bumping into the two scumbags. They merely glanced at her and then hurriedly walked away, with her barely registering their presence.

She returned to the pub and muttered, "Val, I need a coffee." She then shook her head and said, "No, I don't – I need a brandy, and a big one at that!"

"What's going on?" Val asked, panicking. "What happened?"

"Nothing serious. Please—get me a brandy, and I'll tell you."

Val returned with it and one for herself, her forehead furrowed in concern. "What's wrong, Julie? What happened?"

"I just got back from the solicitors, and LeeRoy... he left me a fortune! I'm still trying to process it all."

Val grinned in relief. "Well, that's great, isn't it?"

Julie's forehead remained furrowed in confusion. "Not long ago, I had nothing, was abused by a crazy matron, and had no future. Now, I'm a bloody millionaire – and I'm not even twenty years old."

"Your body might be only twenty, Julie, but your mind is like that of a fifty-year-old," Val said, gently patting Julie's hand. "It's evident how deeply LeeRoy loved you, and he would want you to find happiness and enjoy life."

Julie shook her head sadly. "Val, I'd give it all up to have LeeRoy back."

"I'm sure you would, Julie, but you need to keep moving forward with your life."

Giles drove Julie home in silence, overwhelmed. When she got in, she found a telegram from Sam.

"Hi, Julie, STOP. The funeral is set for next Friday, but don't worry, STOP. I've taken care of everything. STOP. The grave will be next to Barrie's STOP."

Julie called Sam and thanked him for everything. She asked, "What time does the plane land?"

"One fifteen in the afternoon," he replied.

Julie paused thoughtfully. "That's roughly an hour after his mother and sister arrive. It's incredible how that worked out..." She paused, considering something she had been thinking. "Sam, I'm unsure if it's the right decision, but do you think LeeRoy's mother, sister, and I could ride with the coffin in the hearse?"

"No problem. It's already taken care of." Sam said softly. "They have stretch limos—essentially hearses with seats. I've booked one for us."

Julie almost broke down in relief, feeling she didn't want LeeRoy to make his final journey home alone.

Julie chose to delay returning to work until after the funeral. Although she was now unexpectedly rich and didn't need to work, she craved normalcy. Nonetheless, she still needed to handle some arrangements, such as meeting with the accountant, which Sam had scheduled based on the solicitor's advice.

Julie arrived at the accountant's office early for her appointment and was promptly greeted by the receptionist, who introduced her to Mr. Smythe.

He shook her hand and offered her a sincere, sympathetic smile. But following the briefest social pleasantry, he quickly got to the main point.

"I understand that your solicitor explained to you that LeeRoy has left you money in a numbered bank account in Jersey.

"Yes, he did mention that," Julie nodded vaguely. "But I was so overwhelmed with everything else, I didn't fully grasp it or understand what it all meant."

"Not a problem," Smythe smiled. "I will explain everything. LeeRoy has," he quickly corrected himself, "had a numbered bank account." "What's a numbered bank account?" Julie interrupted.

"It's an account that you can only access if you know the number." He leaned over and added in a meaningful tone, "And the contents of it cannot be traced back to the owner."

Julie looked confused, her eyes widening. "I still don't understand. Why would he do something like this? And in Jersey, of all places? Why not just keep it in the same bank here?"

Smythe cleared his throat and folded his hands on the desk. "It's because the money is undeclared, and he didn't want anyone to know about it."

This just seemed even more suspicious to Julie. "Where did the money come from?"

"Julie, do you have any idea what LeeRoy did?" Smythe asked, his eyes fixed on her.

"Sort of," she replied.

"Well, these are the proceeds from some of his deals."

"I don't want it," Julie said, her face white as she was horrified by the thought of LeeRoy's involvement in even more shady deals. The money was too hot to track, and it all became overwhelming for her.

Smythe was taken aback. "What do you mean, you don't want it?"

"Exactly that," Julie said, her lips tight. "Please arrange to give it to a charity anonymously."

Smythe looked bewildered. "Charity, Julie? There's over a quarter of a million pounds in that account."

Julie shuddered. All of this was overwhelming. "I don't care. I don't want it."

"Maybe you should think about it for a while before making any hasty decisions," Smythe warned.

"No," Julie said sharply. "I don't need to consider it. Give it to the orphanage that raised me—a charity runs it." She added, "Yes,

I want them to have it. But only if they remove that dreadful matron."

She immediately regretted her words. "That would be too harsh. Honestly, I should be grateful she was there. Without her, I wouldn't have run away or met LeeRoy. Still, she needs stricter management so she can't mistreat other girls again. Yes, it's St. Catherine's Orphanage in Bexhill. Let them keep the money."

Smythe made a note but still looked doubtful. "Are you sure?"

"Yes, I am. "Besides that nasty woman, the staff there is excellent. Even she was ok with the others. For some reason, it was just me she didn't like."

Smythe observed her, allowing her an opportunity to reconsider. However, from the firmness of her mouth and her intense stare, it was evident she was resolute. He also knew her current account balance precisely.

Finally, he shrugged and said, "Alright. If you're sure, I'll arrange a bank draft to be sent to them. They won't have any idea how the money was made, but one thing's clear – they probably won't be too worried."

Wednesday morning eventually came – the day LeeRoy's body was supposed to arrive.

The traffic heading to the airport was manageable. Giles parked, and they reached the arrival lounge by 11:15, leaving roughly an hour before the first flight landed. Sam was handling all the funeral arrangements, and they planned to meet him later. When they checked the arrivals board, they saw that LeeRoy's mother and sister's flight was on schedule.

"Want a coffee, Julie?"

She agreed, and after their drinks arrived at the table, a brief, tense silence ensued. Giles cleared his throat and asked, "I know this is a delicate matter." Julie looked at him suspiciously, but he pressed on. "And you can tell me to mind my own business, but have you decided about the baby?"

She thoughtfully stirred her coffee. Although she had made her decision, doubts continued to creep in, so she hadn't talked to Giles about it. It felt too personal somehow. And he hadn't pushed her.

"Yes, Giles, I have," she sighed. "I'm holding onto it, hoping it's LeeRoy's. You see, if I keep it, I'll be certain. If I have an abortion, I'll always wonder, and that would drive me insane."

Giles smiled encouragingly. "You know what, Julie? I knew you would."

She frowned, a slight smile spreading across her lips. "Did you now? I didn't!" she asked, her tone filled with surprise. "What made you so sure?"

"Just knew," he replied with a shrug. "You're easy to read, Julie."

"Am I really?" she asked, her eyes locking onto his.

"Yep."

They exchanged a glance, and under different circumstances, they might have laughed out loud. However, it was a difficult day, so a warm look was enough to feel connected.

They wandered through the airport shops, doing nothing, just passing the time. Soon, the plane landed, and they went to Arrivals, waiting more than half an hour before the couple arrived, both looking exhausted. Rosina tried to keep a brave face, but LeeRoy's mother was already crying. They quickly embraced in a tight hug, all three crying. Giles stayed back, out of the way.

Julie pulled Giles over and introduced him to LeeRoy's mother and sister as his friend. He shook their hands with both of his and expressed his deepest condolences.

"He's so proper!" Julie thought to herself. She could always count on Giles to behave appropriately and do the right thing. He's a rock.

"We need to meet Sam at the coffee shop," Julie told the women. When they got there, Sam was already waiting. LeeRoy's mother and sister recognised Sam, and they embraced each other. The woman shed tears once more, and Sam struggled to hold back tears.

Sam said he had scheduled a meeting with the funeral directors in a designated private area at the airport, reserved for such occasions. Together, they moved over, feeling a bit uneasy and anxious, and waited.

The hearse glided through the gates with the coffin inside, and Julie's breath caught in her throat.

More tears followed.

"I'll take the luggage with me," Giles said, as the three women, still crying, got into the hearse. There would be many tears in the days to come.

They arrived home two hours later, finding Giles already there with coffee, having moved the suitcases upstairs to their rooms.

He made his excuses and left them to be alone, saying, "You know where I am if you need anything."

"He seems nice," said LeeRoy's mother, having recovered from her initial grief that day.

"Yes, he's been invaluable," Julie confirmed. "Especially when I was stuck in Ecuador."

"I want to hear exactly what happened, Julie," LeeRoy's mother said earnestly. "And please don't try to hide anything. I know what LeeRoy was doing, so nothing will be a surprise."

Julie sighed. "I'll explain everything over dinner tonight, if that's okay."

LeeRoy's mother nodded.

"I'll show you to your rooms."

"That's fine," said Rosina. "I'll take her. I assume I'll be in my old room, and my mother next door?"

"Yes," Julie replied gratefully. "I'll call you when dinner is ready."

When they sat down for dinner, Julie shared the whole story, including that she had been raped and chose to keep the baby.

LeeRoy's mother took a sharp breath, shook her head slowly, and looked appalled and saddened by what she'd heard. "I don't blame you either way, Julie. I'd love to have a little LeeRoy, but I understand the risk you're taking. I can appreciate you not wanting to be reminded of what you've been through."

Rosina agreed. "It's your choice. We support your decision, whichever way you decide."

The day of LeeRoy's funeral came around. It was a sombre day, to say the least; however, Sam had arranged everything beautifully. The hearse was an elegant black carriage drawn by four sleek, jet-black horses, creating a stunning spectacle, especially with the numerous flower tributes from his friends and colleagues.

LeeRoy arrived at the church for the second time that year, but this time, he wouldn't be leaving.

The whole town seemed to have come out to pay their respects.

Although Giles intended to help Julie personally, he recognised that Rosina and her mother were also supporting each other. As a result, he stayed in the background, overseeing the event as a whole. He remained alert in case the scumbags showed up, ready to step in if needed, but they never arrived.

The funeral went as smoothly as possible, with no issues. LeeRoy was buried beside Barrie, and Julie left flowers on both graves along with many tears.

LeeRoy's mother and sister stayed for the week, promising to keep in touch regularly. Julie felt such immense relief when it was all over, as if a heavy weight had been lifted from her shoulders.

CHAPTER THIRTY-FIVE — *Small World*

As the weeks rolled into months and Julie's belly grew, she continued to visit LeeRoy's grave at least twice a week.

On February 9th at 9 p.m., Julie was in the kitchen chatting with Giles when she suddenly experienced a sharp twinge.

"Are you okay?" Giles asked with concern, frowning. Julie exhaled deeply.

"Ooh! Just a cramp. I think!" she said, rubbing her stomach, believing it was a muscle cramp. However, within thirty minutes, a sharper pain struck her, and she realised the baby was about to arrive.

She had already packed her bag, so Giles took her straight to Canterbury Hospital.

Johnny was born on February 19, 1970, at 5:10 a.m. He was a beautiful light-skinned boy with curly black African hair. His mother instantly recognised that he was LeeRoy's son from his features, and she was overwhelmed with tears of relief. She was overjoyed.

Giles entered to see her and immediately recognized from the big smile on her face that LeeRoy's baby had arrived. She was so happy that Giles's heart also softened. "Look, Giles!" she said excitedly, her eyes bright. "He's perfect! And there's no question—he's LeeRoy's son."

Giles agreed, feeling a wave of relief. He couldn't even begin to imagine what it would've been like if the child had been someone else's, especially a rapist. A constant reminder of her trauma—and yet, a part of her. It was too overwhelming to think about. As if reading his mind, Julie admitted, "I have to tell you this – I honestly don't know what I would've done if he hadn't been LeeRoy's. I know I said it wouldn't matter. And it probably would have been fine, but the doubt was always present." She directed her bright gaze at him. "Oh, Giles! I am so, so happy right now!"

Giles was once again captivated by her beauty, particularly by the gentle expression in her eyes as she smiled at the young boy. He softly kissed her cheek and, hesitantly, inquired, "May I hold the baby?"

Julie cracked a grin, and Giles couldn't help but notice her eyes sparkle. It seemed as if all her love was overflowing, spilling out with plenty to spare. He had never seen her look more radiant.

"Of course, Giles," she smiled, holding her arms out to offer the baby to him, a precious gift. "You're part of the family now."

Giles beamed with pride, feeling honoured by Julie's attention. He puffed out his chest and picked up the small bundle.

Little Johnny was wide awake, staring at Giles with big black eyes. For a moment, Giles felt like he was looking at LeeRoy, and a shiver ran down his spine.

Chas and Val arrived within two hours. When they saw little Johnny, they agreed – there was no mistaking who the father was.

Johnny seemed to love all the attention.

Val was charmed by his tiny hands, tugging at her finger.

"What a handsome little bugger he's going to be! Bet he breaks a few hearts!"

Over the next few months, Giles cared for Johnny as if he were his own, loving that little boy. Julie could see it in his manner. Giles enjoyed playing with him after a day's work in the garden. He often babysat for Julie and loved doing it.

For Julie's next birthday, Giles suggested taking her out to dinner that evening if she could find a babysitter.

Julie smiled. "That would be nice, Giles. I'll call Val. I'm sure she'd be okay with it."

Val said that was fine, as long as they could bring little Johnny to the pub. "You can leave him for the night if you like," she told Julie.

"That's very kind of you, Val, but I couldn't sleep without him."

"Yeah, I can understand that," said Val. "Too bad, I'd love to spoil the little bugger."

Julie put the phone down, happy, and turned to Giles.

"Sorted. Where should we go tonight?"

"There's a pub just outside Sittingbourne called the Plough and Harrow in Oad Street that I've heard has a new chef. How about we try it?"

"Sounds good to me," she replied.

They arrived just before eight, ordered a drink at the bar, and were served by an older woman named Lorna, who had made their reservation. Julie noticed a group of guys playing cards at the bar as she passed by. Anita then showed them to their table, brought over the menu, and handed them the wine list.

"This seems like a pretty friendly little pub," Julie said to Giles.

"Yeah, it does."

The restaurant was half full, and the food was enjoyable. In the end, Julie insisted on paying the bill, but Giles wouldn't hear of it.

"This is my treat," he insisted and triumphed in the argument, giving Anita a generous tip for her efficiency and courtesy.

Keen to make the evening last, Giles asked, "Want to have a drink at the bar?"

Julie agreed. Lorna was very talkative while serving, which annoyed the guys playing cards who were waiting for service. However, Lorna didn't seem to notice. "Don't worry about them," she told Julie. "They don't need it. They've been on it all day, and they're all too fat anyway."

Julie was intrigued by the card game happening across the bar and couldn't stop watching. A lot of money was being added to a small wooden bowl with names carved into it. Every so often, someone would win and take the entire pot.

One man appeared to win more frequently, while another was losing quite a bit. Julie kept glancing at the one who kept losing. She sensed she recognised him from somewhere, but couldn't quite remember and dismissed the thought. Later, she overheard a card player ask, "What do you want, Colin? Masterbrew or Guinness?"

Julie looked up in shock. Colin? The same Colin from Ecuador who had lost everything playing cards. It was hard to believe. How could it be?

Giles saw Julie's expression and asked, "What's wrong, Julie? You look like you've seen a ghost!"

Julie sat silently, mouth gaping, staring at him. "I think I have, Giles."

"What do you mean?"

"Remember when I told you about the coffee farm in Ecuador? Well, I think that guy in the middle, playing cards, is one of those workers! The one I told you about who lost all his money playing cards. His name was Colin, and I just heard someone call him that."

Giles frowned. "Come on, Julie. That's a long shot!"

Julie couldn't tear her eyes away, trying to determine if it was him. "I know, but when we sat here, I thought I recognised him from somewhere, but I couldn't quite place it until I heard his name. Giles, I'm pretty sure it's him." Her eyes shone with excitement.

Giles suddenly felt tense without understanding why. "Go ask him, then," he suggested. Julie recoiled. "No, I couldn't. I'd be too embarrassed if it's not him." She struggled to look away. "But he does look like him."

Lorna, sitting on a stool behind the bar, looked like she was nodding off, so Julie called her over. "I don't know if you can help, but that guy in the middle..." "Who, Colin?" "Yes, do you know him?" "Know him? I practically consider myself his mother," Lorna replied with a laugh.

"Why?"

"Do you know if he was ever in Ecuador?"

"I know he went off to some jungle a million miles away two or three years ago, but I'm not exactly sure where, though. Where did you say?" Lorna asked, looking confused. "Ecuador," Julie repeated. "I'm not certain, but it sounds like the place he often talks about, although no one pays attention to him. You know how men sometimes exaggerate. Why do you ask?"

Julie sat quietly, a small tear forming in her eye, convinced this was the same Colin. "Would you mind telling him that Julie is over here, and see what reaction you get?"

"Do you know him?"

"Sort of. Please, tell him."

Lorna approached the end of the bar and spoke to Colin. He looked over at Julie with a blank expression, not recognising her. Julie, now sure it was him, smiled and waved gently.

The others had ceased their card game and were now watching Julie. Colin remained confused. The only Julie he remembered was the one he met in Ecuador. But surely, that couldn't be her?

He walked around the bar and looked at Julie, his eyes searching her face, taking in every detail, trying to understand the entire situation.

"I don't believe it." He looked stunned and asked in amazement, "You're Julie from Ecuador?"

"Yes, Colin, I am," Julie said, beaming with happiness.

"Bloody hell!" Colin gasped, a bewildered smile spreading across his face. "We wondered what happened to you—if you made it home safely. We lost your phone number, and you know how it is."

His grin broadened as he scanned her expensive attire and impeccably styled hair. "It's clear you got back safely! So nice to see you, Julie."

He looked at Giles and asked, "Would you mind if I gave her a big hug?"

"Be my guest," Giles said, trying to hide his jealousy. He realised he was feeling something he hadn't felt before—protectiveness. He shook off the feeling, telling himself it was just a reaction to the situation.

Colin and Julie were smiling at each other. Giles realised that up close, despite Colin's thinning hair, this man was probably at least ten years younger than him. Much closer in age to Julie, and she seemed happy to see him. Giles took a sip of beer, struggling to swallow.

"How did you get back, Julie?"

"It's a long story, Colin, but basically, I got a passport, and here I am. What about you? How's life treating you these days?"

Colin let out a small laugh. "Guess I never learn my lesson – still playing cards, as you can see."

"Yes," she laughed, her eyes sparkling. "I noticed you giving your money away to all those other nice people over there!"

His friends were all curious why such a beautiful girl showed interest in Colin, so he turned to them and said, "Remember what I told you about that young girl I met in Ecuador? And none of you believed me? Well, here's the proof."

One by one, they got up and came over, shaking hands and smiling. None of them needed another excuse to join Colin, especially to get close to such a beautiful creature.

"Is what he told us true?" one of Colin's friends asked.

Julie looked puzzled. "I have no idea what he told you, so I can't say."

"About the farm? His adventures?"

After the initial introductions and group explanations, Julie retold her story, leaving out the rapes. Even facts that Colin hadn't known at the time.

Lorna, the older barmaid, had been listening to all this, despite people waiting to get served. They could wait. This was far more interesting, as far as she was concerned.

"Oh, my God – your story!" she said to Julie, "That is just unbelievable! It must haunt you every night."

"Not anymore," said Julie. "It was A Long Road Home, but it's a lot easier now." She turned a fond, warm smile towards Giles. "And I have Giles to look after me."

"What does that mean?" Giles wondered, but he let it go. Colin and Julie stood close together, heads nearly touching, chatting nonstop as they updated each other on details. Giles watched

nearby, feeling uneasy, yet he couldn't shake the feeling that something was wrong.

"Still in touch with Franco and the others?" Julie asked animatedly.

"No, no idea where they are nowadays," Colin shrugged. "We didn't stay in touch after we got back. I might have his number somewhere – if I find it, I'll give him a call and let him know you're home safe. He'll be delighted to hear that."

Colin and Julie spent the next hour excitedly talking about their trips to Ecuador and Peru. At the same time, Giles chatted with the other guys, his gaze often drifting toward Julie, always keeping a watchful eye on her.

Finally, Julie checked her watch and turned to Giles.

"It's getting late, and we still need to pick up little Johnny from Val's."

Giles nodded.

"That's a shame," Colin said honestly. "I'm enjoying the evening here."

"Me too," Julie said, thoughtfully twisting her lips as she looked at Giles, who stayed expressionless. "Alright," she concluded. "I'll call Val to see if she can keep Johnny for the night. I probably already know her answer, but it's polite to ask."

Val was more than happy to oblige, so they remained, chatting. Giles moved closer to Julie, attempting to join the conversation, but he still had that nagging sense that something was wrong, though he couldn't quite identify what it was.

The door swung open, and Mark, the landlord, walked in. Mark carried a relaxed demeanour. As a multimillionaire, he didn't have to handle daily tasks himself, so he left the pub's management to the staff. As long as it stayed profitable and trouble-free, he was happy.

Colin introduced Giles and Julie and updated Mark on the situation.

Mark chuckled. "We all thought Colin was just dreaming when he returned with that story! However, I'm delighted everything turned out well for you. Can I buy you both a drink?"

Julie glanced at Giles and knew it had passed last call. "No, thanks," she said. "We need to head back." "Okay," Mark smiled. "Maybe another time, if you're in the area." "I'm sure we'll come back," Julie replied. She gave Colin her phone number and asked him to pass it to Franco if he found his number.

When they were in the car and on the way back down the M2, Julie turned to Giles. "I had a great time tonight, thanks to you!"

He glanced her way.

She went on, "Can you believe it? Running into Colin like that? You'd never think that would happen!"

"It's a small world," Giles said quietly.

"Are you okay, Giles?"

"Of course," he said, his lips tight. "Why?"

"Nothing," Julie said. "You just seem quiet."

"Just thinking, Julie."

"That doesn't sound good," Julie laughed.

"How could I be grumpy with you around, Julie?"

"Maybe you are grumpy," Julie said. "Don't be like that. Tell me what's on your mind."

Giles stared straight ahead, his lips pressed together. "Later, maybe."

"Come on, Giles," Julie said, her tone changing to concern.

"You're not merely my employee, Giles. You're much more—my best friend. I couldn't have gotten through all of this without you."

"Thanks, Julie," Giles said softly. They sat in silence for a moment, both lost in thought.

Then Julie said, "Now tell me what's been bothering you."

He said tightly, "Later."

"Oh. OK. Have it your way, Mr Masterful."

They rode in silence, Julie lost in her memories, and arrived home at 11:45 p.m. Giles pulled up outside the front door to let Julie out, then he parked the Rolls-Royce in the garage. "Thanks, Giles. That was a lovely evening. See you tomorrow." She placed one hand on his forearm, and Giles was acutely aware of her touch. "Okay, Julie, no problem. Sleep tight." "You too, Giles. Night, night."

CHAPTER THIRTY-SIX — *The Line and the Leap*

Giles put the car away and walked down to his chalet, deep in thought. He was just about to open the door when he heard Julie call to him.

"Giles?"

At that moment, he was on high alert, jogging towards the house, where he saw Julie leaning against the doorframe. The moonlight and security light highlighted her blonde hair, making her even more beautiful. He stopped dead in his tracks, captivated.

She had no idea just how stunning she was. She was completely genuine, without a hint of pretence. She was just pure Julie.

"Giles, I'm not tired," she explained with a playful smile.

"Want a cup of coffee?"

He grinned. "Yes, Julie. I'd love one."

When he got to the kitchen, Julie had the coffee percolating.

"Sit down, Giles. You're making the place look untidy." She smiled at him, and he was struck again by how gorgeous she was and how magical the world seemed when she smiled.

Julie poured the coffee and sat down across from Giles. She cleared her throat and gave him a gentle, teasing stare. "Now, Mr Grumpy, spill it."

"What?"

"You know what. Whatever was on your mind on the way home?"

"Oh," he said, blushing. "That."

"Yes. That." An amused smile played on her lips.

Giles took a deep breath. "Okay, it's a little silly. I was thinking how lucky I am. Three years ago, I was walking the streets with nothing to my name. Now, I have an amazing job with an even more amazing employer, who happens to have an amazing little boy I love to death." She swallowed hard. "So, now you know."

"Oh, that's so sweet!" Her face lit up with joy. "That's really nice!"

She followed him to his chair, wrapped her arms around his shoulders, and held him close, her cheek pressed against his. She meant it as a friendly hug, but both of them couldn't ignore the tender warmth of their skin as their faces touched. The feeling was like an electric shock, an overwhelming sensation that made it seem as if something inside them had burst; their chests felt tight. Julie quickly stepped back, startled by her feelings.

Giles turned to face her and looked into her eyes.

She avoided his gaze, her heart pounding.

No, she thought, this can't be real.

She felt lost and unsure of her next move. Eventually, she looked at Giles again, their eyes meeting in a silent, powerful stare as they both searched for words.

As Giles extended his hand, Julie instinctively took it, feeling the warmth of his skin. However, she remained frozen in her spot, staring into his eyes. Giles then firmed his grip and softly drew Julie nearer. She paused for a moment but gradually moved closer to him.

She felt like she was about to faint, and Giles was just as overwhelmed, as if he'd been holding his breath for ages. He stood up, towering over little Julie, and pulled her close. This time, she didn't push him away. As their bodies touched, Giles wrapped his arm around her and held her tight. They fit together perfectly, and it was hard to miss how much they were aware of it. Every sense was on high alert. Julie felt like she wanted to dissolve into him, to become one with him, and she pressed herself against him even harder. So hard that neither of them could breathe easily. Their hearts were pounding, trying to leap out of their chests.

Giles gently reached for the back of Julie's head, his fingers threading through her hair. He tilted her head back and leaned in to examine her angelic face. Her warm breath brushed his cheeks as she softly panted. He lowered his head to give her a gentle kiss on the lips, and she responded, her mouth opening to explore his with her tongue.

Julie's right hand snaked behind Giles's head and pulled him even closer to her. They both felt fantastic. Giles tugged the back of Julie's blouse out and slipped his hand inside, stroking her back. Julie gave a slight wriggle, and Giles wasn't sure if it was because she was enjoying it or if she wanted him to stop.

There was only one way to find out, he thought, and he gently moved his hand around to the front. No resistance.

Giles now had an erection, and Julie could feel it against her. It turned her on, massively. It had been such a long time since she had made love. After LeeRoy's death and the rapes, she had thought she would never be interested again, but now, she felt that nothing was going to stop her. She wanted Giles. She wanted him now – fucked right here and now.

She allowed Giles to caress her breast over her bra. He soon had the clip on the front undone and her bare breast in his right hand. Her nipples were tough, as was his manhood – very, very hard.

He was so aroused that he thought he wouldn't be able to contain himself.

Giles lifted Julie's blouse off over her head and then removed her bra, so she was completely topless. His breath caught in his throat. She was so perfect. He couldn't keep his hands off her: kissing her, caressing her breasts, and rubbing her bottom through her silky skirt with one hand. She had such a tiny, tight behind! Giles gradually pulled her skirt up so his hand was on her bare skin, really enjoying all of her. Bringing his hand around to the front, he slowly rubbed between her legs over her soft underwear. He could feel how turned on she was: so wet; he pressed his fingers against her opening, which made her nearly faint.

Giles then probed from the top of her panties. He deliberately took his time, slowly stroking her pubic hair.

Julie had begun rubbing his crotch over his trousers.

He's not as big as LeeRoy, she thought.

I shouldn't be thinking about LeeRoy right now, but I couldn't help it.

What would he think?

She soon stopped thinking when Giles's fingers entered her. She gasped. She was so wet that it was turning Giles on even more, if that were possible.

Suddenly, Giles stopped and held Julie at arm's length.

"What?" she asked breathlessly, looking up at him, dazed, as if coming to consciousness. "What's the matter, Giles?" "I can't do this, Julie."

"What? Why? What's the matter?" she gasped.

Giles handed Julie her blouse and told her, "Please put it back on."

She snatched it from him, put it back on, and sat down, feeling humiliated and hurt. "Giles, you had better explain."

With his head hanging low, he said, "OK, I'll try. Don't get me wrong. You are a beautiful young lady, and that's where the problem begins."

"What do you mean?" she snapped.

"Please, Julie. Let me explain before you say anything." He stared at her earnestly, his grey eyes serious. "As I said to you earlier, three years ago, I was on the road. Julie, I was a fucking tramp, for God's sake!"

She looked at him, her face a mix of confusion and pain.

"The other issue I have is that you're twenty years younger than me. You have a beautiful house, plenty of money, and a great kid, who, as I've mentioned before, I adore like my own." He raised both hands as if to push her away. "I'm not sure what happened here tonight, but it shouldn't have. And thank goodness we stopped."

"You stopped it, Giles." Julie's voice grew cold. "What would have happened tomorrow morning?" he asked, running his hand through his grey hair in frustration. "Actually, what would have happened tonight? I could have fucked you right here on this table. Is that what you want?"

Just as Julie was about to respond, he cut her off. "Don't say a word until I'm done. If I did, would we say "thank you very much" and act like nothing ever happened in the morning?" His eyes locked onto hers, sincere and genuine. "I couldn't do that, Julie – I respect you too much to pretend like that."

As she sat there, open-mouthed, he kept talking: "Where would it go? Would we do it again? Would we say, "Hey, that was great, we should do it again sometime?" That's not me, Julie, and I know that's not you either. It must have been the drink." He looked crushed. "I'm not saying I don't want to make love to you, Julie. I'd be a total idiot if I didn't want that. But that's what I would want – to make love to you. Not just fuck you on a kitchen table."

She sat there, stunned, unable to respond to his outburst, as he continued with hardly a pause. "I'm probably already making a fool of myself, so I'll keep going and make a complete idiot of myself." Julie looked confused. "Let me try to sum it up. If it were possible, I think I could fall for you. Hell, I might even marry you. I'd be devoted to you and love little Johnny like my own. But I have nothing to offer, and as I've already said, I'm twenty years older than you."

Julie still stood, open-mouthed in wonder.

Fuck it! Thought Giles. *I've gone this far!*

"I love you!" he said, in anguish. "I've loved you for a long time. I didn't realise it was this sort of love, but now I do."

Julie blinked rapidly, taking it all in, but not knowing what to make of it.

"Julie," Giles said, his voice heavy with disappointment. "I think it might be best if I find a new job and a place to live. I was foolish to let this happen tonight."

Julie gazed at him, seeing the pain in his eyes. He slumped into the chair, his head in his hands.

She remained silent for a moment, then spoke. "Okay, Giles, I understand and respect what you just said. I'm also a bit confused, and I don't think it's the alcohol."

Giles's eyes stayed fixed on her, as they always did when she was speaking. He was entirely focused on her, just as he always was.

"So, let's start with you being a tramp. You were on the road because you were down on your luck. You should have seen the state I was in when I was in Peru and Ecuador! You looked well-dressed compared to me, back then! "

Giles shook his head slowly, but she continued speaking. "Why did I look like that? Because, like you, I was down on my luck. So, I believe we're even in that regard, don't you think?" Giles opened his mouth to respond, but she interrupted. "Don't answer, Giles! Let me finish as well. You didn't choose it, and neither did

I. But it happened. So, let's drop the subject. It's not an issue for me."

He could see she was still in the flow, so he didn't even try to respond.

"Next problem. What was it? Oh yes – you're twenty years older than me. So, what does it matter? As far as I remember, it's not illegal, right? Don't respond. So, that's not an issue for me either. Two down, and you haven't won any of them yet, Giles."

Giles knew he wasn't going to win any.

"Next question was – what would have happened tonight if we had fucked on the table? I have no idea, Giles. I'd probably have been very embarrassed, but I certainly wouldn't have just left it there." She fixed him with a stare. "I don't know, Giles. To tell the truth, I was just wrapped up in the moment, which came to an abrupt halt, so I'll never know. The fact that you have just told me you love me is a bit of a shock, because I had no idea."

Giles held his breath, waiting to be hurt and expecting rejection.

Julie gazed at him shyly. "I've just liked you," she said, swallowing hard. "I've loved you for a long time. But until tonight, I thought it was just like I'd love a good friend or a brother. Now..." She let out a frustrated breath. "I'm not sure. I need to think about it. But let me tell you this: if I love you the way I think I do, there's not much we can do about it. We're fucked!"

"Great way to put it, Julie."

And they both had to laugh a little to break the tension, if nothing else.

"One more thing, Giles." She gently pushed him away. "You're not going anywhere, no matter what. I'll lock the gates.

Giles offered a wry smile. "Come here." He spread his arms, and she approached him. They embraced firmly, but this time, they understood it was simply a hug. Their limits were defined, at least for the time being.

"I'm heading out, Julie. We both need some rest."

"Sleep? There's no way I'll be able to sleep tonight...

Maybe I'll have the same problem."

He kissed her innocently on the cheek and left.

Julie lay in bed, her mind consumed by thoughts of Giles.

She thought to herself, *I guess I do love him, but is it genuine? Yes, it is.*

She thought of the way she had felt in the kitchen, especially when he put his hand in her panties.

But was that lust? She didn't think so.

She felt herself getting turned on thinking about it and realised that her hand was between her legs. Her middle finger soon entered her wet opening, and she wished Giles were there with her.

Before she knew it, her left hand was there too, the index finger massaging her clitoris.

She was so turned on that she was having trouble staying quiet, but what did it matter? Johnny was at Val's, and nobody else was in the house. She let out a loud scream as she climaxed in a very wet orgasm.

She went to sleep feeling warm and comforted, thinking of Giles.

And LeeRoy never even crossed her mind.

Giles lay in bed, wide awake, his eyes fixed on the ceiling. In his mind, an image of Julie superimposed itself, making it impossible to focus. There was no question that he was in love with her - a love that went far beyond a brotherly affection. But did she truly feel the same way about him?

He didn't think so. By morning, when she sobered up and realised what had happened, he'd probably be long gone on his bike. She was just a bit drunk, vulnerable, and maybe a little lonely. *Plus, running into Colin had been exciting, he thought.* She was likely lying in bed now, *dreading seeing him in the morning.* He pulled a spare pillow over himself. Hugging it, he imagined it was Julie, holding it close to his heart until he fell asleep.

The next morning, Giles rose at 6 a.m. to make breakfast, but he couldn't bring himself to eat. Instead, he sipped coffee and watched early news on TV, still distracted by last night's events. He saw the light on in Julie's kitchen and wanted to go to her, hold her, and comfort her. However, fear of rejection held him back; now that she had time to think, they both found themselves in this uncertain situation.

His thoughts from the night before raced through his mind again. He realised he was truly in love with her. It wasn't simply brotherly love or paternal concern. When she was a child, those feelings were enough. But then LeeRoy came into the picture. Over the past year, though, everything had shifted. If he were honest with himself, he'd been struggling with these feelings for quite some time. It was genuine, and deep down, he knew he was set to get hurt badly. He questioned how he allowed it to happen.

For her part, Julie was sitting at the same table that Giles had nearly fucked her on the night before, thinking about what might have been. She couldn't get the thought of it out of her mind, nor the fact that she had masturbated about him afterwards.

She only got a few hours of sleep, her mind filled with restless thoughts, and her bed was a mess by morning. Sitting with her elbows on the table, she rested her head in her hands, trying to clear her mind, but it was futile. Giles kept occupying her thoughts, and they refused to fade.

She loved Giles, but she wondered if it was the same love she had felt for LeeRoy. Was it genuine, or merely a fleeting feeling? She wasn't certain.

Please help me, LeeRoy, you bastard. Why did you have to die?

She had long since moved past the idea that she might be betraying LeeRoy. She was realistic, knowing he was gone for good. Yet, she couldn't help but think about him. Though he was gone, he was still not forgotten.

What would LeeRoy think of this? Would he approve?

Would he consider her stupid? She tried to picture how he might react, whether in heaven or wherever he might be, if he even existed. Would he want her to be happy?

After due consideration, she thought, yes, of course! That goes without

question. He was a kind person – to her, anyway – and she knew he would want what was best for her and little Johnny.

I have to be sure.

I am sure, aren't I?

Oh, God, help me, please.

She was starting to get worked up, so she stood up, stepped out the back door, and immediately saw Giles across at the chalet, on the grass in front. She froze, her heart pounding. Not out of fear – she didn't know why; she just froze.

Giles noticed her and started walking toward her. She froze, holding her breath with her heart pounding wildly, as if trying to escape her chest. She wanted to run, but her muscles had become completely stiff, leaving her frozen in place.

Giles decided to play it cool, and as he got closer, he politely asked, "Good night's sleep?"

She couldn't speak; she couldn't move; she wanted the earth to open up and swallow her.

Giles saw the look of horror on her face and thought the worst. This was it, over, finished. He was homeless again.

But as he reached her, she threw her arms around him, hugged him tight, and cried and cried.

Giles was confused, unable to figure out what this meant, but he just held her tightly and said nothing.

Julie was first to speak. "Come inside."

He did so, without saying a word. She sat down at that table and beckoned Giles to do the same.

Giles still said nothing, terrified at what she was going to say.

She looked directly into his eyes and said earnestly, "I do love you. If you love me and want us to be together, I'm willing to give it a try. We've been in each other's lives for a long time, enduring hell both together and alone. I always thought we were just fortunate to have each other as special friends, but last night made us both realise that it's more than that and neither of us knew it."

Giles's throat was so tight with emotion that he couldn't speak. He looked at her, tears filling his eyes. He extended both hands across the table, and Julie took them in hers.

He said, "Julie, you've just made me the happiest man on earth. Of course, I love you! I stayed up most of the night thinking about it, and I couldn't shake it off." He bit his lip. "I did think you'd say last night was a big mistake and that we should just forget it."

"No, Giles," Julie said, squeezing his hands and smiling. "Last night would have been a mistake if you hadn't been strong enough to stop it. I was angry and frustrated at the time, but after thinking about it, I realised it was the right decision. I'm happy you stopped, although a little later." She laughed.

His heart fluttered again, just like before, at her smile. "I honestly have no idea what our morning would look like if we'd gone ahead," Julie admitted. "Would we have treated it as a one-night stand? Enjoyable, but just that? Would we have ended up in bed, or would you have gone back to the chalet? I don't know, Giles, but I'm grateful you were strong. It showed a side of you I like." Giles approached Julie, took her hands, and helped her stand. They hugged tightly, both catching their breath. "What happens next?" he asked. "I don't know," she said with a shrug. "We'll see how things unfold. Maybe I'll pick up Johnny from Val for now. How about I cook dinner for us tonight?"

"That sounds great to me, but I'm going to cook for you."

"Even better," said Julie. "I'm on board with that."

"How about eight?"

"Yep, that sounds good to me. I'll bring Johnny over to your place, and hopefully, he'll sleep most of the evening."

"Tell you what. I'll give you a ride to Val's this morning, and then I'll head out shopping for something special. I know I'll have plenty of time once you two start chatting."

"Ha, ha," she laughed, but she knew he was right.

"Great, now I'd better get to work or I'll be in trouble."

"That you will," she chuckled. She had a mischievous laugh, he thought to himself.

CHAPTER THIRTY-SEVEN — *Candlelight and First Steps*

It was eight o'clock, and Julie was right on time.

"Come on in!" Giles called out when she knocked.

She wheeled Johnny in – he was already fast asleep in his pram.

The table was perfectly arranged, complete with a nice tablecloth, two candles, and a menu. It was romantic, and she appreciated the effort he put into creating it.

Giles finished up what he was doing, wiped his hands, and walked over to Julie. He gave her a gentle kiss on the cheek and said,

"Wine?"

"Yes, please, Giles. I'm sure you have my favourite – Chablis?"

"Right on the nose. First, I have to say hello to the little guy."

"Just don't wake him up, Giles."

Giles peeked in at little Johnny but resisted touching him, just in case he woke up. Then, he'd be in trouble.

He poured them both a glass and said, "Cheers to us."

"Cheers to us!" replied Julie. "Whatever that may be." He gave her a knowing look and assured her, "It'll be what we make it, Julie." She agreed and sat down at the table, picked up the menu, and read.

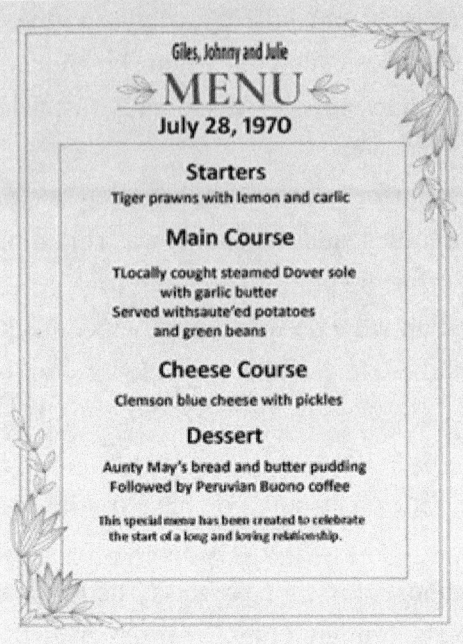

"Wow, Giles, you're talented!" Julie exclaimed, then shot him a mischievous glance. "Or should we wait until we've eaten before I say that?"

He raised an eyebrow and put on a posh, sing-song voice. "May I tell you, madam, that I'm an excellent chef – as you'll no doubt find out very soon."

"Maybe you are, Giles, but not a great choice of coffee, though!"

She couldn't care less if she never heard the word "Peru" again. "Ow! Yes," he winced. "How thoughtless of me! Sorry!"

"Don't worry, Giles. It's just coffee, and that was a long time ago now." Giles, attempting to shift the topic, rubbed his hands together. "Okay, are you ready for the first course?"

She grinned and rubbed her stomach. "Yes, Giles. I'm starving." Giles served the tiger prawns and poured two more glasses of wine. They dug in eagerly.

"These are delicious, Giles. Did you catch them in the lake?" she asked with another heart-stopping smirk.

"Yeah, I was up with the birds this morning. I caught the Dover sole there, too!" "You wish!" she laughed.

They finished the first course, and Giles served up the Dover sole with all the trimmings. She took one bite and looked at him in surprise.

"I could almost believe that you're a chef," Julie joked.

"I was, a long time ago, before I was married and had the farm."

"Really?" Julie couldn't believe there was so much she didn't know about this self-contained, kind man. "Wow! My own real, live chef. I'll never have to cook again!"

He winked at her, and Julie felt a rush of heat.

"That's okay, Julie. You can keep cooking. But I'll spoil you tonight."

They finished the main course, and Julie told Giles that it was the best fish she'd ever eaten. "Please pass on my compliments to the chef."

Giles puffed out his chest and said, "Thanks, ma'am, for the kind words. I hope there's a nice big tip coming my way later."

"I'm sure there will be, Giles," she teased, her eyes boring into his. "I'm sure there will."

Giles thought he knew exactly what she meant. He could feel himself going weak inside, but managed to hide it.

Little Johnny stirred in his pram but didn't wake.

"Are you ready for dessert, ma'am?" Julie sat back and patted her flat tummy. "I think I'd like to wait a bit, Giles, if you don't mind."

"Of course not. Why don't we take the drinks out to the veranda? It's a nice evening, and quite warm."

"Sounds good to me," she replied.

They moved to sit on the lounger outside, and Giles was right — it was a beautiful evening. He glanced at her, her lovely face turned toward the sky like a sunflower, and he felt a strong desire to hold her close and never let go. He kept his composure, but she could tell—she felt the same. They sat quietly for over an hour, exchanging small talk and relishing each other's presence and the secret they shared. Later, Julie mentioned she was getting cold, so they headed back inside.

CHAPTER THIRTY-EIGHT — *The Night, We Chose Each Other*

Giles flashed her a smile and asked, "Ready for the pièce de résistance?" "Yes," She laughed. "I believe I might be."

Giles presented Aunty May's bread and butter pudding, a dish Julie adored, just like the rest of the meal. She was impressed by her new man and had already made up her mind about her feelings for him.

Giles offered coffee once more, apologising that it was from Peru. "I can tease you about that for a while!" she joked. Little Johnny stirred; Giles approached, lifted him from his pram, and cradled him tenderly. Julie watched affectionately, confident that Giles would make a wonderful stepfather, and a tear welled up in her eye. Little Johnny quickly fell asleep again, and Giles carefully placed him back in his pram.

"He's a good-looking boy, Julie."

"He takes after his mother, of course!"

"I won't argue that," Giles replied, "but he's handsome. You are simply beautiful."

She chuckled. "Well, Giles, as they say, flattery will get you wherever you want to go!"

They exchanged a glance, both understanding and desiring what was about to happen. Giles reached out to Julie, and she took his hand. As Giles led her to the bedroom, neither of them spoke.

He started to close the door, but Julie stopped him. "You'd better leave it open a bit, just in case Johnny wakes up," she said.

Giles obeyed, and in that moment, he would have done anything for her.

He wrapped his arms around her, and she snuggled into him. They stayed there, immersed in the moment – a memory they'll both cherish forever.

With a subtle easing of his grip, Giles cupped Julie's head in his left hand. He ran his fingertips through her hair roots, causing her to shiver. Gently, he wrapped a handful of her blonde hair around his fingers and pulled her head back slightly as he looked into her eyes.

He lowered his head, their lips brushing each other in a gentle, butterfly-like touch. Both were electrified, their hearts pounding as Giles continued to press his lips against hers, barely. She wanted to kiss him more passionately, but he restrained her, fingers intertwined in her hair. She realised he was teasing her, and it was having its effect – she almost felt faint. The air pulsed with electricity, her skin alive with his closeness. She was so close, yet still too far away.

You bastard! she thought to herself. *I need you. I need you right now—please, take me now before I pass out.*

He pressed his tongue against her lips, and Julie's tongue immediately met it, full of desperation and longing. She tried to hold back, but she was out of control, and she thrust her tongue fully into Giles's mouth. Still kissing, Giles lifted Julie and carefully laid her on the bed. Her heart was pounding so fiercely she feared it might burst from her chest or cease beating entirely.

With his heart pounding just as fast, Giles lay beside her on the bed, one hand supporting her head and the other at her shoulder. Their eyes locked, and they were instantly drawn together again, their mouths meeting in a passionate kiss. Julie didn't want this moment to end. She longed for him to be inside her, but Giles had other plans.

They kept kissing and clinging to each other tightly, for hours, as far as Julie could tell, it was hours. Giles fondled her breast, and it took her breath away. She struggled to keep up with the kissing, their tongues frantically swirling around each other's; she felt like she was going to suffocate. He gently caressed her breasts over her blouse. He could feel she had no bra on and that her nipples were rock hard.

Giles slowly, very slowly, undid the buttons of her blouse, one at a time, hesitating between each one. He knew how to turn a girl on, and Julie was almost delirious with desire. She was on fire. She needed him then, and with a gasping breath, she said, "Take me, Giles. Take me now. Ple-ease fuck me-ee!"

"You need to be patient," Giles whispered, his tongue brushing her ear. She groaned loudly, waking little Johnny, who started hiccupping and crying, stopping them both cold. Moments later, he screamed in terror. "No, no, not now," Julie whispered, trying to soothe him. "Please, go back to sleep." But Johnny wasn't having it; he needed his mummy.

Julie had no option but to stand up, fasten the two buttons Giles had undone, her body still shaking and wobbling as she walked to the kitchen. She felt faint.

Giles also stood up and followed her, then glanced at Julie, and they both erupted into laughter.

"He did that on purpose," Giles chuckled.

"I think you're right."

"I'll make coffee while you sort out the little bugger," he laughed.

After Julie warmed up Johnny's bottle and fed him, he quickly fell back asleep. Julie even changed his nappy without waking him.

"Very romantic," Giles said in a teasing tone.

"Is this not normal, then?" Julie asked.

"It could become that way, Julie. You never can tell. That might be how LeeRoy keeps watch over you."

Julie's smile faded, and her face fell as she thought about LeeRoy.

"I'm sorry," Giles said quickly. "I shouldn't have said that."

"Oh, that's okay," Julie said with a dismissive wave, her smile returning—though not as happily. "It wouldn't be right to pretend he didn't matter. He was a big part of my life, just as he was part of yours." She approached him and placed her hands on his shoulders. "He thought a lot of you, Giles. I believe he'd be glad we're trying to make this work. "I'm sure he'd approve of you as this little guy's stepdaddy."

"Thanks, Julie. I hope so," Giles said as he looked into the distance, his thoughts wandering back. "He was a good man—especially to those close to him. Despite his past, he was a true gentleman."

"I wish he hadn't gotten involved in all that," she said with a sigh. "But maybe I wouldn't have met him if he hadn't." She turned her captivating eyes back to Giles, giving him her full attention. "It's funny—without LeeRoy, I might never have met you again the second time. Maybe this was meant to be."

"I have no idea. Who knows?"

"Only God, I suppose, and he's definitely keeping it to himself."

Giles sat down in the armchair and slapped his knees, motioning for Julie to come and sit on his lap. She did.

"Now! Where were we?" Giles burst out laughing.

Julie feigned innocence. "Can't remember!"

"Ah, I think I do," he said, pulling her head close and his tongue tracing its way inside her ear. That was all it took for Julie.

The intensity of her feelings, emotions, and the throbbing between her legs came rushing back instantly, and Giles could feel the electricity running through her body.

Giles was still not in a rush and pressed his tongue deeply into her ear. Julie squirmed and wriggled, but he held on tight. She loved it, but at the same time, couldn't handle the erotic shocks it was sending through her body.

How does he do this to me?

Stop! No, don't stop! I don't know what I want. Help me— please!

Just as Julie thought she couldn't take it anymore, Giles loosened his grip, and she shivered, her head dropping onto his shoulder to block her ear from his probing tongue. A thousand thoughts raced through her mind.

If he can make me feel like that with his tongue in my ear, what the hell is he going to be like down there? I can't wait to find out. Hurry up, Giles!

But she knew he would be taking his time. Giles was savouring this moment. He wanted her to crave him more than anything else in the world. He was determined to make that happen tonight, and he was taking his time.

He lifted her head once more, and as his lips brushed her ear, she tensed up at the thought of his tongue going back to it. However, this time, she felt it just brushing her warm, blushing cheek before stopping just shy of her eager, open mouth, ready to receive. His tongue hovered teasingly close but didn't quite reach hers.

Julie's tongue searched, but Giles was holding back, keeping his tongue just out of reach. She tried to move her head, but he held her tightly, making her wait. She was ready to kill him.

She was groaning. Then Giles loosened his grip on her head, and their tongues were immediately locked together – impossible to prise apart.

Julie turned around without letting go of their intertwined tongues, now straddling Giles with both arms wrapped around his head. He was the one trapped, but not complaining.

Giles's hands slowly lowered down her back and onto her bottom.

And what a cute little bottom she has, he was thinking to himself. He was getting as turned on as Julie: he wanted to throw her on the floor and fuck her right there and then, but restrained himself. He gently pulled her blouse up over her breasts. Their mouths broke away, Julie's tongue bereft for a moment, whilst he lifted the blouse off over her head, leaving her completely naked from the waist up.

Giles took a step away and gasped. His eyes strayed from her breasts to her eyes, nose, mouth, chin, her shoulders, and back to her breasts. They were beautiful, and despite having had a baby, they were still firm. Both nipples were hard and erect. His gaze carried on down to her tummy, flat and firm with the cutest little belly button he had ever seen.

He took a step forward, his hands gently cradling her face as he looked into her eyes. His hands gradually moved down, lightly touching the fine hairs on her skin, causing her to shiver with goose bumps. She felt that familiar electric thrill again as he softly touched her breasts with his warm hands.

She wasn't sure if the electricity came from him touching her naked breasts, or if it was as if he was peering straight into her mind. She was convinced he could read her thoughts, but she hoped he couldn't. Ladies shouldn't be thinking the things she was feeling at that moment, right?

Julie leaned forward and yanked Giles's shirt off so quickly that he didn't feel a thing. He had a pretty hairy chest. Julie liked that and ran her fingers through the tangled jungle of coarse grey hairs.

Giles pulled her close, their half-naked, hot, and sweaty bodies entwined again. He stood up, taking Julie with him, and for the second time that night, he carried her to his bed, hoping little Johnny wouldn't wake up again.

Julie was holding him tightly around his neck as he lay her on the bed. She didn't let go, pulling him down on top of her. He lay there with his rigid manhood pressed against her.

She was eager for it and wanted it right away. She shoved him off her and, as he lay on his back, she climbed on top, straddling him with one knee on either side.

He gave in, his arms wide open, and did nothing. She enjoyed that. At last, she was in control. Now it was time to toy with him. She traced her hands over his chest, noticing his nipples were hard, and gave them a gentle pinch.

She then ran her fingers up his body, through the hair on his head, and around to his ears. Her small fingers ran gently around his face, then she slipped her index finger into his mouth. He sucked whilst she started wriggling her crotch over his.

She ran her hands slowly down his body, over his stomach. She shifted back so that she was sitting on his knees and carried on stroking down his body, until she was rubbing his manhood over his trousers. He was very hard, and she wanted him in her, NOW.

She yanked open his leather belt, unbuttoned his pants, then slowly lowered the zipper, being careful not to damage what was about to take her to heaven. She noticed the bulge straining against the fabric. She slid down and off the bed, tugging at his pants until they were off. Standing at the foot of the bed, she gazed at him, her eyes locked on his. He stared back, unbroken silence between them.

Julie leaned forward, grabbed his underpants, and pulled them off. She stood there again, this time not looking at his face, but at what she knew would be inside her soon, just as any woman would. He was big — not as big as LeeRoy, which she couldn't help but compare—but it didn't matter. She loved him and would love whatever he had to offer.

She climbed back astride him. She still had her skirt and panties on and could feel the wet in them. She was turned on more than she could remember being turned on.

She lowered herself onto him. She wanted him in her so badly but also tried to torment him. However, she realised that she was tormenting herself much more. She had to have him inside her.

She wrenched off her skirt and was going to do the same to her panties when Giles, as quick as a flash, reached up and pulled her down on the bed, spinning over so he was now astride her.

"No way," he said. "You've had your fun. Now it's my turn."

He lay on top of her and started to kiss, inevitable tongues embracing, and he pushed his manhood up against her opening. Although she was still wearing her underwear, it sent a shudder down her body. He pushed harder and withdrew, and she began to gasp.

She wanted it, needed it inside her, her vagina aching and swollen with desire, but Giles was not having any of it, not yet anyway. He pushed temptingly up and down, then rolled off as she lay there, still panting.

He gently placed his hand under her head, leaned over, and kissed her again. Her jaw ached from all the kissing and the tension of the muscles involved. Her head was spinning, her mind in a scramble. He started to caress her firm breasts; her nipples were still rock hard. She was getting so turned on that she thought she was going to have an orgasm without intercourse.

She went to put her left hand down inside her panties. She needed something there – anything – to dampen the fire between her legs.

He pushed her hand away, whispering, "That's my job." "I wish you'd just get on with it then," she said. "I'm on fire." "Plenty of time," he whispered back.

He carried on kissing, licking her ear, caressing her breasts, then slowly worked his right hand down, fingering around her belly button. Then his hand crept lower, over her underwear, with her straining upwards for satisfaction. But his hand went teasingly past, landing on the inside of her upper thigh, just lightly stroking his fingers on her skin.

He was tantalizingly close to her, and she opened her legs wide to give him full access. He trailed his fingers up the inside of her thigh, then reached the spot she craved. He gently rubbed over her underwear, feeling the pouting lips between her legs. She couldn't lie still, arching her back, desperate and growing angry with frustration.

He pressed a finger against her opening, and her back arched even more.

He was enjoying this. He ran his hand up a little higher and down inside her underwear. He hesitated over her pubic hair, enjoying both the sensation and her reaction. He knew she wanted him to go all the way, and he would, but in his own time.

Her legs were spread wide, and her knees were up, waiting. But how much longer could she hold out? This was the sweetest kind of torture, but torture all the same. She clutched his head and shoulders tightly.

He slid his hand right down inside her underwear and gently rubbed outside her slick entrance. She was now squirming so much that he thought she'd fall off the bed. His finger slipped in just a little enough to make her writhe and moan even more.

He started to stimulate her clitoris, and she arched her back so hard his hand was forced out of her panties. She crashed back down on the bed, groaning.

He slowly removed her underwear and just looked at her perfect naked body, still trembling on the bed. He didn't need his rock-hard manhood to judge how desirable she was.

He put his tongue into her ear and his finger back onto her clitoris, rhythmically licking and rubbing. She was delirious, thrashing and squealing, and was going to climax at any second.

He could sense how close she was, so he stopped teasing her and just held her tightly, but she was desperate for him to be inside her.

He lowered his head and was sucking on her rock-hard nipple, while his hand was on the inside of her thigh, gently stroking it, but not entering her.

His head gradually went lower, tongue licking around her belly button, then down over her pubic hair and found her entrance. This made her gasp aloud, wriggling and arching her back again, but Giles was holding her buttocks firmly, and his tongue was exploring inside her.

She grasped his head tightly, yanking his hair, desperate to turn his face away. She wanted him to stop, but she also craved more. Her emotions were a tangled mess – she was consumed by a fierce desire, sweating, squirming, overwhelmed. It was as if she were in heaven, then hell, and back to heaven again.

He moved his tongue to her clitoris and gently explored inside her with his finger and found her G-spot. He rubbed the ridges, and she let out a loud cry, violently bucking her hips.

He thought she was having a seizure. She had no idea what was going on with her. Her body was jerking, and she was pounding back against the bed, then arching again, quickly and violently. It felt like her head was almost coming off, exploding, when she had the strongest orgasm she had ever experienced in her short life.

She was shaking violently, her body convulsing in all directions, and her grip on Giles's head was so intense. She screamed uncontrollably, then finally collapsed onto the bed, panting and exhausted, tears streaming down her face. The intensity of the moment had left her physically and emotionally drained.

He gently brushed his finger across her cheeks, wiping away the tears, and she caught a whiff of her scent on him. "Are you all right?" he asked, clearly worried.

She burst out laughing. "Oh, yes!" They both caught their breath. Giles lay on top of her, propped up on his elbows, gazing in wonder at her. At first, he comforted and cuddled her, but then the look in their eyes and his growing hardness made them both serious.

Like a magnet, unable to resist, he involuntarily pushed his manhood against her entrance. She tensed up. She'd thought she'd had enough, but his probing excited her again, and she relaxed as he slowly entered her body, sliding easily into her wetness. He was halfway in, and she knew she wanted more, which he gave her.

He slowly moved backward and forward. Occasionally, he pulled out completely, leaving her feeling empty and breathless, until he gently pushed back in again. She was loving every minute of it. Although she wasn't as electrified as before, she was building up to it again.

Giles carried on, slowly, slowly. Then, with Julie's breath and hips becoming aligned with his, the rhythm changed: faster, faster. Harder and harder. Faster, faster; harder and harder. She was working with him, thrusting against him, fingers digging into his back, her face buried in his neck. She climaxed again and, without realising it, she bit his neck, but he didn't feel a thing, too preoccupied with a loud juddering explosion as he came inside her.

They both collapsed, panting and struggling to catch their breath. He was a heavyweight, and with just a gentle nudge, Julie managed to push him off, providing some relief. But she still felt like she was about to collapse. The darkness was filled with stars dancing before her eyes.

Giles lay on his back next to her, panting. Neither of them spoke a word for at least five minutes. It was Giles who eventually ended the silence. "Are you all right?" "All right?" she chuckled, her breathing coming in heavy gasps. "Yes," she replied between breaths. "Oh, God! That was amazing! I didn't think old men could do that!" "Cheeky!" Giles exclaimed. "I'll do it properly in a few minutes. Then you'll see what an old man can really do," he teased. "No, no, no!" Julie gasped, a laugh threatening to escape her voice. "I didn't mean it. I couldn't take any more. I don't think I'll be able to function properly as it is. You're off-limits for at least a week." "We'll see," he laughed.

"I don't have to tell you this, Giles," she said, thoughtfully. "But this is the first time I've been intimate since LeeRoy passed away. I don't count the times I was raped, and I try to block them out, but it's not easy."

"I can understand that. And I feel honoured you chose me."

"I didn't choose you. You were the last person I thought I'd end up with."

His head spun around to face her, concerned. "Are you regretting it, Julie?"

She shifted onto her elbow to look him in the eye. "No, no; not at all! What about you?"

"Me?" Giles laughed. "No way. I feel like I've won the football pools three weeks in a row."

"Yeah, I understand that." He playfully pinched her, and they cuddled close, their skin warm with love. Giles quickly fell asleep. Julie remained there, deep in thought about her brief life.

I wonder where I would be right now if I hadn't run away. I wonder what might have happened if they had attempted to find me. Did they even try? What if I hadn't met Giles in that old pillbox?

So many unanswered questions...

If LeeRoy hadn't given me Tinky Winky, we wouldn't have run into Giles again. What if we hadn't gone to Peru? What if LeeRoy had managed to escape? What if? What if? What if? Julie, exhausted, eventually fell asleep.

CHAPTER THIRTY-NINE — *Morning, and a Promise*

In the morning, Giles woke up at around seven with an erection that he just had to do something with. He looked across at Julie, who had her back to him. He snuggled up behind her and put his hand down between her legs. She woke up and immediately knew what was going on. Although she was only partly aware, she let go and spread her legs. He shifted down the bed a bit and slowly eased everything inside her, thrusting hard. For Giles, this wasn't about romance, but a need to release, which he did quickly, until he let out a groan, collapsed, and relaxed, still inside Julie, holding her tight.

Julie, now wide awake, asked, "When did you swap places with my stud from last night?"

Giles whispered to her, "Sorry, he was exhausted and needed some help."

Julie laughed, enjoying the feel of Giles's arm around her. "Well, I hope he bounces back soon!"

They remained there for a few minutes until Johnny woke up and began crying. Julie pulled away from Giles and went to check on him. Giles watched her walk across the room, admiring her beautiful, perfect body.

Giles got up and took a shower. He stepped out just as Julie was changing Johnny's nappy. The smell hit him, and he couldn't help but burst out laughing.

Honestly, I have no clue how you do that. I don't think I could. I'd likely vomit if I attempted.

Julie jokingly warned, "You'd better not annoy me, or I might just throw this at you."

Giles shuddered and went to the kitchen to start the coffee.

Julie got Johnny sorted out, fed him, and he was soon back asleep.

Giles called out, "Breakfast is ready, sweetheart."

"Great, I could get used to being spoiled like this, especially in the mornings."

Giles joked, "Thought I was spoiling you before we even got up."

Julie retorted, "Haha. I'm guessing you were using me to get a load off your mind!"

"Very good, like that."

As she passed by, Giles softly reached out, holding her firmly for five seconds in a quiet, meaningful pause. Afterwards, he sat down, still grasping her hand. She took a seat beside him, and he gazed into her eyes.

"Julie, I know it's not been long, but I'm certain about my feelings," he said. She nodded, and he continued, feeling like he was rambling but just wanting to express everything. "I'm completely sure I love you, and if you feel the same — which I believe you do — I'd like us to become an official couple."

"Are you proposing to me?"

"No, no," Giles said hesitantly. "I mean, let's try it and see what happens."

Julie smiled. "After last night, I just assumed that's what would happen. I'd been upset and shocked, otherwise!" Giles grinned in relief. "That's amazing, Julie. I feel like the luckiest guy alive."

"And so, you should," she said with a playful little grin he loved so much.

Giles's tone suddenly became serious again. "There's one thing that worries me, Julie, and I believe it's better to discuss it now rather than later when it might become awkward."

She frowned. "Oh, and what exactly is your problem?"

I would have thought it was clear, Julie. If this relationship progresses, as I hope, and we marry –

"That would depend on you asking me," Julie said teasingly, "and me saying yes, of course!"

"Please don't joke, Julie. This is serious, and it does concern me."

"Okay, sorry."

He looked firmly into her eyes. "All I can give you is my love and loyalty. I understand you might think that's enough," he said,

"Giles!" Julie exclaimed. "I don't need anything else—like, I need money! You know I have more than enough for all of us!"

Giles still looked worried. "But I am concerned about it."

Julie placed her hand on his chest and said earnestly, "Look, Giles. This is all fresh. Let's wait a few months and see how things unfold. If you still have issues, we can discuss it further, even with my solicitor if that helps."

Giles exhaled. "Okay, Julie, I guess I'm getting a little ahead of myself." He stood up quickly, which stirred the air and changed the atmosphere. "Anyway, you're still my boss, and if I don't finish my work, I could get fired."

She grinned. "You're right, of course. Consider this your first verbal warning, and make sure I don't catch you skiving again."

She struggled to keep a straight face. She knew him so well that she instinctively understood what Giles's problem was, but it didn't bother her at all. She had nothing once, so she had no issue sharing what she had now with Giles if it benefited both of them. However, she was going to tease him a little.

CHAPTER FORTY — *Johnny's Questions*

Giles stepped into the garden to clear away some leaves. Inside, the house was quiet. Julie sat at the old oak table, propping her elbows on its surface. She cupped her chin in her hands and began to reflect.

Do I love Giles, though? she asked, trying to be objective for a moment.

Yes, of course. There's no doubt about it, and I'm positive he loves me for who I am, not what I have.

Her mind flicked from thought to thought.

I really miss LeeRoy. God, I miss that man.

Thoughts of LeeRoy, although wistful, caused no regret about her new relationship. LeeRoy was gone, and she had long ago come to terms with it. But

Would LeeRoy approve? *Yes, I think he would. He'd want me to be happy, and he felt the world of Giles.*

Would LeeRoy be happy about Johnny growing up thinking Giles was his daddy?

She shook her head. No way.

He must never forget that Giles is his stepfather. That won't be hard to figure out as he gets older and begins questioning why both of his parents are so much paler than he is.

I'll explain everything to him as soon as he's old enough to understand, and I'll tell him the truth in response to any questions he might ask as he grows up.

The sex from the previous night was great, and Julie wanted more. More importantly, she experienced a sense of stability for the first time in a long while. She had a family, but she also felt more confident and more assertive within herself. Her sense of identity and personal power now felt natural and ingrained.

Whole. I feel whole.

The nightmare through Peru and Ecuador seems a million years away now, but it had indeed been THE LONG ROAD HOME.

She was jolted out of her daydream by Johnny waking up and needing his nappy changed yet again.

This was her reality now.

She smiled while lifting Johnny onto her shoulder and looked out the window, watching Giles bend down to gather some weeds. When he straightened up and saw her, he waved, and his smile lit up her whole being. *This is my real life now.*

Johnny grew quickly, all energy and curiosity. He was the kind of child who couldn't pass a puddle without stepping into it, or see a horse in a field without stopping to watch until it disappeared from sight. There was something in him — a restlessness, a spark — that Giles said came from "the traveller's blood," though Julie never corrected him.

By five, Johnny was already shadowing Giles everywhere he went — to the sheds, the fields, even the farrier's forge at the edge of the village. He loved the scent of oil and smoke, the rhythmic clatter of tools, and the way Giles's big hands could coax a stubborn hinge or a piece of machinery back to life. By seven, he had his own little hammer, more sound than substance, but he swung it with a pride that made Giles laugh.

Julie would watch from the doorway sometimes, wiping her hands on her apron, her heart full and heavy at once. The sound of their laughter filled the air, bright and easy, and though Giles never tried to take the place of Johnny's father, the bond between them was something she could never have hoped for.

When school came, Johnny took to it reluctantly. His heart was never in books or lessons. He preferred the open air — the smell of rain-soaked hay, the hum of bees in the hedgerows, the quiet rhythm of the land. He was happiest when the world was simple and the work was honest.

But as he grew older, questions began to creep in — questions he didn't yet have words for. He'd notice things in the mirror: the darker shade of his skin, the curl in his hair that didn't match his mother's or Giles's. He'd hear it sometimes from the other boys at school, tossed out in cruel laughter or whispered behind his back.

"Mixed blood," one of them said once. "Probably a foreigner."

It came to blows before the teacher could separate them. Johnny went home that day with a torn shirt, one grazed cheek, and eyes full of confusion.

That night, while Julie cleaned the cut on his lip, he looked up at her with a seriousness beyond his years.

"Mum," he said quietly, "why don't I look like you? Or Giles?"

Julie froze, the cloth trembling slightly in her hand, dreading this day. Giles looked up from his chair in the corner, folding his newspaper with deliberate care. The silence that followed was long and heavy — one of those moments where the truth sits just behind the breath, waiting to be spoken.

Julie took a slow breath. "Because your real father was different," she said softly. "He was kind, and brave... and he loved me very much. But he didn't come home from Peru."

Johnny frowned, puzzled. "He died?"

She nodded, the words catching in her throat. "Yes, love. Before you were born."

He was quiet for a long time, tracing the grain of the table with one small finger. "Was he bad?" he asked finally. "The boys at school say I look like... like someone who shouldn't be here."

Julie's eyes filled. "No, sweetheart. He wasn't bad. He just made mistakes — big ones. But he tried to put them right. And he loved you, even if he never got to see you."

Giles rose from his chair, crossing to stand beside them. He placed a rough, steady hand on Johnny's shoulder. "He was a man who got caught in the wrong life," he said. "But your mum saved you both. You've got her heart, lad — and that's worth more than all the rest."

Johnny looked up at him, searching his face for something solid to hold on to. "Can I see him?" he asked.

Julie smiled faintly through her tears. "He's buried in Faversham, at St Mary's. When the weather's kind, we'll go. You can meet him properly."

That night, Johnny lay awake listening to the rain against the windowpane. Somewhere out there, in a quiet churchyard he'd never seen, was the man who gave him his name, his skin, his difference — and, maybe, his restless heart.

The rain had cleared by morning, leaving the sky a washed-out blue and the air sharp with the smell of wet leaves. Julie packed a small bouquet of wildflowers from the garden — the same ones that used to grow behind the manor when she and LeeRoy first met. She wrapped them carefully in brown paper, tied with twine, and set them on the passenger seat beside her.

Johnny sat in the back, unusually quiet. He pressed his forehead to the glass, watching the hedgerows blur past. Giles drove, saying little, his hands steady on the wheel.

When they reached Faversham, the church bells were tolling softly in the distance. St Mary's stood in the middle of the town, its stone walls darkened by time and moss. The churchyard spread wide around it, a quilt of old headstones and leaning crosses.

Julie walked ahead, her steps slowing as memory guided her between the rows. She had stood here before, years ago, her belly round with the child who now followed behind her. She could still remember the smell of damp earth, the murmur of the vicar's voice, the ache of the final goodbye.

She stopped before a modest headstone, its inscription softened by weather:

LeeRoy Mason
1940 – 1969
Beloved Son, Father, and Friend
Gone too soon, but never forgotten.

Johnny stood beside her, his small hand finding hers. "So this is him," he whispered.

Julie nodded, her throat tight. "Yes, love. This is your father."

He crouched down, tracing the letters with his fingertips. "He's been here all this time?"

Giles stepped forward quietly. "Aye. But don't think of him as stuck here. He's part of this place now — the wind, the trees, the sound of the bell."

Johnny looked up at the branches swaying overhead. For a long while, no one spoke. The world felt still, respectful.

Finally, Julie knelt beside her son. "He made mistakes, Johnny, but he was brave. He tried to put things right."

Johnny frowned thoughtfully. "Was he like me?"

"In some ways," Julie said softly. "You've got his courage. But you've got Giles's heart. That's what matters most."

The boy nodded slowly, then laid the flowers at the base of the stone. "Hello, Dad," he murmured. "I wish I'd met you."

The wind lifted, stirring the petals. For just a moment, Julie thought she heard something faint — a sigh, or perhaps the whisper of leaves brushing one another.

She turned her face to the sky, blinking back tears. "Come on," she said gently. "He knows you're here."

As they walked back toward the car, Johnny glanced over his shoulder one last time. The sunlight broke through the clouds and touched the headstone, just enough to make the damp stone gleam.

CHAPTER FORTY-ONE — *Temper and Talent*

In the weeks after the visit to his father's grave, something quiet changed in Johnny. He didn't speak of the grave again, but there was a new stillness in him — not sadness exactly, just thought. He spent more time alone, wandering the grounds or sitting by the lake, skimming pebbles across the glassy surface and watching the ripples fade into the mist that hung there most mornings.

Julie noticed first. "He's thinking too much for a boy his age," she said one evening, folding laundry by the fire.

Giles looked up from mending a broken chair leg. "That's not always a bad thing," he said. "He's finding his feet. Just like we all had to."

But Johnny wasn't just finding his feet — he was searching for his place. He started asking questions, gentle ones at first. About LeeRoy. About what he'd been like. About Peru.

Julie told him the softened version — that his father had gone too far down a dangerous road, that he'd been trying to put things right when his luck ran out. She didn't talk about the prison, or the deal that went wrong, or the men who hadn't come back.

Giles filled in the spaces she couldn't. "Your dad was no saint, lad," he said one evening, "but he wasn't evil either. The world just got hold of him and wouldn't let go."

Johnny listened, turning the words over like stones in his pocket. He wanted to be proud of his father, but he also wanted to understand him — the darkness as well as the good.

By twelve, he'd taken to spending his evenings at the stables up the lane, helping old Fred with the horses. There was something about them — their power, their silence — that made sense to him. When he brushed them down, the world went quiet. When he rode, the noise in his head seemed to fade away.

"He's got a way with them," Fred told Giles once. "Not just skill — something deeper. They listen to him."

Giles smiled at that, pride mixing with unease. "Maybe that's his father in him," he said quietly.

The years rolled on. Johnny grew taller, stronger, and more restless. By fifteen, he was working part-time on a nearby farm, learning the land the way others learned books. But with the strength came temper — flashes of it, quick and sharp, especially when someone mentioned his father's name.

One afternoon, he came home with blood on his knuckles. Julie met him at the gate, her voice trembling with anger and fear. "Johnny, what happened?"

"Nothing," he muttered.

"Don't you lie to me."

He looked away. "Just some lads talking rubbish at school. I sorted it."

Giles appeared in the doorway, arms folded. "You can't fight the whole world, lad."

"They started it," Johnny snapped. "Said my dad was a criminal. Said I'd end up the same."

The words hung there like smoke. Julie's face softened. She reached out, touching his cheek. "You're not your father, Johnny."

He met her gaze, eyes burning. "Aren't I?"

Then he turned and walked away down the lane, fists still clenched, the sky behind him bruised and heavy with rain.

That night, when the thunder rolled across the valley, Julie lay awake listening to it and thought it sounded too much like a warning.

The storm passed, but something in Johnny didn't. He went back to school, did his work, laughed when he was supposed to, but there was a distance in his eyes now — a small, hard glint that hadn't been there before. He still helped at the stables, still came home for supper, but much of his time was spent in the sheds with Giles, tinkering with whatever engine or piece of machinery needed attention.

Giles had always been patient, steady with his tools, but Johnny worked differently. He was quick, instinctive — he could take a motor apart and put it back together almost by feel. "You've got the hands for it," Giles told him one evening as they crouched over a broken generator. "But don't rush. Machines will teach you patience if you let them."

Johnny nodded, though he barely heard. The low hum of the engine filled his mind like a voice he was learning to understand. When it finally sputtered into life, his grin lit the whole shed.

Julie watched from the doorway, her heart full of pride and worry all at once. "You'll make something of yourself yet, Johnny," she said.

"I just like knowing how things work," he replied. "Engines, gears... people."

"People aren't machines," she said softly.

He wiped his hands on a rag and gave a half-smile. "No. They break easier."

By seventeen, Johnny was working full-time on a nearby farm. He drove tractors, repaired balers, and even managed the harvest machinery when the foreman was away. The older men took to him quickly — respectful, clever, strong. But sometimes that temper flared, the same flash Julie had seen in him as a boy. He hated being told he was wrong, hated being spoken down to.

One sweltering afternoon, an argument erupted over a broken axle. Words turned to shouts, then a scuffle. Johnny stormed off across the yard, dust rising behind his boots. Later, he came back and fixed the axle in silence, every turn of the spanner an apology; he didn't know how to speak.

CHAPTER FORTY-TWO — *The Gate on Dean's Hill*

A few months later, the season turned, bringing the soft greys and browns of early autumn. Life had settled into its quiet rhythm again — the same walks, the same suppers, the same steady hum of work that kept them grounded.

Then, one Friday afternoon, Giles came in later than usual, still wearing his coat and boots, with mud flecked on his trousers. He dropped his keys on the kitchen table and nodded toward the window.

"Saw something on the way back from Maidstone," he said. "Up past Dean's Hill. Old farm for sale — big place, needs work, mind, but plenty of land."

Julie looked up from peeling potatoes. "A farm?"

He nodded, easing himself into a chair. "Aye. Been empty a while by the looks of it. Roof's sound, fields overgrown, but I reckon there's good soil under all that mess."

She smiled faintly. "You and your farms. Thought you'd had enough of that life."

"Maybe," he said, rubbing a hand across his chin. "But it caught my eye, that's all. Made me think."

That night, after Johnny had gone to bed, Julie sat by the fire, turning the thought over in her mind. Giles had once owned a smallholding before that fateful day had changed everything — before the debts, the travel, the loss. And Johnny... well, he was happiest outdoors, in the mud and wind, fixing things, finding his rhythm in the work of his hands.

By morning, she'd made up her mind. "Let's go and have a look," she said over breakfast. "If it's not too far gone, maybe it's time we made a proper home again. Something that could be Johnny's one day — his to build on, his to pass down. With your guidance, Giles, it could be everything he needs."

Giles looked at her for a long moment, then smiled, that slow, knowing smile she hadn't seen in years. "All right then. We'll drive out after lunch."

The road wound through narrow lanes lined with hawthorn and ash until it climbed gently toward the top of Dean's Hill. The view opened suddenly — rolling fields, a stand of beech trees, and beyond them, a cluster of old stone buildings standing proud against the horizon.

The sign at the gate was half-rotten, the paint flaking, the words barely legible: *For Sale – Enquiries Within.*

They stopped just short of the drive. The lane was carpeted in leaves, the hedgerows alive with birdsong. The Grange itself stood a little apart — solid, dignified, with ivy curling up one side and a tall chimney rising against the pale sky.

Julie stepped out of the car and took a deep breath. "It's beautiful," she said quietly.

Giles followed, hands in pockets. "Needs work, though."

"That never stopped you before," she replied.

He chuckled softly. "You remember too much."

Johnny had already climbed halfway up the gate, eyes wide. "Can we go in?"

Julie and Giles exchanged a glance — the kind that didn't need words — then nodded. Together they pushed the gate open and walked up the drive toward the house that, though they couldn't have known it then, would one day be called **Ashmore Grange**.

The next morning, Giles made the call.
The estate agent's voice on the other end was brisk and businesslike — "Yes, it's still on the market. The owners passed away several years ago; the property has been empty ever since. Needs attention, but the structure's good. Roof, beams, and foundations are sound."

By lunchtime the next day, an envelope arrived — a glossy brochure tucked neatly inside. Julie laid it out on the kitchen table, flattening the creases with her palms.
The photographs were faded, the colours a little off, but even through the paper's dull sheen, the place had presence.

The Grange stood proud at the top of a long, curving gravel drive, its weathered stone walls softened by ivy that climbed almost to the gables. To the left, a line of old stables and outbuildings leaned gently into the afternoon light, their Kent-peg roofs mottled with lichen. Beyond them, an untamed orchard sloped toward the hedgerow, branches heavy with unpicked fruit.

In one of the photographs, sunlight poured through the high barn doors, striking a beam across the dust-filled air and glinting off the rusted tools still hanging on their pegs — as though the men who'd once worked there had simply stepped out for lunch and never returned. The scene was both peaceful and alive, a portrait of a place that had waited too long to be found again.

Another showed a view across the fields — wide and open, the kind of space that promised both work and peace.

Johnny hovered at her shoulder, peering over. "So that's the place on Dean's Hill," he said. "You can just spot the chimney from the lane — looks huge!"

Julie smiled, tracing a finger over the picture. "It looks very big."

"Yes, it is, but then so is this place." Giles leaned against the counter, studying the details. "Price isn't bad, considering the land. Needs someone who knows what they're doing."

"That would be you," Julie said.

He chuckled. "Maybe once. It's a lot to take on now."

Johnny looked from one to the other, his eyes bright. "We could fix it up together. You'd know what to do, and I can learn."

Julie turned a page. There was a photograph of the farmhouse kitchen — wide stone hearth, heavy oak beams, a sink under a leaded window. She felt something tighten gently in her chest. "It feels like it's been waiting," she said quietly.

Giles met her eyes. "Waiting for what?"

She gave a small smile. "For us, maybe."

The decision wasn't made in that moment, but something settled between them — a quiet understanding that the idea was already growing roots.

By the weekend, they were standing once more at the gate on Dean's Hill, brochure in hand, the autumn light lying soft across the fields. The lane was still and empty, the only sound the rustle of leaves and the distant caw of rooks in the trees.

Julie rested her hand on the top rail of the gate. "Let's go and see if it feels the same up close," she said.

Giles nodded, pushing the gate open. The hinges groaned faintly, like a house clearing its throat after too long asleep.

Together, they walked up the drive — three figures against the pale sky — toward the house that, in time, would carry all their histories within its walls.

CHAPTER FORTY-THREE — *Ashmore Grange*

The gravel crunched softly beneath their boots as they made their way up the drive. The air smelled of damp earth and woodsmoke from distant cottages, the kind of scent that always made Giles feel like life could start fresh if you just worked hard enough.

The closer they came, the more the house revealed of itself — the tall mullioned windows clouded with age, the heavy front door scarred by weather and time. Moss grew thick between the flagstones, and ivy had crept across the lintel as if it meant to pull the building back into the hill.

Julie paused at the threshold, her hand brushing the rough stone. "It feels older than it looks," she murmured.

Giles gave a small smile. "That's a good thing. Old bones hold steady."

Inside, the air was cool and still. Their footsteps echoed through the wide hall, where pale light slanted in through a high window, dust motes drifting in slow motion. The place smelled of emptiness — wood, plaster, and a faint sweetness like dried lavender.

Johnny darted ahead, his boots scuffing across the tiled floor. "It's massive!" he called, his voice bouncing off the walls.

Julie followed more slowly, trailing her fingers across the banister of the old staircase. The timber felt dry but solid beneath her touch. "Someone loved this house once," she said.

"They still do," Giles murmured, half to himself, examining the fireplace in the main room. He could already see the work it would take — the cracked plaster, the sagging lintel, the flue long, cold, and choked with ash. But beneath it all, there was promise.

Johnny's laughter carried from the next room. "Mum! There's a big kitchen! And a window that looks over everything!"

Julie turned toward the sound, her smile widening. "He's already moved in."

They spent the next hour wandering from room to room — the main parlour with its deep alcoves and soot-stained hearth, the back corridor that led to a pantry and a half-collapsed scullery, and upstairs, the bedrooms filled with light that caught on dust and cobwebs.

By the time they returned to the hallway, the sun had shifted westward, filling the upper windows with a soft amber glow. Julie leaned against the doorframe, watching the light slide across the walls.

"It's quiet here," she said. "But not empty. Like it's been waiting for something to happen."

Giles looked at her, then at Johnny, who stood at the window gazing out toward the orchard. "Maybe it's been waiting for us," he said.

Julie's eyes softened. "You think so?"

He shrugged, smiling faintly. "If we've got the nerve for it."

She took his hand. "Then let's have the nerve."

Outside, the first evening breeze rustled the orchard's leaves.

A lone rook wheeled overhead, its cry echoing across the fields.

It felt like the end of one chapter and the beginning of another — the start of something built not from escape, but from the quiet courage to stay.

THE TURN OF SEASONS

Spring came gently to Dean's Hill. The orchard woke first, pale blossoms bursting through months of neglect. The fields followed — green shoots threading through soil Giles swore hadn't breathed properly in years.

The Grange, once silent, found its rhythm again: the steady tap of hammers, the scrape of brushes, the low hum of work and laughter. Julie kept the windows open as she painted, letting the scent of cut grass and linseed oil drift through the rooms.

Johnny thrived. He drove the tractor, mended gates, and learned to listen to the land the way other boys listened to music. Giles watched him with a quiet pride that bordered on awe.

"It's his now," Julie said one evening as they stood by the fence, watching the sun drop behind the trees. "This place will outlive us."

Giles nodded, his arm around her shoulders. "That's how it should be."

But even then, beneath the calm, the house kept its silences. The wind moved differently here — not strange, not haunting, just… watchful.

By the time summer rolled in, the old farm had found a name again — though not one they chose. The local postman, weary of calling it "the old place on Dean's Hill," had written *The Grange* on his route sheet. The name stuck.

And so it began again — a home reborn, a family settled, and a story still unfolding.

Years would pass before anyone else would stand at that same gate, brochure in hand, dreaming of a life waiting to be made.

But the land would remember. It always did.

AUTHOR'S NOTE

The story of Giles, Julie, and their son Johnny marks the end of one journey — but not the end of the road.

Years will pass, the land will change hands, and the echoes of their lives will remain within the walls of the old farmhouse on Dean's Hill — the place that will one day be known as **Ashmore Grange.**

Part Two continues in
Fifty Bales of Hay and a Pair of Jodhpurs
where the past never truly rests, and the choices of one generation cast long shadows over the next.

Thanks to my proofreaders, Derek Watson and Lesley Hazell

All rights reserved. No part of this book may be reproduced or transmitted in any form or by any means, electronic or mechanical, including photocopying, recording, or using any information storage and retrieval system, without permission in writing from the copyright owner.

This is a work of fiction. Names, characters, places, and incidents either are the product of the author's imagination or are used fictitiously, and any resemblance to any actual persons, living or dead, events, or locales is entirely coincidental.

Printed in Dunstable, United Kingdom